The Northern Lights

spun and played in the sky. It was quiet and desolate and cold. Then suddenly Imnak cried out, pointing upward.

In the lights in the sky, in those shimmering, subtle, shifting streaks and curtains of light, some hundreds of miles in height, clearly portrayed, though it was for a moment only, was the gigantic hideous visage of a Kur.

There was no mistaking that towering face etched in the auroral lights against the darkness. Its outline was shaggy. Its eyes seemed to blaze, as though fires burned behind them. Its mouth was fanged. Then the visage faded and disappeared, and the aurora too and we saw only the stars and the polar night.

I looked up at the sky, and smiled to myself. I had come, after long trekking, to the brink of the camp of my enemy, to the brink of the camp of Half-Ear.

"I think, Imnak," I said, "that I am close to finding him whom I have sought."

"Perhaps, already, he has found you," said Imnak.

JOHN NORMAN

books available from DAW:

HUNTERS OF GOR
MARAUDERS OF GOR
TRIBESMEN OF GOR
SLAVE GIRL OF GOR
BEASTS OF GOR
TIME SLAVE
IMAGINATIVE SEX
EXPLORERS OF GOR

BEASTS OF GOR

John Norman

DAW BOOKS, INC.
DONALD A. WOLLHEIM, PUBLISHER

1301 Avenue of the Americas
New York, N. Y.   10019

FIRST PRINTING, MARCH 1978

5 6 7 8 9

PRINTED IN U.S.A.

Contents

1   THE SLEEN

"There is no clue," Samos had said.

I lay awake on the great couch. I stared at the ceiling of the room. Light from a perforated lamp flickered dimly. The furs were deep and soft. My weapons lay to one side. A slave, sleeping, lay chained at my feet.

There was no clue.

"He might be anywhere," had said Samos. He had shrugged. "We know only that somewhere he is among us."

We know little about that species of animal called the Kur. We do know it is blood-thirsty, that it feeds on human flesh and that it is concerned with glory.

"It is not unlike men," had once said Misk to me, a Priest-King.

This story, in its way, has no clear beginning. It began, I suppose, some thousands of years ago when Kurii, in internecine wars, destroyed the viability of a native world. Their state at that time was sufficiently advanced technologically to construct small steel worlds in orbit, each some pasangs in diameter. The remnants of a shattered species then, as a world burned below them, turned hunting to the plains of the stars.

We do not know how long their hunt took. But we do know the worlds, long ago, entered the system of a slow-revolving, medium-sized yellow star occupying a peripheral position in one of nature's bounteous, gleaming, strewn spiral universes.

They had found their quarry, a world.

They had found two worlds, one spoken of as Earth, the other as Gor.

One of these worlds was a world poisoning itself, a pathological world insane and short-sighted, greed-driven and self-destructive. The other was a pristine world, virginal in its beauty and fertility, one not permitted by its masters, called the Sardar, or Priest-Kings, to follow the example of its tragic sister. Priest-Kings would not permit men to destroy Gor. They are not permissive; they are intolerant of geocide. Perhaps it is hard to understand why they do not permit men to destroy Gor. Are they not harsh and cruel, to deny to men this pleasure? Perhaps. But, too, they are rational. And one may be rational, perhaps, without being weak. Indeed, is not weakness the ultimate irrationality? Gor, too, it must be remembered, is also the habitat of the Sardar, or Priest-Kings. They have not chosen to be weak. This choice may be horrifying to those of Earth, so obsessed with their individualism, their proclaimed rights and liberties, but it is one they have chosen to make. I do not defend it. I only report it. Dispute it with them who will.

"Half-Ear is now among us," Samos had said.

I stared at the ceiling, watching the shifting shadows and reflections from the small, perforated lamp.

The Priest-kings, for thousands of years, had defended the system of the yellow star against the depredations of the prowling Kurii. Fortunes had shifted perhaps dozens of times, but never had the Kurii managed to establish a beachhead on the shores of this beautiful world. But some years ago, in the time of the Nest War, the power of the Priest-Kings was considerably reduced. I do not think the Kurii are certain of this, or of the extent of the reduction.

I think if they knew the truth in these matters the code-words would flash between the steel worlds, the ports would open, and the ships would nose forth, turning toward Gor.

But the Kur, like the shark and sleen, is a cautious beast.

He prowls, he tests the wind, and then, when he is certain, he makes his strike.

Samos was much disturbed that the high Kur, it referred to as Half-Ear, was now upon the surface of this world. We had discovered this from an enciphered message, fallen into our hands, hidden in the beads of a necklace.

That Half-Ear had come to Gor was taken by Samos and Priest-Kings as evidence that the invasion was imminent.

Perhaps even now the ships of Kurii flamed toward Gor, as purposeful and silent as sharks in the waters of space's night.

But I did not think so.

I did not think the invasion was imminent.

It was my surmise that the Kur, it called Half-Ear, had come to prepare the way for the invasion.

He had come to make smooth the path, to ready the sands of Gor for the keels of the steel ships.

He must be stopped.

Should he discover the weakness of the Priest-Kings, or construct a depot adequate to fuel, to shield and supply the beaching ships, there seemed little reason to suppose the invasion would not prove successful.

Half-Ear was now upon the surface of Gor.

"He is now among us," had said Samos.

The Kurii moved now, at last, with dispatch and menace. Half-Ear had come to Gor.

But where was he!

I almost cried with anger, my fists clenched. We did not know where he might be.

There was no clue.

The slave at my feet stirred, but did not awaken.

I rose on one elbow and looked down at her. How incredibly beautiful and soft she seemed; she was curled in the furs; she was half covered by them; I lifted them away, that I might see her fully; she stirred; her hands moved a bit on the furs; she drew her legs up; she reached as though to pull the furs more about her but her hands did not find them; she drew her legs up a bit more and snuggled down in the furs; there is perhaps nothing in the world as beautiful as a naked slave girl; a heavy iron collar, with chain, was locked on her throat; the chain ran from a ring fixed in the bottom of the great couch, circular, and some twenty feet wide, around the circumference of the couch to the right and was lifted and coiled to one side, on the left. Her skin, she was very fair-skinned and dark-pelted, seemed very soft and reddish, subtly so, glowingly so, vulnerably so, in the light of the tiny perforated lamp. I found her incredibly beautiful. Her hair, dark and lovely, half covered the heavy collar that encircled her neck. I looked at her. How beautiful she was. And I owned her. What man does not want to own a beautiful woman?

She stirred, and reached again for the furs, chilled. I took her by the arm and drew her beside me, roughly, and threw her on her back. She opened her eyes suddenly, startled, half crying out. "Master!" she gasped. Then I had her swiftly. "Master! Master!" she whispered, clutching me. Then I was finished with her. "Master," she whispered. "I love you. I love you." One has a slave girl when and as one wishes.

She held me closely, pressing her cheek against my chest.

Sex is an implement which may be used in controlling a slave girl. It is as useful as chains and the whip.

"I love you," she whispered.

Sex in a woman, I think, is a more complicated phenomenon than it is in a man. She, if properly treated, and by properly treated I do not mean treated with courtesy and gentleness, but rather correctly treated, as her nature craves,

9

is even more helplessly in the grasp of its power than a man. Sex in a woman is a very subtle and profound thing; she is capable of deep and sustained pleasures which might be the envy of any vital organism. These pleasures, of course, can be used by a man to make her a helpless prisoner and slave. Perhaps that is why free women guard themselves so sternly against them. The slave girl, of course, cannot guard herself against them, for she is at the mercy of her master, who will treat her not as she wishes, but precisely as he wishes. Then she yields, as she must, and as a free woman may not, and her will is yielded in ecstasy to his. The needs of a woman, biologically, are deep; it is unfortunate that some men regard it as wrong to satisfy them. The correct treatment of a female, which is only possible to administer to a girl who is owned, is adjusted to her needs, and is complex and subtle. The least girl contains wonders for the master who understands her. Two things may perhaps be said. The correct treatment of a girl does not always preclude courtesy and gentleness no more than it always involves them. There is a time for courtesy and gentleness, and a time for harshness. The master must remember that he owns the girl; if he keeps this in mind he will generally treat her correctly. He must be strong, and he must be capable of administering discipline if she is not pleasing. Sex in a woman, as in a man, is not only richly biological but psychological as well, and the words suggest a distinction which is somewhat misleading. We are psycho-physical organisms, or better perhaps, thinking, feeling organisms. Part of the correct treatment of a woman is treating her as *you* wish; she has genetic dispositions for submission bred into every cell of her body, a function of both natural and sexual selection. Accordingly, what might seem brutal or quick to a man can be taken by a woman in the dimensions of her sentience as irrefutable evidence of his domination of her, her being owned by him, which thrills her to the core for it touches the ancient biological meaning of her womanhood. He simply uses her for his pleasure, because he wished to do so. He is her master.

I did not thrust her from me.

"May I speak your name, Master?" she begged.

"Yes," I said.

"Tarl," she whispered. "I love you."

"Be silent, Slave Girl," I said.

"Yes, Master," she whispered.

I watched the shadows on the ceiling. I sensed her lips softly kissing me.

You may judge and scorn the Goreans if you wish. Know as well, however, that they judge and scorn you.

They fulfill themselves as you do not.

Hate them for their pride and power. They will pity you for your shame and weakness.

Half-Ear stood somewhere upon Gor.

I did not know where.

Perhaps there was never a time for courtesy and gentleness with an owned woman.

The girl beside me, Vella, was an owned woman.

I laughed. I wondered if I had been tempted to weakness. She trembled then. Still she kissed me, but now frightened, trying to placate me.

How small and weak she was. And how beautiful. How I relished the owning of every bit of her!

I wondered if I had been tempted to weakness. Courtesy and gentleness for a slave? Never!

"Please me," I said. My voice was hard.

"Yes, Master," she whispered. She began to lick and kiss at my body.

In time I ordered her to desist and put her again to her back. I lifted aside the chain which ran to her collar.

"Oh," she said, softly, as I claimed her.

I felt her fingernails in my arms.

She looked up at me, her eyes filled with tears. How helpless she was in my arms.

Then she began to cry out, softly. "Please, please," she begged, "let me speak your name."

"No," I told her.

"Please," she begged.

"What am I to you?" I said.

"My master," she said, frightened.

"Only that," I said.

"Yes, Master," she said.

I did not let her speak further then, but forced the slave, as my whim had it, to endure the lengthy tumult of a bond girl's degradation, lying chained in the arms of a master who does not choose to show her mercy.

I had her as what she was, a slave.

In a quarter of an Ahn her beauty squirmed helplessly; my arms bled from her fingernails; her eyes were wild and piteous. "You may speak," I informed her. She threw back her head and screamed, jolting with spasms, "I yield me your slave! I yield me your slave!" she cried. How beautiful a woman is in such a moment! I waited until she drew trem-

11

blingly quiescent, looking at me. Then I cried out with the pleasure of owning her, and claimed her. She clutched me, kissing me. "I love you, Master," she wept. "I love you."

I held her to me closely, though she was a slave. She looked up at me. Her eyes were moist. "I love you, Master," she said. I brushed back hair from her forehead. I supposed one could be fond of a slave.

Then I recalled that she had once betrayed Priest-Kings, and had pointed me out to my enemies. She had served the Kurii in the Tahari. She had smiled at me when in a court at Nine Wells she had testified falsely against me. Once, from a window of the kasbah of the Salt Ubar she had blown me a kiss and tossed me a token to remember her by, a scarf, perfumed and of slave silk, to taunt me, when I was to be marched chained to the pits of Klima. I had returned from Klima and had made her my slave. I had brought her back with me from the Tahari to the house of Bosk, captain, and merchant, of Port Kar.

I kept her in the house, slave. Much work was she given. Sometimes, as this night, I let her sleep chained at my feet.

"I love you, Master," she said.

I looked angrily to the slave whip upon the wall.

She trembled. Would I use the lash on her? She had felt it more than once.

Suddenly I lifted my head a bit. I smelled the odor of sleen.

The door to my chamber which, in my house, I did not keep locked, moved slightly.

Instantly I moved from the couch, startling the chained girl. I stood, bent, tensed, beside the couch. I did not move.

The snout of the beast thrust first softly through the opening, moving the door back.

I heard the girl gasp.

"Make no sound," I said. I did not move.

I crouched down. The animal had been released. Its head was now fully through the door. Its head was wide and triangular. Suddenly the eyes took the light of the lamp and blazed. And then, the head moving, its eyes no longer reflected the light. It no longer faced the light. Rather it was watching me.

The animal was some twenty feet in length, some eleven hundred pounds in weight, a forest sleen, domesticated. It was double fanged and six-legged. It crouched down and inched forward. Its belly fur must have touched the tiles. It wore a leather sleen collar but there was no leash on the leash loop.

12

I had thought it was trained to hunt tabuk with archers, but it clearly was not tabuk it hunted now.

I knew the look of a hunting sleen. It was a hunter of men.

It swiftly inched forward, then stopped.

When in the afternoon I had seen it in its cage, with its trainer, Bertram of Lydius, it had not reacted to me other than as to the other observers. It had not then, I knew, been put upon my scent.

It crept forward another foot.

I did not think it had been loose from its cage long, for it would take such a beast, a sleen, Gor's finest tracker, only moments to make its way silently through the halls to this chamber.

The beast did not take its eyes from me.

I saw its four hind legs begin to gather under it.

Its breathing was becoming more rapid. That I did not move puzzled it.

It then inched forward another foot. It was now within its critical attacking distance.

I did nothing to excite it.

It lashed its tail back and forth. Had it been longer on my scent I think I might have had less time for its hunting frenzy would have been more upon it, a function in part of the secretions of certain glands.

Very slowly, almost imperceptibly, I reached toward the couch and seized one of the great furs in my right hand.

The beast watched me closely. For the first time it snarled, menacingly.

Then the tail stopped lashing, and became almost rigid. Then the ears lay back against its head.

It charged, scratching and scrambling, slipping suddenly, on the tiles. The girl screamed. The cast fur, capelike, shielding me, enveloped the leaping animal. I leaped to the couch, and rolled over it, and bounded to my feet. I heard the beast snarling and squealing, casting aside the fur with an angry shaking of its body and head. Then it stood, enraged, the fur torn beneath its paws, snarling and hissing. It looked up at me. I stood now upon the couch, the ax of Torvaldsland in my hand.

I laughed, the laugh of a warrior.

"Come my friend," I called to it, "let us engage."

It was a truly brave and noble beast. Those who scorn the sleen I think do not know him. Kurii respect the sleen, and that says much for the sleen, for its courage, its ferocity and its indomitable tenacity.

13

The girl screamed with terror.

The ax caught the beast transversely and the side of its head struck me sliding from the great blade.

I cut at it again on the floor, half severing the neck.

"It is a beautiful animal," I said. I was covered with its blood. I heard men outside in the hall. Thurnock, and Clitus, and Publius, and Tab, and others, weapons in hand, stood at the door.

"What has happened?" cried Thurnock.

"Secure Bertram of Lydius," I said.

Men rushed from the door.

I went to fetch a knife from my weapons. They lay beside and behind the couch.

I shared bits of the heart of the sleen with my men, and, together, cupping our hands, we drank its blood in a ritual of sleen hunters.

"Bertram of Lydius has fled," cried Publius, the kitchen master.

I had thought this would be true.

I had looked into the blood, cupped in my hands. It is said that if one sees oneself black and wasted in the blood, one will perish of disease; if one sees oneself torn and bloody, one will perish in battle; if one sees oneself old and gray one will die in peace and leave children.

But the sleen did not speak to me.

I had looked into the blood, cupped in my hands, but had seen nothing, only the blood of a beast. It did not choose to speak to me, or could not.

I rose to my feet.

I did not think I would again look into the blood of a sleen. I would look rather into the eyes of men.

I wiped the blood from my hands on my thighs.

I turned and looked at the naked girl on the furs, half tangled in her chain, it running about her ankle and leg, looped, and lifting to the ring on the heavy collar. She shrank back, her hand before her mouth.

"Bertram of Lydius approached a guardsman," said Publius, "who suspected nothing, Bertram of Lydius being guest in the house. He struck him unconscious. With a rope and hook he descended the delta wall."

"The tharlarion will have him," said a man.

"No," I said. "There would be a boat waiting."

"He cannot have gotten far," said Thurnock.

"There will be a tarn in the city," I said. "Do not pursue him."

14

I regarded the circle of men about. "Return to your rest," I said.

They moved from the room.

"The beast?" asked Clitus.

"Leave it," I said. "And leave me now."

Then I and the slave were alone. I closed the door. I slid shut the bolts, and turned to face her.

She looked very small and frightened, chained on my couch.

"So, my dear," I said, "you labor still in the service of Kurii."

"No, Master," she cried, "no!"

"Who tended my chamber afore this morning?" I asked.

"It was I, Master," she said. It is common to let the girl who is to spend the night at your feet tend your chamber the preceding day. She scrubs and cleans it, and tidies it. It is not a full day's work and she has hours in it in which she has little to do but wait for the master. She readies herself. She plans. She anticipates. When the master arrives, and she kneels before him, she is eager and anxious, vulnerable and stimulated, well ready both physically and psychologically for the mastery to which she will have no choice but to be joyfully subjected. Even the performance of small servile tasks, such as the polishing of his tarn boots, which she must perform, plays its role in her preparation for the night. The performance of such small tasks teaches her, incontrovertibly, in the depths of her beauty, that she truly belongs to him, and that he is truly her master. She is then well ready when he gestures her to the furs to perform for him exquisitely the most delicious and intimate of her assigned tasks, her most important tasks, those of the helpless love slave.

"Kneel on the tiles," I told her.

She slipped from the couch and knelt on the tiles before me. She knelt in the blood of the sleen.

"Position," I said.

Swiftly she assumed the position of the pleasure slave. She knelt back on her heels, her knees wide, her hands on her thighs, her back straight, her head up. She was terrified. I looked down at her.

I crouched before her, and took her by the arms. I was covered with the blood of the sleen. "Master?" she asked. I put her to her back on the tiles in the sleen's blood. I held her so she could not move, and entered her. "Master?" she asked, frightened. I began to caress her from within, deeply, with my manhood. The warm closeness of her body, so beau-

15

tiful, so helpless, that of an owned slave, clasped me. She began to respond to me, frightened.

"You labor still for Kurii," I said.

"No, Master," she wept, "no!"

I felt her spasmodically squirm beneath me. "No!" she wept. Her haunches shuddered.

"Yes," I said.

"No," she said, "no, Master!"

"The beast must have been put upon my scent," I said.

"I am innocent!" she said. Then she writhed beneath me. "Please do not make me yield to you this way, Master," she wept. "Oh," she cried. "Oh!"

"Speak," I told her.

She closed her eyes. "Have mercy!" she begged.

"Speak," I told her.

"I was taking the tunics to the tubs," she said. "I would have put them in with the others!" She half reared up beneath me, struggling, her eyes open and wild. She was strong for a girl, but girls are weak. I thrust her back down, shoulders and hair into the blood. Her head was back. She writhed, impaled and held. How weak she was. How futile were her struggles.

"There is no escape," I told her. "You are mine."

"I know," she said. "I know."

"Speak further," I said.

"Oh," she cried. "Oh!" Then she wept, "Please, Master, do not make me yield this way!"

"Speak further," I said.

"I was tricked," she cried. "Bertram of Lydius, in the halls, followed me. I thought little of it. I thought only he wanted to see my body move in the livery of the house, that he only followed me as a man will upon occasion follow a slave girl, idly, for the pleasure in seeing her."

"And this flattered you, did it not, you slut?" I asked.

"Yes, Master," she said. "I am a slave girl."

"Go on," I said.

"Please, Master," she wept, clutching me. "Oh, oh!" she cried.

"Go on," I said.

"Yes," she cried, angrily. "I was pleased! He was handsome, and strong, and Gorean, and I was a female slave. I thought he might ask for my use, and that it would be granted him by you in Gorean courtesy!"

It was true. Had a guest expressed interest in Vella, Elizabeth, a former secretary from Earth, one of my slaves, I

16

would surely have given her to him for his night's pleasure. And if he were not fully pleased, I would have had her whipped in the morning.

"He spoke to me," she said, "so I turned and knelt before him, the tunics clutched in my arms. 'You are pretty,' he said to me. This pleased me." Slave girls relish compliments. Indeed, there is a Gorean saying to the effect that any woman who relishes a compliment is in her heart a slave girl. She wants to please. Most Gorean men would not think twice about collaring a girl who responds, smiling, to compliments. It is regarded as right to enslave a natural slave. Most masters, incidentally, make a girl they own earn her compliments. She must struggle to be worthy of complimenting. She so struggles. Gorean compliments are generally meaningful, for they tend to be given only when deserved, and sometimes not then. A girl desires to please her master. When she is complimented she knows she has pleased him. This makes her happy, not simply because then she knows she is less likely to be punished, but because she, in her heart, being a woman, truly desires to please one who is her complete master. " 'Do you know me?' he asked," she said. " 'Yes, Master,' I said, 'you are Bertram of Lydius, guest in the house of my Master.' 'Your master has been kind to me,' said he. 'I would make him a gift to show my appreciation. It would be unfitting for me to accept his hospitality without in some small way expressing the esteem in which I hold him and my gratitude for his generosity.' 'How may I aid you, Master?' I asked. 'In Lydius,' said he, 'we encounter often the furs of snow sleen, fresh and handsome and warm. Too, we have there cunning tailors who can design garments with golden threads and secret pockets. I would make a gift of such a garment, a short coat or jacket, suitable for use in the tarn saddle, for your master.' "

"Few," I said, "in Port Kar think of me as a tarnsman. I did not so speak myself to Bertram of Lydius in our conversations."

"I did not think, Master," she said.

"Did you not think such a gift strange for a merchant and mariner?"

"Forgive a girl, Master," she said. "But surely there are those in Port Kar who know you a tarnsman, and the gift seems appropriate for one to proffer who is of Lydius in the north."

"The true Bertram of Lydius would not be likely to know me a tarnsman," I said.

"He was not then what he seemed," she whispered.

"I do not think so," I said. "I think he was an agent of Kurii."

I thrust into her, savagely. She cried out, looking at me. She was hot with sweat. The collar was on her throat.

"I think we have here, too," I said, holding her, "another agent of Kurii."

"No," she said, "no!" Then I began to make her respond to me.

"Oh," she wept. "Oh. Oh!"

"He wanted my tunic," I told her, "to take its measurements, that the jacket of the fur of the snow sleen might be well made."

"Yes," she wept. "Yes! But only for moments! Only for moments!"

"Fool," I said to her.

"I was tricked," she wept.

"You were tricked, or you are a Kur agent," I said.

"I am not a Kur agent," she wept. She tried to rise up, but I held her down, her small shoulders down to the tiles in the blood. She could not begin to be a match for my strength.

"Even if you are a Kur agent," I said, softly, "know, small beauty, that you are first my slave girl."

I looked down into her eyes.

"Yes, Master," she said. She twisted miserably, her head to one side. "He had the garment for only moments," she said.

"Was it always in your sight," I asked.

"No," she said. "He ordered me to remain in the hall, to wait for him."

I laughed.

"He had it for only moments it seemed," she said.

"Enough time," I said, "to press it between the bars of the sleen cage and whisper to the beast the signal for the hunt."

"Yes!" she wept.

Then I thrust again and again into her, in the strong, increasingly intense rhythms of a savage master until the collared she of her, once that of a civilized girl, screamed and shuddered, and then lay mine, without dignity or pride, shattered, only a yielded, barbarian slave, in my arms.

I stood up, and she lay at my feet collared, in the sleen's blood.

I reached to the great ax of Torvaldsland. I stood over her, looking down at her, the ax grasped in my hands.

She looked up at me. One knee was lifted. She shook her

18

head. She took the collar in her hands and pulled it out from her neck a bit, lifting it toward me.

"Do not strike me, Master," she said. "I am yours."

I looked at the collar and chain. She looked up at me, frightened. She was well secured.

My grip tightened on the ax.

She put her hands to the side, helplessly, and, frightened, lifted her body, supplicatingly, to me.

"Please do not strike me, Master," she said. "I am your slave."

I lowered the ax, holding it across my body with both hands. I looked down at her, angrily.

She lowered her body, and lay quietly in the blood, frightened. She placed the backs of her hands on the tiles, so that the palms were up, facing me, at her sides. The palms of a woman's hands are soft and vulnerable. She exposed them to me.

I did not lift the ax.

"I know little of sleen," she said. "I had thought it a sleen trained to hunt tabuk, in the company of archers, little more than an animal trained to turn and drive tabuk, and retrieve them."

"It is thus that the animal was presented to us," I said. That was true. Yet surely, in the light of such a request, one for a garment, a sleen in the house, her suspicions should have been aroused.

"He wanted a garment," I said.

"I did not think," she said.

"Nor did you speak to me of this thing," I said.

"He warned me not to speak to you," she said, "for the gift was to come as a surprise."

I laughed, looking at the sleen.

She put her head to one side, in shame. She turned then again to look at me. "He had it for only a few moments," she said.

"The cage could be opened later, and was," I said. "The hunt then began, through the halls of the house, in the silence and darkness."

She closed her eyes in misery, and then opened them again, looking at me.

I heard the ship's bell, in the great hall, striking. I heard footsteps in the hall outside.

"It is morning," I said.

Thurnock appeared at the door to my chamber. "Word has

19

come," said he, "from the house of Samos. He would speak with you."

"Prepare the longboat," I said. We would make our way through the canals to his house.

"Yes, Captain," he said, and turned and left.

I put aside the ax. With water, poured into a bowl, and fur, I cleaned myself. I donned a fresh tunic. I tied my own sandals.

The girl did not speak.

I slung a sword over my left shoulder, an admiral's blade.

"You did not let me tie your sandals," she said.

I fetched the key to the collar, and went to her, and opened the collar.

"You have duties to attend to," I said.

"Yes, Master," she said. On her knees she suddenly grasped my legs, weeping, looking up at me. "Forgive me, Master," she cried. "I was tricked! I was tricked!"

"It is morning in Port Kar," I said.

She put down her head to my feet. She kissed my feet. She then looked up at me. "If I do not please you this day, Master," she said, "impale me."

"I will," I told her. Then I turned and left her.

2 THE MESSAGE OF THE SCYTALE; I CONVERSE WITH SAMOS

"The arrogance of Kurii may yet prove their undoing," said Samos.

He sat, cross-legged, behind the low table. On it were hot bread, yellow and fresh, hot black wine, steaming, with its sugars, slices of roast bosk, the scrambled eggs of vulos, pastries with creams and custards.

"It is too easy," I said. I did not speak clearly with my mouth full.

"It is a sport for them," he said, "this war." He looked at me, grimly. "As it seems to be for some men."

"Perhaps to some," I said, "those who are soldiers, but

20

surely not to Kurii in general. I understand their commitment in these matters to be serious and one involving their deep concern."

"Would that all men were as serious," said Samos.

I grinned, and washed down the eggs with a swig of hot black wine, prepared from the beans grown upon the slopes of the Thentis mountains. This black wine is quite expensive. Men have been slain on Gor for attempting to smuggle the beans out of the Thentian territories.

"Kurii were ready once," said I, "or some party of them, to destroy Gor, to clear the path to Earth, a world they would surely favor less. Willingness to perform such an act, I wager, fits in not well with the notion of vain, proud beasts."

"Strange that you should speak of vain, proud beasts," said Samos.

"I do not understand," I said.

"I suppose not," said Samos. He then drank from his cup, containing the black wine. I did not press him to elucidate his meaning. He seemed amused.

"I think the Kurii are too clever, too shrewd, too determined," said I, "to be taken at their face value in this matter. Such an act, to deliver such a message, would be little better than a taunt, a gambit, intended to misdirect our attention."

"But can we take this risk?" he asked.

"Perhaps not," I said. With a Turian eating prong, used in the house of Samos, I speared a slice of meat, and then threaded it on the single tine.

Samos took from his robes a long, silken ribbon, of the sort with which a slave girl might bind back her hair. It seemed covered with meaningless marks. He gestured to a guardsman. "Bring in the girl," he said.

A blond girl, angry, in brief slave livery, was ushered into the room.

We were in Samos' great hall, where I had banqueted many times. It was the hall in which was to be found the great map mosaic, inlaid in the floor.

She did not seem a slave. That amused me.

"She speaks a barbarous tongue," said Samos.

"Why have you dressed me like this?" she demanded. She spoke in English.

"I can understand her," I said.

"That is perhaps not an accident," said Samos.

"Perhaps not," I said.

"Can none of you fools speak English?" she asked.

"I can communicate with her, if you wish," I told Samos.

21

He nodded.

"I speak English," I informed her, speaking in that intricate, beautiful tongue.

She seemed startled. Then she cried out, angrily, pulling downward at the edges of the livery in which she had been placed, as though that would hide more of her legs, which were lovely. "I do not care to be dressed like this," she said. She pulled away, angrily, from the guard, and stood before us. "I have not even been given shoes," she said. "And what is the meaning of this?" she demanded, pulling at a plain ring of iron which had been hammered about her throat. Her throat was slender, and white, and lovely.

Samos handed the hair ribbon to a guardsman, gesturing to the girl. "Put it on," he said to her, in Gorean.

I repeated his command, in English.

"When am I to be permitted to leave?" she asked.

Seeing the eyes of Samos she angrily took the ribbon, and winding it about her head, fastened back her hair. She blushed, angrily, hotly, knowing that, as she lifted her hands gracefully to her hair, she raised the lovely line of her breasts, little concealed in the thin livery. Then she stood before us, angrily, the ribbon in her hair.

"Thus it was she came to us," said Samos, "save that she was clad in inexplicable, barbarous garments." He gestured to a guardsman, who fetched and spilled open a bundle of garments on the edge of the table. I saw that there were pants of some bluish, denim-type material, and a flannel, long-sleeved shirt. There was also a white, light shirt, short-sleeved. Had I not realized them to have been hers, I would have assumed them the clothing of an Earth male. They were male-imitation clothing.

The girl tried to step forward but the shafts of two spears, wielded by her flanking guardsmen, barred her way.

There was also a pair of shoes, plain, brown and low, with darker-brown laces. They were cut on a masculine line, but were too small for a man. I looked at her feet. They were small and feminine. Her breasts, too, and hips, suggested that she was a female, and a rather lovely one. Slave livery makes it difficult for a girl to conceal her sex.

There was also a pair of colored socks, dark blue. They were short.

She again tried to step forward but this time the points of the guards' spears prevented her. They pressed at her abdomen, beneath the navel. Rep-cloth, commonly used in slave livery, is easily parted. The points of the spears had gone

22

through the cloth, and she felt them in her flesh. She stepped back, for a moment frightened and disconcerted. Then she regained her composure, and stood before us.

"This garment is too short," she said. "It is scandalous!"

"It is feminine," I told her. "Not unlike these," I said. I indicated the brassiere, the brief silken panties, which completed the group of garments on the table.

She blushed redly.

"Though you imitated a man outwardly," I said to her, "I note that it was such garments you wore next to your flesh."

"I don't know what you're talking about," she said.

"Here," I said, "You wear one garment, which is feminine, and where it may be seen, proclaiming your femininity, and you are permitted no other garments."

"Return my clothing to me," she demanded.

Samos gestured to a guardsman, and he tied up the bundle of clothing, leaving it on the table.

"You see," said Samos, "how she was."

He meant, of course, the ribbon in her hair. She stood very straight. For some reason it is almost impossible for a woman not to stand beautifully when she wears slave livery and is in the sight of men.

"Give me the ribbon," said Samos. He spoke in Gorean, but I needed not translate. He held out his hand. She, lifting her arms, blushing, angrily, again touched the ribbon. She freed it of her hair and handed it to a guard, who delivered it to Samos. I saw the guards' eyes on her. I smiled. They could hardly wait to get her to the pens. She, still a foolish Earth girl, did not even notice this.

"Bring your spear," said Samos to a guard. A guard, one who stood behind, gave his spear to Samos.

"It is, of course, a scytale," I said.

"Yes," said Samos, "and the message is in clear Gorean."

He had told me what the message was, and we had discussed it earlier. I was curious, however, to see it wrapped about the shaft of the spear. Originally, in its preparation, the message ribbon is wrapped diagonally, neatly, edges touching, about a cylinder, such as the staff of a marshal's office, the shaft of a spear, a previously prepared object, or so on, and then the message is written in lines parallel with the cylinder. The message, easily printed, easily read, thus lies across several of the divisions in the wrapped silk. When the silk is unwrapped, of course, the message disappears into a welter of scattered lines, the bits and parts of letters; the coherent message is replaced with a ribbon marked only by mean-

23

ingless, unintelligible scraps of letters; to read the message, of course, one need only rewrap the ribbon about a cylindrical object of the same dimension as the original object. The message then appears in its clear, legible character. Whereas there is some security in the necessity for rewrapping the message about a cylinder of the original dimension, the primary security does not lie there. After all, once one recognizes a ribbon, or belt, or strip of cloth, as a scytale, it is then only a matter of time until one finds a suitable object to facilitate the acquisition of the message. Indeed, one may use a roll of paper or parchment until, rolling it more tightly or more loosely, as needed, one discovers the message. The security of the message, as is often the case, is a function not of the opacity of the message, in itself, but rather in its concealment, in its not being recognized as a message. A casual individual would never expect that the seemingly incoherent design on a girl's ribbon would conceal a message which might be significant, or fateful.

From the girl's reactions I gathered that she understood now that the ribbon bore some message, but that she had not clearly understood this before.

"It is a message?" she asked.

"Yes," I said.

"What does it say?" she asked.

"It is none of your concern," I said.

"I want to know," she said.

"Do you wish to be beaten?" I asked.

"No," she said.

"Then be silent," I said.

She was silent. Her fists were clenched.

I read the message. "Greetings to Tarl Cabot, I await you at the world's end. Zarendargar. War General of the People."

"It is Half-Ear," said Samos, "high Kur, war general of the Kurii."

"The word 'Zarendargar'," I said, "is an attempt to render a Kur expression into Gorean."

"Yes," said Samos. The Kurii are not men but beasts. Their phonemes for the most part elude representation in the alphabets of men. It would be like trying to write down the noises of animals. Our letters would not suffice.

"Return me to Earth!" demanded the girl.

"Is she still a virgin?" I asked Samos.

"Yes," he said. "She has not even been branded."

"With what brand will you mark her?" I asked.

"The common Kajira brand," he said.

24

"What are you talking about?" she demanded. "Give me my clothing," she demanded angrily.

Again the points of the two spears pressed against her abdomen. Again they penetrated the loosely woven cloth. Again she stepped back, for the moment disconcerted.

I gathered that she had been accustomed to having her demands met by men.

When a woman speaks in that tone of voice to a man of Earth he generally hastens to do her bidding. He has been conditioned so. Here, however, her proven Earth techniques seemed ineffectual, and this puzzled her, and angered her, and, I think, to an extent frightened her. What if men did not do her bidding? She was smaller and weaker, and beautiful, and desirable. What if she discovered that it were she, and not they, who must do now what was bidden, and with perfection? A woman who spoke in that tone to a Gorean man, if she were not a free woman, would find herself instantly whipped to his feet.

Then she was again the woman of Earth, though clad in Gorean slave livery.

"Return me to Earth," she said.

"Take her below to the pens," said Samos, "and sell her off."

"What did he say!" she demanded.

"Is she to be branded?" asked the guard.

"Yes," said Samos, "the common brand."

"What did he say!" she cried. Each of the two guards flanking her had now taken her by an arm. She looked very small between them. I thought the common Kajira mark would be exquisite in her thigh.

"Left thigh," I suggested.

"Yes, left thigh," said Samos to one of the guards. I liked the left-thigh branded girl. A right-handed master may caress it while he holds her in his left arm.

"Give me back my clothing!" she cried.

Samos glanced at the bundle of clothing. "Burn this," he said.

The girl watched, horrified, as one of the guardsmen took the clothing and, piece by piece, threw it into a wide copper bowl of burning coals. "No!" she cried. "No!"

The two guards then held her arms tightly and prepared to conduct her to the pens.

She looked with horror at the burnt remnants, the ashes, of her clothing.

25

She now wore only what Gorean men had given her, a scrap of slave livery, and a ring hammered about her neck.

She threw her head about, moving the ring. For the first time she seemed truly aware of it.

She looked at me, terrified. The guards' hands were on her upper arms. Their hands were tight.

"What are they going to do!" she cried.

"You are to be taken to the pens," I said.

"The pens!" she asked.

"There," I said, "you will be stripped and branded."

"Branded?" she said. I do not think she understood me. Her Earth mind would find this hard to understand. She was not yet cognizant of Gorean realities. She would learn them swiftly. No choice would be given her.

"Is she to be sold red-silk?" I asked Samos.

He looked at the girl. "Yes," he said. The guards grinned. It would be a girl who knew herself as a woman when she ascended the block.

"I thought you said I would be stripped and branded," she said, laughing.

"Yes," I said, "that is precisely what I said."

"No!" she screamed. "No!"

"Then," I said, "you will be raped, and taught your womanhood. When you have learned your womanhood, you will be caged. Later you will be sold."

"No!" she cried. "No!"

"Take her away," said Samos.

The guards' hands tightened even more on the beauty's arms. She might as well have been bound in steel. She must go as they conducted her. "Wait! Wait!" she cried. She struggled, squirming in their grasp, her feet slipping on the tiles. Samos motioned that they wait, momentarily. She looked at me, and at Samos, wildly. "What place is this?" she asked.

"It is called Gor," I told her.

"No!" she said. "That is only in stories!"

I smiled.

"No!" she cried. She looked about herself, at the strong men who held her. She threw her head back, moaning, sensing the ring on her throat. "No, no!" she wept. "I do not want to be a woman on Gor! Anything but a woman on Gor!"

I shrugged.

"You are joking," she said, wildly.

"No," I said.

26

"What language is it here which they speak?" she asked.

I smiled.

"Gorean," she said.

"Yes," I said.

"And I must learn it quickly?" she said.

"Yes," I said. "You must learn it quickly, or be slain. Gorean men are not patient."

"—Gorean," she said.

"It is the language of your masters," I said.

"—Of my masters?" she asked.

"Yes," I said. "Surely you know that you are a slave girl."

"No!" she cried. "No! No! No! No!"

"Take her away," said Samos.

The girl was dragged, screaming and sobbing, from our presence, to the pens.

How feminine she seemed then. No longer did she seem an imitation male. She was then only what she was, a slave girl being taken to the pens.

Samos, thoughtfully, began to unwind the long ribbon, that which the girl had worn, and which formed the scytale, from the spear's shaft.

We heard her screaming down the corridor, and then she cried out in pain, and was silent. The guards, wearied by her outcries, had simply cuffed her to silence. Sometimes a girl is permitted to scream. Sometimes she is not. It depends on the will of the man. When she is branded a girl is commonly permitted to scream, at least for a time. But we would not hear that screaming, for, when it was done, she would be below, and far away, in the pens.

I dismissed her from my mind, for she was a slave. Her history as a free woman had terminated; her history as an imbonded beauty had begun.

Samos, the ribbon freed from the spear's shaft, the spear retrieved by the guardsman, looked down at the table, at the ribbon, which now seemed only a ribbon, with meaningless marks.

"Greetings to Tarl Cabot," I said, recalling the message. "I await you at the world's end. Zarendargar. War General of the People."

"Arrogant beasts," he said.

I shrugged.

"We had no clue," he said. "Now we have this." He lifted the ribbon, angrily. "Here is an explicit message."

"It seems so," I said.

We did not know where lay the world's end, but we knew

27

where it must be sought. The world's end was said to lie beyond Cos and Tyros, at the end of Thassa, at the world's
edge. No man had sailed to the world's end and returned. It
was not known what had occurred there. Some said that
Thassa was endless, and there was no world's end, only the
green waters extending forever, gleaming, beckoning the mariner and hero onward, onward until men, one by one, had
perished and the lonely ships, their steering oars lashed in
place, pursued the voyage in silence, until the timbers rotted
and one day, perhaps centuries later, the brave wood, warm
in the sun, sank beneath the sea.

"The ship is ready," said Samos, looking at me.

Others said, in stories reminiscent of Earth, and which had
doubtless there had their origin, that the world's end was protected by clashing rocks and monsters, and by mountains that
could pull the nails from ships. Others said, similarly, that the
end of the world was sheer, and that a ship might there
plunge over the edge, to fall tumbling for days through emp-
tiness until fierce winds broke it apart and the wreckage was
lifted up to the bottom of the sea. In the maelstroms south
and west of Tyros shattered planking was sometimes found.
It was said that some of this was from ships which had
sought the world's end.

"The ship is ready," said Samos, looking at me.

A ship had been prepared, set to sail to the world's end. It
had been built by Tersites, the half-blind, mad shipwright,
long scorned on Gor. Samos regarded him a genius. I knew
him for a madman; whether he might be, too, a genius, I did
not know. It was an unusual ship. It was deep-keeled and
square-rigged, as most Gorean ships are not. Though it was a
ramship it carried a foremast. It possessed great oars, which
must be handled by several men, rather than one man to an
oar. Instead of two side-hung rudders, or oars, it carried a
single oar, slung at the vessel's sternpost. Its ram was carried
high, out of the water. It would make its strike not below, but
at the waterline. It was a laughing stock in the arsenal at Port
Kar, but Tersites paid his critics no attention. He worked as-
siduously, eating little, sleeping at the side of the ship, super-
vising each small detail in the great structure. It was said the
deep keel would slow the ship; that the two masts would take
too long to remove in the case of naval combat; that so large
an oar would constitute an impractical lever, that it could not
be grasped by a man, that the oarsmen could not all sit during the stroke, that if more than one man controlled an oar
some would shirk their work. Why one rudder rather than

28

two? With lateen rigging one could sail closer to the wind. Of what use is a ram which makes its strike so high?

I was not a shipwright, but I was a captain. It seemed to me such a ship would be too heavy to manage well, that it would be clumsy and slow, that it might be better fitted to cargo service when protected in a convoy than entrusted to confront, elude or brave the lean, lateen-rigged wolves of gleaming Thassa, hungry for the cargoes of the ineffectual and weak. Were I to hunt the world's end I would prefer to do so with the Dorna or the Tesephone, a sleep ship whose moods and gifts I well knew.

Yet the ship of Tersites was strong. It loomed high and awesome, mighty with its strakes, proud with its uprearing prow, facing the sea canal. Standing beside the ship, on the ground, looking up at that high prow, so far above me, it seemed sometime that such a ship, if any, might embark upon that threatening, perhaps impossible voyage to the world's end. Tersites had chosen to build the ship in such a way that its prow faced west; it pointed thus not only to the sea canal; it pointed also between Cos and Tyros; it pointed toward the world's end.

"The eyes have not yet been painted," I said. "It is not yet alive."

"Paint its eyes," said he to me.

"That is for Tersites to do," I said. He was the shipwright. If the ship did not have eyes, how could it see? To the Gorean sailor his ships are living things. Some would see this as superstition; others sense that there is some sort of an inexplicable reality which is here involved, a difficult and subtle reality which the man of the sea can somehow sense, but which he cannot, and perhaps should not attempt to explain to the satisfaction of men other than himself. Sometimes, late at night, on deck, under the moons of Gor, I have felt this. It is a strange feeling. It is as though the ship, and the sea, and the world were alive. The Gorean, in general, regards many things in a much more intense and personal way than, say, the informed man of Earth. Perhaps that is because he is the victim of a more primitive state of consciousness; perhaps, on the other hand, we have forgotten things which he has not. Perhaps the world only speaks to those who are prepared to listen. Regardless of what the truth should be in these matters, whether it be that man is intrinsically a mechanism of chemicals, or, more than this, a conscious, living animal whose pain and meaning, and defiance, emergent, must transcend the interactions of carbon and oxygen, the exchange of

29

gases, the opening and closing of valves, it is undeniable that some men, Goreans among them, experience their world in a rich, deep way that is quite foreign to that of the mechanistic mentality. The man of Earth thinks of the world as being essentially dead; the Gorean thinks of his world as being essentially alive; one utilizes the metaphor of the blind machine, the other the metaphor of the living being; doubtless reality exceeds all metaphors; in the face of reality doubtless all metaphors are small, and must fail; indeed, what are these metaphors but instruments of fragile straw with which we, pathetic, wondering animals, would scratch at the gates of obdurate, granite mystery; yet if we must choose our way in which to fail I do not think the Gorean has made a poor choice; his choice, it seems to me, is not inferior to that of the man of Earth. He cares for his world; it is his friend; he would not care to kill it.

Let it suffice to say that to the Gorean sailor his ships are living things. Were they not, how could he love them so?

"This ship is essentially ready," said Samos. "It can sail soon for the world's end."

"Strange, is it not," I asked, "that when the ship is nearly ready that this message should come?"

"Yes," said Samos. "That is strange."

"The Kurii wish us to sail now for the world's end," I said.

"Arrogant beasts!" cried Samos, pounding down on the small table. "They challenge us now to stop them!"

"Perhaps," I admitted.

"We have sought them in vain. We were helpless. We knew not where to look. Now they in their impatient vanity, in their mockery of our impotence, boldly announce to us their whereabouts!"

"Have they?" I asked.

" 'We are here,' they say. 'Come seek us, Fools, if you dare!' "

"Perhaps," I said. "Perhaps."

"Do you doubt the message?" asked Samos.

"I do not know," I said. "I simply do not know."

"They taunt us," said Samos. "War is a sport for them."

"Perhaps," I said.

"We must act," he said.

"In what way?" I asked.

"You must sail immediately to the world's end." Samos looked at me, grimly. "There you must seek out Half-Ear, and destroy him."

"None have returned from the world's end," I said.

"You are afraid?" asked Samos.

"Why," I asked, "should the message be addressed to me?"

"The Kurii know you," said he. "They respect you."

I, too, respected them. I was a warrior. I enjoyed sharing with them the cruel, mortal games of war. They were cunning, and fierce, and terrible. I was a warrior. I found them precious foes.

"Does not the fate of worlds weigh upon you?" asked Samos.

I smiled.

"I know you," he said, bitterly, "you are a warrior, a soldier, a mercenary, an adventurer. You fight for the exhilaration. You are frivolous. In your way you are as despicable as the Kur."

"Perhaps I am an adventurer," I said. "I do not truly know. I have stood against the Kur. I have met men with steel. I have had the women of enemies naked at my feet, suing to be my slaves."

"You are a mercenary," he said.

"Perhaps," I said, "but I choose my wars with care."

"It is strange," said Samos.

"What?" I asked.

"We fight for civilization," said Samos, "against the barbarism of the Kur."

I smiled that Samos should see himself so.

"And yet," said he, "in the world for which we strive we would have no place."

I looked at him.

"In a civilized world, Captain," said he, "there would be no place for such as you."

"That is true," I said.

"Is it not a paradox?" asked Samos. "Men need us in order to bring about a world in which we may be scorned and disregarded."

I said nothing.

"Men seldom recall who it was who brought them the fruits of victory."

"It is true," I conceded.

"Civilized men," said Samos, "the small and pale, the righteous, the learned, the smug, the supercilious, the weak-stomached and contemptuous, stand upon the shoulders of forgotten, bloody giants."

I shrugged.

"You are such a bloody giant," he said.

31

"No," I said. "I am only a tarnsman, a nomad in unusual conflicts, a friend of the sword."

"Sometimes," said Samos, "I weep." He looked at me. I had never before seen him in such a mood.

"Is our struggle, if successful," he asked, "to issue only in the victory of defeat, the triumph of the trivial and placid, the glorification of mediocrity?"

"Perhaps," I said.

"Will our blood have been shed," he asked, "to bring about so miniscule an achievement, the contentment of the herd browsing among the dunes of boredom?"

"They will have their petty concerns," I said, "which will seem important to them."

He looked down, angrily.

"And they will have their entertainments and their stimulations. There will be industries which will attempt to assuage their boredom."

"But will nothing truly matter?" he asked.

"Perhaps men must sleep before they wake," I said.

"I do not understand," he said.

"There are the stars," I said.

"The Kurii stand between us and the stars," said Samos.

"Perhaps we labor," said I, "to open the gates to the stars."

"Men will never seek them," said Samos.

"Some men will," I said.

"But the others will not help them, and the adventure will fail," said Samos.

"Perhaps," I said. "I do not know." I looked at him. "Much depends on what men are," I said.

"His measure has not yet been taken," said Samos.

"And perhaps it will never be taken," I said, "and cannot be taken. Every bound you set him will show him a place beyond which he can place his foot or hand."

"Perhaps," smiled Samos.

"I have hunted, and I have been hunted," I said.

"Why do you say this?" he asked.

"And in hunting, and in being hunted," I said, "I have been alive."

"Yes," said Samos. "But why are you saying this?"

"Do you not see?" I asked him. "The conflict, the struggle, even if it should issue in the triumph of the leveled herd, each smiling and trying to be the same as the other, will yet have been ours, and cannot be taken from us."

"Yes," said Samos.

"Ours will have been the war," I said.

"Yes," he said.

"It is our hand that will have grasped the hilt of the sword. It is we, not they, who will have met the enemy. Let them weep that they were not there."

"Yes," said Samos, "I would not be other than I am, and I would not be other than where I am."

"The meaning of history," I said, "lies not in the future. It is like a range of mountains with many summits. Great deeds are the meaning of history. There are many meanings and many summits. One may climb different mountains at different times, but each mountain glows in the same sun."

"The Kurii must be met!" said Samos.

"Perhaps we will choose to do so," I said.

"You are a monster, Captain," he laughed.

"I am of the warriors," I said.

"I know your sort," he said. "It is the fight you relish. What a wicked sort you are, and yet how useful!"

I shrugged.

"You see a fight you want, you take it," he said. "You see a woman you like, you take her."

"Perhaps if she pleased me," I said.

"You would do as you wished," he said.

"Of course," I said.

"Warrior!" said he.

"Yes, Warrior," I said.

"The eyes will be painted, and the ship will be launched at dawn," he said.

I rose to my feet. "Let us not be precipitate," I said.

He looked at me, startled.

"Supplies must be laid in," I said. "Too, a crew must be recruited. Too, there must be an acceptable preliminary voyage, to test the handling of the ship, and its seaworthiness."

"Time is crucial!" he said. "I can give you supplies, men."

"I must think of these things," I said. "And if I am to sail with men I must pick them myself, for our lives would depend upon one another."

"Half-Ear waits at the world's end!" cried Samos.

"Let him wait," I said.

Samos looked at me, irritated.

"If he is truly waiting," I said, "there is no great hurry." I looked at Samos. "Besides," said I, "it may take months to reach the world's end, if it can be reached at all."

"That is true," said Samos.

"Besides," I said, "it is En'Kara."

"So?" asked Samos.

"It is time for the Kaissa matches at the Fair of En'Kara, at the Sardar," I said. I found it hard to think that this was not on the mind of Samos. "Centius of Cos," I said, "is defending his title against Scormus of Ar."

"How can you be concerned with Kaissa at a time like this?" he asked.

"The match is important," I pointed out. Anyone who knew anything of Kaissa knew this. It was the talk of Gor.

"I should have you whipped, and chained to an oar," said Samos.

"I have been whipped," I said, "at various times, and, too, I have been chained to an oar." I had felt the leather. I had drawn the oar.

"Apparently it taught you little," he said.

"I am difficult to teach," I admitted.

"Kaissa!" grumbled Samos.

"The planet has waited years for this match," I said.

"I have not," said Samos.

It had been delayed because of the war between Ar and Cos, having to do with piracy and competitive commercial claims on the Vosk. The war persisted but now both players had been brought to the Sardar by armed men from their respective cities, under a special flag of truce, agreed upon by Lurius of Jad, Ubar of Cos, and Marlenus of Ar, called the Ubar of Ubars, who ruled in Ar. Hostilities between the two cities were suspended for the duration of the match. Kaissa is a serious matter for most Goreans. That Samos did not seem sufficiently impressed with the monumentality of the confrontation irritated me somewhat. It is hard to understand one who is not concerned with Kaissa.

"We all have our limitations," I said.

"That is true," he said.

"What did you say?" I asked. He muttered something.

"I said," said Samos, "that Kaissa is a disease."

"Oh," I said. If it was a disease, and that seemed not unlikely, it was at least one which afflicted perhaps a majority of Goreans. I expected to have to pay a golden tarn disk for standing room in the amphitheater in which the match would take place. A golden tarn disk would purchase a trained war tarn, or several women.

"If there was a crucial act to be done at a given time," said Samos, "and the fate of two worlds hung upon that act, and it interfered with a Kaissa match, what would you do?"

I grinned. "I would have to think about it," I told him. "Who would be playing?"

Samos rose to his feet, exasperated, but grinning. "Come with me," he said.

He conducted me to a place in the hall, where he pointed down to that portion of the intricate map mosaic which lay there.

"Cos and Tyros," I said.

He pointed beyond them. For most practical purposes, except for a few small, close islands, of little or no importance, the mosaic ended there. No one knew what lay beyond Cos and Tyros to the west, once the small islands were passed.

"You should have your mind not on Kaissa," said Samos, "my dear Captain, but on the world's end." He pointed to a place on the floor. It contained only small, smooth white tiles.

"Perhaps the world's end," I said, "is on the other side of the wall."

We did not know where it might be, in the scale of the map mosaic.

"Perhaps," laughed Samos. "Perhaps."

He glanced about at the mosaic. For an instant his eye stopped, near its top.

"What is it?" I asked. I had noticed a bit of hesitation in him, a small movement in his shoulder, the sort of thing which suggests that a casual thought, unimportantly troubling, has occurred to someone.

"Nothing," he said. He had dismissed the thought.

"No," I said, curious. "What is it?"

He gestured to a guardsman to bring a lamp, for we were far from the light of the bowl of coals now, and of various torches set in the walls.

We walked slowly toward the back of the hall. The guardsman brought him the lamp there.

"As you know," said Samos, "this house is an intelligence center, in which we receive many reports. Much of what we hear is trivial and unimportant, simply meaningless. Yet we try to remain informed."

"Naturally," I said. Who knew when, or if, a pattern might emerge.

"Two items of information we have received seem to us peculiar. We have received them at different times. They are in their nature, unrelated. Yet each is provocative."

"What are they?" I asked.

"See," said Samos, crouching down, holding the lamp about a foot above the floor, "here is Kassau, and the Skerry of Vars."

"Yes," I said.

35

"And Torvaldsland, northwards," he said, "and Ax Glacier."

"Yes," I said.

"Have you heard," he asked, "of the herd of Tancred?"

"No," I said.

"It is a herd of northern tabuk," said Samos, "a gigantic herd, one of several. The herd of Tancred winters in the rims of the northern forests south and east of Torvaldsland. In the spring, short-haired and hungry, they emerge from the forests and migrate northward." He indicated the map. "They follow this route," he said, "emerging from the forest here, skirting Torvaldsland here, to the east, and then moving west above Torvaldsland, to the sea. They follow the shore of Thassa north, cross Ax Glacier here, like dark clouds on the ice, then continue to follow the shore north here, until they then turn eastward into the tundra of the polar basin, for their summer grazing. With the coming of winter, long-haired and fat, they return by the same route to the forests. This migration, like others of its kind, occurs annually."

"Yes?" I said.

"It seems not to have occurred this year," he said.

I looked at him, puzzled.

"Red hunters of the polar basin, trading for tea and sugar, have reported the failure of the herd to appear."

"That is puzzling," I said.

"It is more serious than that," he said. "It means the perishing of the men of the polar basin, or their near starvation. They depend on the tabuk in the summer for food."

"Is there anything that can be done?" I asked.

"I think not," said Samos. "Their winter stores of food, from the ice hunting, will last them for a time. Then they must hunt elsewhere. Perhaps some can live by fishing until the fall, and the return of the black sea sleen."

The red hunters lived as nomads, dependent on the migrations of various types of animals, in particular the northern tabuk and four varieties of sea sleen. Their fishing and hunting were seasonal, and depended on the animals. Sometimes they managed to secure the northern shark, sometimes even the toothed Hunjer whale or the less common Karl whale, which was a four-fluked, baleen whale. But their life, at best, was a precarious one. Little was known of them. Like many simple, primitive peoples, isolated and remote, they could live or die without being noticed.

"Send a ship north," I said, "with supplies."

"The waters north of Ax Glacier are ruthless," said Samos.

"Send it," I said.

"Very well," he said.

"There was something else," I said.

"It is nothing," he said.

"Tell me," I said.

"Here," he said, moving a bit, "here." He crouched over the mosaic where it delineated the sea, an arm of Thassa, crescentlike, extending northward and eastward, tangent upon the polar shores. The sea in this area was frozen for more than half the year. Winds and tides broke the ice, crushing and piling it in fantastic shapes, wild, trackless conformations, the sport of a terrible nature at play, the dreaded pack ice of the north.

Samos put the lamp down on the floor. "Here," he said, pointing. "It lies somewhere here."

"What?" I asked. Nothing was indicated on the map.

"The mountain that does not move," he said.

"Most mountains do not move," I smiled.

"The ice mountains of the polar sea," he said, "drift eastward."

"I see," I said.

Samos referred to an iceberg. Some of these are gigantic, pasangs in width, hundreds of feet high. They break from glaciers, usually in the spring and summer, and drift in Thassa, moving with the currents. The currents generally moved eastward above the polar basin. Gorean has no expression specifically for an iceberg. The same expression is used for both mountain and iceberg. If a reference should be unclear the expression is qualified, as by saying, "ice mountain." A mountain is a mountain to Goreans, regardless of whether it be formed of soil and stone, or ice. We tend to think of mountains as being land formations. The Gorean tends to think more of them as being objects of a certain sort, rather than objects of a certain sort with a particular location. In a sense, English does, too, for the expression 'berg' is simple German for 'mountain', and the expression 'iceberg', then is a composite word which, literally translated would yield 'ice mountain' or 'mountain of ice'. 'Berg', of course, in actual German, would be capitalized, for it is a noun. Interestingly, Goreans, although they do not capitalize all nouns do capitalize many more of them than would be capitalized in, say, English or French. Sometimes context determines capitalization. Languages are diverse and interesting, idiosyncratic and fascinating.

I will generally use the expression 'iceberg' for it is easier for me to do so.

"There is here an iceberg," said Samos, pointing to the map, "which is not following the parsit current." Samos had said, literally, of course, 'ice mountain'. The parsit current is the main eastward current above the polar basin. It is called the parsit current for it is followed by several varieties of migrating parsit, a small, narrow, usually striped fish. Sleen, interestingly, come northward with the parsit, their own migrations synchronized with those of the parsit, which forms for them their principal prey. The four main types of sea sleen found in the polar seas are the black sleen, the brown sleen, the tusked sleen and the flat-nosed sleen. There is a time of year for the arrival of each, depending on the waves of the parsit migrations. Not all members of a species of sleen migrate. Also, some winter under the ice, remaining generally dormant, rising every quarter of an Ahn or so to breathe. This is done at breaks in the ice or at gnawed breathing holes.

"An iceberg which does not drift with the current, which does not move with its brothers," I said.

"Yes," said Samos.

"It is a thing of myth," I said.

"I suppose so," said Samos.

"You grow too tense with your responsibilities, Samos," I told him. "Obviously such a thing cannot be."

Samos nodded. He grinned. "You are right," he said.

"Where did you hear of this?" I asked.

"It was told by a man of the polar basin who had come south to sell skins at the Sardar."

"Had he himself seen this?" I asked.

"No," said Samos.

I smiled.

"And how was it that he spoke of it?" I asked.

"He was given a coin," said Samos, "to speak of anything strange or unusual of which he might have heard."

"He well earned his coin," I said.

"Wily sleen," said Samos.

I laughed. Samos, too, laughed.

"They are clever fellows," I said.

"It is not often I am outwitted," said Samos.

Samos and I rose to our feet and returned to the small table. He put the lamp down on the table.

"You will sail then, soon, for the world's end?" asked Samos.

"It is my intention," I said. I turned to leave.

"Captain," said he.

I turned to face him. "Yes," I said.

"Do you think," he asked, "that if ever the gate to the stars should be opened, that men will remember the name of Tarl Cabot?"

"No," I said.

"I wish you well," he said.

"I, too, wish you well, Samos, first captain of Port Kar," I said.

"Who will win," he asked, "Centius of Cos or Scormus of Ar?"

"Scormus of Ar," I said. "He is invincible. Centius of Cos is a fine player, but he is beyond his prime. He is weary now. He has had his day. He will be no match for Scormus."

I remembered Scormus of Ar, whom I had seen in the house of Cernus, of Ar, some years ago. He was an incredibly handsome fellow, young, brilliant, arrogant, haughty, lame. He lived much by himself. It was said he had never touched a woman. He ruled the high bridges of Ar with his Kaissa board. No other player might call "Kaissa" on those bridges until he had bested the young Scormus. His play was swift, decisive, brilliant, merciless; more than one player had given up the game after being indulged, and then toyed with and humiliated by the genius of Scormus. Kaissa was for him a weapon. He could use it to destroy his enemies. Centius of Cos, on the other hand, was an older man; no one knew how old: it was said the stabilization serums had not taken their full effect with him until he had seen fifty winters; he was slight and gray-haired; he was quite different in personality and character from the young Scormus; he was quiet, and soft-spoken, and gentle; he loved Kaissa, and its beauty. He would often ponder a board for hours, by himself, searching for a supreme combination. "It eludes me," he would say. Once he had been bested by Sabo of Turia, at the Tharna tournaments, and he had wept with joy and embraced the victor, thanking him for letting him participate in such a beautiful game. "Winning and losing," he had said, "do not matter. What matters is the game, and the beauty." Men had thought him mad. "I had rather be remembered as the loser in one beautiful game," he said, "then as the winner in a thousand flawed masterpieces." He had always sought for the perfect game. He had never found it. Beauty, I suspect, lies all about us. The craftsman can find it in a turning of leather, where I might never see it. A musician may find it in a sound which I cannot detect. And one who plays Kaissa may find it in the arrangements of tiny bits of wood on a board of red and yellow squares. Centius of Cos had sought always for the perfect game. He had never found it.

"When will you return?" asked Samos.

"After the matches," I said.

"You will see others, too," he asked.

"Of course," I said. "Do you know that Philemon of Teletus will play Stengarius of Ti, and that Hobart of Tharna will match wits with Boris of Turia?"

"No," said Samos, ruefully. "It escaped my attention."

I shrugged. Samos, I decided, was hopeless.

He conducted me even to the first gate of his house, where I threw about myself the cloak of the admiral.

In a few moments, I sat at the tiller of the longboat, for the simple task of guiding the craft pleased me, and was being rowed to my house. I saw the silken head of an urt in the canal, a few feet from the boat. It was a large urt, some forty pounds in weight. They live on garbage cast into the canals, and on bound slaves who have not been pleasing.

I looked back at the house of Samos. The slim, blond-haired girl would have been branded by now. We had not heard her scream for she, when it was done, would have been below, far away, in the pens.

I thought of the message:

> Greetings to Tarl Cabot,
>> I await you at the world's end.
>> Zarendargar.
> War General of the People.

I smiled to myself.

The prow of the ship of Tersites pointed even now to the world's end.

None had returned from the world's end.

The canal turned then and I guided the craft about the corner. As we turned I glanced once more at the house of Samos. It loomed high and formidable, over the canal, a slaver's house, a high, dark, frightening fortress.

In the pens far below the fortress there was a new slave, a slim, blond-haired Earth girl. She would be caged now. I wondered if she seized the bars of her cage, pressing her face against them, trying to understand what had happened to her. She had mixed in the affairs of worlds. She was now a slave. Probably she lay naked on her stomach on the cement floor-

40

ing of her kennel, her hands over her head, screaming. On the exterior of her left thigh there would be a brand. On the interior of her thigh there would be blood. She had mixed in the affairs of worlds. It had not turned out well for her. She was now a slave. She would be soon sold off.

I wondered if she would learn swiftly to be pleasing to a master.

Another urt's head, sleek and glistening, surfaced near the boat, then it submerged.

I expected she would learn swiftly.

I considered the upcoming match between Centius of Cos and Scormus of Ar.

I would wager heavily on Scormus of Ar. I did not expect, however, that I would get good odds.

3   THE FAIR OF EN'KARA

"Make way! Make way!" laughed the brawny young fellow. He had a naked girl over his shoulder, bound hand and foot. He had won her in Girl Catch, in a contest to decide a trade dispute between two small cities, Ven and Rarn, the former a river port on the Vosk, the second noted for its copper mining, lying southeast of Tharna. In the contest a hundred young men of each city, and a hundred young women, the most beautiful in each city, participate. The object of the game is to secure the women of the enemy. Weapons are not permitted. The contest takes place in an area outside the perimeters of the great fair, for in it slaves are made. The area is enclosed by a low wooden wall, and spectators observe. When a male is forced beyond the wall he is removed from the competition and may not, upon pain of death, re-enter the area for the duration of the contest. When a girl is taken she is bound hand and foot and thrown to a girl pit, of which there are two, one in each city's end of the "field." These pits are circular, marked off with a small wooden fence, sand-bottomed, and sunk some two feet below the surface of the "field." If she cannot free herself she counts as a catch. The object of the male is to remove his opponents from the field

41

and capture the girls of the other city. The object of the girl, of course, is to elude capture.

"Make way!" he called. "Make way!" I, with others in the crowd, stepped aside.

Both the young men and women wear tunics in this sport. The tunics of the young women are cut briefly, to better reveal their charms. The young man wears binding fiber about his left wrist, with which to secure prizes. The young women, who are free, if the rules permit, as they sometimes do not, commonly wear masks, that their modesty be less grievously compromised by the brevity of their costume. Should the girl be caught, however, her mask is removed. The tunics of the girls are not removed, however, except those of the girls of the losing city, when the match has ended and the winner decided. The win is determined when the young men of one city, or those left on the field, have secured the full hundred of the women of the "enemy." A woman once bound and thrown to the girl pit, incidentally, may not be fetched forth by the young men of her city, except at the end of the match, and on the condition that they have proved victorious. The captured women of the victorious city at the conclusion of the contest are of course released; they are robed and honored; the girls of the losing city, of course, are simply stripped and made slaves. This may seem a cruel sport but some regard it as superior to a war; surely it is cleaner and there is less loss of life; this method of settling disputes, incidentally, is not used if it is felt that honor is somehow involved in the disagreement. Honor is important to Goreans, in a way that those of Earth might find hard to understand; for example, those of Earth find it natural that men should go to war over matters of gold and riches, but not honor; the Gorean, contrariwise, is more willing to submit matters of honor to the adjudication of steel than he is matters of riches and gold; there is a simple explanation for this; honor is more important to him. Strangely the girls of the cities are eager to participate in this sport. Doubtless each believes her standard will be victorious and she will return in honor to her city.

The young man brushed past me. The girl's hair was still bound, knotted, on her head; it had not yet even been loosened, as that of a slave girl. Looped about her neck, locked, was a slender, common, gray-steel slave collar. He had wired a tag to it, that she might be identified as his. She had been of Rarn, probably of high caste, given the quality of her beauty. She would now be slave in the river port of

42

Ven. The man appeared to be a young bargeman. Her lips were delicate and beautiful. They would kiss him well.

I watched him press on through the crowds, toward the looming palisade which ringed the Sardar mountains, black and snow-capped, behind it.

The numbers in the game are set at a hundred young men and a hundred young women, in order that there be a young woman for each winning male.

This was the first year, incidentally, in which masks had been permitted to the young women in some of these contests. The masks, however, had been brief and feminine. They concealed little and did little more than to excite the men and stimulate them to the beauty's pursuit, culminating in her rude assault, capture and unmasking. Still I suspected the innovation, next year, would be dropped. It is easier to gamble on the taking of given girls, and how long they will be at large, if their beauty is better visible to the bettors.

I looked after the young man. He was going to the palisade. There he would climb one of the platforms and, putting the girl on her knees, her ankles and wrists crossed and bound, at his feet, facing the Sardar, he would unbind her hair. Then he would lift her in his arms, hair unbound, before the mountains of the Sardar, rejoicing, and giving thanks to Priest-Kings that she was now his.

"Where are the merchant tables," I asked a fellow from Torvaldsland, with braided blond hair and shaggy jacket, eating on a roast hock of tarsk, "where the odds on the Kaissa matches are being given?"

"I do not know," he said. "They play Kaissa only in the North."

"My thanks, fellow," said I. It was true that the Kaissa of the north differed in some respects from tournament Kaissa in the south. The games, however, were quite similar. Indeed, Kaissa was played variously on the planet. For example, several years ago Kaissa was played somewhat differently in Ar than it was now. Most Gorean cities now, at least in the south, had accepted a standard tournament Kaissa, agreed upon by the high council of the caste of players. Sometimes the changes were little more than semantic. For example, a piece which once in Ar had been called the "City" was now identified officially as the "Home Stone" even in Ar. Indeed, some players in Ar had always called it the Home Stone. More seriously there were now no "Spear Slaves" in common Kaissa, as there once had been, though there were distinctions among "Spearmen." It had been argued that

43

slaves had no right upon the Kaissa board. One might note also, in passing, that slaves are not permitted to play Kaissa. It is for free individuals. In most cities it is regarded, incidentally, as a criminal offense to enslave one of the caste of players. A similar decree, in most cities, stands against the enslavement of one who is of the caste of musicians.

The man of Torvaldsland bit a large chunk from his hock of roast tarsk. "Where are the slave markets?" he asked.

"There are many," I said. Indeed, one might buy slaves here and there, publicly and privately, at many places in the Fair of En'Kara, one of the four great annual fairs at the Sardar. It is not permitted to fight, or kill, or enslave within the perimeters of the fairs, but there is no prohibition against the buying and selling of merchandise within those precincts; indeed, one of the main functions of the fairs, if not their main function, was to facilitate the buying and selling of goods; the slave, of course, is goods. The fairs, too, however, have many other functions. For example, they serve as a scene of caste conventions, and as loci for the sharing of discoveries and research. It is here, for example, that physicians, and builders and artisans may meet and exchange ideas and techniques. It is here that Merchant Law is drafted and stabilized. It is here that songs are performed, and song dramas. Poets and musicians, and jugglers and magicians, vie for the attention of the crowds. Here one finds peddlers and great merchants. Some sell trinkets and others the notes of cities. It is here that the Gorean language tends to become standardized. These fairs constitute truce grounds. Men of warring cities may meet here without fear. Political negotiation and intrigue are rampant, too, generally secretly so, at the fairs. Peace and war, and arrangements and treaties, are not unoften determined in a pavillion within the precincts of the fairs. "The nearest," I told the fellow from Torvaldsland, pointing down a corridor between pavillions and booths, "lies some quarter of a pasang in that direction, beyond the booths of the rug merchants. The largest, on the other hand, the platforms of slave exhibition and the great sales pavillion, lie to your left, two pasangs away, beyond the smithies and the chain shops."

"You speak clearly for one of the south," he said. He thrust the hock of roast tarsk to me. I took it and, holding it with both hands, cut at it with my teeth. I tore away a good piece of meat. I had not had food since the morning, when I arrived at the fair.

"My thanks," I said.

44

"I am Oleg," he said.

"I have been called Jarl Red Hair in the north," I said.

"Jarl!" he cried. "Forgive me, I did not know!"

"The meat is good," I said. I handed it back to him. It was true that in the north, by the word of Sevin Blue Tooth, I had stood upon the shields as Jarl.

"I fought with you," he said, "at the camp of the beasts. I saw you once near the tents of Thorgard of Scagnar."

"It was a good fight," I said.

"It was," said he, smacking his lips.

"Is the north quiet?" I asked. "Is there Kur activity in Torvaldsland?"

"No," said he, "no more than an occasional stray. The north is quiet."

"Good," I said. The Kurii were not active in Torvaldsland. They had been driven from that bleak, rocky land by the mighty men of the high-roofed halls.

He grinned at me.

"Good hunting," said I, "in the slave markets."

"Yes, Jarl," said he, grinning, lifting the hock of roast tarsk. He turned toward the nearest market. In a few moments he hurled the bone of the tarsk from him, wiping his hands on the sides of his jacket. Over his shoulder hung the great ax of Torvaldsland.

It had rained in the night, and the streets of the fair were muddy.

The Sardar fairs are organized, regulated and administered by the Merchant Caste.

I heard a girl screaming, being lashed. She was on her knees, to one side, between two tents; she was chained at a short stake, about which she had wrapped her arms, holding it for support. The side of her cheek was against the stake. The prohibition against violence at the Sardar, of course, does not extend to slaves. They may there, as elsewhere, be lashed, or tortured or slain, as it should please the master. They are slaves.

I turned down one of the muddy streets, making my way between booths featuring the wares of potters and weavers. It seemed to me that if I could find the fair's street of coins, that the makers of odds might well have set their tables there. It was, at any rate, a sensible thought.

"Where is the street of coins?" I asked a fellow, in the tunic of the tarnkeepers.

"Of which city?" he asked.

"My thanks," I said, and continued on. The fairs are large, covering several square pasangs.

I turned another corner.

"Buy the silver of Tharna," called a man. "Buy the finest silver on all Gor."

He was behind a counter at a booth. At his belt, as did the men of Tharna, he wore two yellow cords, each about eighteen inches long. At the back of the booth, kneeling, small, her back low, her head and hair down to the mud, naked, collared, was a woman.

I stepped to one side to make way for a procession of initiates, who, with a ringing of bells, and shaking of bowls on chains, containing burning incense, passed me on their way to the palisade. An initiate in the lead carried a standard on which was mounted the sign of the Priest-Kings, a golden circle, that which has no beginning or end, the symbol of eternity, the symbol of Priest-Kings.

They were white-robed and chanting, and shaven-headed. The caste of initiates is rich on Gor.

I glanced to the kneeling woman in the booth of the man from Tharna. She had not dared so much as to raise her head. She had not been given permission. There are few free women in Tharna. One of the most harsh and cruel slaveries on Gor, it is said, is that of the slave girls of Tharna.

"Where are odds made on the Kaissa matches," I asked the fellow from Tharna.

"I do not know," he said.

"My thanks," I said, and turned away. The woman remained kneeling as she had been placed.

I hoped the fellow from Torvaldsland would be able to buy a good piece of meat at the market.

"Where are odds made on the Kaissa matches?" I asked a small fellow, in the garb of the leather workers. He wore the colors of Tabor on his cap.

"I would ask you that," he said.

"Do you favor Scormus of Ar?" I inquired.

"Assuredly," he said.

I nodded. I decided it would be best to search for a merchant who was on the fair's staff, or find one of their booths or praetor stations, where such information might be found.

I stepped again to one side. Down the corridor between tents, now those of the carvers of semiprecious stones, came four men, in the swirling garb of the Tahari. They were veiled. The first led a stately sand kaiila on which a closed, fringed, silken kurdah was mounted. Their hands were at

46

their scimitar hilts. I did not know if the kurdah contained a free woman of high state or perhaps a prized female slave, naked and bejeweled, to be exhibited in a secret tent and privately sold.

I saw two men of the Wagon Peoples pass by, and, not a yard from them, evincing no concern, a fellow in the flowing robes of Turia. The fairs were truce ground.

Some six young people, in white garments, passed me. They would stand before the palisade, paying the homage of their presence to the mysterious denizens of the Sadar, the mysterious Priest-Kings, rulers of Gor. Each young person of Gor is expected, before their twenty-fifth birthday, to make the pilgrimage to the Sardar, to honor the Priest-Kings. These caravans come from all over known Gor. Most arrive safely. Some are preyed upon by bandits and slavers. More than one beauty who thought to have stood upon the platforms by the palisade, lifting laurel wreaths and in white robes singing the glories of the Priest-Kings, has found herself instead looking upon the snow-capped peaks of the Sardar from the slave platforms, stripped and heavily chained.

Colorful birds screamed to one side, on their perches. They were being sold by merchants of Schendi, who had them from the rain forests of the interior. They were black-visaged and wore colorful garments.

There were many slave girls in the crowd, barefoot, heeling their masters.

Schendi, incidentally, is the home port of the league of black slavers. Certain positions and platforms at the fairs are usually reserved for the black slavers, where they may market their catches, beauties of all races.

I stopped to watch a puppet show. In it a fellow and his free companion bickered and struck one another with clubs.

Two peasants walked by, in their rough tunics, knee-length, of the white wool of the Hurt. They carried staves and grain sacks. Behind them came another of their caste, leading two milk verr which he had purchased.

I returned my attention to the puppet show. Now upon its tiny stage was being enacted the story of the Ubar and the Peasant. Each, wearied by his labors, decides to change his place with the other. Naturally this does not prove fruitful for either individual. The Ubar discovers he cannot tax the bosk and the Peasant discovers his grain cannot grow on the stones of the city streets. Each cannot stop being himself, each cannot be the other. In the end, of course, the Ubar returns gratefully to his throne and the peasant, to his relief,

47

manages to return to the fields in time for the spring planting. The fields sing, rejoicing, upon his return. Goreans are fond of such stories. Their castes are precious to them.

A slave girl in the crowd edged toward me, and looked up at me. She was alone.

I saw a short fellow in the street crowd. He was passing by. He was squat and broad, powerful, apparently very strong. Though the weather was cool in the early spring he was stripped to the waist. He wore trousers of fur, and fur boots, which came to the knee. His skin was dark, reddish like copper; his hair was bluish black, roughly cropped; his eyes bore the epicanthic fold. About his shoulder he had slung some coils of braided rope, fashioned from twisted sleen hide, and, in his hand, he carried a sack and a bundle of tied furs; at his back was a quiver containing arrows, and a short bow of sinew-bound, layered horn.

Such men are seldom seen on Gor. They are the natives of the polar basin.

The herd of Tancred had not appeared in the north. I wondered if he knew this.

I had arranged with Samos to have a ship of supplies sped northward.

Then he was gone, lost in the crowd.

The slave girl put her head down. I felt her timidly biting at my sleeve.

She lifted her eyes to mine. Her eyes were dark, moist, pleading.

Slave girls often need the caress of men.

"I followed you," she said, "in the crowds."

"I know," I said. I had known this, for I was of the warriors.

"I find you very attractive, Master," she whispered.

She held my arm, closely, looking up at me. Her breasts, sweet, pendant, white, were lovely in the loose rep-cloth of her tunic.

"Please, Master," she whispered.

"Are you on an errand for your master?" I asked.

"No, Master," she said. "I am not needed until supper."

I looked away from her.

Her hands, small and piteous, grasped my arm. "Please, Master," she said.

I looked down into her eyes.

There were tears in them.

"Please, Master," she said, "take pity on me. Take pity on the miserable needs of a girl."

"You are not mine," I told her. "You are a pretty little thing, but I do not own you."

"Please," she said.

"Your master," I said, "if he chooses, will satisfy your needs. If he does not, he will not." For all I knew she might be under the discipline of deprivation. If that were so, I had no wish to impair the effectiveness of her master's control over her. Besides I did not know him. I did not wish to do him dishonor, whoever he might be.

"Does your master know you are begging in the streets?" I asked.

"No," she said, frightened.

"Then," said I, "perhaps I should have your hands tied and write that upon your body."

"Oh, no!" she cried.

"Is this girl bothering you?" asked a merchant, one whose head bore the talmit of the fair's staff. Behind him were two guardsmen, with whips.

"No," I said. Then I said, "Where are the tables for the gambling on Kaissa?"

"They have been arranged but this morning," he said. "They may be found in the vicinity of the public tents near the amphitheater."

"My thanks, Officer," said I.

"The lines are long," he said.

"I wish you well," I said.

"I wish you well," he said. They left.

"Thank you, Master," said the girl. At a word from me, she would have been lashed.

"Kneel and kiss my feet," I said.

She did so.

She then looked up.

"Run now to your master," I said. "Crawl to him on your belly, and beg his touch."

"Yes, Master," she said. She leaped to her feet, frightened, and sped away.

I watched her disappear in the crowds.

I laughed. What a meaningless, lovely, delicious little slave she was. How helpless she was in her needs.

Another slave girl in the crowd smiled at me. I grinned at her, and turned away.

It is pleasant to live on a world where there are female slaves. I would choose to live on no other sort of world.

Before I left the fair I would inspect the major market, that beyond the smithies and chain shops, where the most numerous exhibition platforms were erected, near the great sales pavillion of blue and yellow silk, the colors of the slavers.

If I found girls who pleased me I could arrange for their transportation to Port Kar. The shipment and delivery of slaves is cheap.

I turned down the street of the dealers in artifacts and curios. I was making my way toward the public tents in the vicinity of the amphitheater. It was there that the tables for the odds on the Kaissa matches might be found.

In traversing the street I saw the fellow from the polar basin, he stripped to the waist, with fur trousers and boots. He was dealing with a large fellow, corpulent and gross, who managed one of the booths. There was a thin scribe present as well behind the counter. The fellow in the furs, the rope coiled over his shoulder, apparently spoke little Gorean. He was taking objects from the fur sack he had carried with him. The large fellow behind the booth's counter was examining them. The objects would not stand on the counter, for they were rounded, as are shapes in nature. They were intended to be kept in a pouch and, from time to time, taken forth and examined. All details must be perfect, from every perspective, as in nature. Some collectors file such objects that they may be more easily displayed on a shelf or in a case. The native of the polar basin, on the other hand, holds them when he looks at them, and they have his attention as he does so. He is fond of them. He has made them. There were carvings of sea sleen, and fish, and whales, and birds, and other creatures, large and small, of the north.

Other objects, too, other carvings, were in the bag. The carvings were of soft bluish stone and ivory, and bone.

I continued on my way.

In a few minutes I had come to the area of the public tents, and there was there no difficulty in determining where the Kaissa lines were to be found. There were dozens of tables, and the lines were long at each.

I would stay in one of the public tents tonight. For five copper tarsks one may rent furs and a place in the tent. It is expensive, but it is, after all, En'Kara and the time of the fair. In such tents it is not unusual for peasants to lie crowded, side by side, with captains and merchants. During En'Kara, at the Fair, many of the distinctions among men and castes are forgotten.

Unfortunately meals are not served in the tents. For the price it seems one should banquet. This lack, however, is supplied by numerous public kitchens and tables. These are scat-

50

tered throughout the district of the fair. Also there are vendors.

I took my place at the end of one of the long lines, that which I conjectured to be the shortest.

There are some compensations in the public tents, however. One may have paga and wines there. These are served by slave girls, whose comforts and uses are also included within the price of the lodging.

"Soup! Soup!" called a man.

"Soup!" I called, raising my hand. I purchased from him, for a copper tarsk, a bowl of soup, thick with shreds of hot bosk and porous chunks of boiled sul.

"Whom do you favor in the great match?" I asked.

"Scormus of Ar," said he.

I nodded. I handed him back the soup bowl. I feared the odds would be too high on Scormus. Yet I would wager him the winner. I was not pleased, however, that I might have to bet a golden tarn to win a silver tarsk.

I could see on hills, on either side of the amphitheater, a golden tent pitched. One of these was for Scormus of Ar, the other, on the other side of the great amphitheater, was for Centius of Cos.

"Have they drawn yet for yellow?" I asked.

"No," he said.

Normally much betting would wait until it was known which player had yellow, which determines the first move, and the first move, of course, determining the opening.

But already the betting was heavy.

I speculated on the effect which the draw for yellow might have on the odds in the match. If Centius drew yellow, I reasoned, the odds favoring Scormus might be reduced a bit, but probably not much; if Scormus, on the other hand, drew yellow, the odds might rise so in his favor as to preclude a rational wager. Few people would accept a bet of even twenty to one under such circumstances. Already I suspected I would have to wager at least ten to one to bet on Scormus, who would be champion. I noted a fellow from Cos a few men ahead of me in the line. "On whom do you wager?" I asked him. "On Centius of Cos," he said, belligerently. I smiled to myself. We would see. We would see. I wondered if his patriotism would last all the way to the betting table. Often, incidentally, the first move in a match is decided by one player's guessing in which hand the other holds a Spearman, one of the pieces of the game. In this match, however, a yel-

51

low Spearman and a red Spearman were to be placed in a helmet, covered with a scarlet cloth. Scormus of Ar and Centius of Cos would reach into the helmet and each draw forth one Spearman. He who held the yellow Spearman had the first move.

I was now some twenty men from the table.

"Look," called a man.

Two parties of men, one party from each of the tents, began to make their way toward the amphitheater. Somewhere in those parties were Scormus of Ar and Centius of Cos. The chief officer of the caste of players, with representatives of both Cos and Ar, would be waiting for them on the stone stage of the amphitheater, with the helmet.

I breathed more easily. I was confident now I would have my bet placed before the draw. If Scormus should draw yellow, and I were to place my bet after this fact was generally known, I would stand to win almost nothing, even should I wager a good deal.

"Hurry!" called a man. "Hurry!"

The two parties of men had now, from opposite sides, entered the amphitheater.

"A silver tarsk on Scormus of Ar," said the man from Cos, who stood now at the table.

"They will be raising the standard of Ar or Cos any moment!" cried a man.

In moments I was two men from the table.

Then there was only one man before me.

"Next," called the odds merchant.

I stood before the table.

"Fourteen to one favoring the champion of Ar," he said.

"Fourteen hundred tarns of gold," said I, "on Ar's champion."

"Who are you?" asked the odds merchant. "Are you mad?"

"I am Bosk," I said, "of Port Kar."

"Done," said he, "Captain!"

I signed his sheet with the sign of the bosk.

"Look!" cried a man. "Look!"

Above the amphitheater, on its rim, a man lifted the standard of Ar.

I stepped aside. There was much shouting. Men of Ar in the crowd embraced one another. Then, beside he who bore the standard of Ar, there stood one in the garb of the players, the red and yellow checkered robe, and the checkered cap, with the board and pieces slung over his shoulder, like a war-

52

rior's accouterments. He lifted his hand. "It is Scormus!" they cried. "It is Scormus!" The young man then lifted the standard of Ar himself.

Men of Ar wept. Then the young man returned the standard to him who had first carried it to the amphitheater's rim and withdrew from sight.

There was much cheering.

"Next," said the odds merchant.

The next man then stood before the table.

"Thirty-six to one, favoring the champion of Ar," he said.

The man groaned.

I grinned, and left the vicinity of the tables. I would have preferred to have had better odds, but I had managed to place my bet before they had more than doubled against poor Centius of Cos. I stood now to win a hundred golden tarns. I was in a good mood.

I turned my steps toward the main market. I would look at the goods on the long wooden platforms. Perhaps I would buy a girl for the night and sell her in the morning.

In a few minutes I saw the silken summit of the gigantic sales pavillion, its pennons fluttering, its blue and yellow silk billowing in the wind.

I saw male slaves thrusting a cart filled with quarry stones. It left deep tracks in the rain-softened earth.

I smelled verr, closed in shallow pens, more than a pasang away. The air was clear and sparkling.

I came to the great sales pavillion, but it was now roped off and quiet. There was much activity, and bustle, however, among the platforms. Here and there slaves were being thrown food.

I mingled with the crowds among the platforms. There are hundreds of such platforms, long, raised about a foot from the ground, far more than one could easily examine in a day's browsing. They are rented to individual slavers, who, reserving them before the fairs, would rent one or more, or several, depending on their riches and the numbers of their stock. Small signs fixed on the platforms identify the flesh merchant, such as 'These are the girls of Sorb of Turia' or 'These slaves are owned by Tenalion of Ar'.

I penetrated more deeply among the platforms. A girl, kneeling and naked, heavily chained, extended her hands to me. "Buy me, Master!" she begged. Then I had passed her and she was behind me. I saw two girls standing, back to back, the left wrist of each chained to the right wrist of the other. "Handsome master, consider me!" cried a girl as I passed her. Most of the girls knelt or sat on the platforms. All were secured in some fashion.

"Scandalous," said a free woman, to another free woman, who was passing near me.

"Yes," said the other free woman.

"Candies! Candies!" called a hawker of sweets near me in the crowd. "Candies of Ar!"

"Buy this candy of Ar, Master!" laughed a chained girl to me. I roughly fondled her head, and she seized my wrist suddenly in her chained hands and desperately began to press kisses upon it. "Please," she wept. "Please!" "No," I said. I pulled my wrist away and continued on. She sobbed, and knelt back in her chains.

"I will make you a superb love slave," called another girl to me. I did not respond to her.

On a rounded wooden block a naked slave girl knelt, her wrists braceleted behind her. Her head was back. One of the physicians was cleaning her teeth.

By another platform a slaver's man was moving along the platform. He carried a large, handled copper tureen filled with a watery soup. The slaver's beauties, chained together by the neck, knelt at the edge of the platform. Each dipped her cupped hands twice into the tureen, and lifted them, drinking and feeding, to her mouth. They then licked and sucked their fingers and wiped their hands on their bodies.

Sales take place at night in the pavillion, from a sawdust-strewn block, under the light of torches, but girls may also be sold directly from the platforms. Indeed, many girls are sold from the platforms. Given the number of girls at the fair, and the fact that new ones are constantly being brought to the platforms, it is impractical to hope to market them all from the block. It is just not feasible. At the end of every fair there are always some hundreds of girls left unsold. These are usually sold in groups at wholesale prices in sales restricted to professional slavers, who will transport them to other markets, to dispose of them there.

"Do you think you could make me kneel to you?" asked a girl sitting on a platform, with chained neck and ankles, her knees drawn up, chewing on a larma fruit. She smiled at me, over the fruit, Then she turned white. "Forgive me, Master!" she cried. She had seen my eyes. She knelt before me on the boards, trembling, her head down. Would she be permitted to live? The fruit lay discarded beside her. I took the fruit and bit into it. I watched her for a time, and then I said, "Lift your head." She did so. I threw the fruit back to her, and

54

she, fearfully, caught it. She held it in her hands, looking at me. "Finish it," I said, "and then, for an Ahn, lie on your belly." "Yes, Master," she said.

I looked up, beyond the crowds and platforms. From where I stood I could see the great palisade, and the black, snow-capped mountains of the Sardar.

I moved on, pushing past a man who was examining the legs of a slave girl, feeling them. He was considering her purchase.

"Where are the new slaves?" asked one man of another.

"They are on the western platforms," said the respondent. Those platforms are commonly used for processing and organization. Girls are not often sold from them. They wait there, usually, when they are brought in, before they are conducted to their proper platforms, those on which they will be displayed, those having been rented in advance by their masters.

Since I had time to spare I took my way to the western platforms. If something good might be found there perhaps I could find on which platform she was to be vended, and might then arrange to be at that platform when she arrived. As soon as the locks snap shut on a girl's chain at the platform she is available to be bid upon. Perhaps I would find something good.

I was soon at the western platforms.

It is easy to tell among girls which are familiar with their condition and which are not. Once a girl truly understands that she is a slave, and that there is no escape for her, once she understands it truly, emotionally, categorically, intellectually, physiologically, totally, deeply, profoundly, in every cell in her beautiful body, a fantastic transformation occurs in her. She then knows she is truly a slave. She then becomes wild, and free, and sexual, and cares not that she might be scorned by the free either for her miserable condition or helpless appetites; she knows she will be what she must; she has no choice; she is slave. Women, in their heart, long to submit; this is necessary for the slave girl; she must submit or die; submitted, she is thrilled to the core; she lives then for love and service, bound to the will of her master. The joy of the slave girl may seem incomprehensible to the free but it is a reality.

I heard the lamentations of girls in chains.

It must be clearly understood that the life of the slave girl, of course, can often be far from joyful.

After all, she is slave. Her wills mean nothing.

She can be bought and sold.

She is subject to the whip, and torture and even death should the master please.

She does not know who will buy her.

Her condition is objectively degrading.

Often she must labor with perfection to please a harsh master to whom she is nothing.

The glory of the slave girl is that she is a slave; and the misery of the slave girl is that she is a slave.

But all in all chains are right for a woman. They belong in them.

I looked at some of the new platforms. I could easily detect girls who were fresh to the collar. They were clumsy and tight, not yet liberated and free, not yet women.

Even as I walked about the new platforms wagons, drawn by draft tharlarion, waited to unload their lovely wares. The markets of the Sardar fairs are large and important ones in the Gorean economy. Most of the wagons were common slave wagons, with a parallel bar running down the center of the wagon box, about which the ankles of the girls were chained; others, however, were flat wagons fixed with an iron framework; two lines of girls kneel back to back on such a wagon, their ankles and necks locked into the framework; on the flat wagons I saw the wrists of the beauties were braceleted behind them.

I inspected more of the new platforms.

It is painful for a girl to be locked in the framework of a flat wagon but, of course, she is well displayed enroute.

On some of the new platforms the women were still clothed or partly clothed.

I was about to leave the area of the western platforms when I saw something which interested me, a set of four girls.

I walked casually over to the vicinity of the platform, standing back somewhat.

Three were dark-haired and one was blond. The wrists of each were chained; the ankles, too, of each were chained. Their wrists were separated by some six inches of chain, their ankles by about a foot of chain.

They were kneeling.

They wore collars, fastened together by a chain.

What I found interesting about these girls was that they wore Earth raiment.

The girl on the end, blond, wore very brief denim shorts, faded and blue. They were low on her belly, revealing her navel, and tattered about the hems. They had round metal snaps. She wore a blue, workman's shirt, the tails of which were tied under her breasts, to display her midriff. She was tanned, and blue eyed. Her blond hair was loose and there were tiny rings in her ears. The next girl, dark-haired, lovely, wore black, feminine slacks; these were apparently of some synthetic Earth material; the left leg of the slacks was torn from the knee downward; she also wore what had probably been a soft, red, turtle-necked pull-over; it, too, was rather feminine; perhaps that is why it had been half torn from her; her right breast was exposed; when I looked at her she looked down, frightened, and with one chained hand drew a shred of the pull-over before her, to conceal herself; I smiled; how meaningless was the gesture; did she not know where she was; she was on Gor; she was on the platform; she, too, wore ornaments in her ear lobes, tiny jewellike disks, very small; the next two girls, too, were both dark-haired, and dark-eyed, and were attired, save for the colors of their shirts, identically; both wore blue trousers of denim; both wore flannel shirts, one a plaid flannel and the other a beige flannel; both wore small earrings of gold. I thought, of course, of the girl in the house of Samos and the raiment she had worn, which had been burned in her presence. She and the last two girls would have been extremely similarly attired; they all wore, or had worn, the male-imitation uniform which I gathered must be popular among such girls, girls apparently striving to copy a masculinity which hormonally and anatomically would be forever denied to them; better to be an imitation man they seemed to reason than to dare to be what they were, women; it seemed to me permissible that a woman should be a woman, but I suppose the matter is more complex than this simplicity would suggest; I wondered if such girls feared the promptings of their sex, the stirrings in them of a biology antedating the caves; but perhaps male imitation was only an unconscious step, a scarcely understood phase, ingredient to the possibly inexorable unfolding dynamics of a machine culture, a step or phase leading to what would be the proper fulfillment of the needs of the machine, sexless, tranquil, utilizable units, suitable components, functionality and neuterism triumphant. The machine and the animal must, I suspect, forever be at war, or until one conquers. On Gor slaves know to whom they belong.

I looked at the girls on the platform. How little they would understand a biological world. And yet each wore adornments in her ears, which required the literal piercing of her

57

ears, the softness of her beauty yielding therein to the emblematic spike of penetration. On Gor only slave girls have pierced ears. On Gor these girls, with pierced ears, could be only slaves. Yet how feminine was this, that they had had their ears pierced, they, though girls of Earth. Gorean free women often envied slave girls their pierced ears, though this would seldom be admitted. How barbaric that an ear should be pierced that it may wear an adornment selected by a master. Their ears had been pierced. I admired this small, almost meaningless symbol of their femininity, this small, pathetic gesture protesting to the machine and the lies that they were really women; too, I recalled the undergarments of such girls; they, too, protested the cause of their beauty in the alien country of the machine. From the lineaments of the garments they wore I did not think, however, that their masters had permitted them their customary undergarments. Certainly the dark-haired girl in the torn red pull-over had no longer been permitted her brassiere. It is common to permit a Gorean slave girl only one layer of clothing, if any. That they had been permitted to retain for the time what they now wore rather than, say, brassiere and panties, or nothing, was doubtless due only to the whim of the slaver who owned them.

"I wish to speak to someone," said the girl on the end, addressing a slaver's man who was passing them. He stopped, surprised that she had dared to speak.

"Send someone to me who is in authority who speaks English," she demanded.

He cuffed her. "Be silent," he said to her, in Gorean. The girl had been struck back in her chains. She seemed utterly startled. Her eyes were wide. She put her fingers to her mouth. There was blood there.

"He hit me," she said. "He hit me."

The girls looked about themselves, frightened. The girl in the brief shorts, the blond on the other end, knelt back, making herself small.

"He hit me," said the girl who had been struck. There was a strange, frightened look in her eye. She looked after the man, and then looked again to the other girls.

"Yes," whispered the girl in the torn red pull-over, shrinking back in her chains.

The girl who had been struck again looked after the fellow who had cuffed her. There was a look in her eyes which was akin to awe. Then again they looked at one another, frightened. I gathered they had never seen a girl cuffed before. It might be done, they realized, to any one of them.

The girl in denim shorts, whom I would have originally thought would have been the least frightened of her native sexuality, looked at the others. "What if they make us kiss them?" she asked. "What will we do?"

"Kiss them," said the girl in the torn red pull-over.

"Do you think they will want anything like that?" asked the dark-haired girl in the plaid flannel shirt.

"Who knows what they will want," said the girl in the pull-over.

"We have rights!" said the blond girl in the shorts.

"Do we?" asked the girl in the red pull-over. She seemed the most feminine of all.

The girls were silent for a time. Then one spoke, the girl in the shorts. "What sort of prisoners are we?" she asked.

"Let us hope," said the girl in the red pull-over, "that we are just prisoners."

"I do not understand," said the girl in the shorts. "What else might we be?"

"Can you not guess?" asked the girl in the red pull-over.

"No," said the blond girl, in the brief shorts, frightened.

"Perhaps we are slaves," said the girl in the red pull-over.

"Don't joke," said the blond girl, aghast.

The girl in the red pull-over shrugged and looked away.

"Please don't joke," whispered the blond girl. The girl in the red pull-over did not respond to her.

I considered the slaves. The fact that the blond had worn shorts and had tied her shirt as she had made it clear to me that she was willing to display her body. From this I would have originally thought that she might have been the least frightened of her sexuality. I now understood that she, in spite of her attire, deeply feared her native drives. Indeed, perhaps she had dressed as she did to try to convince herself, and others, that she did not fear them. Her behavior, however, made manifest the nature of her terror. Doubtless she had sensed in her dreams, and in inadvertent moments, what men might do to her. But that she had displayed her body as she did, even if in compensation for her fears, which she would scarcely admit to herself, indicated the strength of the drives against which she fought. She had dressed her body as a challenge to men, though she feared them. Her mode of dress suggested powerful drives, which might, by a master, be well exploited. It was interesting to note that the garb of both the blond and the girl in the red pull-over were variations of the uniform of male imitation; the blond wore the uniform, except that she altered it to brazenly display that it was she, actually a female, and an attractive one, who wore it. The garb of the dark-haired girl, the black slacks of some synthetic material and the soft, red pull-over, was also a variation from the conformist raiment of the two girls on the end. She wore pants, of course, for slacks are a form of pants, and her garments, in general, were body-concealing; these features they had in common with the male-imitation garb of the two girls on the end; on the other hand the slacks were not as body concealing as they might have been for they were cut, actually, subtly, in such a way as to betray her figure; the soft pull-over, too, would leave no doubt as to her femininity, particularly now that her masters had removed her brassiere from her. The slacks, I conjectured, were custom tailored. She had probably been rich. She was now a slave. The blond girl, I would have conjectured, would have been from the middle class. She, too, now, was a slave. Both girls were now identical, only slaves. The fact that the dark-haired girl had worn the garments she did suggested that she had felt, for some time, her femininity, though doubtless it had never been adequately exploited on Earth. She would have lived in unfulfilled frustration. Her garments, in their own way, like those of the blond girl, suggested that she, too, had deep feminine drives. She seemed more honestly to recognize them than the blond girl. I did not know which of them would have the deepest, richest sexuality. Both, I conjectured, would be prizes. I had little doubt the dark-haired girl would come most quickly to lick her chains. The other two girls, I felt, were far behind their chain sisters. They were still, in effect, almost imitation boys. It might take months for them to suddenly, in the throes of the female slave orgasm, become true women.

Another slaver's man walked past them. They shrank back.

I wondered if these girls had been in the same shipment as the girl I had met in the house of Samos. I supposed at one time each, unconscious, had worn locked on her left ankle the steel identification anklet of the Kur slaver. They wore now, as it was easy to see, only rounded ankle rings. Their feet were all bare, of course. Slavers do not put chains or bonds over stockings; similarly, if wrists are to be chained or bound, gloves would be removed; bonds are not placed over clothing. Gorean slave girls, incidentally, almost always go barefoot; it is a rare girl, and a high girl, who is permitted sandals. I looked again at the four girls. Earth-girl slaves, thanks to the raids of Kur slavers, are not as rare on Gor as they used to be. Earth girls are thought to make superb slaves. Gorean men will pay for them. Earth-girl names, incidentally, are thought of on Gor as slave names. Even many slave girls of Gorean origin wear them. That Earth-girl names are thought of on Gor as slave names is an indication of the regard in which Gorean men hold Earth girls. They are thought to be natural slaves. I believe, incidentally, that this hypothesis is true. She is not herself until she wears a collar and kneels at the feet of a master.

I turned away from the girls, for I had become hungry. I would eat at one of the public restaurants set up in the district of the fair.

I had considered buying the two girls on the end, those on the chain's left, as I faced it, the blond and the dark-haired girl in the red pull-over, but I decided against it. They were not yet broken in, and I felt my men might kill them. Both girls I felt had an amazing potentiality, even beyond that of most Earth girls, for being superb slaves. It would be unfortunate if this potentiality were to be rudely terminated while they thrashed, bound, in the canals under the teeth of urts.

I glanced back once at the four girls, kneeling closely together, chained, on the platform. The collars they wore seemed somewhat incongruous with their upper garments, the blue workman's shirt of the blond girl, the soft pull-over of the dark-haired girl, the flannel shirts of the two dark-haired girls on the end, but, still, somehow, they seemed correct, and even beautiful, on their throats. Their wrists, in the two-inch-high, steel cuffs, were small and lovely. Their feet, in the confining ankle loops, were small and beautiful. I was pleased. Their chains looked well on them. This is a way of telling what girls are true slaves. But do chains not look well on any woman? But is not any woman a true slave? I commended the taste and judgment of the Kur slavers. Such girls, yielded, would nestle well in a man's arms. I saw two slaver's men advancing toward them. The first carried a knife, the second, over his arm, carried some brief, white, platform tunics.

I swilled down the last of the Cal-da. I had not had it since Tharna.

In the restaurant where I had eaten there were some two hundred tables, under tenting.

I wiped my mouth on my sleeve and rose to my feet.

There were many at the tables who were singing the songs of Ar.

61

"I am looking forward to the game," had said Centius of Cos to Scormus of Ar.

"I shall destroy you," had said Scormus of Ar.

I wondered what thoughts occupied these giants of Kaissa on the eve of their confrontation. Scormus, it was said, walked the tiers of the amphitheater, alone, restlessly, eagerly, like a pacing, hungry beast. Centius of Cos, in his tent, it was said, seemed unconcerned with the match. He was lost in his thoughts, studying a position which had once occurred a generation ago in a match between the minor masters Ossius of Tabor, exiled from Teletus, and Philemon of Aspericht, not even of the players, but only a cloth worker. The game had not been important. The position, however, for some reason, was thought by Centius of Cos to be intriguing. Few masters shared his enthusiasm. It had occurred on the twenty-fourth move of red, played by Philemon, Physician to Physician Six, generally regarded as a flawed response to Ossius' Ubar to Ubara's Scribe Five. Something in the position had suggested to Centius of Cos a possible perfection, but it had never materialized. "Here, I think," had said Centius of Cos, "the hand of Philemon, unknown to himself, once came close to touching the sleeve of Kaissa."

I saw a fellow several tables away, his back to me, leave the tenting. Something vaguely bothered me about him. I could not place it. I did not see his face. I did not think he had seen me.

I left the tenting. One pays before the meal, and carries a disk, a voucher, to the table. The meal itself is brought to his place, marked on an identical disk, by a slave girl. One surrenders the disk to her and she places the meal before you. The girl wears a leather apron and an iron belt. If one wants her one must pay more.

Outside the tent I again mingled in the crowds. There was nothing pressing until tomorrow's forenoon when the match would begin.

The singing of the men of Ar was now behind me.

A slaver's man, pounding on a bar with a metal rod, called that the sales in the pavillion would begin within the Ahn.

"Rent her! Rent her!" called a man, moving through the crowds. Before him, thrust ahead of him on a control stick, her wrists braceleted behind her, was a naked slave girl. There is a chain loop at the end of the control stick, which is about two feet in length. The loop goes about her neck and, by means of a trigger, may be tightened or slightly loosened. The girl may be signaled by means of the chain. I saw her

62

neck and head move, jerking under the chain. She knelt quickly before me and began to bite at my tunic. "Only a quarter tarsk!" called the man. I brushed her aside. At the other end of the control stick there is a leather loop. This goes about the right wrist of the master. Behind me I heard the girl cry out in pain and struggle to her feet. "You worthless slut," said the man to her. And then he again was calling out, "Rent her! Rent her, kind masters!"

Some jugglers, to one side, were exhibiting their astonishing talents with colored plates and torches.

I passed some booths where rep-cloth was being sold in bolts. Peasant women were haggling with the vendors.

In another area boiled meat hung on ropes. Insects swarmed about it.

I wanted to watch the sales, or some of them, this evening. I wished to pick up some girl flesh for my men.

But there seemed little point in arriving before they had begun. Indeed, there is not much point, usually, in coming early to a sale. Merchants usually exhibit their best merchandise only later in the evening.

The thought of the fellow whom I had seen in the restaurant briefly troubled me. Then I dismissed it.

I made my way toward the platforms.

I saw the fellow from the polar basin again, him with the fur trousers and boots, and the rope and short bow. I recalled he had sold carvings to a dealer in curios earlier in the day.

I was curious to see the Earth girls again. When I had last seen them two slaver's men had been approaching them, one with a knife and the other with some brief, white, platform tunics. I was curious to see what they would look like in clothing which would make clear their femininity rather than conceal or deny it.

"Where are the platforms of Tenalion of Ar?" I asked a man. They had been his property.

The fellow pointed to the two hundreds.

"My thanks, Sir," said I. Tenalion is a well-known slaver.

Most girls on the platforms are exhibited naked in their chains. Some, on the other hand, are attired, usually briefly and in platform tunics, which may be opened. It is thought that sometimes a clothed girl is more intriguing to a buyer. When he comes forward and asks to see the girl, and the tunic is opened, he is, of course, already there and interested. The slaver or the slaver's man, then, can talk with him, discussing, praising and pointing out the values of the commodity. This would not be easy if the fellow had merely glanced upon the wares and passed by. Girls are seldom, if ever, of course, sold clothed. It is said that only a fool would buy a clothed woman. That is certainly true. Would you buy a girl you had not had a chance to examine in detail?

In the two hundreds Tenalion's platforms were numbered from two hundred and forty through two hundred and eighty, inclusive.

How pleased I was to see the slaves. It was now clear they were beauties. But many of the slaves of Tenalion were beautiful.

They still wore neck collars and were chained together. But now the neck collars were fantastically beautiful on them. No longer did they now wear their distracting, meaningless Earth raiment, but Gorean platform tunics. The tunics were white, with deep, plunging necklines, well revealing and setting off the collars, completely sleeveless, and terribly brief. They knelt. There was about a yard of chain between the collars, fastening them in a four-girl coffle.

"I hardly dare move," said the blond girl. She knelt, as the others did, with her knees pressed closely together.

Their wrists were now in steel cuffs behind their backs. No longer would they be able to conceal themselves if their tunics were opened.

"Nor I," said the girl on the end. "What is being done with us?" she asked.

"I don't know," said the third girl. "I don't know!"

A man walked by, slowly, appraising them.

They shrank back.

Their ankles were confined in loose, steel ankle loops, but they could not slip them. A common chain ran though rings on the loops. No longer were their ankles confined with a foot of chain between them. Their ankles, now, for the chain running through the loop-rings was long, could be moved as closely together or as widely apart as they, or their masters, might wish. There were round, pierced metal balls at each end of the ankle chain, to prevent its slipping through the rings entirely. One such ball was to the right of the blond's right ankle and the other was to the left of the left ankle of the last girl on the chain. This ankle-chain arrangement, permitting much plasticity of movement, makes it easier to display a girl.

"We have rights!" whispered the blond girl.

"Do you think so?" asked the dark-haired girl, who had worn the black slacks and the soft, torn red pull-over.

"Yes!" said the blond girl.

"Look at their eyes," said the dark-haired girl.

The blond girl shrank back in the chains.

"Do you still think we have rights?" asked the dark-haired girl.

The blond was silent.

"Do you think a woman could have rights with such men?" asked the dark-haired girl. "Do you think we are still on Earth?" she asked.

"What has become of us?" asked the girl on the end.

"Is it not obvious?" asked the dark-haired girl. Her face was narrow, but delicate and very beautiful. Her figure was slight, but exquisite. Her hair was short, and very dark. She had lovely legs, marvelously revealed by the brevity of the platform tunic. I thought her the most beautiful of all. I also thought her the most intelligent. The next most valuable meat in the coffle was, in my opinion, the blond, who was sweetly slung and exciting.

"No!" said the girl on the end. "No! It is not obvious!"

The slender dark-haired girl shrugged, and, with a rustle of chain, turned away.

Then all the girls suddenly shrank back, frightened, for another fellow was passing by, slowly, examining them.

"I do not wish to be dressed like this," said the third girl on the chain.

"Be pleased," said the first girl on the chain, the blond, "that they have given you anything to wear."

Within sight of them, on other platforms, there were numerous, naked chained beauties.

"You will note, of course," said the dark-haired girl, second on the chain, who had worn the torn pull-over, "the nature of the garments in which we have been placed."

The left side of the brief tunic overlapped the right side of the tunic. It was held in place by a light, white cord, which passed through two loops and was loosely knotted at the right hip. If the cord were jerked loose the garment would fall open and could be easily brushed aside, to fall back, loose, behind them, on their cuffed, chained wrists.

"What about it?" asked the girl at the end of the chain, belligerently.

"Do you think it would be difficult to open?" asked the dark-haired girl.

"They wouldn't dare!" said the blond girl.

The dark-haired girl did not respond to her.

"You think you are so clever because you are rich!" hissed the blond.

"Do you think any of us have anything now?" demanded the dark-haired girl, angrily. "Do you think we own even the chains we wear?"

"I do not understand what you are saying!" said the girl, angrily, at the end of the line.

The dark-haired girl did not respond to her.

"What sort of place is this!" cried out the girl on the end. She jerked her cuffed wrists futilely. She could bring one of them to a position behind her left hip or her right hip, but could not bring either before her body.

"Struggle if you will," said the dark-haired girl. "It is not the intention of the men that you escape." She smiled. "Therefore you will not escape." The dark-haired girl looked out, over the crowds. "Besides, where would you escape to?" she asked. "There is nowhere to escape to," she said.

"I hate you!" said the girl who had struggled.

The dark-haired girl shrugged.

Two more men walked by, casually casting a glance upon the confined goods.

The girls were silent, and knelt back, small.

The men saw nothing of interest in them. There were many beauties on display.

"I cannot stand the way they look at us," said the blond.

"What does it mean?" asked the third girl on the chain.

"Masters!" called a girl, in Gorean, some yards down the platform, accosting the two men who were passing. She knelt on one knee, and flexed and extended her other leg, beautifully, touching the boards of the platform with her toes. She lifted her body and thrust forth her lovely breasts to them. "Masters," she whimpered, "take me home with you!"

"Do you beg to be purchased?" asked one of the men.

"Yes, Master!" she said.

"Slave," said he, scornfully.

"Yes, Master!" she said.

"Do you find her of interest?" asked the first man, he who had questioned her, to his fellow.

"Stand, Slave," said the second man.

She stood before them, beautifully, almost nude in the platform tunic.

A slaver's man, seeing their interest, came to where they stood.

"Would you care to see the pretty little slut?" he asked.

The four Earth girls, though they could not speak Gorean, watched, horrified, the enactment of a common Gorean ep-

66

isode, the attempt on the part of a slave to interst masters in her purchase.

The blond girl gasped and shrank back when the slaver's man, joining the girl on the platform, jerked loose the cord at her right hip and, with two hands, standing behind the girl, held back the tunic, well displaying her to the gaze of the inquirers.

They could not, of course follow the conversation, but it was clearly one of appraisal, and of commerce.

Then the Earth girls, with the exception of the dark-haired girl, who watched, fascinated, eyes shining, turned their eyes away, shuddering. One of the men had joined the slaver's man and the girl on the platform. The girl cried out, startled, being ruthlessly appraised. Then she writhed on the platform, obedient to the touch of the masters.

"Look!" said the dark-haired girl.

The other three girls then looked too, in horror and fascination.

They saw the beauty being swiftly put through slave paces.

Then they saw her sold. There was a clear exchange of money. The girl was released from her chains and braceleted by one of the men. She was put in a collar and leash and led from the platform. Behind then was left only the discarded chains and a discarded, crumpled tunic. The girl was gone.

"Do you still ask what manner of place this is?" asked the dark-haired girl bitterly of the girl at the chain's end.

That girl, dark-haired, too, shook her head with horror. "It cannot be," she whispered.

The dark-haired girl, who had worn the pull-over, turned angrily to the blond, at the other end of the chain. "Do you still think," she asked, "they will not 'dare' to look at your precious body?"

The blond shrank back, terrified in the chains.

"Do you truly think now," pressed the dark-haired girl, furiously, "that you have rights, you foolish little thing? Do you think before such men you would have rights? These are not men of Earth!"

The blond girl looked at her with horror.

"These men will have their way with women," she said. "Can you not see it in their eyes? They will have what they want from women." And she laughed bitterly, "And we are women," she said.

"This place then—" stammered the girl at the end of the chain.

"Yes," said the dark-haired girl. Then she looked at the

blond. "Do you still think," she asked, "that we are merely some sort of prisoners?"

"No, no," wept the blond girl.

"This is a slave market," said the dark-haired girl, "and we are slaves."

The blond girl moaned and threw her head back. The third and fourth girl began to sob.

"Accept it, my dear," said the dark-haired girl, "our reality is now transformed."

They looked at her.

"We are now slave girls on a strange world."

"No," whispered the girl on the end.

"I am for sale," said the dark-haired girl, "and so, too, are you, and the rest of us."

"Yes," whispered the blond, suddenly shuddering, "I—I am for sale."

"As are the rest of us," said the dark-haired girl.

The girls then subsided, and were quiet.

After a time the dark-haired girl spoke. "I wonder," she said, "what it will be like, being a slave girl."

"I cannot even think of it," said the blond-haired girl.

"I wonder what it will be like, being owned by a man," mused the dark-haired girl.

"Perhaps a woman will buy us," said the girl on the end.

The blond girl, and the dark-haired girl, looked at her, apprehensively.

"We would have less to fear from a woman," said the girl on the end.

"Do you want to be owned by a woman?" asked the dark-haired girl.

"No," said the girl on the end.

"Nor would I," said the third girl.

"Nor would I," said the dark-haired girl.

"—Nor would I," said the blond.

"That is interesting, is it not?" asked the dark-haired girl, thoughtfully. She looked out at the crowd. "Have you ever seen such men?" she asked. "I had never dreamed such men could exist."

"No," whispered the blond girl.

"Do you not find them disturbing?" asked the dark-haired girl.

"Wicked girl!" cried the girl on the end.

"I will tell you something," said the dark-haired girl. "They make me feel warm inside, and hot and wet."

"Wicked girl! Wicked girl!" cried the girl on the end.

"I have never felt feelings like this before," said the dark-haired girl. "I do not know what I would do if one of them touched me."

"Feminine! Feminine!" scolded the girl on the end, who had worn the beige flannel shirt.

The dark-haired girl in the brief platform tunic, who had worn the red pull-over, knelt back. "Yes," she said, "feminine."

"If they so much as touch me, I'll scream," said the blond.

But there seemed little chance of this for there appeared to be much more choice merchandise for sale upon those long, darkly varnished, slatted platforms. I had stood back in the crowd, interested to hear them speak. But now I would move on. It was nearly time to go to the pavillion. I did see in the crowd, some platforms away, the fellow from the polar basin. He was looking at women. The rawhide rope was looped about his shoulder.

"Look," I heard a fellow say, "it is Tabron of Ar."

I turned about. A tarnsman, in the scarlet leather of his war rights, tall, was moving through the crowd. He casually stopped before the four girls.

The blond shrank back as his eyes examined her in the collar, chains and platform tunic.

He looked upon the dark-haired girl. To my surprise and pleasure I saw her kneel very straight and lift her body before him. Then he looked past her to the other two girls and continued on his way. She knelt back in her chains.

"I saw you!" said the girl on the end, who had worn the beige flannel shirt.

"He was very handsome," said the dark-haired girl. "— And I am a slave."

"He didn't buy you," sneered the third girl, who had worn the plaid flannel shirt, "you rich tart!"

"He didn't buy you either," retorted the dark-haired girl, "you low-class idiot."

I smiled. They were both only slaves.

"I am more beautiful than you," said the third girl.

I was pleased to see that the third girl seemed now much more sensitive to her femaleness than earlier. Perhaps she would not take as long as I had thought to discover her womanhood. Gorean males, I conjectured, might teach it to her quickly. She would look lovely, I thought, crawling to her master, his sandals in her teeth.

"If we must discuss that sordid sort of thing," said the girl on the end, who had worn the beige flannel shirt, "I am the most beautiful of us four."

"I am," said the dark-haired girl, angrily, indignantly.

"No," said the blond. "I am surely the most beautiful!"

"You do not even want a man to touch you," said the dark-haired girl.

"No," said the blond. "But I am still the most beautiful."

The dark-haired girl looked out over the crowd. "They will decide who is most beautiful," she said.

"They?" asked the blond.

"The masters," said the dark-haired girl.

"Masters?" stammered the blond.

"Yes," said the dark-haired girl, "the masters, those men out there, those who will buy us, our masters, they will decide who is most beautiful."

The girls knelt back in their chains. They knelt back easily, on their heels.

"Oh!" cried the blond girl.

A stout fellow, in the garb of the tarn keepers, smelling of the tarn cots, stood looking at her. She pulled back, and shook her head, "No." Her eyes were frightened.

The stout fellow looked about, and caught the eye of one of the slaver's men who, seeing him, made his way through the crowds to his side.

"These are new slaves?" asked the tarn keeper.

"Fresh to the collar," said the slaver's man.

"I need a wench," said the man, "one who will cost me little, one to keep in the cots by day, to shovel the excrement of tarns, one to keep in my hut by night, as a pot-and-mat girl."

"These four wenches," said the slaver's man, expansively, indicating the small coffle, "are comely candidates for such a post." He stepped upon the platform, and crouched upon its surface. "Consider this one," he said, indicating the blond, who was first upon the chain.

He reached to her tunic.

"Don't touch me," she cried, drawing back.

"A barbarian," said the tarn keeper.

"Yes," said the slaver's man.

"And the others?" asked the tarn keeper.

"They are all barbarian, Master," said the slaver's man.

The dark-haired girl, seeing the tarn keeper's eyes upon her, shrank back.

The tarn keeper turned and walked away. The girls looked at one another, frightened, and knelt back. They seemed relieved. This relief, however, was surely premature. Another slaver's man joined his colleague at the platform. "We will never sell these," said the first. "They are raw girls, untrained, inept, clumsy, meaningless sluts. They do not even speak Gorean."

"Tenalion has no intention of putting them on the main block in the pavillion," said the second. He had a five-bladed slave whip at his belt.

"It would be a waste of block time," said the first. "Who would want girls this worthless and ignorant?" he asked. "We shall surely have to transport them back to Ar."

"Who of Ar would want them?" asked the second man, grinning.

"We will have to take them back to Ar," said the first man.

"We could sell them for sleen feed here," said the second.

"That is true," granted the first.

"Attend to the forty through forty-five platforms," said the second man, who seemed to have greater authority than the first. "I shall stay in this vicinity for the time."

The other man nodded, and turned away.

The second slaver's man regarded the four girls, who did not meet his eyes. He wore blue and yellow, a tunic. He wore studded leather wristlets. At his belt hung the whip. The girls now seemed apprehensive. I did not blame them. One in whose charge they were now stood near them. I saw them look at his whip, but there was no real comprehension of it in their eyes. They did not yet understand the whip, or what it might do to them. I gathered they had never been whipped.

"The bids have begun in the pavillion," I heard.

"Move forward," said the slaver's man to the girls, in Gorean. They did not understand his words, but his gesture was clear. Frightened, they, on their knees, crept forward to the edge of the platform. They were now quite near the crowd. Before they had been back about a yard or so on the platform. When a girl is back somewhat it is easier to see her. On the other hand, the proximity of female flesh to the buyer can in itself, of course, be a powerful inducement to her purchase. What man, truly close to a beautiful female, can fail to feel her in his blood, and want to own her?

The slaver, I conjectured, knew his business.

The girls looked at one another, terrified. They were now close to the men.

"Please, don't!" begged the blond girl. A man in the crowd, passing her, had put his hand on her thigh.

The slaver's man looked at her, angrily. She looked at him,

71

tears in her eyes. Did he not know what the beast, in passing, had done? He looked away.

What did it matter that someone had touched, even intimately caressed, a woman who was only a slave?

She tried to creep back, but the slaver's man, seeing this, irritably removed his whip from his belt and, with its coils, indicated the place on the platform where her knees must be. They were placed in such a way as to be a quarter of an inch over the edge of the platform. The other girls, too, made certain their knees were perfectly aligned. The robes of passing men then brushed their knees.

"I would look at this one," said a leather worker, who stopped before the blond, first on the chain.

She shrank back.

"She is a beauty, isn't she?" smiled the slaver. "Open her tunic. See what she has to offer you," he invited.

The leather worker reached toward the girl, but she scrambled back. "Don't touch me!" she cried. The dark-haired girl cried out with pain, dragged by her collar back, too. She fell twisted, on her side, in the chain.

"I'll scream," warned the blond girl.

The leather worker was quite puzzled. "I do not think I am interested," he said. "Too, this one is a barbarian. She is not broken to the collar."

"Break her to your collar," said the slaver's man.

"I do not want to take the time to break a girl in," he said.

"Wait, kind sir," said the slaver. "Wait! See what delights would await you."

The man hesitated.

"Prodicus!" called the slaver's man.

In a moment the first slaver's man, who had gone to supervise the forty through forty-five platforms, those in the two hundreds, joined his colleague.

The second slaver's man, who carried the whip, which he now uncoiled, unnoticed, I am sure, by the girls, indicated the blond with his head.

The fellow called to the platform scrambled onto it and swiftly knelt the blond before the slaver's man with the whip and the leather worker. The fellow on the platform then jerked loose the knot at the blond's right hip, which held the wrap-around tunic closed. "No!" she screamed. He jerked it back, away from her, exposing her. She was very beautiful. It lay behind her, over her chained wrists. He kicked her knees apart. Then he crouched behind her, holding her by the upper arms. She struggled, twisting, on her knees. She began to

72

scream miserably, her head back. She pressed her knees closely together. The slaver's man with the whip angrily leaped to the platform. He kicked her knees open again. She was sobbing and screaming. Men about laughed. "See, Master?" asked the slaver's man with the whip, but the leather worker had gone. The slaver's man glared down, in fury, at the chained blond. Another man in the crowd reached to take the ankle of the dark-haired girl in his hand and she, with a rattle of chain, jerked it away. She looked at him, terrified. "They are all barbarians," said a man, "all of them." Puzzled by the reactions of the blond and the dark-haired girl other men in the crowd reached out to touch the last two girls on the chain. One held with his two hands the thighs of the third girl, who had worn the plaid flannel shirt. She screamed in the collar. Another man took the fourth girl, who had worn the beige flannel shirt, under the arms, and pulled her to him. She fought to pull her lips back, that they might not touch his. She struggled in his arms. She screamed. He thrust her back on her side on the platform, and left her. The man who had held the thighs of the third girl, too, released her. There was much laughter in the crowd. She scrambled back in her chains, sobbing. The slaver's man was furious. He looked from one girl to the other, to the stripped, chained blond, to the cowering dark-haired girl, her neck cut by the collar, from its movement, to the third girl, sobbing and looking up at him, to the fourth girl, lying on her side, her legs drawn up, crying. He gestured to his colleague. This man went to the second girl and jerked back her tunic, and to the third and jerked back her tunic, and to the fourth and jerked back her tunic. Then they lay in their chains, exposed at his feet. Then he put them under the whip.

In moments they writhed at his feet, slave girls, screaming for mercy.

Tenalion of Ar, the slaver, their master, stood at the edge of the platform. He was not pleased.

"They are worthless," said the man with the whip, coiling it.

The girls lay on the platform, sobbing. Stripes were on their bodies.

"Take anything for them," said Tenalion, and turned away.

"Two," said a voice. "Two. How much?"

It was the fellow from the polar basin, who wore no jacket, but fur trousers and boots, with the bow at his back, and the rawhide rope on his shoulder. In his left hand he carried a bundle of furs, smaller now, than it had been, and a sack,

73

which was now less bulky than it had been when I had seen it earlier near the puppet theater. I remembered he had sold carvings to a corpulent, gross fellow, one whose booth had been set up in the street of the dealers in artifacts and curios. It was not far from the puppet theater.

I moved in more closely, thinking he might have difficulty in communicating with the slaver's man.

"Those," said the coppery-skinned fellow, pointing to the blond and the dark-haired girl, freshly whipped, crying in their chains.

"Yes?" asked the slaver's man.

"Cheap?" asked the man, a red hunter from the bleak countries north even of Ax Glacier.

"These two?" asked the slaver's man.

The hunter nodded.

The slaver's man knelt the two stripped girls before the hunter.

They looked at him with fear.

He was a man. They had felt the whip.

"Yes cheap. Very cheap," said the slaver's man. "Do you have money?"

The hunter pulled a pelt from the bundle of furs he carried. It was snowy white, and thick, the winter fur of a two-stomached snow lart. It almost seemed to glisten. The slaver's man appreciated its value. Such a pelt could sell in Ar for half a silver tarsk. He took the pelt and examined it. The snow lart hunts in the sun. The food in the second stomach can be held almost indefinitely. It is filled in the fall and must last the lart through the winter night, which lasts months, the number of months depending on the latitude of his individual territory. It is not a large animal. It is about ten inches high and weighs between eight and twelve pounds. It is mammalian, and has four legs. It eats bird's eggs and preys on the leem, a small arctic rodent, some five to ten ounces in weight, which hibernates during the winter.

"Not enough," said the slaver's man. The hunter grunted. He had guessed this. I did not think the slaver's man was out to defraud the hunter. For one thing, the fellow, this far south, probably had some conception of the values of the furs. For another thing the hunters of the north, though a generally kind, peaceable folk, except with animals, think little of killing. They are inured to it. As hunters they live with blood and death.

The hunter drew forth from the bundle of furs two tiny

pelts of the leem. These were brown, the summer coats of the animals.

"Look," said the slaver's man, gesturing at the two girls, the blond and the dark-haired girl. "Two beauties!"

The hunter drew forth two more pelts of the leem.

"Not enough," said the slaver's man.

The hunter grunted and bent down, retying the bundle of furs. He picked up the bundle and began to leave.

"Wait!" laughed the slaver's man. "They are yours!"

The girls reacted. "We have been sold," whispered the dark-haired girl. I recalled she had worn soft, black, custom-fitted feminine slacks, a soft, delicious, turtle-necked, red pull-over. It had been a beautiful top and had doubtless been quite expensive. I recalled that she had been rich. She was now the naked slave girl of a red hunter.

The slaver's man put the pelts in a pouch which hung from his belt.

With his right hand he pulled the head of the blond girl down, until it was at her knees. He did the same with the head of the dark-haired girl. They knelt as they had been placed. They had felt the whip.

The slaver then went behind them and freed their ankles from the steel ankle loops. He then unlocked the two-inch-high steel cuffs which had held the hands of the girls behind them. Their platform tunics, loose, he then let fall to the boards of the platform. The hunter, meanwhile, with a knife, had cut a length from the rope of twisted sleen hide which he wore over his shoulder. He fastened the two girls together by the neck. The slaver then unlocked the slaves' throat collars and tossed them, with the chain, to the platform.

The two beauties were drawn by the hunter from the platform and they then stood, frightened, tied together by the neck, before it.

The third and fourth girl looked upon these proceedings with unfeigned terror. They knew they themselves could be as easily the objects of so casual a transaction, putting them in the total power of a buyer, their master.

The red hunter, with two short lengths of the leather rope, jerked the hands of the beauties behind them and, swiftly, expertly, fastened them together. The blond-haired girl winced. "Oh," said the dark-haired girl, suddenly. I saw the hunter had tied women before. They were totally helpless.

The red hunters are generally a kind, peaceable folk, except with animals. Two sorts of beasts are kept in domestica-

75

tion in the north; the first sort of beast is the snow sleen; the second is the white-skinned woman.

"Ho," said the red hunter, and strode from the platform. The two beasts he had purchased hurried after him.

"Theirs will be a hard slavery," I said to the slaver's man.

"They will learn to pull a sled under the whip," he said.

"Yes," I said. Such women were used as draft animals. But they would serve, too, as slave girls do, many other purposes.

"Wait until the red women get hold of them," laughed the slaver's man.

"They may kill them," I said.

"They have one chance for life," he said, "to obey with total perfection."

"But," I asked, "is that not every slave girl's one chance for life?"

"True," he said. Then he turned and looked at the third and fourth girl.

They looked at him with terror. Beside them, on the platform, were two pairs of opened, empty ankle loops, two pairs of opened, empty wrist cuffs, two opened, empty collars, and some chain, and two platform tunics, discarded.

"I think," I said, "that these two girls might now be moved back on the platform and have their hands chained before their bodies rather than behind."

"I think you are right," he said, chuckling. He climbed to the platform and moved the girls back. He then unlocked the left cuff of the first girl and then recuffed her, this time with her small hands before her body. He did the same with the second. In doing this he had discarded their platform tunics. He then rejoined me before the platform.

They now knelt back on the platform in normal display location, their hands chained before them. They looked at him.

The slaver's man, with the whip, gestured broadly, expansively, to the passing crowd. He grinned at the girls.

The fourth girl, who had once worn the denim pants and beige flannel shirt, extended her chained hands to the crowd. "Buy me, Masters!" she cried out. "Buy me for your lover and slave. I am beautiful. I will serve you well!" She called out in English, for she knew no Gorean, but there could be little misinterpretation of her intent or of the desperate, piteous nature of her entreaties. "Buy me! Buy me!" she begged.

"I am even more beautiful!" cried the other suddenly. "Buy me instead!"

I saw men gathering about them. The girls redoubled their piteous efforts to please. "Buy me, Master!" cried one. "Buy

76

me, kind masters!" cried the other. They sought the eyes of men in the crowd. I could see they now, though they were barbarian, excited interest. Some men like a barbarian girl. And if a girl is not fully broken to the collar, one can always teach her. There is always the whip.

"How much do you want for them?" asked a man.

"They are not cheap," said the slaver's man.

I smiled to myself and left the area of the platform. They would soon be sold.

I pressed through the crowds.

The sales in the pavillion would already have begun. "Buy these girls! Buy these girls!" I heard, as I made my way between the platforms toward the pavillion. "Buy me, Master!" called a girl, with long dark hair, naked, lying on her side on one of the darkly varnished platforms, her body half covered with chains bound about her.

"A tarsk bit to enter, Master," said a slaver's man at the entrance to the pavilion.

I handed him a tarsk bit from my pouch, and pushed through the canvas.

My nostrils flared, my blood moved now faster in my veins. There is something charged and exhilarating about a slave market, the color, the movement, the excitement of the crowds, the bidding, the intensity, the lovely women being sold.

"Four copper tarsks!" was a bid called from the floor.

The girl stood on the block, her right side to the bidders. Her hands were behind her head, and her body was arched back. Her left leg was behind her, her right leg, flexed, thrust forth.

"Six!" was another bid.

She then faced the bidders, half crouched, her hands at her head, throwing her hair forward over her face. She regarded them angrily, sullenly, through her hair. Yet there was in her eyes a sultry need recognized by Gorean buyers. Taken home, she would soon become a satisfactory, hot slave, piteous and eager at her master's feet. She was directed by the auctioneer, responding to his voice commands and the light, deft, guiding touches of his whip.

I moved through the crowds, to get somewhat closer to the block. The girl was sold for fifteen copper tarsks to a metal worker from Tor.

I looked about in the crowd.

The next girl was a willowy blond Earth girl. She was sent to the block in what are regarded as the odd undergarments of Earth females. Both the upper undergarment and the lower were white. Her hands were braceleted behind her and the auctioneer, his whip in his belt, controlled her by the hair. She was hysterical. Her brassiere was first removed, then the panties. The latter garment, by Goreans, is regarded as a peculiarly strange one. It, silken and brief, is obviously a slave's garment, but it is closed at the bottom. It would take a man an extra moment to rape such a slave.

She was sold for four copper tarsks. I did not see who bought her. I think it was a locksmith from Ti.

I bought a slice of rolled meat, filled with sauce, in a waxed paper, from a vendor.

It was then that I saw him. Our eyes met. He turned white. Immediately, flinging aside the food, I began to thrust through the crowd toward him. He turned and, squirming and thrusting, fought his way toward the side of the tent.

I knew him now. He was the fellow whose back I had seen in the restaurant, from a distance. I had not been able to place at that time his identity. He no longer now wore the brown and black common to professional sleen trainers. He wore, as I, merchant robes.

I did not speak, or call out to him. Rather I pursued him. He looked back once and then, thrusting men aside, fought his way to the tent's side.

I pursued him who had called himself Bertram of Lydius, he who had, in my house, set a sleen upon me.

I wanted his throat in my hands.

When I thrust through the cut side of the tent, where he had slashed it open, he was not in sight.

I cursed and struck my fist upon my thigh. He was gone.

Behind me, from the tent, I heard the calls and the bidding. Another girl was on the block.

I looked out over the crowds. Thousands were at the fair of the Sardar.

My chances of finding one man in that crowd, and one who knew I searched for him, would be negligible. I looked angrily about. Behind me two men slipped into the tent, through the cut canvas. I no longer wished to attend the market. I turned away from the tent and, angrily, no clear destination in mind, mingled with the crowds. In time I found myself near the palisade ringing the Sardar mountains. I climbed one of the high platforms there. From these platforms one may look upon the Sardar. I stood alone on the platform, and gazed at the snow-capped mountains, glistening under the mingled light of the three white moons. From the

78

platform, too, I could see the fair, with its lights and fires, and tents and shelters, and the amphitheater in the distance, where Scormus of Ar and gentle Centius of Cos would meet tomorrow on the opposite sides of a small board marked with red and yellow squares. The district of the fair covered several square pasangs. It was very beautiful at night.

I descended the stairs of the platform and turned my steps toward the public tent where I had, earlier in the morning, reserved a lodging for myself.

I lay thinking in the furs, my hands behind my head, looking up at the ceiling of the tent above me. There was little light in the tent, for it was late. It was difficult for me to sleep.

More than a thousand men slept in this great tent.

The ceiling of the tent above me billowed slightly, responsive to a gentle wind from the east.

There were small lamps hung here and there in the tent. They hung on tiny chains. These chains were suspended from metal projections on certain of the tent poles.

I turned to my side, to watch her approach.

She moved carefully through the furs.

She knelt beside me.

A string was knotted about her waist. Over this string, in the front, there was thrust a single, simple narrow rectangle of vulgar, white rep-cloth, some six inches in width, some twelve inches in length.

She wore on her throat a high, gold collar, with, in front, a large golden loop, some two inches in width. Threaded through this loop loose, was a golden chain. This chain terminated, at each end, with high, golden slave bracelets. When the girl stands her hands may fall naturally at her sides, each in its bracelet, each bracelet attached to the same chain, which passes through the collar loop.

It is a very beautiful way of chaining a girl.

"Master," she whispered.

"I remember you," I said. She had been the slave who had followed me earlier in the day, who had bitten at my sleeve near the puppet theater, whom I had saved from a beating by the guardsmen under the aegis of the officer of the fair's merchant staff. She had begged me to take pity on her needs. I had not done so, of course. She might have been under the discipline of deprivation. Too, there had seemed no point in perhaps doing her master dishonor. I did not even know him. I had told her, after I had had her kneel and kiss my feet, to

79

run to her master, and crawl to him on her belly and beg his touch. "Yes, Master," she had said, and she had then leaped to her feet, frightened, and sped away.

"I did not know you were a slave in the public tents," I said to her.

"Yes, Master," she said, putting her head down. "I am a tent slave here."

"Why did you not tell me?" I asked.

"Is a girl to be permitted no pride?" she asked.

"No," I told her.

"Yes, Master," she said.

"Would it have made any difference?" she asked.

"No," I said.

"I thought not," she said.

"When you ran to your master," I asked, "as I commanded you, and crawled to him on your belly and begged his touch, what did he do?"

"He kicked me from his feet, and gave me over to a servant for switching," she said.

"Excellent," I said.

She looked down.

"Doubtless, by now," I said, "you have been much pleasured in these furs."

"There are other tent slaves here," she said, "many more beautiful than I, and men come late to the furs, tired and drunk. It is hard for us to compete with the beauties of the paga tents."

"I see," I said.

There were tears in her eyes. She reached forth her right hand, timidly, to touch my thigh. This caused the chain to slip a bit through the collar loop.

"Take pity on a slave, Master," she said.

I looked at her.

She backed away a bit and then, on her belly, crawled to me. She timidly pulled back the furs and pressed her lips to my thigh. Her lips were soft and wet. She looked up at me, tears in her eyes. "I crawl to my master on my belly," she said, "and beg for his touch."

I smiled.

I, a guest in the tent, now stood to her, of course, as master. Such girls come with the price of the lodging.

"Please, Master," she wept, "take pity on me. Take pity on the miserable needs of a girl."

I threw off the furs, and motioned her to my arms. She crept into them, sobbing.

80

"You are kind, Master," she said.

"Do you think so?" I asked.

She looked at me, frightened.

I drew her right hand away from her body, until the slave bracelet on her left wrist was against the golden collar loop. I then doubled the chain and formed from it a slip loop, which I dropped over her head. I jerked it tight. Her wrists now, both, were held at the collar loop. She looked up at me, frightened. I put her on her back, in the cradle of my left arm. She moved her small wrists in the cuffs; she tried to move her hands; they were held, confined, at the golden loop. I then pulled away the rectangle of rep-cloth she wore and wadded it and thrust it in her mouth. She looked at me, frightened. Then I began to touch her.

4 I REWARD TWO MESSENGERS, WHO HAVE RENDERED GOOD SERVICE

"Will he use the Two Tarnsmen opening?" asked a man.

"I wager," said another, "he will use the Physician's Gambit."

"That would permit the Turian Defense," said another.

I felt good. I had had a splendid night's rest. I had had an excellent breakfast.

The slave I had used had been helpless and spasmodically superb. She had not been permitted to use her hands; they had been chained; her bit of a garment had been thrust in her mouth; she could not cry out; she must endure in helpless squirming silence, as a slave girl, what sensations I chose to inflict upon her body. I was pleased; I had put her through pleasures which would have made a Ubara beg for the collar. I do not think she slept all night. In the morning, red-eyed, lying at my thigh, she had piteously begged that I buy her.

The morning was cool and the air was bright and clear. It would be a good day for the match.

I had arranged to have the pretty little slave lashed and then sent to Port Kar. I think she was a good buy. She cost me only a quarter of a silver tarsk.

"On whom do you wager?" asked a man.

"On Scormus of Ar," I responded.

"I, too," he said.

I was no longer as angry as I had been that the man I had seen last night in the pavillion had escaped me. I did not expect to see him again. If I did, that would be time enough to conduct him beyond the fair's perimeter and kill him.

I was restless and eager for the gates of the amphitheater to open. Already, even in Port Kar, I had reserved a seat for the match. It had cost me two golden tarns.

I found myself in the vicinity of the palisade. Initiates moved about, and many others. They performed ceremonies and sacrifices. In one place a white, bosk heifer was being slaughtered. Incense was being burned and bells were being rung; there was singing and chanting.

Then I was among the high platforms near the palisade.

Tied by the neck to the foot of a post, one of several supporting one of the long, high platforms near the palisade, kneeling, naked, their hands tied behind them, were two slave girls. They looked at me in terror. They had spent their first night in a man's power. Their thighs were bloodied; the dark-haired girl's arm was bruised. The red hunters are not gentle with their animals.

I climbed the stairs to the platform. I would look upon the Sardar in the morning light. At this time, particularly in the spring, the sun sparkling on the snow-strewn peaks, the mountains can be quite beautiful.

I attained the height of the platform and found the view breath-taking, even more splendid than I had hoped. I stood there very quietly in the cool, sunlit morning air. It was very beautiful.

Near me, on the platform, stood the red hunter. He, too, it seemed, was struck to silence and awe.

Then, standing on the platform, he lifted his bare arms to the mountains.

"Let the herd come," he said. He had spoken in Gorean. Then he reached into a fur sack at his feet and, gently, took forth a representation of the northern tabuk, carved in blue stone. I had no idea how long it took to make such a carving. It would take many nights in the light of the sloping, oval lamps.

He put the tiny tabuk on the boards at his feet, and then

again lifted his arms to the mountains. "Let the herd come," he said. "I give you this tabuk," he said. "It was mine, and it is now yours. Give us now the herd which is ours."

Then he lowered his arms and reached down and closed the sack. He left the platform.

There were other individuals, too, on the long platform. Each, I supposed, had their petition to make to Priest-Kings. I looked at the tiny tabuk left behind on the boards. It looked toward the Sardar.

Below, the red hunter freed the kneeling, tethered girls of the post. They stood. He kept them neck-linked by the rawhide rope. Their hands remained bound behind them. He then made his way from the foot of the platform. I remembered that one of the Earth girls had been rich, the dark-haired girl; the other, the blond, I supposed had been middle class, perhaps upper middle class; I did not know; at any rate, whatever they might have been, that was now behind them, a world away; social distinctions no longer divided them; social distinctions, like their clothing, had been taken away; they were now the same, identical; both, whatever they might once have been, were now only naked slaves. They followed the red hunter, their master.

I looked at the amphitheater. I could see it easily from the height of the platform.

I saw that now the Kaissa flag, with its red and yellow squares, flew from a lance on the amphitheater's rim. Flanking it, on either side, were the standards of Cos and Ar. That of Ar was on the right, for Scormus had won yellow in the draw; it had been his hand which, under the scarlet cloth, had closed upon the tiny, wooden, yellow spearman in the helmet, the possession of which determined the first move and, with it, the choice of opening.

I would win a hundred golden tarns.

The amphitheater was now open. I hurried down the stairs of the platform.

There was a great cheer in the amphitheater and men stood upon the tiers, waving their caps and shouting.

"Scormus of Ar!" they shouted. "Scormus of Ar!"

I could hear the anthem of Ar being sung now.

It was hard to see.

"He is here!" cried a man next to me.

I climbed on the tier and stood. I could now see, in the robes of the players, Scormus of Ar, the fiery, young champion of Ar. He was with a party of the men of Ar. The table with the board was set in the center of the stage, at the foot of the huge, sloping, semicircular amphitheater. It seemed small and far away.

Scormus lifted his hands to the crowd, the sleeves of his robe falling back over his arms.

He wore a cape, which was removed from him by two other players of Ar.

He threw his cap into the crowd. Men fought wildly to possess it.

He lifted again his arms to the crowd.

There was then another cheer, for Centius of Cos, with the party of Cos, had emerged upon the stage. I heard now the anthem of Cos being sung.

Centius of Cos walked to the edge of the stone stage, some five feet above the pit, and lifted his hand to the crowd. He smiled.

The amphitheater, of course, is used for more than Kaissa. It is also used for such things as the readings of poets, the presentations of choral arrangements, the staging of pageants and the performances of song dramas. Indeed, generally the great amphitheater is not used for Kaissa, and the Sardar matches are played in shallow fields, before lengthy sloping tiers, set into the sides of small hills, many matches being conducted simultaneously, a large vertical board behind each table serving to record the movements of the pieces and correspond to the current position. The movements of the pieces are chalked on the left side of the board, in order; the main portion of the board consists of a representation of the Kaissa board and young players, in apprenticeship to masters, move pieces upon it; one has thus before oneself both a record of the moves made to that point and a graphic representation of the current state of the game. The movements are chalked, too, incidentally, by the young players. The official scoring is kept by a team of three officials, at least one of which must be of the caste of players. These men sit at a table near the table of play. Games are adjudicated, when capture of Home Stone does not occur, by a team of five judges, each of which must be a member of the caste of players, and three of which must play at the level of master.

"Scormus of Ar will destroy him," said a man.

"Yes," said another.

Behind the table of play on the stage, and a bit to the right, was the table for those who would score. There was a man there from Ar, and one from Cos, and a player from Turia, Timor, a corpulent fellow supposed to be of indisputable integrity and one thought, at any rate, to be of a city far enough removed from the problems of Cos and Ar to be impartial. Also, of course, there were hundreds of men in the tiers who would simultaneously, unofficially, be recording the match. There was little danger of a move being incorrectly recorded. An official in such a situation insane enough to attempt to tamper with the record of the moves would be likely to be torn to pieces. Goreans take their Kaissa seriously.

I saw now upon the stage Reginald of Ti, who was the elected administrator of the caste of players. A fellow with him carried the sand clocks. These clocks are arranged in such a way that each has a tiny spigot which may be opened and closed, this determining whether sand falls or not. These spigots are linked in such a way that when one is open the other must be closed; the spigot turned by a given player closes his own clock's sand passage and opens that of his opponent; when the clocks must both be stopped, as for an adjournment of play, they are placed on their side by the chief judge in the match, in this case Reginald of Ti. There are two Ahn of sand in each player's clock. Each player must complete forty moves before his clock is empty of sand, under penalty of forfeit. The clocks improve tournament play which otherwise could become contests not of Kaissa but of patience, the victory perhaps going to him who was most willing to outsit his opponent. There was a movement among some of the younger players to divide the sand in such a way that each player would have one Ahn for the first twenty moves, and one Ahn for the second twenty moves, subject to the same forfeiture conditions as the two-Ahn clock. The point of this, I was told, would be to improve Kaissa in the second Ahn. It was true that many times even masters found themselves in time pressure in the second Ahn, having perhaps only a few Ehn sand left for eight or ten moves. On the other hand, there seemed little likelihood of this innovation being accepted. Tradition was against it, of course. Also, it was felt preferable by many for a player to be able to decide for himself, under the conditions of a given game, the duration of his speculations on a given move. He is thought by many better able to govern his own play when there is only a single time pressure to be considered, that of the full two Ahn, I rather agree with the latter view. There are precision chronometers on Gor, incidentally, and a more mechanical method of time control is technically feasible. The sand clocks, on the other hand, tend to be a matter of tournament tradition.

Centius of Cos tossed his cap into the crowd and men, too, fought to possess it.

He lifted his arms to the crowd. He seemed in a good mood.

He walked across the stage, in front of the table of play, to greet Scormus of Ar. He extended his hand to him in the comraderie of players. Scormus of Ar, however, angrily turned away.

Centius of Cos did not seem disturbed at this rebuff and turned about again and, lifting his hands again to the crowd, returned to the side of the stage where his party stood.

Scormus of Ar paced angrily on the stage. He wiped the palms of his hands on his robe.

He would not look upon, nor touch, Centius of Cos in friendship. Such a simple gesture might weaken his intensity, the height of his hatreds, his readiness to do battle. His brilliance, his competitive edge, must be at its peak. Scormus of Ar reminded me of men of the caste of Assassins, as they sometimes are, before they begin their hunt. The edge must be sharp, the resolve must be merciless, the instinct to kill must in no way be blunted.

The two men then approached the table.

Behind them, more than forty feet high, and fifty feet wide, was a great vertical board. On this board, dominating it, there was a giant representation of a Kaissa board. On it, on their pegs, hung the pieces in their initial positions. On this board those in the audience would follow the game. To the left of the board were two columns, vertical, one for yellow, one for red, where the moves, as they took place, would be recorded. There were similar boards, though smaller, at various places about the fair, where men who could not afford the fee to enter the amphitheater might stand and watch the progress of play. Messengers at the back of the amphitheater, coming and going, delivered the moves to these various boards.

A great hush fell over the crowd.

We sat down.

The judge, Reginald of Ti, four others of the caste of players behind him, had finished speaking to Scormus and Centius, and the scorers.

There was not a sound in that great amphitheater.

Centius of Cos and Scormus of Ar took their places at the table.

The stillness, for so large a crowd, was almost frightening.

I saw Scormus of Ar incline his head briefly. Reginald of

Ti turned the spigot on the clock of Centius of Cos, which opened the sand passage in the clock of Scormus.

The hand of Scormus reached forth. It did not hesitate. The move was made. He then turned the spigot on his clock, ceasing its flow of sand, beginning that in the clock of Centius.

The move, of course, was Ubara's Spearman to Ubara five.

There was a cheer from the crowd.

"The Ubara's Gambit!" called a man near me.

We watched the large, yellow plaque, representing the Ubara's Spearman, hung on its peg at Ubara five. Two young men, apprentices in the caste of players, on scaffolding, placed the plaque. Another young man, also apprenticed in the caste of players, recorded this move, in red chalk, at the left of the board. Hundreds of men in the audience also recorded the move on their own score sheets. Some men had small peg boards with them, on which they would follow the game. On these boards they could, of course, consider variations and possible continuations.

It was indeed, I suspected, that opening. It is one of the most wicked and merciless in the repertoire of the game. It is often played by tournament masters. Indeed, it is the most common single opening used among masters. It is difficult to meet and in many of its lines has no clear refutation; it may be played accepted or declined; it would be red's hope not to refute but to neutralize in the middle game; if red could manage to achieve equality by the twentieth move he might account himself successful. Scormus of Ar, though almost universally a versatile and brilliant player, was particularly masterful in this opening; he had used it for victory in the Turian tournaments of the ninth year of the Ubarate of Phanias Turmus; in the open tournaments of Anango, Helmutsport, Tharna, Tyros and Ko-ro-ba, all played within the past five years; in the winter tournament of the last Sardar Fair and in the city championship of Ar, played some six weeks ago. In Ar, when Scormus had achieved capture of Home Stone, Marlenus himself, Ubar of the city, had showered gold upon the board. Some regarded winning the city championship of Ar as tantamount to victory at the Fair of En'Kara. It is, in the eyes of many followers of Kaissa, easily the second most coveted crown in the game. Centius of Cos, of course, would also be a master of the Ubara's Gambit. Indeed, he was so well versed in the gambit, from both the perspective of yellow and red, that he would doubtless play now for a draw. I did not think he would be successful. He

87

sat across the board from Scormus of Ar. Most players of the master level, incidentally, know this opening several moves into the game in more than a hundred variations.

"Why does Centius not move?" asked the man next to me.

"I do not know," I said.

"Perhaps he is considering resigning," said a fellow some two places down the tier.

"Some thought Scormus would use the Two Tarnsmen Opening," said another fellow.

"He might have," said another, "with a lesser player."

"He is taking no chances," said another man.

I rather agreed with these thoughts. Scormus of Ar, no irrational fool, knew he played a fine master, one of the seven or eight top-rated players on the planet. Centius of Cos, doubtless, was past his prime. His games, in recent years, had seemed less battles, less cruel, exact duels, than obscure attempts to achieve something on the Kaissa board which even many members of the caste of players did not profess to understand. Indeed, there were even higher rated players on Gor than Centius of Cos, but, somehow, it had seemed that it was he whom Scormus of Ar must meet to establish his supremacy in the game. Many regarded Centius of Cos, in spite of his victories or defeats or draws, as the finest player of Kaissa of all time. It was the luminosity of his reputation which had seemed to make the grandeur of Scormus less glorious. "I shall destroy him," had said Scormus. But he would play him with care. That he had chosen the Ubara's Gambit indicated the respect in which he held Centius of Cos and the seriousness with which he approached the match.

Scormus would play like an Assassin. He would be merciless, and he would take no chances.

Centius of Cos was looking at the board. He seemed bemused, as though he were thinking of something, something perhaps oddly irrelevant to the game at hand. His right hand had lifted, and poised itself over his own Ubara's Spearman, but then he had withdrawn his hand.

"Why does he not move?" asked a man.

Centius of Cos looked at the board.

The correct response, of course, whether the Ubara's Gambit be accepted or declined, is to bring one's own Ubara's Spearman to Ubara five. This will contest the center and prohibit the advance of the opposing spearman. Yellow's next move, of course, is to advance the Ubara's Tarnsman's Spearman to Ubara's Tarnsman's five, attacking red's defending spearman. Red then elects to accept or decline the gambit, accepting by capturing the Ubara's Tarnsman's spearman, but surrendering the center in doing so, or declining the gambit, by defending his spearman, and thus constricting his position. The gambit is playable both ways, but not with the hope of retaining the captured spearman for a material advantage. We wished Centius to move the Ubara's Spearman to Ubara five, so that Scormus might play the Ubara's Tarnsman's Spearman to Ubara's Tarnsman's five. We were then eager to see if Centius would play the gambit accepted or declined.

"Does he not know his clock is open?" asked a man.

It did seem strange that Centius did not move swiftly at this point in the game. He might need this time later, when in the middle game he was defending himself against the onslaughts and combinations of Scormus or in the end game, where the contest's outcome might well hang upon a single, subtle, delicate move on a board almost freed of pieces.

The sand flowed from the clock of Centius.

Had the hand of Centius touched his Ubara's Spearman he would have been committed to moving it. Too, it might be mentioned, if he should place a piece on a given square and remove his hand from the piece, the piece must remain where it was placed, subject, of course, to the consideration that the placement constitutes a legal move.

But Centius of Cos had not touched the Ubara's Spearman. No scorer or judge had contested that.

He looked at the board for a time, and then, not looking at Scormus of Ar, moved a piece.

I saw one of the scorers rise to his feet. Scormus of Ar looked at Centius of Cos. The two young men who had already picked up the Ubara's Spearman's plaque seemed confused. Then they put it aside.

Centius of Cos turned the spigot on his clock, opening the clock of Scormus.

We saw, on the great board, the placement not of the Ubara's Spearman at Ubara five, but of the Ubar's Spearman at Ubar five.

It was now subject to capture by yellow's Ubara's Spearman.

There was a stunned silence in the crowd.

"Would he play the Center Defense against one such as Scormus?" asked a man.

That seemed incredible. A child could crush the Center Defense. Its weaknesses had been well understood for centuries.

The purpose of the Center Defense is to draw the yellow

Spearman from the center. Yellow, of course, may ignore the attack, and simply thrust deeper into red territory. On the other hand, yellow commonly strikes obliquely, capturing the red spearman. Red then recaptures with his Ubar. Unfortunately for red, however, the Ubar, a quite valuable piece, rated at nine points, like the Ubara, has been too early centralized. Yellow simply advances the Ubara's Rider of the High Thalarion. This exposes the advanced Ubar to the immediate attack of the Initiate at Initiate one. The Ubar must then retreat, losing time. Yellow's Initiate, of course, has now been developed. The move by the capturing yellow spearman, too, of course, has already, besides capturing the red spearman, developed the yellow Ubara.

The Center Defense is certainly not to be generally recommended.

Still, Centius of Cos was playing it.

I found this intriguing. Sometimes masters develop new variations of old, neglected openings. Old mines are sometimes not deficient in concealed gold. At the least the opponent is less likely to be familiar with these supposedly obsolete, refutable beginnings. Their occasional employment, incidentally, freshens the game. Too often master-level Kaissa becomes overly routine, almost automatic, particularly in the first twenty moves. This is the result, of course, of the incredible amount of analysis to which the openings have been subjected. Some games, in a sense, do not begin until the twentieth move.

I looked at the great board.

Scormus, as I would have expected, captured the red spearman.

Some of the most brilliant games on record, incidentally, have been spun forth from openings now often regarded as weak or anachronistic.

The Center Defense seemed an implausible candidate however from which to project a brilliancy, unless perhaps the brilliancy might involve some swift and devastating exploitation of red's temerity by yellow.

Still Centius of Cos seemed prepared to meet Scormus with the Center Defense.

The crowd was quite restless.

But Centius of Cos did not play to retake with the Ubar.

The crowd watched, stunned.

Centius of Cos had moved his Ubar's Tarnsman's Spearman to Ubar's Tarnsman four.

It was undefended.

The Center Defense was not being played. Men looked at one another. Centius of Cos had already lost a piece, a spearman. One does not give pieces to a Scormus of Ar.

Most masters, down a spearman to Scormus of Ar, would tip their Ubar.

But another spearman now stood *en prise*, vulnerably subject to capture by the threatening, advancing spearman of yellow.

"Spearman takes Spearman," said a man next to me. I, too, could see the great board.

Red was now two spearmen down.

Red would now advance his Ubar's Rider of the High Tharlarion, to develop his Ubar's Initiate and, simultaneously, expose the yellow spearman to the Initiate's attack.

"No! No!" cried a merchant of Cos.

Instead Centius of Cos had advanced his Ubar's Scribe's Spearman to Ubar's Scribe three.

Another piece now stood helplessly *en prise*.

I grew cold with fury, though I stood to win a hundred golden tarns.

Scormus of Ar looked upon Centius of Cos with contempt. He looked, too, to the scorers and judges. They looked away, not meeting his eyes. The party of Cos left the stage.

I wondered how much gold Centius of Cos had taken that he would so betray Kaissa and the island of his birth. He could have done what he did more subtly, a delicate, pretended miscalculation somewhere between the fortieth and fiftieth move, a pretended misjudgment so subtle that even members of the caste of players would never be certain whether or not it was deliberate, but he had not chosen to do so. He had chosen to make his treachery to the game and Cos explicit.

Scormus of Ar rose to his feet and went to the table of the scorers and judges. They conversed with him, angrily. Scormus then went to the party of Ar. One of them, a captain, went to the scorers and judges. I saw Reginald of Ti, high judge, shaking his head.

"They are asking for the award of the game," said the man next to me.

"Yes," I said. I did not blame Scormus of Ar for not wishing to participate in this farce.

Centius of Cos sat still, unperturbed, looking at the board. He set the clocks on his side, that the sand would not be draining from the clock of Scormus.

The party of Ar, and Scormus, I gathered, had lost their petition to the judges.

Scormus returned to his place.

Reginald of Ti, high judge, righted the clocks. The hand of Scormus moved.

"Spearman takes Spearman," said the man next to me. Centius of Cos had now lost three spearmen.

He must now, at last, take the advancing yellow spearman, so deep in his territory, with his Ubar's Rider of the High Tharlarion. If he did not take with the Rider of the High Tharlarion at this point it, too, would be lost.

Centius of Cos moved his Ubara to Ubar's Scribe four. Did he not know his Rider of the High Tharlarion was *en prise!*

Was he a child who had never played Kaissa? Did he not know how the pieces moved?

No, the explanation was much more simple. He had chosen to make his treachery to Kaissa and the island of Cos explicit. I thought perhaps he was insane. Did he not know the nature of the men of Gor?

"Kill Centius of Cos!" I heard cry. "Kill him! Kill him!"

Guardsmen at the stage's edge, with shields, buffeted back a man who, with drawn knife, had tried to climb to the level where sat the table of the game.

Centius of Cos seemed not to notice the man who had been struck back from the edge of the stage. He seemed not to note the angry cries from the crowd, the menace of its gathering rage. I saw many men rising to their feet. Several raised their fists.

"I call for a cancellation of all wagers!" cried a man from Cos. He had, I assumed, bet upon the champion of Cos. It would indeed be a sorry way in which to lose one's money. Several men had bet fortunes on the match. There were few in the audience who had not put something on one or the other of the two players.

But among the angriest of the crowd, interestingly, were hot-headed men of Ar itself. They felt they would be cheated of the victory were it so fraudulently surrendered to them.

I wondered who had bought the honor of Centius of Cos, to whom he had sold his integrity.

"Kill Centius of Cos!" I heard.

I did not think my hundred tarns were in danger, for it would be madness on the part of the odds merchants to repudiate the documented bargainings they had arranged. I did think, however, that I would not much relish my winnings.

Guardsmen, with spear butts and cruel shield rims, forced back two more men from the stage's edge.

Scormus of Ar moved a piece.

"Spearman takes Rider of the High Tharlarion," said the man next to me, bitterly.

I saw this on the great board. Yellow's pieces, as they are arranged, begin from their placements at the lower edge of the great board, red's pieces from their placement at its upper edge.

Centius of Cos had now lost four pieces, without a single retaliatory or compensating capture. He was four pieces down, three spearmen and a Rider of the High Tharlarion. His minor pieces on the Ubar's side had almost been wiped out. I noted, however, that he had not lost a major piece. The response of Centius of Cos to the loss of his Rider of the High Tharlarion was to retake with his Ubar's Initiate.

There was a sigh of satisfaction, of relief from the crowd. Centius of Cos had at least seen this elementary move. There were derisive comments in the audience, commending this bit of expertise on his part.

This move, of course, developed the Ubar's Initiate. I also noted, as I had not noted before, that red's Ubar's Scribe was developed. This was the result of the earlier advance of red's Ubar's Tarnsman's Spearman. The Ubara, of course, as I have mentioned, had been developed to Ubar's Scribe four. The Ubar, too, I suddenly realized, stood on an open file. I suddenly realized that red had developed four major pieces.

Scormus, on his sixth move, advanced his Ubar's Spearman to Ubar four. Ubar five would have been impractical because at that point the spearman would have been subjected to the attack of red's Ubara and Ubar. Scormus now had a spearman again in the center. He would support this spearman, consolidate the center and then begin a massive attack on red's weakened Ubar's side. Scormus would place his Home Stone, of course, on the Ubara's side, probably at Builder one. This would free his Ubar's side's pieces for the attack on red's Ubar's side.

Centius of Cos then, on his sixth move, placed his Ubar at Ubar four. This seemed too short a thrust for an attack. It did, however, place his Ubar on the same rank with the Ubara, where they might defend one another. The move seemed a bit timid to me. Too, it seemed excessively defensive. I supposed, however, in playing with a Scormus of Ar, one could not be blamed for undertaking careful defensive measures.

On his seventh move Scormus advanced his Ubar's Tarnsman's Spearman to Ubar's Tarnsman five. At this point it

93

was protected by the spearman at Ubar four, and could soon, in league with other pieces, begin the inexorable attack down the file of the Ubar's Tarnsman.

Scormus of Ar was mounting his attack with care. It would be exact and relentless.

I suddenly realized that yellow had not yet placed his Home Stone.

The oddity in the game now struck me.

No major piece had yet been moved by yellow, not an Initiate, nor a Builder, nor a Scribe, nor a Tarnsman, nor the Ubar nor Ubara. Each of these major pieces remained in its original location. Not one piece had yet been moved by yellow from the row of the Home Stone.

I began to sweat.

I watched the great board. It was as I had feared. On his seventh move Centius of Cos advanced his Rider of the High Tharlarion to Ubara's Builder three. This would prepare for Builder to Builder two, and, on the third move, for placement of Home Stone at Builder one.

The crowd was suddenly quiet. They, too, realized what I had just realized.

Anxiously we studied the board.

If Scormus wished to place his Home Stone at either Ubar's Builder one or Ubara's Builder one, it would take three moves to do so. It would also take three moves if he wished to place it at Ubar's Initiate one, or at Ubara's Scribe one, Ubara's Builder one or Ubara's Initiate one. He could place the Home Stone, of course, in two moves, if he would place it at Ubar's Tarnsman one, or Ubar's Scribe one, or Ubar one, or Ubara one, or Ubara's Tarnsman one. But these placements permitted within two moves left the Home Stone too centralized, too exposed and vulnerable. They were not wise placements.

Already, though he had red, Centius of Cos was moving to place his Home Stone.

Now, on his eighth move, Scormus of Ar angrily advanced his Rider of the High Tharlarion to Builder three. His attack must be momentarily postponed.

On his own eighth move Centius of Cos advanced his Ubara's Builder to Builder two, to clear Builder one for placement of Home Stone.

On his ninth move Scormus of Ar, following suit, advanced his Ubara's Builder to Builder two, to open Builder one for the positioning of the Home Stone on the tenth move.

We watched the great board.

Centius of Cos placed his Home Stone at his Ubara's Builder one. He had done this on his ninth move. It needed not be done before the tenth move. His tenth move was now free, to spend as he would.

Scormus of Ar, on his tenth move, inexplicably to many in the crowd, though he possessed yellow, a move behind, placed his Home Stone at Builder one.

The two Home stones, at their respective locations, faced one another, each shielded by its several defending pieces, Scribe and Initiate, one of the central spearmen, a flanking spearman, a Builder, a Physician, and a Rider of the High Tharlarion.

Scormus might now renew his attack.

"No," I cried suddenly. "No, look!"

I rose to my feet. There were tears in my eyes. "Look!" I wept. "Look!"

The man next to me saw it, too, and then another, and another.

Men of Cos seized one another, embracing. Even men of Ar cried out with joy.

Red's Ubar's Initiate controlled the Ubar's Initiate's Diagonal; the red Ubara controlled the Ubar's Physician's Diagonal; the red Ubar controlled the Ubar's Builder's Diagonal; the Ubar's Scribe controlled the Ubar's Scribe's Diagonal. Red controlled not one but four adjacent diagonals, unobstructed diagonals, each bearing on the citadel of yellow's Home Stone; the red Ubara threatened the Ubara's Scribe's Spearman at Ubara's Scribe two; the Initiate threatened the Ubara's Builder at Builder two, positioned directly before yellow's Home Stone; the Ubar threatened the Rider of the High Tharlarion at Builder three; the Scribe threatened the Ubara's Flanking Spearman at Ubara's Initiate three. I had never seen such power amassed so subtly in Kaissa. The attack, of course, was not on the Ubar's side but on the side of the Ubara, where Scormus had placed his Home Stone. Moves which had appeared to weaken red's position had served actually to produce an incredible lead in development; moves which had appeared meaningless or defensive had actually been deeply insidious; the timorous feint to the Ubar's side by red with the Ubara and Ubar had, in actuality, prepared a trap in which Scormus had little choice but to place his Home Stone.

On his tenth move Centius of Cos moved his Rider of the High Tharlarion, which had been at Builder three. obliquely to Builder four. This opened the file of the Builder. The

95

power of this major piece now, in conjunction with the might of the Ubar, focused on yellow's Rider of the High Thar-larion. The attack had begun.

I shall not describe the following moves in detail. There were eleven of them.

On what would have been his twenty-second move Scor-mus of Ar, saying nothing, rose to his feet. He stood beside the board, and then, with one finger, delicately, tipped his Ubar. He set the clocks on their side, stopping the flow of sand, turned, and left the stage.

For a moment the crowd was silent, stunned, and then pandemonium broke out. Men leaped upon one another; cushions and caps flew into the air. The bowl of the am-phitheater rocked with sound. I could scarcely hear myself shouting. Two men fell from the tier behind me. I scrambled onto my tier, straining to see the stage. I was buffeted to one side and then the other.

One of the men of the party of Cos which had now re-turned to the stage stood on the table of the game, the yellow Home Stone in his grasp. He lifted it to the crowd. Men be-gan to swarm upon the stage. The guards could no longer re-strain them. I saw Centius of Cos lifted to the shoulders of men. He lifted his arms to the crowd, the sleeves of the player's robes falling back on his shoulders. Standards and pennons of Cos appeared as if from nowhere. On the height of the rim of the amphitheater a man was lifting the standard of Cos, waving it to the crowds in the fields and streets be-low.

The stage was a melée of jubilant partisans.

I could not even hear the shouting of the thousands outside the amphitheater. It would later be said the Sardar itself shook with sound.

"Cos! Cos! Cos!" I heard, like a great drumming, like thunderous waves breaking on stone shores.

I struggled to keep my place on the tier.

Pieces were being torn away from the great board. One sleeve of the robe of Centius of Cos had been torn away from his arm.

He waved to the crowds.

"Centius! Centius! Centius!" I heard. Soldiers of Cos lifted spears again and again. "Centius! Cos!" they cried. "Centius! Cos!"

I saw the silvered hair of Centius of Cos, unkempt now in the broiling crowd. He reached toward the man on the table

96

who held aloft the yellow Home Stone. The man pressed it into his hands.

There was more cheering.

Reginald of Ti was attempting to quiet the crowds. Then he resigned himself to futility. The tides of emotion must take their course.

Centius of Cos held, clutched, in his hand, the yellow Home Stone. He looked about in the crowd, on the stage, as though he sought someone, but there was only the crowd, surgent and roiling in its excitement and revels.

"Cos! Centius! Cos! Centius!"

I had lost fourteen hundred tarns of gold. Yet I did not regret the loss nor did it disturb me in the least. Who would not cheerfully trade a dozen such fortunes to witness one such game.

"Centius! Cos! Centius! Cos!"

I had, in my own lifetime, seen Centius of Cos and Scormus of Ar play.

On the shoulders of men, amidst shouting and the upraised standards and pennons of Cos I saw silver-haired Centius of Cos carried from the stage.

Men were reluctant to leave the amphitheater. I made my way toward one of the exits. Behind me I could hear hundreds of men singing the anthem of Cos.

I was well pleased that I had come to the Sardar.

It was late now in the evening of that day on which Centius of Cos and Scormus of Ar had met in the great amphitheater. There seemed little that was discussed in the fair that night save the contest of the early afternoon.

"It was a flawed and cruel game," Centius of Cos was reported as having said.

How could he speak so of the masterpiece which we had witnessed?

It was one of the brilliancies in the history of Kaissa.

"I had hoped," had said Centius of Cos, "that together Scormus and I might have constructed something worthy of the beauty of Kaissa. But I succumbed to the temptation of victory."

Centius of Cos, it was generally understood, was a strange fellow.

"It was the excitement, the press, the enthusiasm of the crowds," said Centius of Cos. "I was weak. I had determined to honor Kaissa but, on the first move, I betrayed her. I saw, suddenly, in considering the board what might be done. I did

97

it, and followed its lure. In retrospect I am saddened. I chose not Kaissa but merciless, brutal conquest. I am sad."

But any reservations which might have troubled the reflections of the master of Cos did not disturb those of his adherents and countrymen. The night at the fair was one of joy and triumph for the victory of Cos and her allies.

His response to Ubara's Spearman to Ubara's Spearman five, sequential, in its continuation, was now entitled the Telnus Defense, from the city of his birth, the capital and chief port of the island of Cos. Men discussed it eagerly. It was being played in dozens of variations that very night on hundreds of boards. In the morning there would be countless analyses and annotations of the game available.

On the hill by the amphitheater where sat the tent of Centius of Cos there was much light and generous feasting. Torches abounded. Tables were strewn about and sheets thrown upon the ground. Free tarsk and roast bosk were being served, and Sa-Tarna bread and Ta wine, from the famed Ta grapes of the Cosian terraces. Only Centius of Cos, it was said, did not join in the feasting. He remained secluded in the tent studying by the light of a small lamp a given position in Kaissa, one said to have occurred more than a generation ago in a game between Ossius of Tabor, exiled from Teletus, and Philemon of Asperiche, a cloth worker.

On the hill by the amphitheater, where sat the tent of the party of Ar, there was little feasting or merriment. Scormus of Ar, it was said, was not in that tent. After the game he had left the amphitheater. He had gone to the tent. He was not there now. No one knew where he had gone. Behind him he had left a Kaissa board, its kit of pieces, and the robes of the player.

I turned my thoughts from Centius of Cos and Scormus of Ar. I must now think of returning to Port Kar.

There was little now to hold me at the fair. Overhead, with some regularity, I saw tarns streaking from the fair, many with tarn baskets slung beneath them, men and women returning to their cities. More than one caravan, too, was being harnessed. My own tarn was at a cot, where I had rented space for him.

I thought that I would leave the fair tonight. There seemed little point now in remaining at the fair.

I thought of the ship of Tersites, its high prow facing toward the world's end. That unusual, mighty ship would soon be supplied and fitted. It could not yet see. Its eyes had

98

not yet been painted. This must be done. It would then be ready to seek the sea and, beyond it, the world's end.

I was troubled as I thought of the great ship. I was troubled as I thought of the world's end. I was not confident of the design of the ship. I thought I might rather ply toward the horizon beckoning betwixt Cos and Tyros in the Dorna or the small, swift Tesephone.

Tersites, it was clear, was mad. Samos thought him, too, however, a genius.

Oddly, for there seemed no reason for it, I found myself thinking, in a mentally straying moment, of the herd of Tancred, and its mysterious failure to appear in the polar basin. I hoped the supplies I had sent north would mitigate what otherwise might prove a catastrophe for the red hunters, the nomads of the northern wastes. I recalled, too, the myth of the mountain that did not move, a great iceberg which somehow seemed to defy the winds and currents of the polar sea. Many primitive peoples have their stories and myths. I smiled to myself. It was doubtless rather the invention of a red hunter, bemused at the request of the man of Samos, months ago, for reports of anything which might prove unusual. I wondered if the wily fellow had chuckled well to himself when placing the tarsk bit in his fur pouch. Seldom would his jokes and lies prove so profitable I suspected. The foolishness of the man of Samos would make good telling around the lamp.

I was making my way toward the tarn cot where I had housed the tarn on which I had come to the fair, a brown tarn, from the mountains of Thentis, famed for its tarn flocks. My belongings I had taken there earlier, putting them in the saddlebags. I had had supper.

I was looking forward to the return to Port Kar. It is beautiful to fly alone by night over the wide fields, beneath the three moons in the black, star-studded sky. One may then be alone with one's thoughts, and the moons, and the wind. It is beautiful, too, to so fly, with a girl one has desired, bound over one's saddle, tied to the saddle rings, commanded to silence, her white belly arched, exposed to the moons.

I turned down the street of the rug makers.

I was not dissatisfied with my stay at the fair and I did not think my men would be either.

I smiled to myself.

In my pouch were the receipts and shipping vouchers for five slave girls, she whom I had purchased at the public tent this morning and four others, recently acquired on the platforms near the pavillion. I had had good buys on the four, as well as the first. A new shipment had come in, from which I had bought the four. I had had almost first pick of the chain beauties. The market had been slow, as I had thought it would be, and as I had hoped it would be, because of the game earlier between the Kaissa titans, Centius of Cos and Scormus of Ar. Indeed the market had been almost empty, save for the displayed wares and their merchants. The girls must wait, chained, for buyers, while men discuss Kaissa. The four I had purchased I had obtained from the platforms of Leander of Turia. His caravan had been delayed in arriving at the Sardar because of spring floods on the Cartius. None of the girls was an Earth wench. All were Gorean. Each was woman enough to survive when thrown naked and collared among men such as mine. I had had the lot for a silver tarsk, a function of the slowness of the market, a slowness which I had anticipated and on which I had been pleased to capitalize. I happily slapped the pouch at my side which contained the receipts for the fair merchandise and the shipping vouchers. My favorite I thought would be the girl I had bought from the public tent. She could not help herself but turn hot and open when a man's hand so much as closed on her arm. What marvelous slaves women make, when men are strong.

I turned down the street of the cloth makers now. Most of the booths were closed.

I thought again of the herd of Tancred, which had not appeared in the north, and of the "mountain that did not move," the great iceberg which seemed, somehow, independent and stable, maintaining its position, fixed and immobile, in the midst of the restless, flowing waters of the polar sea. But I dismissed consideration of the latter, for that was obviously a matter of myth. That the herd of Tancred, however, had not appeared in the north seemed to be a matter of fact, a puzzling anomaly which, in Gorean history, had not, as far as I knew, hitherto occurred.

The herd has perhaps been wiped out by a disease in the northern forests.

I hoped the supplies I had had Samos send northward would save the red hunters from extinction.

I made my way down the street of the cloth makers. There were few people in the street now.

The ship of Tersites intrigued me. I wondered if its design was sound.

"Greetings to Tarl Cabot," had read the message on the

scytale, "I await you at the world's end. Zarendargar. War General of the People."

"It is Half-Ear," had said Samos, "high Kur, war general of the Kurii."

"Half-Ear," I thought to myself. "Half-Ear."

Eyes must be painted on the ship of Tersites. It must sail.

It was then that I heard the scream, a man's scream. I knew the sound for I was of the warriors. Steel, unexpectedly and deeply, had entered a human body. I ran toward the sound. I heard another cry. The assailant had struck again. I tore aside a stake on which canvas was sewn and forced my way between booths. I thrust aside boxes and another sheet of canvas and stumbled into the adjacent street. "Help!" I heard. I was then in the street of the dealers in artifacts and curios. "No!" I heard. "No!" Other men, too, were hurrying toward the sound. I saw the booth, closed, from which the sounds came. I tore aside the roped canvas which, fastened to the counter and to the upper framework of the booth, closed off the selling area. Inside, crouching over a fallen man, the merchant, was the attacker, robed in swirling black. In his hand there glinted a dagger. Light in the booth was furnished by a tiny lamp, dim, burning tharlarion oil, hung from one of the booth's ceiling poles. The merchant's assistant, the scribe, his face and arm bleeding, stood to one side. The attacker spun to face me. In his hand, his left, he clutched an object wrapped in fur; in his right he held the dagger, low, blade up. I stopped, crouched, cautious. He had turned the dagger in his hand as he had turned to face me. It is difficult to fend against the belly slash.

I must approach him with care.

"I did not know you were of the warriors, he who calls himself Bertram of Lydius," I smiled. "Or is it of the assassins?"

The struck merchant, bleeding, thrust himself back from the attacker.

The attacker's eyes moved. There were more men coming. Gorean men tend not to be patient with assailants. Seldom do they live long enough to be impaled upon the walls of a city.

The assailant's hand, that bearing the object of his quest, some curio wrapped in fur, flashed upward, and I turned my head aside as flaming oil from the lamp splashed upon me, the lamp itself struck loose from its tiny chains and flying past my head. I rolled to one side in the sudden darkness, and then scrambled to my feet. But he had not elected to attack. I heard him at the back of the booth. I heard the dag-

101

ger cutting at the canvas. He had elected flight, it seemed. I did not know this for certain, but it was a risk I must take. Darkness would be my cover. I dove at the sound, low, rolling, to be under the knife, feet first, presenting little target, kicking, feet scissoring. If I could get him off his feet I might then manage, even in the darkness, regaining my feet first, to break his diaphragm or crush his throat beneath my heel, or, with an instep kick to the back of his neck to snap loose the spinal column from the skull.

But he had not elected flight.

The cutting at the canvas, of course, had been a feint. He had shown an admirable coolness.

But I had the protection of the darkness. He, waiting to one side, leaped downward upon me, but I, twisting, squirming, proved an elusive target. The blade of the dagger cut through the side of the collar of my robes and my hand then was on his wrist.

We rolled in the darkness, fighting on the floor of the booth. Curios on shelves fell and scattered. I heard men outside. The canvas at the front of the booth was being torn away.

We struggled to our feet, swaying.

He was strong, but I knew myself his master.

I thought him now of the assassins for the trick with the canvas was but a variant of the loosened door trick, left ajar as in flight, a lure to the unwary to plunge in his pursuit into the waiting blade.

He cried out with pain and the knife had fallen. We stumbled, locked together, grappling, to the back of the tenting, and, twisted, tangled in the rent canvas, fell to the outside. A confederate was there waiting and I felt the loop of the garrote drop about my neck. I thrust the man I held from me and spun about, the cord cutting now at the back of my neck. I saw another man, too, in the darkness. The heels of both hands drove upward and the head of the first confederate snapped back. The garrote was loose about my neck. I turned. The first man had fled, and the other with him. A peasant came about the edge of the booth. Two more men looked through the rent canvas, who had climbed over the counter. I dropped the garrote to the ground. "Don't," I said to the peasant. "It is already done," he said, wiping the blade on his tunic. I think the man's neck had been broken by the blow of my hands under his chin, but he had still been alive. His head now lay half severed, blood on the peasant's sandals. Gorean men are not patient with such as he. "The

102

other?" asked the peasant. "There were two," I said. "Both are gone." I looked into the darkness between the tents.

"Call one of the physicians," I heard.

"One is coming," I heard.

These voices came from within the booth.

I bent down and brushed aside the canvas, re-entering the booth. Two men with torches were now there, as well as several others. A man held the merchant in his arms.

I pulled aside his robes. The wounds were grievous, but not mortal.

I looked to the scribe. "You did not well defend your master," I said.

I recalled he had been standing to one side when I had entered the booth.

"I tried," said the scribe. He indicated his bleeding face, the cut on his arm. "Then I could not move. I was frightened." Perhaps, indeed, he had been in shock. His eyes though had not suggested that. He was not now in shock. Perhaps he had been truly paralyzed with fear. "He had a knife," pointed out the scribe.

"And your master had none," said a man.

I returned my attention to the struck merchant. The placement of the wounds I found of interest.

"Will I die?" asked the merchant.

"He who struck you was clumsy," I said. "You will live." I then added, "If the bleeding is stopped."

I stood up.

"For the sake of Priest-Kings," said the man, "stop the bleeding."

I regarded the scribe. Others might attend to the work of stanching the flow of blood from the wounds of the merchant.

"Speak to me," I said.

"We entered the booth and surprised the fellow, surely some thief. He turned upon us and struck us both, my master most grievously."

"In what was he interested?" I asked. Surely there was little in a shop of curios to interest a thief. Would one risk one's throat and blood for a toy of wood or an ivory carving?

"In that, and that alone," said the merchant, pointing to the object which the thief had held, and which he had dropped in our struggle. It lay wrapped in fur on the ground within the booth. Men held cloth against the wounds of the merchant.

"It is worthless," said the scribe.

103

"Why would he not have bought it?" asked the merchant. "It is not expensive."

"Perhaps he did not wish to be identified as he who had made the purchase," I said, "for then he might be traced by virtue of your recollection to the transaction."

One of the men in the tent handed me the object, concealed in fur.

A physician entered the booth, with his kit slung over the shoulder of his green robes. He began to attend to the merchant.

"You will live," he assured the merchant.

I recalled the assailant. I recalled the turning of the blade in his hand. I remembered the coolness of his subterfuge at the back of the booth, waiting beside the rent canvas for me to thrust through it, thus locating myself and exposing myself for the thrust of the knife.

I held the object wrapped in fur in my hands. I did not look at it.

I knew what it would contain.

When the physician had finished the cleansing, chemical sterilization and dressing of the merchant's wounds, he left. With him the majority of the watchers withdrew as well. The scribe had paid the physician from a small iron box, taken from a locked trunk, a tarsk bit.

A man had lit the tiny lamp again and set it on a shelf. Then only I remained in the booth with the scribe and merchant. They looked at me.

I still held the object, wrapped in fur, in my hand.

"The trap has failed," I said.

"Trap?" stammered the scribe.

"You are not of the scribes," I said. "Look at your hands." We could hear the flame of the lamp, tiny, soft, in the silence of the tent.

His hands were larger than those of the scribe, and scarred and roughened. The fingers were short. There was no stain of ink about the tips of the index and second finger.

"Surely you jest," said the fellow in the robe of the scribe.

I indicated the merchant. "Consider his wounds," I said. "The man I fought was a master, a trained killer, either of the warriors or of the assassins. He struck him as he wished, not to kill but in the feigning of a mortal attack."

"You said he was clumsy," said the fellow in the scribe's blue.

"Forgive my colleague," said the merchant. "He is dull. He did not detect that you spoke in irony."

104

"You work for Kurii," I said.

"Only for one," said the merchant.

I slowly unwrapped the object in my hands, moving the fur softly aside.

It was a carving, rather roundish, some two pounds in weight, in bluish stone, done in the manner of the red hunters, a carving of the head of a beast. It was, of course, a carving of the head of a great Kur. Its realism was frightening, to the suggestion of the shaggy hair, the withdrawn lips, exposing fangs, the eyes. The left ear of the beast, as indicated with the patient fidelity of the red hunter, was half torn away.

"Greetings from Zarendargar," said the merchant.

"He awaits you," said the man in blue, "—at the world's end."

Of course, I thought. Kurii do not care for water. For them, not of Gorean background, the world's end could mean only one of the poles.

"He said the trap would fail," said the merchant. "He was right."

"So, too," I said, "did the earlier trap, that of the sleen."

"Zarendargar had naught to do with that," said the merchant.

"He disapproved of it," said the fellow in the robes of the scribe.

"He did not wish to be cheated of meeting you," said the merchant. "He was pleased that it failed."

"There are tensions in the Kurii high command," I said.

"Yes," said the merchant.

"But you," I said, "work only for Zarendargar?"

"Yes," said the merchant. "He will have it no other way. He must have his own men."

"The assailant and his confederates?" I asked.

"They are in a separate chain of command," said the merchant, "one emanating from the ships, one to which Zarendargar is subordinate."

"I see," I said.

I lifted the carving.

"You had this carving," I asked, "from a red hunter, a bare-chested fellow, with rope and bow about his shoulders?"

"Yes," said the merchant. "But he had it from another. He was told to bring it to us, that we would buy it."

"Of course," I said. "Thus, if the trap failed, I would supposedly detect nothing. You would then give me this carving, in gratitude for having driven away your assailant. I, seeing

105

it, would understand its significance, and hurry to the north, thinking to take Half-Ear unsuspecting."

"Yes," said the merchant.

"But he would be waiting for me," I said.

"Yes," said the merchant.

"There is one part of this plan, however," I said, "which you have not fathomed."

"What is that?" asked the merchant. Momentarily he gritted his teeth, in pain from his wounds.

"It was the intention of Half-Ear," I said, "that I understand full well, and with no possible mistake, that I would be expected."

The merchant looked puzzled.

"Else," I said, "he would have given orders for both of you to be slain."

They looked at one another, frightened. The fellow with whom I had grappled, who had called himself Bertram of Lydius, would have been fully capable of dispatching them both with ease.

"That would have put the badge of authenticity on the supposedly accidental discovery of the carving," I said.

They looked at one another.

"That you were not killed by one of the skill of the assailant," I said, "makes clear to a warrior's eye that you were not intended to die. And why not? Because you were confederates of Kurii. A twofold plan is thus manifested, a trap and a lure, but a lure which is obvious and explicit, not so much a lure as an invitation." I looked at them. "I accept the invitation," I said.

"Are you not going to kill us?" asked the merchant.

I went to the counter and thrust back the canvas. I slipped over the counter, feet first, and then turned to regard them.

I lifted the carving, which I had rewrapped in its fur. "I may have this?" I asked.

"It is for you," said the merchant.

"Are you not going to kill us?" asked the fellow in blue.

"No," I said.

They looked at me.

"You are only messengers," I said. "And you have done your work well." I threw them two golden tarn disks. I grinned at them. "Besides," I said, "violence is not permitted at the fair."

5 I TAKE MY DEPARTURE FROM THE HOUSE OF SAMOS

"The game," I said, "was an excellent one."

Samos rose to his feet, storming with rage. "While you sported at the fair," said he, "here in Port Kar catastrophe has struck!"

I had seen the flames in the arsenal as I had returned on tarn from the perimeters of the Sardar.

"He was mad," I said. "You know this to be true."

"Only he could have so approached the ship, only he could have done this!" cried Samos.

"Perhaps he was not satisfied with the design," I suggested. "Perhaps he feared to paint the eyes, perhaps he feared to commit his dream to the realities of Thassa."

Samos sat down, cross-legged, behind the low table in his hall. He wept. He struck the table with his fist.

"Are you sure it was he?" I asked.

"Yes," said Samos, bitterly. "It was indeed he."

"But why?" I asked.

"I do not know," said Samos. "I do not know."

"Where is he now?" I asked.

"He has disappeared," said Samos. "Doubtless he has thrown himself into the canals."

"It meant so much to him," I said. "I do not understand it. There is a mystery here."

"He took a fee from Kurii agents," said Samos.

"No," I said. "Gold could not buy dreams from Tersites."

"The ship," said Samos, "is destroyed."

"What remains?" I asked.

"Ashes," said he, "blackened timbers."

"And the plans?" I asked.

"Yes," said he, "the plans."

I nodded. "Then it might be rebuilt," I said.

"You must take the Dorna," said he, "or the Tesephone."

"It makes little sense to me," said I, "that Tersites would fire the ship."

"It is the end of our hopes," said Samos, "to meet Half-Ear at the world's end."

"I have spoken to you of that matter," I said.

"Yes," said Samos, bitterly, "I have seen your carving. Can you not recognize that as a ruse to mislead you northward, while Kurii pursue unimpeded their fierce schemes at the world's end?"

"Perhaps," I said. "But I sense that there is an honesty in this, as of the cruel sport of war. I think I sense the nature and being of this Zarendargar."

"Kurii," said Samos, "are without honor."

"There is a brotherhood of professional soldiers," I said, "which I suspect crosses the boundaries of species."

"We have only one choice," said Samos. "You must take another ship, the Dorna or the Tesephone, or you may take my flagship, the Thassa Ubara."

"But there is little hope," I smiled, "that such ships may reach the world's end."

"None have hitherto done so, or have done so and returned," said Samos. He looked at me. "I do not, of course, command that you undertake such a journey."

I nodded.

No sane leader could command this of a subordinate. A journey so far and terrible could be undertaken by none but volunteers.

"I am sorry about the ship," I said, "and I do not understand what has happened there, but I had previously determined, my dear Samos, that in any case I would venture not to the west but the north."

Samos looked at me, angrily.

"I hope, of course," said I, "to discover one day what occurred in the arsenal."

"I can command you," said Samos, "as one loyal to Priest-Kings, to remain in Port Kar."

"I am in my way a mercenary," I said. "I command myself. I choose my wars. I choose my loyalties."

"Would you betray Priest-Kings?" asked Samos.

"I will keep faith with them in my own way," I said.

"I order you to remain in Port Kar," said Samos, coldly.

I smiled at him. "That is an order you have no authority to issue," I told him. "I am a free soldier."

"You are a brigand and an adventurer!" he cried.

"I am curious to see the north," I said.

"The ship may have been destroyed by Tersites, in fee to Kurii," snapped Samos, "precisely to prevent you from reaching the world's end!"

"Perhaps," I admitted.

"That is where Zarendargar waits for you!" said Samos.

"We think of the world's end as lying betwixt Tyros and Cos, at the end of a hundred horizons," I said, "but who knows where a Kur would see it to be." I rose to my feet and strode to the map mosaic on the floor of the great hall. I pointed downwards. "There," I said, "may well be what a Kur regards as the world's end." I indicated the frozen north, the polar sea, the ice of the lonely pole. "Is that not a world's end?" I asked.

"Only red hunters can live in such a place," whispered Samos.

"And Kurii?" I asked.

"Perhaps," he said.

"And perhaps others?" I asked.

"Perhaps," he said.

"It is my belief," I said, "that Zarendargar waits in the north."

"No," said Samos. "The carving is a trick, to lure you away from the locus of their true efforts, those at the true world's end, there." He indicated the western edge of the map, the *terra incognita* beyond Cos and Tyros, and the scattered, farther islands.

"A judgment must be made here," I said. "And I have made it."

"I will make the judgment," said Samos. "I am commanding you to remain in Port Kar."

"But I am not under your command," I pointed out. "I am a free captain. Apprise yourself of the articles of the Council of Captains."

I turned and strode to the door.

"Stop him," said Samos.

The two guards, their spears crossed, barred my way. I turned to regard Samos.

"I am sorry, my friend," he said. "You are too valuable to risk in the north."

"Am I to understand," I asked, "that it is your intention to prevent me by force from leaving your house?"

"I will cheerfully accept your word," said he, "that you will remain in Port Kar."

"I do not, of course, accord you that word," I grinned.

"Then I must detain you by force," he said. "I am sorry. I

will see that your accommodations are in keeping with your station as a captain."

"I trust," I said, "you can make clear the benevolence of your intentions to my men."

"If the house is stormed," said Samos, "my defenses will be found to be in order. It would be my hope, however, that you would not see fit, under the circumstances, to encourage useless strife. We are both, surely, fond of our men."

"To be sure," I said, "I expect they could find better things to do than die on your walls."

"I ask only your word, Captain," said Samos.

"It seems I have little choice," I said.

"Forgive me, Captain," said Samos.

I turned and seized the crossed spears of the guards, twisting and pulling them toward me, flinging them, they surprised, not swiftly enough releasing the weapons, to the tiles.

"Stop!" cried Samos.

I slipped through the door and, with one of the spears, which I had retained, sliding the shaft through the great handles, closed the door. Instantly they were pounding on it. I seized the mallet of an alarm bar which hung in the hall, and began to pound it madly. It served to drown out the noise. Men's feet began to pound in the halls; I heard the clank of weapons. I hurried down the hall and struck another alarm bar.

A guardsman appeared. "There!" I cried. "In the great hall! Hurry!"

Four more guards appeared.

"Come!" cried the first guard.

They ran down the hall.

Other guardsmen appeared.

"To the hall!" I cried.

They fled past me.

In a moment I was at the double portal, the first barred, of the house of Samos.

"What is it, Captain?" asked one of the guards there.

"I think it is nothing," I said. "A new guardsman, affrighted at a shadow or noise sounded the alarm."

"Is it a false alarm?" said the man.

"I think so," I said.

"Perhaps a sleen is loose," said another guard.

"That would be serious," I admitted.

"Perhaps we should assist," said one of the guards.

"I think you should remain at your post," I said.

"He is right," said another.

110

"Is my boat ready?" I asked.

"Yes," said one of the guardsmen. He opened the interior gate, and then the heavy iron portal.

"Stop him!" we heard. "Stop him!" These shouts came from down the hall.

"It sounds as though there is an intruder," I said.

"He will not get past us," said one of the guardsmen.

"Good man," I commended him.

"I wish you well, Captain," said the man.

"I wish you well, too, Guardsman," said I. Then I stepped across the narrow court before the house of Samos and down into the waiting longboat.

"To the house, Captain?" asked Thurnock.

"Yes," I said.

6 TWO GIRLS ARE MADE SLAVES; I PROCEED NORTHWARD TO LYDIUS

I lay on my belly before the small pond, and, with the palm of my hand, lifted water to my mouth.

When I heard the sound of the tharlarion, some four or five of them, I rose to my feet.

"Have you see aught of a sport slave?" she asked.

"No," I said.

She was very lovely and attractive in her hunting costume, brief tunic and long hose, brown, a scarlet cape and cap, the cap with a feather. She carried a short, yellow bow, of Kala-na wood, which could clear the saddle of the tharlarion, its missile being easily released to either side. Her black boots, slick and shining, were spurred. A quiver of arrows, yellow, was at the left of her saddle.

"Thank you, Warrior," she said, and wheeled the light saddle tharlarion, its claws scattering pebbles by the side of the pond.

She was with four men, also on upright tharlarion. They followed her as she sped away.

She had had dark hair, dark eyes.

111

I did not envy the sport slave.

I stood in the midst of fields south of the Laurius river, some forty pasangs inland from the shore of Thassa, some one hundred and twenty pasangs south of the river port of Lydius, lying at the mouth of the Laurius river, on its farther side. My tarn was foraging. I had brought it inland where game was more plentiful.

I had had at that time no intention of stopping at Lydius. My business lay far to the north.

I did not know how long it would take my tarn to make a kill and return. Usually this can be done within the Ahn. There is little scarcity of game on Gor, save in relatively populated areas. Usually one spots game from the saddle and calls "Tabuk," which is the tarn's hunting signal. I had, however, spotted little suitable game, and so had released the tarn to do his own foraging. When the tarn takes game one may either retain the saddle or not. If there is no press of time I have usually surrendered it, if only to stretch my legs. Too, the feeding of a tarn is not pleasant to witness.

From a distance, approaching, I could see a small retinue, not more than some fourteen persons.

A free woman, robed in white, veiled, was being carried in a sedan chair by four draft slaves. Beside the chair, on either side, afoot, walked a girl. Each was veiled but bare-armed. From the fact that their arms had been bared to the gaze of men I knew they were slaves.

The journey from Port Kar north had been long.

I felt in a good humor.

Besides the women and the draft slaves, the latter chained by the wrists and neck to the sedan chair, there were seven warriors, six spearmen and their captain.

I walked about the edge of the pond, to meet them. They were approaching the pond, presumably to draw water.

I waited, standing, my helmet over my back, my shield behind my left shoulder, leaning on my spear.

The retinue stopped, seeing me. Then, at a gesture from the robed figure in white, it proceeded again. It stopped some fifteen feet from me.

"Tal," said I, lifting my right hand to them, palm facing the left.

They did not respond.

The captain stepped forth. They did not seem then to me to be pleasant fellows.

"Who are you?" asked the captain.

"One who has greeted you," I said.

112

"Tal," said he, lifting his hand.

"Tal," I rejoined.

"We have seen nothing of the sport slave," he said.

"I do not hunt him," I said.

"Where is your tharlarion?" asked one of the men.

"I have none," I said.

"Do not block our way," said the captain.

"I mean you no harm," I said. "I greet you in peace and friendship."

"Who are you?" asked the captain.

"I am one who is of the warriors," I said. "And I am a traveler, a visitor now in this country."

"What is your business?" he asked.

"It lies in the north," I said.

"He is a brigand from the forests north of Laura," said the lady.

"No, Lady," said I, deferentially. I inclined my head to her, for she was free, and obviously of high station.

"You have been greeted," she said, icily. "Now stand aside."

I thought her tone surly.

I did not move.

"This is the retinue of Constance, Lady in Kassau, enroute to Lydius, returning from the sights of Ar."

"She must be rich," I said. Surely this was true, for her to travel as she did, not in public caravan.

"Stand aside," said the captain.

"A moment, Captain," said I. I looked to the free woman. "I am a man, dear lady," said I, "and am of the warriors. I have journeyed far."

"I do not understand," she said.

"I assume," said I, "that you will linger briefly here, to fill the flasks of water, if not camp for the night."

"What does he want?" she asked.

"He is of the warriors, milady," said the captain.

"Forgive me, Lady," said I, "but my need is much upon me."

The two slave girls, bare-armed and veiled, quickly glanced to one another.

"I do not understand," said the graceful figure in the sedan chair. She was free.

I grinned at her. "I have food," I said. "I have water. But I have not had for four days a woman."

She stiffened. The night before I had left Port Kar I had had Vella sent naked to my room. I had used her ruthlessly

113

several times, before sleeping and, early in the morning, when I had awakened. "Take me with you," she had begged. "So that you might with another Bertram of Lydius," I asked, "conspire against me?" "He tricked me, Master," she wept. "He tricked me." "I should have you lashed to within an inch of your life, Slave Girl," I had told her. "I am innocent, Master," she had wept. I had then turned my back on her and left her, naked, chained in the furs at the foot of my couch.

But that had been four days ago.

I gestured to the two girls with the free woman. One of them slightly lowered her veil.

"I will pay well for the use of one of these slaves," I said to the free woman.

"They are my personal slaves," she said.

"I will give a silver tarsk for the brief use of one, either that you might indicate," I said.

The warriors looked at one another. The offer was quite generous. It was unlikely that either of the girls would bring so much on the block.

"No," said the free woman, icily.

"Permit me then to buy one," I said, "for a golden tarn."

The men looked at one another, the draft slaves, too. Such a coin would fetch from the block a beauty fit for the gardens of a Ubar.

"Stand aside," said the free woman.

I inclined my head. "Very well, Lady," said I. I moved to one side.

"I deem myself to have been insulted," she said.

"Forgive me, Lady," said I, "but such was not my intent. If I have done or said aught to convey that impression, however minutely, I extend to you now the deepest and most profound of apologies and regrets."

I stepped back further, to permit the retinue to pass.

"I should have you beaten," she said.

"I have greeted you in peace and friendship," I said. I spoke quietly.

"Beat him," she said.

I caught the arm of the captain. His face turned white. "Have you raised your arm against me?" I asked.

I released his arm, and he staggered back. Then he slung his shield on his arm, and unsheathed the blade slung at his left hip.

"What is going on!" demanded the woman.

"Be silent, foolish woman," said the captain.

114

She cried out with rage. But what did she know of the codes?

I met his attack, turning it, and he fell, shield loose, at my feet. I had not chosen to kill him.

"Aiii!" cried one of the draft slaves.

"Kill him! Kill him!" cried the free woman. The slave girls screamed.

Men shouted with rage.

"Who is next?" I asked.

They looked at one another.

"Help me," said the captain. Two of the men went to him and lifted him, bleeding, to his feet. He looked at me, held between his men.

I stood ready.

He looked at me, and grinned. "You did not kill me," he said.

I shrugged.

"I am grateful," he said.

I inclined my head.

"Too," said he, "I know the skills of my men. They are not poor warriors, you understand."

"I am sure they are not," I said.

"I do not choose to spend them," he said. He looked at me. "You are a tarnsman," he said.

"Yes," I said.

"I thought it would be so," he said. He looked at me. "I give you greetings of the caste of warriors," he said.

"Tal," said I.

"Tal," said he.

"Kill him!" cried the free woman. "Kill him!"

"You have wronged this man," said the captain. "And he has labored within the permissions of his codes."

"I order you to kill him!" cried the free woman, pointing to me.

"Will you permit us to pass, Warrior?" asked the captain.

"I am afraid, under the circumstances," I said, "that is no longer possible."

He nodded. "Of course not," he said.

"Kill him!" cried the free woman.

"We are six now who can fight," said the captain. "It is true that we might kill him. I do not know. But never have I crossed swords with one such as he. There is a swiftness, a sorcery, a savageness in his steel which in a hundred fights to the death I have never encountered. And yet I now stand

115

alive beside your chair to explain this to you, who are incapable of understanding it."

"He is outnumbered," she pointed out.

"How many will he kill?" asked the captain.

"None, of course!" she cried.

"I have crossed steel with him, Lady," said the captain. "Do not explain to me the nature of swordplay and odds." He looked to his men. "Do you wish to fall upon him, Lads?" he asked, smiling wryly.

"Command us, and we shall attack," said one of the men.

I thought their discipline good.

The captain shook his head ruefully. "I have crossed steel with him, Lads," said he. "We shall withdraw."

"No!" screamed the free woman.

The captain turned, supported by two men.

"Cowards!" she cried.

The captain turned to face her. "I am not a coward, Lady," said he. "But neither am I a fool."

"Cowards!" she cried.

"Before I send men against one such as he," said the officer, "it will be to defend a Home Stone."

"Coward! Cowards!" she screamed.

"I have crossed steel with him," said the captain. He then, held between his men, withdrew. More than one of them cast glances at me over their shoulder. But none, I think, wished to return to do contest.

I resheathed the blade.

"Turn about," said the free woman to the draft slaves. She would follow the retreating warriors.

"Do not turn about," I said to them.

They obeyed me. The sedan chair stayed as it was. "Why did you not kill them?" asked one of the draft slaves.

"You were of the warriors?" I asked.

"Yes," said he.

"It seems not fitting you should be chained to a lady's chair," I said.

He grinned, and shrugged.

"Will you not permit me to withdraw, Warrior?" asked the free woman.

"These seem fine fellows," I said. "Doubtless you have the key to these chains in your possessions."

"Yes," she said.

"Give it to her," said I, indicating one of the slave girls. This was done, and, at my gesture, the girl freed the draft slaves.

They rubbed their wrists, and moved their heads, no longer in the iron circle of the collars.

The sedan chair rested still on their shoulders. They looked at me, well pleased.

"I will let you have the use of one of the girls for a silver tarsk," said the free woman.

I looked up at her. "It is a bit late for that, my dear Lady Constance," I said.

"I will sell one of them to you for a golden tarn," she said.

"That seems a high price to ask for a slave girl," I said.

She lifted up her veiled head. "You may have the use of one or both for free," she said.

"Lady Constance is generous," I said.

She did not lower her head to so much as glance upon me. "I give them to you," she said.

"Lower the chair," I said to the draft slaves. The chair was lowered.

"Free them," I said, indicating the draft slaves.

They stood about her, looking at her. She sat nervously in the chair. "You are free," she said. "You are free."

They grinned, and did not move.

"You may go," she said. "You are free."

I nodded to them and, together, grinning and striking one another in their pleasure, they withdrew. One remained for a moment. "My thanks, Warrior," he said.

"It is nothing," said I, "—Warrior."

He grinned, and turned, hurrying after the others.

The two slave girls looked at one another.

"Remove your veils," said the free woman.

The two girls pulled away their veils. Both were pretty.

I smiled at them. They blushed, basking in my smile.

"They are yours, of course, if you wish," said the free woman, gesturing with her head to the two girls.

One of the girls looked at me, and I nodded.

"No!" cried the free woman. One of the girls had lifted aside the first of the free woman's veils, and the other had brushed back the first of her hoods.

"No!" cried the free woman. Then, despite her protest, the first girl drew aside the last veil which concealed her features, and the second girl brushed back the final hood, revealing her hair, which was blond. The free woman's blue eyes looked at me, frightened. She had been face-stripped. I saw that she was beautiful.

"Stand," I said to her.

She stood.

117

"I will pay you well to conduct me to safety," she said. Her lip trembled.

"If the beauty of your body matches that of your face," I said, "it is the collar for you."

"It will be the collar for her, Master!" cried one of the slave girls, delightedly.

"Fina!" cried the free woman.

"Forgive me, Mistress!" said the girl.

The two girls lifted aside the free woman's robes, until she stood displayed before me.

I walked about her. "Yes," I said, "it is the collar for you, Lady Constance."

"Daphne! Fina!" cried the free woman. "Protect me!"

"Do you not know enough to kneel before your master, foolish slave?" chided Fina.

Numbly the Lady Constance knelt.

"In my belongings, over there," I said to one of the girls, she called Daphne, "there is a collar. Bring it."

"Yes, Master," she cried happily, running to where I had indicated, a place beside a small tree some fifty yards from the pond. I had made a temporary camp there, while awaiting the return of the tarn. I scanned the skies. It was not in sight.

"On your hands and knees, head down," I said to the Lady Constance.

She assumed this posture, her blond hair hanging forward, downward, over her head.

I roughly collared her and she sank moaning to her stomach in the grass.

I then tied the hands of the two slave girls behind their backs and knelt them by the sedan chair. I then took what valuables and moneys there were in the chair, kept in the cabinets at its sides, and slung them, some scarfed and others placed in pouches, about the necks of the two slave girls. I was surprised. The owner of the chair had been rich indeed. There was a fortune there, and the notes for other fortunes. I would keep none of this. I had what I wanted. She lay collared in the grass.

"Stand," I said to the two slave girls.

They stood, obediently. I pointed off, over the grass. The former slaves could be seen in the distance. "Do you see the men?" I asked. "Yes, Master," they said. "Here in the wilderness, bound, alone, you will die," I pointed out. "Yes, Master," they said, frightened. "Follow the men," I said to them. "Beg them to keep you, and the riches you bear." "We shall,

118

Master," they said. "I think they will be agreeable," I conjectured. "Yes, Master," they said, looking down. "And that you may appear more worth keeping about, and to facilitate your pursuit of the men," I said, "I will take the liberty of shortening your tunics." "Yes, Master," they said, pleased. But when I had finished my work they looked at me, frightened. They shrank back. "Hurry now," said I, "after the men, before I rape you myself." They laughed and turned and ran after the men. "Overtake them before dark," I said, "for sleen may soon be prowling." "Yes, Master," they cried. I laughed, watching them stumble, weighted with riches, after the former draft slaves.

I returned to where the girl lay in the grass. She was on her stomach. Her hands had dug into the dirt. She sensed I stood near her. I stood a bit behind her and to her left.

"Am I a slave?" she whispered.

"Yes," I said.

"You can do anything with me you want?" she asked.

"Yes," I said.

Her head was to one side. There were tears on her cheek.

"What are you going to do with me, Master?" she asked.

"Whatever pleases me," I said.

"I ordered my men to kill you," she said. "Are you going to slay me for that?"

"Of course not," I said. "That was the act of the Lady Constance. She no longer exists."

"A slave girl is now in her place," whispered the girl.

"Yes," I said.

"It seems I have escaped easily," she said.

"Not really," I said. "It is only that now you are subject to new risks and penalties, those of a slave girl."

She clutched the grass. She knew well of what I spoke.

"You may now be slain for as little as an irritable word, or for being in the least displeasing. Indeed, you may be slain upon the mere whim of a master, should it please him."

She sobbed.

"Do you understand?" I asked.

"Yes, Master," she said. Then she looked up at me. "Are you a kind master?" she asked.

"No," I said.

"I do not know how to be a slave," she said.

"Men will teach you," I said.

"I will try to learn swiftly," she said.

"That is wise," I said.

"My life will depend on it?" she asked.

"Of course," I said. I grinned. Gorean men are not patient with their girls.

"This morning," she said, "I was free."

"You are now a slave," I said.

"Yes, Master," she said.

I looked up at the late afternoon skies. The tarn had not yet returned. Yet I was not displeased.

I looked down at the girl. "Go to my things," I said. "Spread furs upon the grass."

"I am a virgin," she said.

"You are white-silk," I said.

"Please do not use that vulgar expression of me," she begged.

"Do not fear," I said. "It will soon be inappropriate."

"Show me mercy," she begged.

"Spread the furs," I said.

"Please," she begged.

"I have no slave whip at hand," I said, "but I trust my belt will serve."

She leaped to her feet. "I will spread the furs, Master," she said.

"Then lie on them on your belly," I said.

"Yes, Master," she said.

She spread the furs on the grass by the tree, and then lay on them, on her belly.

"Throw your hair forward and over your head," I said.

She did so. The collar was now clearly visible on her neck. I stood behind her, and dropped my accouterments to the side.

"Why did you make me a slave?" she whispered.

"It pleased me," I said.

I crouched beside her and took her by the right arm and hair, and turned her to her back on the furs. She was delicately beautiful. She would ravish well.

"In Torvaldsland," I said, "it is said the woman of Kassau make superb slaves." I looked at her. "Is it true?" I asked.

"I do not know, Master," she said frightened.

"How marvelously beautiful you are," I said.

"Please be kind to me, Master," she begged.

"I have not had a woman in four days," I told her. Then she cried out.

The three moons were high.

The night was chilly. I felt her kissing softly at my thigh.

120

"Is it true," she asked, "what they say in Torvaldsland, that the women of Kassau make superb slaves?"

"Yes," I said.

"I never knew that I could feel this way," she said. "It is so different, so total, so helpless."

I touched her head.

"It is only the feelings of a slave girl," I said.

"Yes, Master," she said.

I lay on my back, looking upward.

"Please, Master," she whispered, "subject me again to slave rape."

"Earn your rape," I told her.

"Yes, Master," she said, kissing me.

"Stop," I said.

"Master?" she asked.

"Be quiet," I said. I was listening. I rolled from her side and crouched in the furs. I was now certain that I heard it. I slipped my tunic over my head and looped the scabbard at my left shoulder. She crouched in the furs naked, beside me.

I drew the blade.

I could see him coming now, running over the fields, stumbling.

He was a large man, exhausted. At his hips he wore a rag. An iron collar, with broken chain, was at his neck.

He came near us and then stopped, suddenly. He stood unsteadily. "Are you with them?" he asked.

"With whom?" I asked.

"The hunters," he said.

"No," I said.

"Who are you?" he asked.

"A traveler, and a slave girl," I said. She shrank back in the furs, pulling them about her throat.

"You are of the warriors?" he said.

"Yes," I said.

"You will not kill me, nor hold me for them?" he asked.

"No," I said.

"Have you seen them?" he asked.

"A girl, and four guardsmen?" I asked.

"Yes," he said.

"Earlier today," I said. "You are then the sport slave?" I said.

"Yes," said he, "purchased from the pens at Lydius, for a girl's hunting."

I recalled the dark-eyed, dark-haired girl, vital and trim in her carefully tailored hunting costume, with the tunic and

121

hose, the boots, cape and feathered cap. It was an attractive oufit.

"You have done well to elude them this long," I said. "Would you care for food?"

"Please," said he.

I threw him meat and he sat down, cross-legged. Seldom had I seen a man so tear at food.

"Would you care for paga?" I asked.

"No," he said.

"I see that it is your intention to survive," I said.

"That is my intention," he said.

"Your chances," I said, "are slim."

"I now have food," he said.

"You are a courageous fellow," I said.

"Did they have sleen?" he asked.

"No," I said. "They were, it seems, making it truly a sport."

"Those well-armed and mounted can afford nobility," he said.

"You sound bitter," I said.

"If they do not find me tonight," he said, "they will return with sleen in the morning."

"That," I said, "would be the end." The sleen can follow a track better than a larl or a Kur. It is tireless and tenacious, and merciless.

"I have one chance," he said.

"What is that?" I asked.

"They had formed a hunting line," said he, "the girl in the center. It was in her path that I left a bit of rag, and did not deign thenceforward to conceal my trail. She should have come upon the bait by now."

"She will summon her guardsmen," I said, "and you will be finished."

"I assess her vanity differently," he said. "It is her sport, not theirs. She will pull away from her guardsmen to be first to the quarry."

"They will pursue," I said.

"Of course," he said.

"You will have little time," I said.

"True," he said.

"Do you think that you, afoot, will be able to elude a mounted archer, be she even female?" I asked.

"I think so," he said.

"There is little cover," I said. I looked at the fields.

"There is enough," he said. Then he rose to his feet and

122

wiped his hands on his thighs. Then he walked over to the pond several yards away. He lay down on his belly and drank from the water.

"Yes," I said. "There is cover. He is a clever fellow."

The man left tracks by the side of the pond, and then waded into the chill water. He broke off a reed and then waded deeper into the water.

I felt the girl beside me touch me, timidly. "May I labor now to earn my rape, Master?" she asked.

"Yes," I said.

I smiled to myself. The slave fires, which lurk in any woman, had been particularly easy to arouse in this girl. I recalled that the men of Torvaldsland regarded the women of Kassau as superb slaves. I saw now the justice of this assessment. Gorean girls, however, who are aware of the cultural implications of their collar, and its meaning, usually spend little time, once it is helplessly locked on their throats, in fighting their womanhood. They must bend, or die. In bending, in submission, in total, will-less submission to a master, they find themselves free for the first time from the chains of egoism, liberated from the grasping pursuits of the self, readied for the surrenders of love.

"Disgusting!" said the free woman, on the tharlarion, in the hunting costume.

I rolled over, looking up. The blond girl by my side, the slave, cried out with misery, and dared not meet the eyes of her free sister.

"Greetings," I said.

"Do not permit me to interfere with your pleasures," she said cooly.

The slave girl whimpered and put down her head. How shamed she was before the freedom and grandeur of the free woman.

"Have you found your sport slave yet?" I inquired.

"No," she said. "But he is quite near."

"I have not been paying much attention," I said.

"You have been otherwise engaged," she said loftily. I wondered at the hatred which free women seem to bear to their imbonded sisters. This hatred, incidentally, is almost never directed at the master, but almost always at the slave. Do they envy the slaves their collar?

"That is true," I admitted.

"It is fortunate I am here," said the free woman. "You might need my protection."

"You think there is a dangerous fellow lurking about?" I asked.

"I am sure of it," she said.

"We shall be on our guard," I said.

"I will take him soon," she said. "He is not far." She wheeled the tharlarion away. "Return to the pleasures of your slut," she said.

"But we must be on our guard," I called.

"There is little need," she said. "I will take the fellow within minutes."

I turned to the girl beside me, who was crying.

"Are you shamed?" I asked her.

"Yes," she said.

"Good," I said.

She looked at me.

"You are a slave," I said.

"Yes, Master," she said, her head down.

"Watch," I said. She lifted her head.

The free woman was at the edge of the pond. She did not dismount. Her bow was ready. In an instant it might clear the saddle to either side. From the saddle she studied the tracks in the moonlight. She moved the tharlarion into the water. Doubtless she thought the pond had been waded, to obscure tracks, which would emerge on the other side. Had she been a more experienced hunter she would have circled the pond to determine this for certain.

The blond girl beside me kissed me. "What does she know of being a woman?" she asked.

"Very little," I said. "But perhaps by tomorrow at noon she will know more."

"I do not understand, Master," said the girl.

"Watch," I said.

The girl, astride the tharlarion, moved deeper into the pond.

"She is an arrogant girl, is she not, Master?" asked the slave.

"Yes," I said.

Suddenly emerging from the water at the very side of the tharlarion there was the large, fierce figure of a man. His hand closed on the girl's left arm and dragged her swiftly, forcibly from the saddle, she crying out, startled, dashing her shoulder and headfirst into the water at his side. He thrust her under the surface following her under.

"She knew too little of men even to fear them," I said.

In a moment the figure of the man reared up, shaking his

124

head to clear his eyes of water. The girl's knife was in his right hand; his left hand held her head, grasped by the hair, beneath the surface. He looked about. He jerked her head up from the water and she gasped and sputtered. When she could scream he thrust her head again beneath the surface. The tharlarion moved about, water at the stirrup, shifting, tossing its head about. Then its reins hung in the water. It was a small, hunting tharlarion, controlled by bit and bridle. The large upright tharlarion, or war tharlarion, are guided by voice commands and the blows of spears. The man put the knife in his teeth and, fiercely, smote the tharlarion. It grunted and, splashing, fled from the water, running in its birdlike gait across the fields. The man again pulled up the girl from the water. She spit water into the pond, and vomited, and coughed. The man then tore the belt from her and fastened her hands behind her back. He thrust the knife he had held in his teeth in his belt. He broke off a tube of reed. The girl looked at him, frightened. In the distance I could see the four guardsmen, moving swiftly, trying to catch up with the girl who had broken away from them in the rash vanity of her hunt, desiring to be first upon the prize. She had apparently broken the hunting line without informing them. Perhaps, too, her tharlarion was swifter than theirs. It bore less weight. I saw the man take the tube of reed he had broken off and thrust it in her mouth; then the knife he carried, hers, lay across her throat; I saw her eyes, wild, in the moonlight, and then he, another bit of reed in his mouth, pulled her quietly below the surface.

In a few moments the four guardsmen, distraught, reined up beside my furs.

I looked up from the collared slave in my arms.

"Tal," said their leader.

"Tal," I said.

"Have you seen aught of the Lady Tina of Lydius?" inquired one of the men.

"The huntress?" I asked.

"Yes," he said.

"She was here, inquiring about a sport slave," I said.

"Where did she go?" asked one of the men.

"Have you not taken the sport slave yet?" I asked. "It is late."

"Have you see the Lady Tina?" asked the leader of the men.

"Yes," I said, "earlier."

"Where did she go?" asked the leader.

"Are there tracks?" I asked.

"Here," said one of the men, "here, see here. There are tracks."

They followed the tracks to the side of the pond. Had they crossed the pond they might, in the breadth of their passage, have struck the submerged couple. These men, however, apparently more skilled than the girl, first circled the pond to discover emergent tracks. They found these, of course, almost immediately, those of the running tharlarion. In their haste, and in their desire to overtake their lovely charge, they sped into the night. It was not even clear to me that they, in their concern with the tracks of the tharlarion, observed the tracks of the man leading to the pond. Too, as I determined later, his tracks had been, for the most part, obscured by the tracks of the beast of his lovely huntress. Some of the more obvious ones, too, I had erased with a branch.

I assumed the couple might be chilled upon emerging from the water and so I took the liberty of building a fire. The wood was gathered by my slave, whom I named Constance.

In time I saw the man's head lift slowly, almost imperceptibly, from the pond. He reconnoitered, and then, dragging the girl with him, her wrists bound behind her back, approached the fire.

"You had better get out of those wet clothes," I told the girl.

She looked at me with horror.

"Don't," she begged her captor.

She squirmed, held, as he cut the tunic and cape from her, and then she was thrown on her belly on the grass and the wet hose and boots were drawn from her. He then knelt across her body and freed her hands. With the knife he slit the belt into narrow strips, improvising binding fiber. He then retied her hands behind her back and, crouching beside her, crossed and bound her ankles. She struggled to her knees. She faced us.

"I am the Lady Tina of Lydius," she said. "Free me!"

We looked at her.

"I am the Lady Tina of Lydius," she said. "I demand to be immediately freed."

I thought she would look well dancing naked in a paga tavern before men.

"Free me!" she cried.

I had once owned a slave named Tina, who also had been from Lydius. It is not that uncommon a name. The Tina whom I had known was now free, an esteemed member of the caste of thieves in Port Kar, one of the most skillful in the city. She was doing well for herself.

I looked at this Tina. She was obviously too beautiful to free. She would be kept as a slave for men.

"You have won," she said to the slave. "I acknowledge that in the generosity of my freedom. Release me now and I shall petition that you not be slain."

"In the morning," he said, "they will bring sleen."

"Yes," she said.

"Will you discuss the matter with them?" he asked.

"Perhaps they will be leashed," she said.

The man laughed. "Do you think me a fool?" he asked. "They will be run free from the kennels. Do you think they want me alive?"

"I own you," she said to the man. "Free me!" I recalled that he had been purchased from the pens of Lydius for her sport. Apparently she had stood the purchase price. Her arrogance, and airs, suggested that she might well have done so.

"You seem rich and educated," I said.

"I am both," she said. "I am of the high merchants."

"I, too, was of the merchants," said Constance.

"Be silent, Slave Girl," snapped the free woman.

"Yes, Mistress," stammered Constance. She placed a branch upon the fire. She withdrew. She was new to her collar.

The free woman glared at the man who had captured her. "Free me, now!" she said.

He looked at her, fingering the knife he had taken from her.

The free woman squirmed in her bonds, frightened. She looked at me. "You are free," she said, "protect me!"

"What is your Home Stone?" I asked.

"That of Lydius," she said.

"I do not share it," I said.

The man crouched near her. His hand was behind her neck, holding her. The point of the dagger was in her belly.

"I free you! I free you!" she said.

"Have some meat," I said to him. I had been roasting some bosk over the small fire.

He, now a free man, came and sat near me, across the fire from me. The free woman shrank back, in the shadows. Constance knelt behind me and to my left, making herself unobtrusive. Occasionally she fed the fire.

The free man and I fed. "What is your name?" I asked. I

threw a bit of meat to Constance, which she snatched up and ate.

"Ram," said he, "once of Teletus, but friendless now in that island, one banished."

"Your crime?" I asked.

"In a tavern," he said, "I slew two men in a brawl."

"They are strict in Teletus," I said.

"One of them stood high in the administration of the island," he said.

"I see," I said.

"I have been in many cities," he said.

"How do you work your living?" I asked. "Are you a bandit?"

"No," said he. "I am a trader. I trade north of Ax Glacier for the furs of sleen, the pelts of leem and larts."

"A lonely work," I said.

"I have no Home Stone," he shrugged.

I pitied him.

"How is it," I asked, "that you fell slave?"

"The hide bandits," he said.

"I do not understand," I said.

"They have closed the country north of Ax Glacier," he said.

"How can this be?" I asked.

"Tarnsmen, on patrol," said he. "I was seized and, though free, sold south as a slave."

"Why should these men wish to close off the north?" I asked.

"I do not know," he said.

"Tarns cannot live at that latitude," I said.

"In the summer they can," said he. "Indeed, thousands of birds migrate each spring to the nesting cliffs of the polar basin."

"Not tarns," I said.

"No," said he. "Not tarns." Tarns were not migratory birds.

"Surely men can slip through these patrols," I said.

"Doubtless some do," he said.

"You were not so fortunate," I said.

"I did not even know they came as enemies," he laughed. "I welcomed them. Then I was shackled." He chewed on a piece of meat, then swallowed it. "I was sold at Lydius," he said. He looked up, again chewing, at the free woman. "I was bought there by this high lady," he said. He swallowed down the meat.

"What are you going to do with me?" she asked.

"I can think of many things," he said, regarding her.

"It would be simple to untie her ankles," I said.

"Do not touch me!" she said. "I am free."

"Perhaps you are a slave," he said.

"No," she said. "No! I am free!"

"We shall see," he said.

"I do not understand," she said.

He turned away from her, wiping his hands on his thighs. He went over to the edge of the pond, and, kneeling down beside the water, drank. When he got up he looked at the tracks there. When he returned, he smiled. "My thanks," said he.

I nodded.

I scanned the skies for the tarn. Game must indeed be scarce, I thought.

Constance put more wood on the fire. She glanced at the Lady Tina.

"Do not look at me, Slave!" hissed the Lady Tina.

"Forgive me, Mistress," said Constance. She looked away, frightened. She did not wish to be beaten.

"Sir," said the free woman, addressing her captor, Ram, once of Teletus.

"Yes," he said.

"My modesty is offended," she said. "I find it disagreeable to be unclothed before a slut of a slave who is not even my personal maid."

"In the morning," said he, "you will be partially clothed."

She looked at him, puzzled.

"May I command your girl," he asked.

"Yes," I said.

"Constance," said he.

"Yes, Master," she said.

"Look well and carefully upon our prisoner," he said.

"Yes, Master," she said.

The free woman turned her head away, in fury.

"Do you think," he asked, "that she might make a pretty slave."

"I am not a man, Master," said Constance, "but I should think she might make even a beautiful slave."

"Please!" protested the free woman.

"Look upon her when and as you wish," said Ram.

"Yes, Master," smiled Constance. I saw her make a tiny face at the Lady Tina.

129

"Oh!" cried the Lady Tina, in fury, squirming in the leather.

"What do you think?" asked Ram of me.

"She squirms well," I said. "I think she is excellent meat for marking."

"I hate you all!" said the Lady Tina. "And I will never be a slave! You cannot make me a slave! Never, never will I be a slave. No man can make me a slave!"

"I shall not even try," said Ram.

She looked at him, startled.

"I shall not make you my slave," he said. "unless you beg to be my slave."

She threw back her head and laughed. "I would die first," she said.

"It is late now," I said. "I think we should sleep."

"What is your name?" he asked.

"Tarl," said I. "Let that suffice."

"Accepted," he said, smiling. He would not pry further into my affairs. Doubtless he assumed I was bandit, fugitive or assassin.

I took Constance by the arm, and threw her to his feet. It was a simple act of Gorean courtesy.

Constance looked at me, wildly.

"Please him," I said.

"Yes, Master," she whispered.

"Yes, slut," called the free woman. "Please him! Please him well, you stinking little slave!"

"My thanks, my friend," said the fellow once from Teletus. He took Constance by the arm to one side and threw her on the grass beneath him.

In a few Ehn she crept to my side in the furs, shuddering. He was asleep.

I looked over at the free woman. She was struggling in the narrow leather which confined her. But she would be unable to free herself. She had watched in fury, and, I think, ill-concealed envy at the rapine which had been worked upon Constance.

I, in the light of the subsiding fire, watched the Lady Tina fight weeping with her bonds.

He had said that in the morning he would partially clothe her. I had not understood this.

I observed her struggling. I thought she would look well in a slave collar. Then I went to sleep.

"Hear it?" I asked.

It was early morning. Ram sat upright in the grass. I stood near the tarn, which had returned in the night, its beak smeared with blood and the hairs from the small yellow ta-buk, of the sort which frequent Ka-la-na thickets. I cleaned its beak and talons with dried grass. I had already saddled the beast.

Constance lay to one side, curled in the furs. The free woman, the Lady Tina of Lydius, too, slept, lying on her side, exhausted from her struggles of the night. The sky was overcast, and gray.

"Yes," he said. "Sleen."

We could hear their squealing in the distance. There must have been four or five of the beasts.

"Master?" asked Constance, rubbing her eyes.

"It is sleen, in the distance," I said. "Get out of the furs, lazy girl."

She was frightened.

"We have time," I said.

"What weight can the tarn carry?" asked Ram.

"It is strong," I said. "It can carry, if need be, a rider and freighted tarn basket."

"Might I then request passage?" he smiled.

"It is yours," I said.

I rolled the furs in which Constance had lain, and put them across the back of the saddle, fastening the two straps which held them.

We could hear the sleen cries quite clearly now. I do not think they were more than a pasang away.

"This ring," I said to Ram, pointing to a ring at the left of the saddle, "will be yours."

"Excellent," he said.

"Come here, Constance," I said.

"Yes, Master," she said, running to me.

"Awaken, Lady Tina," I heard Ram say. He was bending near her.

"Cross your wrists before your body," I said to Constance. She did so and I lashed them together. I then carried her to the right side of the saddle and placed her left foot in a ring there, which I had wrapped with fur. Her tied wrists I looped over the pommel.

I, standing in the stirrup, looked over the fields. There were five sleen. They were about a half of a pasang away, excited, squealing, their snouts hurrying at the turf.

"I have an extra tunic here," I said to Ram, throwing it to him.

"What are you doing?" demanded the Lady Tina.

He had taken the rags he had worn about his hips and was, with what had been her dagger, punching holes in them. Through these holes he threaded a strip of her belt. He knotted the rags about her hips. Because of the lovely flare of her hips, the smallness of her waist, the sweet, exciting swelling of her breasts, she would be unable, her hands tied behind her, to pull or scrape the garment from her.

"Is your modesty less offended now?" he asked. He slipped on the tunic which I had thrown him.

"What is that sound I hear?" she asked.

"Sleen," he said.

"I do not understand," she said, tremulously.

He cut the leather strips which had bound her ankles. "You will now be able to run," he said.

"I do not understand," she said.

"You soon will," he said.

I climbed to the saddle. Ram placed his left foot in the ring which I had designated and looped his left arm about the pommel of the saddle.

She struggled to her feet. "Where are you going?" she cried.

"To Lydius, Lady Tina," I informed her. I had not originally intended to go to Lydius, but I had acquired a girl in the fields. She was not yet branded. I would have her marked in Lydius.

The sleen were now within a few hundred yards of the tarn. I took the tarn straps in my left hand, the one-strap in my right.

Their squealing was loud. I could see them moving swiftly toward us.

Suddenly Lady Tina went white. "Oh, no! No!" she cried. She tried with her bound wrists to tear away the rags which she wore but they, because of the knotted belt strip, were perfectly fastened upon her.

"No!" she screamed.

The rags she wore, of course, were rich and heavy with the scent of him who had been her quarry. Such rags would have been used to put the sleen on his track.

"No!" she screamed. "No! They will tear me to pieces!"

The sleen were now no more than two hundred yards away. The squealing was wild now, as they caught sight of the bound girl in the field.

"They will tear me to pieces!" she wept.

"Run, Lady Tina," suggested Ram.

132

"They will tear me to pieces!" she wept, screaming.

"It is the same chance," said he, "which I in your place would have had."

The five sleen stopped now, tails thrashing, crouched down, shoulders high, heads low, eyes blazing. They were some fifty yards from the girl. Their nostrils were flared, their ears laid back against the sides of their broad, triangular heads. I saw the tongue of one darting in and out.

They crept forward, there must be no mistake of losing the prey.

The girl turned and fled, bound, the rag on her hips to the legs of the tarn. She knelt in the grass. She looked up, her eyes wild.

"Take me with you!" she wept.

"There is no room for free women here," said Ram.

"But I am a slave!" she cried.

"Are you a natural slave?" asked Ram.

"Yes, yes," she wept. "I have known for years in my heart that I was truly a slave. I lack only the brand and collar!"

"Interesting," said Ram.

"Make me your slave!" she wept.

"But perhaps," said he, "I do not want you."

"Want me! Want me!" she begged.

"Do you acknowledge yourself a true slave?" asked Ram.

"Yes, yes!" she cried.

"Do you beg to be my slave?" he asked.

"Yes, Master," she said, on her knees.

"Then beg," said he.

"I beg to be your slave, Master," she said.

The sleen charged. Ram, with his left hand on the tarn harness, managed to get his right hand on her arm. The tarn, given the sudden force on the one-strap, reared and, smiting the air with his mighty wings, lifted itself into the air. The girl screamed, dangling. One of the sleen leaped more than twenty feet into the air, tearing at her, but fell back to the turf, twisting, squealing. She who had been the Lady Tina was held safe in the arms of Ram, her master. He freed her hands that she might hold to him. With his knife he cut the rags from her hips and we watched them fall among the angry sleen who tore them to pieces.

"It seems we have a new slave girl," said Constance.

She who had been the Lady Tina looked at her with fear.

"Yes," I said.

I turned the head of the tarn toward Lydius.

"We are flying in the direction of Lydius, Master," said Constance, her hair lifted by the wind.

"We shall stop there for a time," I said. "I acquired a girl in the fields. She has not yet been branded. It is my intention to have her marked."

She turned white.

"Did you expect to escape the brand?" I asked.

"No, Master," she said. She, Gorean, knew well that slave girls are marked.

She was silent.

I would let her anticipate the iron.

"I, too, acquired a girl in the fields," said Ram. "I may, in Lydius, as well, see that her thigh is clearly marked, that identifying her as what she is, a slave."

I looked at the naked girl, clinging fearfully, helplessly to Ram. "She is so beautiful," I said, "there could be little doubt in anyone's mind that she is a slave, whether she is branded or not."

"She is comely," admitted Ram. "But I will nonetheless have her incontrovertibly marked."

"The mark will improve her beauty," I said, "making it doubly desirable."

"True," said Ram, "perhaps even infinitely more desirable."

"Perhaps," I said. It was true that a brand incredibly enhanced the beauty of a female. Some women did not know what male lust was, until they became slaves, and found themselves, suddenly, vulnerably exposed to its full predations.

She who moments before had been free held to Ram, her master, clutching him, desperately, that she might not fall.

I let her hold to Ram for a while; then I said to her, "Extend your wrists to me, crossed."

"I will fall," she wept.

"If your master pleases," I said, "he will hold you."

"Hold me, Master," she wept. "I beg you!'

"Perhaps," he said.

She extended her wrists to me, crossed. I lashed them together with binding fiber.

She knew that it was only her master's hands on her which prevented her from falling to the ground, hundreds of feet below. She depended on him totally for her life, that he would hold her.

Then her hands were bound, and I drew her up and over the saddle. I then lifted up Constance's arms and thrust the

134

new slave's tied wrists over the pommel, then placed Constance's bound wrists over hers.

The load was thus balanced on the tarn, the weight of the two beauties on one side, that of Ram on the other.

I had placed Constance's bound wrists over those of the new slave for Constance was first girl. She would be first to be lifted from the pommel.

"You are first girl," I told Constance.

"Yes, Master," she said.

"Constance is first girl," I told her who had been the Lady Tina of Lydius.

"Yes, Master," said she who had been the Lady Tina of Lydius.

"Address her as Mistress," I told the former free girl.

"Mistress," said she who had been the former Lady Tina of Lydius, frightened, to Constance.

"Slave," responded Constance to her, confirming the former free woman as second girl.

"Now, on to Lydius!" I said.

"Yes, Master," said the two girls, the blond and the brunet, first girl and second girl, yet both really new slaves, neither of whom had as yet even been branded.

7 I AM CARELESS IN LYDIUS: I AM TAKEN CAPTIVE

I kicked in the door. It splintered inward. I was through the door, sword drawn.

The man at the desk leaped up.

"Where is Bertram of Lydius?" I asked.

"I am he," said the man, in fur jacket. "What do you want? Are you an assassin? You do not wear the dagger. What have I done?"

I laughed. "You are not the man I seek," I said. "One in the south who meant me harm, who seemed a sleen master, had assumed your identity. I thought perhaps he might truly have been Bertram of Lydius."

135

"I do not know you," said the man.

"Nor I you," I said.

I described to him the man who had called himself Bertram of Lydius. But he could not identify him for me. I wondered at who he might truly be.

"You have an excellent name in sleen training," I said. "It is known even in the south. Else I would not have permitted the man to my house."

"I am pleased I am not he whom you seek," said Bertram of Lydius. "I do not envy him."

"The one I seek," I said, "is skilled with the knife. He is, I suspect, of the assassins."

I threw a tarsk bit to the desk. "Your door will need repairing," I said.

Then I turned and left the place. I had not thought the man at my house, he, too, whom I had seen in the tent of the curio dealer, had been truly Bertram of Lydius, but I had wished to clarify that. Too, I had thought he might be one known to Bertram of Lydius, if it were not he. It is easier to assume an identity where one knows a subject reasonably well. Yet one, to assume that identity, would have to know little more than the streets of Lydius and the training of sleen. I hoped to renew my acquaintance with the fellow. Little love is lost betwixt the castes of warriors and assassins. Each deems himself the superior of, and the natural foe, of the other. The sword of the warrior, commonly, is pledged to a Home Stone, that of the assassin to gold and the knife.

I walked through the streets of Lydius until I came to the small metal worker's shop, one out of the main ways of the city.

I entered the shop.

"Are you still crying?" I asked Constance.

She sat in the straw beside an anvil. A chain ran from the anvil and was padlocked about her neck.

"My brand hurts, Master," she said.

"Very well," I said, "cry."

"There," said the metal worker. He eased the heavy iron collar, with the short, dangling chain, from Ram's neck.

"Ah," said Ram.

Beside him, on the floor, knelt Tina, which was now her slave name.

Ram directed the metal worker to saw away an inch and a half of the opened collar. He put it in a vise on his workbench and did so.

"Did you find Bertram of Lydius?" asked Ram.

136

"Yes," I said.

"You slew him?" asked Ram.

"No," I said. "He was not the man I sought."

"Oh," said Ram.

"I did not think he would be," I said.

I looked down at Tina. "Show me your thigh, Girl," I said. She did so.

"How did she take the iron?" I asked.

"She screamed like a she-sleen," he said, "but she is quiet now."

"The brands," I said, "are excellent, both of them."

"Thank you, Master," said Constance, smiling. Tina, too, I noted, straightened herself a bit.

I threw the metal worker a silver tarsk.

"My thanks, Warrior!" he said.

Both of the girls had been beautifully branded. I was pleased.

The metal worker finished sawing the portion off the heavy collar Ram had worn.

Ram then pulled Tina to the feet by her hair and forced her head down on the anvil.

The metal worker looked at him.

"Put it on her neck," he said.

I watched while the heavy collar, shortened now to fit a woman, was curved expertly about her neck by blows of the hammer, and then, decisively, struck shut.

"Lift your head, Slave Girl," said Ram.

She did so, tears in her eyes. The chain on the collar dangled between her breasts.

I signaled the metal worker to free Constance of the chain on her neck. I tossed both girls a light, white rep-cloth slave tunic which I had purchased in the city.

Gratefully, half sobbing, they drew them on. I smiled. Did they not know, to a man's eye, they were almost more naked in such a garment than without it? Garments are an additional way, incidentally, in which to control slave girls. Knowing that the master may not permit her even such a rag if he chooses tends to make her more eager to please him, that she not be sent into the streets without it.

"I will march her barefoot, clad so, through the streets of Lydius," said Ram.

"Excellent," I said. It would be a rich joke. Who would recognize in her the former lofty lady of Lydius, the rich Lady Tina, who had often trod these streets aloof and hidden, probably escorted, in her several veils and multitudinous robes of concealment? Looking upon her, and look they would, they would see only a bond girl, only a lovely, half-naked slave at the heels of her master.

"I will have her serve me paga, publicly, in her own city," said Ram.

"Let us go to the tavern of Sarpedon," I said. "It is a fine tavern." I had been there before, some years earlier. I remembered a girl who had once been wench there, named Tana. It was I who had informed Sarpedon, her master, of her skill in dancing. She had been danced that very night for the patrons, but I had had business, and had not dallied to see her perform.

In less than a quarter of an Ahn we had come to the tavern of Sarpedon.

It was, however, in an angry mood. On the wharves leading to the tavern, in many places, I had seen bales of hide. It was hide of the northern tabuk.

"I must leave Lydius tonight," I said. "There is much here I do not understand. It must be investigated."

"I shall accompany you," said Ram.

"I am a tarnsman," I said. "It is better that you remain."

"The reins of a tarn are not unfamiliar to me," said Ram.

"You are a tarnsman?" I asked.

"I have done many things," he said. "In Hunjer I worked with tarn keepers."

"Do you know the spear, the bow, the sword?" I asked.

"I am not a warrior," he shrugged.

"Remain behind," I said.

"Do masters desire aught?" asked the proprietor, a paunchy man, in leather apron.

Ram and I sat behind one of the small tables. Our girls knelt by us.

"Where is Sarpedon?" I asked.

"He visits in Ar," said the man. "I am Sarpelius, who is managing the tavern in his absence." He regarded the girls. "Lovely," he said. "Would masters care to sell them? I can always use such wenches in the alcoves."

"No," I said.

The girls seemed then less tense.

"There are many bales of hide on the wharves," I said.

"From Kassau, and the north," he said.

"Did the herd of Tancred this year emerge from the forests?" I asked.

"Yes," said the man. "I have heard so."

"But," said I, "it has not yet crossed Ax Glacier?"

138

"I would not know of that," he said.

"On the wharves," I said, "there are thousands of hides."

"From the northern herds," he said.

"Are there traders come south from the north?" asked Ram.

"Few," said the man.

"Is it common," I asked, "for the hides to be so plentiful in Lydius in the spring?" Normally hide hunters prefer the fall tabuk, for the coats are heavier.

"I do not know," said the man. "I am new in Lydius." He looked at us, smiling. "May I serve, Masters?" he asked.

"We will be served by our own girls," said Ram. "We will send them shortly to the vat."

"As masters wish," beamed Sarpelius, and turned about and left us.

"Never have there been hides in this quantity in Lydius," said Ram to me, "either in the spring or fall."

"They are perhaps from the herd of Tancred," I said.

"There are other herds," he said.

"That is true," I said. But I was puzzled. If the herd of Tancred had indeed emerged from the forests why had it not yet crossed Ax Glacier? Surely hunters, even in great numbers, could not stay the avalanche of such a herd, which consisted of doubtless two to three hundred thousand animals. It was one of the largest migratory herds of tabuk on the planet. Unfortunately for the red hunters, it was also the only one which crossed Ax Glacier to summer in the polar basin. To turn such a herd from its migratory destination would be less easy than to turn the course of a flood. Yet, if reports could be believed, the ice of Ax Glacier had not yet, this year, rung to the hooves of the herd.

I was now more pleased than ever that I had had Samos send a ship with supplies north.

But I was suddenly afraid that the ship might not have gotten through. Ram had said that the north was closed.

"Worry upon the morrow," suggested Ram. "Tonight let us divert ourselves with the pleasures of slave girls and paga."

I put a golden tarn on the table. "Remain," I said. "But I fear I must go. There is much here which is seriously amiss. I fear the worst."

"I do not understand," he said.

"Farewell, my friend," said I. "Tonight I take tarn for the north."

"I will accompany you," he said.

"I cannot share this business," I said. "My flight will be

fraught with peril, my work is dangerous." I thought of Zarendargar, Half-Ear, waiting for me at the world's end. Now, more than ever was I certain that the works of the Kurii flourished concealed among the snows of the northern wastes. The pattern was forming. The north was closed. The red hunters were to die by starvation. The frozen north, in its wind-swept desolation, was to keep its secrets in silence from men. "No, my friend," I said. "You cannot accompany me." I turned and strode to the door.

At the door I encountered Sarpelius. "Master asked many questions," he observed.

"Stand aside," I said.

He did so, and I brushed past him. Constance fled after me, in the brief tunic of white rep-cloth. Outside the tavern I turned and looked at her. She had slim, lovely legs, and sweet breasts. She was very beautiful in my collar. I knew where, on the wharves, there was a slave market. I had once bought a dark-haired, captured panther girl named Sheera there. I had broken her swiftly to my collar. She had been excellent in a man's arms. Months later I had freed her. What a fool I had been. It was not a mistake I would make again with a woman. Keep them slaves. They belong in collars.

"Master?" asked Constance.

"It will not be hard to sell you," I said. "You are quite beautiful."

"No!" she begged. "Do not sell me, Master!"

I turned my back upon her. I thought I would probably obtain a silver tarsk for her. She was new to the collar, but she had incredible potentialities. Any slaver could determine that.

With a few more havings I thought she would be helpless, and paga hot.

I strode toward the market. I must leave soon. The girl stumbled after me, weeping. "Please, Master!" she wept. I did not tell her to heel. It was not necessary. She was slave.

I thought she would bring me a tarsk.

Suddenly I heard her cry out, startled. I spun about. "Do not unsheath your blade, Fellow," said a man.

I was covered with four crossbows, the quarrels set. Fingers were tense at the triggers.

I raised my hands.

Two woven canvas straps, some two inches in width, had been looped about the girl's throat and drawn close about it. She was bent backward. Her fingers pulled futilely at the straps. She could scarcely breathe. The man behind her, the straps looped about his fists, tightened them slightly and instantly, terrified, eyes wild, she stopped all attempts to resist.

"In there, between the buildings," said the man, the leader of the others.

Angrily I moved between the buildings and stood in the half darkness of the alley, my hands raised. The girl, rudely, the straps on her throat, was dragged into the darkness with us.

"The bolts," said the man, indicating the missiles at rest in the guides of the weapons, "are tipped with kanda. The slightest scratch from them will finish you."

"I see you are not of the assassins," I said. It is a matter of pride for members of that caste to avoid the use of poisoned steel. Too, their codes forbid it.

"You are a stranger in Lydius," said the man.

"I scarcely think you are magistrates investigating my business," said I. "Who are you? What do you want?" I was angry. My thoughts had been too filled with fear and tumult, and fury at the mysteries of the north. I, though a warrior, had been insufficiently alert. I had been careless.

"I do not think he will be missed," said one of the men.

"You are not common robbers," I said.

"Welcome to Lydius," said the leader of the men. He proffered to me a metal cup. He had filled this from a verrskin canteen slung at his left hip, behind the scabbard.

"Why do you not simply loose your quarrels?" I asked.

"Drink," said he.

"Paga," I said. I had smelled the drink.

"Drink," said he.

I shrugged. I threw back my head and drained the cup. I held the metal cup in my right hand. Then it fell from my hand.

One of the men had set aside his crossbow. I saw the wadding of a slave hood thrust deep in Constance's mouth and then, behind her neck, secured in place with two narrow, buckled straps. The hood itself was then drawn over her head and buckled shut under her chin. The fellow removed the straps from her throat.

I leaned back against the wall.

I saw Constance's hands pulled behind her and snapped in slave bracelets.

I sank to one knee, and then I fell on my shoulder to the stones of the alley. I tried to push myself up, but fell again.

"He will be useful at the wall," said a man.

The boots of the men about me blurred, and then were clear, and then blurred again.

"Yes," said another man.

The voice had seemed far away. Things began to go black. I was dimly aware of them removing my belt and pouch, and the strap with scabbard and sword. Then I lost consciousness.

8   I FIND MYSELF PRISONER IN THE NORTH

"There seems to be no end of them," said a man's voice. "We kill hundreds a day, and yet more come."

"Increase then," said a girl's voice, "the ratios of your slaughtering."

"The men are weary," said the voice.

"Double then the fees," she snapped.

"It will be done," said the voice.

"The wall weakens a pasang east of the platform," said another man's voice.

"Strengthen it," she said.

"Logs are now few," he said.

"Use stone," she said.

"It will be done," said the voice of the man who had spoken.

I lay on a wooden floor, of heavy, rough boards. I shook my head.

I felt the roughness of the boards with my shoulder. I was stripped to the waist. I wore loose trousers of fur, tied about my waist, and fur boots. My hands were manacled behind my back.

"This is the new one?" asked the girl's voice.

"It is he," said a man's voice.

"Arouse him," she said.

I was dragged to my knees and struck with the butts of spears.

I shook my head, and regarded her.

"You are Tarl Cabot," she said.

"Perhaps," I said.

"What men could not do," she said, "I have done. I have taken you."

"There were some men in Lydius," I said.

"They were in my fee!" she said. "Thus, it is I who have taken you."

"Of course," I said.

"We have been watching for you," she said. "We were warned that you might be foolish enough to venture northward."

I said nothing.

"You are a strong, sensuous brute," she said. "Is it true that you are so dangerous?"

I saw no point in responding to her.

"Your acquisition," she said, "will earn me a promotion with my superiors."

"Who might they be?" I asked.

"Ones who are not Priest-Kings," she smiled. She went to a table. I saw belongings of mine upon the table, doubtless fetched from Lydius.

"It was clear quite early," she said, "that you were no common ruffian from the docks of Lydius." She sifted golden tarn disks through her fingers. She drew forth the blade from the sheath. "I am told," said she, "this is a finely tempered blade, keen, subtly balanced, the weapon of one who is of the warriors."

"Perhaps," I said.

She unwrapped from its fur the carving, in bluish stone, of the head of a beast. "What is this?" she asked.

"Do you not know?" I asked.

"The head of a beast," she said.

"That is true," I said.

She placed it back in the fur. It seemed clear to me that she did not understand its import. Kurii, like Priest-Kings, often work through men, concealing themselves from those who would serve them. Samos, for example, had little inkling of the nature of Priest-Kings.

"You are a woman," I said.

I regarded her. She wore trousers and a jacket of whitish fur, of the sea sleen; the jacket had a hood, thrown back, rimmed with lart fur, on which human breath does not freeze. Her boots were of the fur of sea sleen, trimmed, too, with lart fur. The jacket was held about her waist, closely, by a narrow belt, black, and shining, with a golden catch. To this belt, on two small straps, hung a dagger sheath; the

143

handle of the weapon was ornamented with red and yellow swirls. Over her shoulder, across her body, was a second belt, from which hung, at her right hip, a pouch and, on a ring, a slave whip, its blades folded, and four coils of narrow, rawhide rope.

"You are perceptive," she said.

"And one who is perhaps beautiful," I said. Surely her face was beautiful. It was one which, like that of Constance, was very feminine and delicate. It did not comport well with what I took to be the harshness of her charge in the north. Her complexion was very fair; her eyes were softly blue; her hair, fallen about her shoulders, revealed by the thrown-back hood, was a soft, lush auburn in color.

"What do you mean 'one who is perhaps beautiful'?" she asked.

"The furs obscure my vision," I said. "Why do you not remove them?"

She strode toward me, angrily, and struck me across the mouth with her small hand.

She could not hit me hard, for she was too weak. I did not think she weighed more than one hundred and twenty Earth pounds. She was about five feet five inches in height.

I laughed. "I suppose you would bring something in the neighborhood of a silver tarsk in the market," I said.

She struck me again, and again. And then desisted, in fury.

"I will make you regret your insolence," she said.

"Do you know the dances of a Gorean slave girl?" I asked.

"Beast!" she screamed.

"You are of Earth," I said. "Your accent is not Gorean." I looked at her. "American, aren't you?" I asked her, in English.

"Yes," she hissed, in English.

"That explains," I said, "why you are unfamiliar with the dances of the Gorean slave girl."

She looked at me in fury.

"But you might be taught," I said.

She pulled the whip from her belt in a rage and hysterically, holding it with both hands, began to strike me with it. It was not pleasant, but she did not have the strength to make the blows tell. I had been whipped by men. Finally, angrily, she stepped back.

"You are too weak to hurt me," I said. "But I am not too weak to hurt you."

"I will have you whipped by my men," she said.

I shrugged.

144

"What is your name?" I asked.

"Sidney," she said.

"What is your first name?" I asked.

"That is my first name," she said, not pleasantly. "I am Sidney Anderson."

" 'Sidney'," I said, "is a man's name."

"Some women have it," she said. "My parents gave it to me."

"Doubtless they wanted a boy," I said. Then I added, "They were fools."

"Do you think so," she asked.

"Certainly," I said, "both sexes are utterly splendid. One is fortunate to have either. Women are rich, and subtle and marvelous."

"I did not think you respected women," she said.

"I do not," I said.

"I do not understand," she said.

"The man who respects a woman does not know what else to do with her," I said. "I meant only to indicate that women are inordinately precious and desirable."

"We look well in collars," she said, acidly.

"You belong in collars," I said, "at the feet of men."

She turned away, angrily. I could not see her face.

"Are you still attempting to be the boy your parents wished?" I asked.

She spun about, in fury.

"In such a task," I said, "you will never be successful."

"You will be lengthily and sufficiently beaten," she said.

I looked away, at the room. It was high, and of wood, and with an arched roof. There was a dais at one end, on which, in a rough-hewn curule chair, she had sat. There was a rug of sleen skin beneath the chair, and another before the dais. A table was to one side, on which were some of my things. There was a hearth to one side, in which wood burned.

I turned my attention back to the auburn-haired girl.

"Are you well paid?" I asked.

"Yes," she said.

"Do you understand the nature of the cause in which you work?" I asked.

"Of course," she said. "I labor in the cause of Sidney Anderson."

"You are a true mercenary," I smiled.

"Yes," she said, proudly, "I am a mercenary." She looked at me. "Do you think a woman cannot be a mercenary?"

"No," I said, "I see no reason why a woman cannot be a mercenary."

She came over to me and touched me on the cheek with the whip.

"I will put you to work on the wall," she said.

"What wall?" I asked.

"You will see," she said.

"Are you a virgin?" I asked.

She struck me across the face with the whip. "Yes," she said.

"I shall be the first to have you," I told her.

She struck me again, savagely. "Be silent!" she said.

"Surely you are curious about your sexuality," I said.

"Do not use that word before me!" she said.

"It is obvious," I said. "Consider how closely you have fastened the belt on your furs. That is done, even if only unconciously, to draw attention to your figure, accenting and emphasizing it."

"No!" she said.

"Have you never considered," I asked, watching her, "what it would be like to be naked on a slave block, being sold to men, what it would be like to be a nude slave, owned, at the command of a master?"

"No! No! No!" she cried.

"You have seen slaves," I said. "Surely you are curious what it would be like to be one."

"No!" she screamed.

The intensity of her responses had conveyed to me the information in which I was interested.

"There is a slave in you," I said. "I will collar her."

I closed my eyes that I be not blinded by the blows of the whip.

Then she stopped and, angrily, fastened the whip at her belt.

"Sidney Anderson," she said, "will never be a man's slave. Never!"

"When I own you," I told her, "I will give you a girl's name, an Earth girl's name, a slave name."

"And what name would that be?" she asked, curious.

"Arlene," I said.

Momentarily she trembled. Then she said, "That is only a girl's name."

"And you are only a girl," I said.

"I see," she said. She backed away from me a few feet,

146

and regarded me. "You are clever," she said. "You seek to anger me."

"No," I said, "I merely, in response to your request, informed you of the name I would give you, when I own you."

"You are my prisoner," she said.

"For the time," I said.

"I will teach you to fear me," she said.

"It is you who will be taught to fear me," I said, "when I am your master."

She threw back her head and laughed.

I saw that she, too, as had the Lady Tina of Lydius, knew too little of men to fear them. I supposed she had known only the men of Earth and, on Gor, those who were her subordinates in the discipline of the Kurii cause.

I saw the sense of the Kurii enlisting such women. They owed no Gorean allegiances. They possessed no Home Stones. They were aliens on this world.

Did they not know that they, not having a Home Stone, were subject to any man's collar?

She looked at me. She had laughed, but I saw that she seethed with fury. Too, in her eyes there was another emotion. I think she was wondering what it would be like to be owned by me. She would learn.

"The mighty Tarl Cabot," she said, "a manacled, kneeling prisoner."

Too, such women, in their frustrations, so desperately fighting their femininity, made excellent agents.

"Where men have failed to take you," she said, "I have succeeded."

Too, their sex and alien origin, being from Earth, gives them an excellent distance from their subordinates.

She pulled the loops of rawhide rope from the ring at her belt, the same ring which held the hook on the whip, and tied one end of the rope about my neck, knotting it tightly.

Yes, I thought, such women would make excellent tools for the Kurii.

"There," she said, "the feared Tarl Cabot is tethered, kneeling on a woman's rope."

I was puzzled only that the Kurii would enlist such obviously feminine, genuinely feminine, even beautiful, women in their cause. Surely they could find more masculine women upon Earth. Why did they not use harder, harsher, more manlike females?

I looked up at her. She jerked the rawhide rope, testing it.

"An interplanetary force," she said, "unknown to the fools

of Earth, lays siege to this solar system. Its programs will culminate in conquest. I, participating in this struggle, will find high place in the ranks of the victors."

"Priest-Kings oppose them," I said.

"I understand Priest-Kings are weak," she said. "Do they move other than defensively?" she asked.

"Upon occasion," I said.

Yet it was true, surely, that Priest-Kings were not an aggressive species. It did not seem to me, objectively, that it was unlikely they would eventually be supplanted in the system by a fiercer, more territorial, more aggressive form of life. Kurii, it seemed to me, were well fitted to become the dominant life form in the system.

"I shall be on the winning side," she said.

"The mercenary speaks," I said.

"Yes," she said.

I regarded her. She was slim, blue-eyed, auburn-haired, delicately beautiful and feminine.

"Do you truly think," I asked, "that if the Kurii are victorious you will stand high in the ranks of the victors?"

"Of course," she said.

I smiled to myself. I now knew why such women had been brought to Gor. When they had served their purpose, they would be made slaves.

She jerked the rope. "On your feet, Beast," she said.

I rose to my feet.

I looked down on the beauty. She had been brought to Gor, ultimately, to wear a man's collar.

I determined that it would be mine.

"Come, Beast," she said, leading me leashed from the room. "I will show you our work in the north. Later, as I choose and direct, you will labor for us." She turned and looked at me. "You have opposed us long enough," she said. "Now you will, in your humble way, contribute, if only by carrying stone and wood, to our cause."

9

I SEE THE WALL;
I AM TO BE WHIPPED

"Impressive, is it not?" she asked.

We stood on a high platform, overlooking the wall. It extended to the horizons.

"It is more than seventy pasangs in length," she said. "Two to three hundred men have labored on it for two years."

Beyond the wall there milled thousands of tabuk, for it had been built across the path of their northward migration. They stretched for pasangs to the south, grazing.

On our side of the wall was the compound, with the hall of the commander, the long houses of the guards and hunters, and the roofed, wooden pens of the laborers. There was a cook shack, a commissary, a smithy and other ancillary structures. Men moved about their work.

"What are in the storage sheds?" I asked.

"Hides," she said, "thousands, not yet shipped south." "The slaughtering," she said, "takes place largely at the ends of the wall, to prevent animals from taking their way northward."

"It seems many would escape," I said.

"No," she said. "The ends of the wall are curved, to turn the beasts back. When they mill the hunters fall upon them. We kill several hundred a day."

"Can you skin so many?" I asked.

"No," she said. "We content ourselves with prime hide. Most of the animals we leave for the larts and sleen, and the jards." The jard is a small scavenger. It flies in large flocks. A flock, like flies, can strip the meat from a tabuk in minutes.

"Even the jards die, gorged with meat," said the man near us on the platform.

"May I present my colleague," said my lovely captor, "Sorgus."

"The hide bandit?" I asked.

"Yes," she said.

The man did not speak to me, nor look at me.

149

"Such men," she said, "have been useful. No longer are they confined to robbing the hides of honest hunters. We give them harvests beyond the loots which might be reaped from a hundred seasons of thievery."

"But I note," I said, "that higher men aid you as well."

I looked to the other fellow on the platform.

"We meet again," he said.

"It seems so," I agreed. "Perhaps now," I said, "you might succeed in striking me with your dagger."

"Release him," said he to my captor, "that I may with blades, he, too, armed, dispatch him."

"The silly pride of men offends me," said she.

"Free him," said he.

"No," she said. "He is my prisoner. I do not wish for you to kill him."

"It seems," said he to me, "that you will live, if only for an Ahn longer."

"It is you, perhaps," said I, "whose life she thusly prolongs."

He turned away, to look out over the railing on the platform, and out over the high wall, to the thousands of animals, like cattle, beyond.

"Can you truly do your own killing," I asked, "or do you need, as in my house, to enlist the services of a female slave to aid you?" I recalled Vella. She had given him a jacket of mine, that he might use it to give my scent to the sleen. What a traitress she was! I had known she had once served Kurii. I had not known at that time that the pretty little slave, the former secretary on Earth, still licked their claws. She would no longer receive an opportunity to betray me. Death was too good for her. When I returned to Port Kar I would plunge her into a slavery deeper than she would believe possible.

The man, angry, did not respond to me.

"You are not Bertram of Lydius," I said to him. "Who are you?"

"I do not speak to slaves," he said.

My fists clenched in the manacles.

"Did you truly enlist the services of a female slave in his house?" asked my captor.

"I do not wish to speak before him," said the man.

"Do so," she snapped.

I saw him look at her, angrily. I read the look in his eyes. I smiled to myself. I saw that it had been to him that she, when her work was done, had been promised as a slave.

"I am waiting," she said.

150

"Very well," said he. "It is true that I enlisted the services of a lowly bond girl in his house, to obtain material from which I might give scent to the sleen."

"She is a spy there?" she asked.

"No," he said, "I tricked her. I used her as a mere dupe in my scheme. It was not difficult. She was only a woman."

My captor's eyes flashed.

"Only a slave girl," he said.

"That's better," she said. Then she said, "Slave girls are so stupid."

"Yes," he said, "that is true."

I was amused. I wondered if she would change her opinion as to the intelligence of slave girls when she herself wore the collar. As a matter of fact intelligence is one of the major criteria used by Gorean slavers when scouting an Earth girl for capture and abduction to the chains of Gor. The other two major criteria appear to be beauty and femininity. Intelligent, beautiful, feminine women make the best slaves. Who would want a stupid slave? Too, intelligent women can feel their slavery much more keenly than their simpler sisters. This makes it much more amusing to keep them in bondage. Too, because of their intelligence they more swiftly realize the biological rightness of their predicament, though they may fight it longer. The intelligent woman is more apt to trust her own intelligence, and intuitions and feelings than the duller woman, who is more apt to be a naive function of the stereotypes and images with which she has been conditioned. The more intelligent woman is quicker to realize, though more tardy to admit, that it is right for her beauty to be enslaved. Her yielding, too, to her secret realities, when she yields honestly and fully to them, is a glorious thing. At last she whispers, on her knees, to him, "I am a slave, Master." "Go to the furs," he says, gently. "Yes, Master," she says, and obeys.

But many highly intelligent women have fought these battles out in their heart long before they see a chain or the steel of a collar.

They live waiting for a master. They wait for the man who will look into their eyes and see what they truly are, and into whose eyes they will look, and see that he knows their secret. When they are alone, he will say to her, softly, "Kneel, Slave." They kneel. They are then truly a slave, his.

"Tell him your name," she ordered the fellow on the platform.

"I do not speak to slaves," he said.

"Obey me!" she said.

He turned and went down the stairs of the platform.

"He is called Drusus," she said. "He is of the metal workers."

"He is not a metal worker," I said. "He is of the Assassins."

"No," she said.

"I have seen him use a knife," I said. "He did not obey you," I observed.

She looked at me, angrily.

"Your days in authority here," I said, "are numbered."

"I am in command here!" she said.

"For the time," I said. I looked out over the milling tabuk.

They were northern tabuk, massive, tawny and swift, many of them ten hands at the shoulder, a quite different animal from the small, yellow-pelted, antelopelike quadruped of the south. On the other hand, they, too, were distinguished by the single horn of the tabuk. On these animals, however, that object, in swirling ivory, was often, at its base, some two and one-half inches in diameter, and better than a yard in length. A charging tabuk, because of the swiftness of its reflexes, is a quite dangerous animal. Usually they are killed from a distance, often from behind shields, with arrows.

My thoughts strayed to Vella, once Elizabeth Cardwell. Apparently she had not knowingly collaborated with Drusus, he who had called himself Bertram of Lydius. He had tricked her in the matter of the sleen. She had been his dupe. It would not then be necessary to be too hard on her. It would be sufficient, when I returned to Port Kar, merely to have her whipped for her stupidity.

I put her from my mind, for she was only slave.

"It must be difficult to place the logs of the wall," I said, "because of the permafrost."

"How difficult you will learn," she said. She was still angry that her authority had been flouted in my presence.

At this latitude, even in the summer, the earth only thaws to a depth of some two feet. Beneath this depth one strikes still frozen ground. It is almost like stone. Picks and drive bars ring upon it.

The construction of the wall was, in its way, a considerable engineering feat. That it had been accomplished by men, with simple tools, said much for the determination of the Kurii, and the rigors imposed upon its laborers by their guardsmen.

"You will see who is in authority here," she said, angrily. I felt the line on my neck jerk tight. I accompanied her down the stairs of the platform.

"Guards!" she called. Some four guardsmen came to her, running.

"Bring Drusus to me," she said, "if necessary in chains."

They hurried from her. In a few moments they returned, he who called himself Drusus with them.

She pointed arrogantly to the ground at her feet. "Kneel," she said to him.

Angrily he knelt.

"Tell him your name," she said to him.

The man looked up at me, in fury. "I am Drusus," he said.

"Attend now to your duties, Drusus," she said.

He got to his feet and left. I saw that she was truly in authority. If her tenure of authority were to be soon terminated there was as yet no sign of it. She looked at me, and tossed her head arrogantly. She was supreme among these men.

"It was Drusus who identified you for me," she said.

"I see," I said.

"Three prisoners have been captured," said a man, coming up to her.

"Bring them before me," she said.

The three prisoners, their hands bound behind their backs, were brought forward. One was a man, the other two were girls, slave girls. The man was on an individual neck tether, in the hand of a guard. The girls were on a common tether, the throat of each tied at a different end of a long strap; it served as their common leash, a guard grasping it in the center. The man was the red hunter I had seen at the fair. He no longer possessed his bow or other accouterments. The two girls were the slaves he had purchased at the fair, the Earth girls, one blond, the other dark-haired, who had worn the torn red pullover. He was dressed as he had been at the fair, in trousers and boots of fur, but bare-chested. The two girls now, however, wore fur wrapped on their feet, tied with hide string, and brief fur tunics. The hair of each was tied behind her head with a red string. Under the tether on the throat of each there was tied an intricately knotted set of four leather strings. In such a way the red hunters identify their animals. The owner of the beast may be determined from the knotting of the strings.

"Kneel," said a guard.

The two slave girls immediately knelt, obedient to a master's command.

My lovely captor regarded them with contempt.

153

The red hunter, he of the polar basin, had not knelt. Perhaps he did not speak Gorean well enough to understand the command. There are several barbarian languages spoken on Gor, usually in more remote areas. Also, some of the dialects of Gorean itself are almost unintelligible. On the other hand, Gorean, in its varieties, serves as the *lingua franca* of civilized Gor. There are few Goreans who cannot speak it, though with some it is almost a second language. Gorean tends to be rendered more uniform through the minglings and transactions of the great fairs. Too, at certain of these fairs, the caste of scribes, accepted as the arbiters of such matters, stipulate that certain pronounciations and grammatical formations, and such, are to be preferred over others. The Fairs, in their diverse ways, tend to standardize the language, which might otherwise disintegrate into regional variations which, over centuries, might become mutually unintelligible linguistic modalities, in effect and practice, unfortunately, separate languages. The Fairs, and, I think, the will of Priest-Kings, prevents this.

"No," said the red hunter. He had spoken in Gorean.

He was struck to his knees by the blows of spears. He looked up, angrily. "Free our tabuk!" he said.

"Take him away and put him to work on the wall," said my lovely captor.

The man was dragged away.

"What have we here?" Sidney Anderson asked, regarding the two girls.

"Polar slaves, beasts of the red hunters," said a man.

"Look up at me," she said.

The girls looked into her eyes.

"You have the look of Earth girls," said my captor, in English.

I thought her perceptive. They could still be distinguished from Gorean collar girls. There was still something about them which, to a discerning eye, betrayed their intricate, constricted Earth origin. Later, if they had the proper master or series of masters, it would no longer be possible to do this by sight. They would be betrayed then, if their teeth were not carefully inspected, only by their accent. A filling found in a tooth is usually a sign of an Earth girl. It is not an infallible sign, however, for not all Earth girls have fillings and some dental work is done upon occasion by the caste of physicians on Gorean girls. Cavities are rare in Goreans because of their simple diet and the general absence of cruel emotional stress, with its physiological and chemical consequences, during

154

puberty. Gorean culture tends to view the body, its development, its appetites and needs, with congeniality. We do not grow excited about the growth of trees, and Goreans do not grow excited about the growth of people. In some respects the Goreans are, perhaps, cruel. Yet they have never seen fit, through lies, to inflict suffering on children. They seem generally to me to be fond of children. Perhaps that is why they seldom hurt them. Even slave children, incidentally, are seldom abused or treated poorly, and are given much freedom, until they reach their young adulthood. It is then, of course, that they are taught that they are slaves. Men come, and the young male is tied and taken to the market. If the young slave is a female she may or may not be sent to a market. Many young slave maidens are raised almost as daughters in a home. It is often a startling and frightening day for such a girl when, one morning, she finds herself suddenly, unexpectedly, put in a collar and whipped, and made to begin to pay the price of her now-blossomed slave beauty.

"Are you not Earth girls?" asked blue-eyed, auburn-haired Sidney Anderson of the two kneeling girls, in their short fur tunics, the strings on their throats, and tethers, their hands tied behind their backs.

"Yes! Yes!" said the blond girl suddenly, "Yes!"

Sidney Anderson, I conjectured, was the first person on Gor whom they had met who spoke English.

"What are you?" asked Sidney Anderson.

"We are slaves, Mistress," said the blond girl.

"What are your names?" asked my lovely captor.

"Barbara Benson," said the blond girl. "Audrey Brewster," said the dark-haired girl.

"I scarcely think," said my captor, "that those names would have been given to you by an Indian."

I had not really thought of the red hunter as an Indian, but I supposed this was true. The men of the polar basin are usually referred to as the red hunters in Gorean. Certainly they were culturally distinct from the red savages, tarn riders, of the countries north and east of the Thentis mountains, who maintained a feudal nobility over scattered agricultural communities of white slaves. Those individuals, more than the red hunters, I thought of as Indians. Yet, doubtless the red hunters, too, if one were to be strict about such matters, were Indian. On the other hand the children of the red hunters are born with a blue spot at the base of the spine and those of the red savages, or red tarn riders, are not. There is, thus, some sort of racial disaffinity between them. There are also

155

serological differences. Race, incidentally, is not a serious matter generally for Goreans, perhaps because of the inter-mixtures of people. Language and city, and caste, however, are matters of great moment to them, and provide a sufficient basis for the discriminations in which human beings take such great delight.

The blond-haired girl looked up at Sidney Anderson. "I am Thimble," she said.

"I am Thistle," said the dark-haired girl.

How beautiful they looked, kneeling, with their hands bound behind them.

"Are you not shamed to be slaves?" asked Sidney Anderson.

"Yes, yes!" wept the blond-haired girl. I remembered she had once worn the brief, denim shorts, raveled, and the man's shirt, tied under her breasts.

"Good," said Sidney Anderson.

They looked at her.

"Look at yourselves," she said. "Consider your attire. You should be ashamed."

"Are you going to free us?" breathed the blond-haired girl. Then she added, "—Mistress?"

Sidney Anderson regarded them with contempt.

"Some women," she said, "should be slaves."

"Mistress," protested the blond-haired girl.

"I look upon you," said Sidney Anderson, "and I see women who deserve to be only meaningless slaves."

"Mistress!" protested the blond-haired girl.

"Take them away," said Sidney Anderson.

"Do you want them killed?" asked a guard.

"Wash and comb them," she said, "and then chain them in the long house for the guards."

"It will be done," said the man.

The girls were dragged away.

"Doubtless you have other girls, too," I said, "kept for the men."

"Those are the only two," she said. "I have given orders that our sutlers not peddle slave sluts in the camp."

"When I was captured," I said, "a blond slave named Constance was taken, too. I would have thought she would have been brought here."

"No," said my lovely captor.

"Where was she taken?" I asked.

"I do not know," she said.

She tugged on the rawhide leash I wore. Then she reached

156

up and removed it from my neck, and coiled it, and replaced it on the ring on her belt.

"The sun is beautiful in your auburn hair," I said.

"Oh?" she asked.

"Yes," I said. "Did you know that girls with auburn hair often bring higher prices on the slave block?" I asked.

"No," she said, "I did not." Then she said to guardsmen who stood about. "Take him to the whipping frame. Secure him there and beat him well. Use the snake. Then pen him and chain him. Tomorrow put him to work on the wall."

"The red hunters depend on the tabuk," I told her. "Without it they will starve."

"That is not my concern," she said.

The men put their hands on my arms.

"Oh," she said, "incidentally you may know of a ship of supplies which had been bound for the high north."

"I know of such a ship," I said.

"It has been sunk," she said. "Its crew doubtless will greet you tomorrow. They, too, labor on the wall."

"How could you take the ship?" I asked.

"There are five tarnsmen here," she said, "though now they are on patrol. They fired the ship from the air. Its crew, abandoning the ship, were apprehended later. The ship, burned to the waterline, was steered onto the rocks and fell awash. In the rising of the tide it was freed and sank. Sharks now frequent its hold."

I looked at her.

"We are thorough," she said.

"The red hunters will starve," I told her.

"That is not my concern," she said.

"Why are you holding the tabuk?" I asked. "What have you to gain?"

"I do not know," she said. "I am merely discharging my orders."

"The red hunters," I said.

"They are not my concern," she said. Then she said, "Take him away."

Two men seized me and conducted me from her presence. I was confident that I saw the point of stopping the tabuk. Its role in the plans of Kurii seemed clear to me. I was puzzled that the girl did not see its import.

She knew no more, it seemed, than she needed to know.

10 WHAT OCCURRED IN THE VICINITY OF THE WALL

"Is he still alive?" asked a man.

I lay chained in the slave pen.

"Yes," said the red hunter.

"He is strong," said another man.

I wanted the woman in my power who had had me beaten. I struggled to a sitting position.

"Rest now," said Ram. "It is nearly dawn."

"They have you, too," I said. I had left him in Lydius, in the paga tavern.

He grinned wryly. "Late that night," said he, "in the alcove they surprised me with Tina. At sword point I was hooded and chained."

"How was the girl?" I asked.

"In a quarter of an Ahn," he said, "I had her screaming herself mine." He licked his lips. "What a slave she is!" he marveled.

"I thought she would be," I said. "Where is she?" I asked.

"Is she not here?" he asked.

"No," I said.

"Where have they taken her?" he asked.

"I do not know," I said.

"I want her back," he said.

"She is only a slave," I said.

"I want to own her again," he said.

"Do you think she is your ideal slave?" I asked.

"Perhaps," he said, "I do not know. But I will not be content until she is again at my feet."

"But did you not make her serve you paga publicly in her own city, and as a slave girl?"

"Of course," he said. "And then I took her by the hair to the alcove."

"Is that the way you treat your ideal slave?" I asked.

"Of course," he said.

"Excellent," I said. I saw that Ram was a true master. The girl's helplessness was doubtless in part a response to his strength. Slave girls are seldom in doubt as to which men are their masters and which are not.

"What is your name?" I asked the red hunter. "Forgive me," I said.

Red hunters are often reluctant to speak their own name. What if the name should go away? What if it, in escaping their lips, should not return to them?

"One whom some hunters in the north call Imnak may share your chain," he said.

He seemed thoughtful. Then he seemed content. His name had not left him.

"You are Imnak," I said.

"Yes," he said.

"I am Tarl," I said.

"Greetings, Tarl," he said.

"Greetings, Imnak," I said.

"I have seen you before," said a man.

"I know you," I said. "You are Sarpedon, who owns a tavern in Lydius.

"I sold the little slave whom you knew," he said.

"I know," I said. "She is now collared in my house."

"A superb wench," he said. "I often used her for my pleasure."

"Your tavern, now," I said, "seems to be managed by one called Sarpelius."

"I know," he said. "I would that I could get my hands on the rogue's throat."

"How came you here?" I asked.

"I was voyaging upstream on the Laurius," he said, "to see if panther girls had caught any new slave girls, whom I might purchase from them for arrow points and candy, for use in the tavern as paga sluts. But unfortunately it was I, taken by five tarnsmen on the river, who found myself chained. It was part of a plan, of course. My assistant, Sarpelius, was in league with them."

"Your tavern is being used to recruit workers for the wall," said Ram.

Several men grunted angrily.

"Put Sarpelius in my grasp," said Sarpedon, "and I will see you receive rich satisfaction for your inconvenience."

"Admiral," said a man.

"I know you," I said. "You are Tasdron, a captain in the fee of Samos."

159

"The ship was fired, and then sunk," said he, "the supply ship, that bound for the north."

"I know," I said.

"I am a failed captain," said he.

"It is difficult to defend against tarn attack, the sheets of burning oil to the sails."

"They came again and again," he said.

"You were not a ram ship," I said, "not craft set for war."

"Who would have thought there would be tarnsmen north of Torvaldsland," said Ram.

"It is possible in the spring and summer," said Sarpedon.

"You saved your men," I said. "You did well."

"What ship is this?" asked Imnak.

"I had a ship sent north," said I, "with food for the men of the polar basin, when I heard the herd of Tancred had not yet trod the snows of Ax Glacier."

Imnak smiled. "How many skins would you have demanded in payment for this provender?" asked he.

"I had not thought to make a profit," I said.

Imnak's face darkened.

The people of the north are proud. I had not meant to demean him or his people.

"It is a gift," I said. He would understand the exchange of gifts.

"Ah," he said. Gifts may be exchanged among friends. Gifts are important in the culture of the men of the polar basin. There need be little occasion for their exchange. Sometimes, of course, when a hunter does not have food for his family another hunter will invite him to his house, or will pay a visit, bearing meat, that they may share a feast. This pleasantry, of course, is returned when the opportunity presents itself. Even trading in the north sometimes takes on the aspect, interestingly, of the exchange of gifts, as though commerce, obvious and raw, might somehow seem to offend the sensibility of the proud hunters. He who dares to pursue the twisting, sinuous dangerous sea sleen in the arctic waters, fended from the teeth and sea by only a narrow vessel of tabuk skin and his simple weapons and skill, does not care to be confused with a tradesman.

"I know you are wise and I am stupid," said Imnak, "for I am only a lowly fellow of the polar basin, but my peoples, in the gathering of the summer, in the great hunts, when the herd comes, number in the hundreds."

"Oh," I said. I had not realized there were so many. One ship would have done little to alleviate the distress, the danger of starvation, even had it managed to slip through the air blockade of the Kurii's tarnsmen.

"Too," said Imnak, "my people are inland, waiting for the herd to come to the tundra grazing. It gives me pleasure to know that you understood this, and knew where to find them, and had considered well how to transport the gifts to them, so many sleeps across the tundra."

"There was only one ship," I said. "And I had not realized the difficulty of getting the supplies to where they would be most needed."

"Do my ears deceive me?" asked Imnak. "I cannot believe what I am hearing. Did I hear a white man say he had made a mistake?"

"I made a mistake," I said. "One who is wise in the south may be a fool in the north."

This admission took Imnak aback for a moment.

"You are wiser than I," I added, for good measure.

"No," he said, "you are wiser than I."

"Perhaps I am wiser in the south," I said, "but you are wiser in the north."

"Perhaps," he said.

"And you are a great hunter," I said.

He grinned. "I have done a little hunting," he said.

"Rouse up! Rouse up!" called a guard, beating on the wooden bars of the pen with his spear. "It is time for your gruel, and thence to your labors."

Two guards were then amongst us, prodding men awake and up.

"Release this man from the chain," said Ram, indicating me. "Yesterday he was beaten with the snake."

It was not unusual that men died under the lash of the snake, that heavy coil laced with wire and flecks of iron.

"It is ordered," said the guardsman, "that he labors today."

Ram looked at me, startled. I was already on my feet. My lovely captor, I recalled, had said that I would labor today. I was to well understand whose prisoner I was. "I am hungry," I said.

The guard backed away from me. He went to check the ankle chains of the others.

We were soon shuffled from the pen. In making our way to the cook shack we passed the large, wooden dais on which the whipping frame had been erected. It was some twelve feet square, and some four feet in height, its surface reached by steps. The whipping frame itself, vertical, consisted of two heavy uprights, some six inches square and eight feet high, and a crossbeam, some six inches square and some seven feet in length. Each upright was supported by two braces, each also six inches square. A heavy ring was bolted on the underside of the high crossbeam; it was from this ring that a prisoner, bound by the wrists, might be suspended. A matching ring was bolted in the beams of the dais, under the upper ring. It was to the lower ring that the prisoner's feet, some six inches above the wood, crossed and tied, might be bound. This prevents undue swinging under the lash.

We were knelt outside the cook shack. We were given wooden bowls. We were served gruel, mixed with thick chunks of boiled tabuk, by the blond, she who had once been Barbara Benson, now Thimble, and the dark-haired girl, who had once been the rich girl, Audrey Brewster, now the slave girl, Thistle. Thimble had been made first girl. She made Thistle carry the metal bucket of gruel while she, with a ladle, filled the bowls. Neither girl any longer wore the strings on her throat, identifying them as a hunter's beasts, nor her brief furs nor the fur wrappings on their feet. Both had been placed in belted woolen camisks, an open-sided garment sometimes worn by female slaves. Though it was chilly both were barefoot.

Blond Thimble cried out, seized by one of the men in the chain. She struck at him with the ladle. She was thrown to the ground beneath him. Instantly guards were on the fellow, striking him with spear butts and pulling him from the girl. They struck him cruelly. "She is for the guards," they told him.

Terrified, Thimble, her camisk half torn away, stumbled back, away from the chain.

"Fill their bowls again," said the head guard. "They have much work to do today."

Thimble and Thistle began again at the far end of the line to my right. They swayed back, frightened, as far as they could from the line, in their serving.

They knew the terror of slave girls, among men hungry for women.

There were some forty men in my chain. Along the some seventy pasangs of the wall there were several such chains, with their own pens and facilities. Somewhere between three and four hundred men, with their guards, labored at one place or another along the wall. I do not think it was a mistake that I was in one of the more central chains. My lovely captor, doubtless, had so decreed it. She was quite proud of my capture, which she regarded as a function of her own

162

merits. She wanted me in a position of maximum security, nearer the wall's center, closer to her headquarters. Too, I think she relished the pleasure of seeing me in her chains.

We were marched past the high platform overlooking the wall.

She was on the platform, with two guards.

"She is up early this morning," said one of the men.

Near the platform there were piled some logs and heavy stones, carried there by other laborers the preceding afternoon. Tools, also, wrapped in hide, were there.

"Lift these logs," said a guard. "Carry these stones."

I, with Ram and Imnak, and Tasdron, who had been the captain in the fee of Samos, he whose ship had been lost to the tarnsmen, shouldered one of the logs.

My lovely captor looked down on us. Her face was flushed with pleasure.

"She wears a man's furs," said Imnak.

That was true, at least from the point of view of a red hunter. Women of the red hunters are furred differently from the hunters. Their boots, soft, of sleenskin, are high, and reach the crotch, instead of the knee. Instead of trousers of fur they wear brief panties of fur. When they cover their breasts it is commonly with a shirt of beaded lartskin. In cold weather they, like the men, wear one or more hooded parkas of tabuk hide. Tabuk hide is the warmest pelt in the arctic. Each of the hairs of the nothern tabuk, interestingly, is hollow. This trapped air, contained in each of the hollow hairs, gives the fur excellent insulating properties. Air, incidentally, is extremely important, generally, in the effectiveness of the clothing of the red hunters. First, the garments, being of hide, are windproof, as most other garments are not. Cold air, thus, cannot penetrate the garment. The warming factor of the garment is a function of air trapped against the skin. This air, inside the garment, is warmed by the body, of course. The garment, because of the hood, and the weight of the garment on the shoulders, tends to trap this warm air inside. It does not escape from the bottom because warm air, being less dense than cold air, tends to rise. The major danger of these garments, interestingly, is the danger of the wearer becoming overheated. Perspiration in the arctic winter, which can freeze on the body, and soak the clothing, which can then become like ice, brittle and useless, is a peril to be avoided if at all possible. Yet the garment's design permits this danger to be nullified. When the hunter becomes overheated he pulls down the neck of the parka. This permits the warm air to escape and its place is taken by fresh, cold air from the bottom. He thus, by closing or opening the throat of the garment, regulates its effectiveness according to his needs. The warmth of most normal clothing, incidentally, is a function of layers of cloth, not of trapped, warmed air. These many layers of clothing are, of course, heavy, cumbersome and difficult to work in. Also, of course, since this sort of clothing is not normally windproof cold air penetrates the garment and, meeting the warm air of the body, tends to precipitate moisture. The garments thus become wet and more heavy, and more dangerous, at low temperatures. Also, there is no simply way of avoiding this danger. One may, of course, remove layers of clothing, but this, in arctic temperatures, can be dangerous in itself. Also, when one wishes to replace the clothing, it may be, by then, frozen. At arctic temperatures moisture in a garment can turn to ice in a matter of seconds. The armholes in a parka, incidentally, are cut large enough to allow a man to pull his arms and hands inside and warm them, if he wishes, against the body. The clothing of the arctic hunter seems ideally suited to his needs in the north. It is warm, light in weight and permits great freedom of movement.

"Work well, Tarl Cabot," called my lovely captor from the height of the platform.

"Move," said a guardsman.

We strode forth, moving in unison, on the left foot. Our right ankles, chained in coffle, followed.

The log was heavy.

"It is like stone," said Ram. He drove the iron bar, which he gripped in fur, downward. It struck the layer of permafrost, and rang.

I, too, drove the bar into the hole. A bit of frozen dirt was chipped away.

We made our hole at a diagonal, for the logs we were to set now were bracing logs, which would help support the wall at this place. It was some half a pasang from the platform. It was weakened at this point. I had heard of this yesterday, before I had been conducted by my fair captor from her headquarters. Some work had been done yesterday, with logs and stone. More remained to be done now. This weakness was to the left of the platform, looking out toward the tabuk. The center of the wall had been built across the main run of the tabuk migration. The animals, frustrated, sometimes tended to press against the wall. Sometimes, too, animals at the wall

164

were forced against it, pinned against it, by the weight of animals behind them. Sometimes, in open places, huge, massive bucks, heads down, would charge and strike the wall with their horns. The animals did not understand this obstruction in their path. It was incomprehensible to them, and, to many, maddening. Why did it not yield?

Two or three times, at certain points, I learned, the wall had buckled, but, each time, men managed to repair it in time.

"Put stone here," said a guardsman.

Men, carrying stone, placed it against the wall. Such support, however, would not be as effective as the log braces which we were laboring to set in place.

On the other side of the wall there were thousands of tabuk. New thousands arrived each day, from the paths east of Torvaldsland.

"With the permafrost," I said to Ram, "the logs of the wall cannot be too deeply fixed."

"They are deeply enough fixed," he said. "They could not be withdrawn without sufficient labor."

"Surely we have sufficient labor," I said.

"Perhaps you could discuss the matter with the guards," he said.

"They might not be agreeable," I pointed out.

"What is your plan?" he asked.

We two were chained together, but apart from the others, to facilitate our labors. Several other pairs, too, were so chained. The coffle, in virtue of the arrangements of chains and ankle rings, could be broken up into smaller work units.

"Imnak," I said, "would you like to go home?"

"I have not seen the performance of a drum dance in four moons," he said.

"Tasdron," said I, "would you like a new ship?"

"I would fit it to fight tarnsmen," said he. "Let them then try to take her."

"Do not be foolish," said a man. "Escape is hopeless. We are chained. Guards, if not here, are many."

"You have no allies," said another man.

"You are mistaken," I said, "our allies number in the thousands."

"Yes!" said Ram. "Yes!"

The keys to our ankle rings were in the keeping of the chief guard, the master of our coffle.

"Speak less," said a guard. "You are here to reinforce the wall, not spend your time in talk like silly slave girls."

"I fear the wall is going to buckle here," I said, indicating a place at the wall.

"Where?" he asked, going to the wall, examining it with his hands.

I did not think it wise on his part to turn his back on prisoners.

I thrust his head, from behind, into the logs. It struck them with considerable force. I gestured to the men about, that they join me at the wall. The fallen guard could not be seen amongst us. His sword I now held in my hand.

"What is going on there?" called the chief guard.

"You will get us all killed," said a man.

He pushed his way amongst us, striking to the left and right. Then he saw his fallen fellow. He turned, white-faced, his hand at the hilt of his sword. But the sword I carried was at his breast.

Ram relieved him swiftly of the keys he bore. He released me, and then himself, and then gave the keys to Tasdron.

"There is no escape for you," said the chief guard. "You are pinned with the wall on one side, the guardsmen who may be swiftly marshaled on the other."

"Call your fellow guards to your side," I said.

"I do not choose to do so," he said.

"The choice is yours," I granted him. I drew back the blade.

"Wait," he said. Then he called out, "Jason! Ho-Sim! To the wall!"

They hurried over. We had then four swords, and two spears. They did not carry shields, for their duties had only involved the supervision of a work crew.

"Captain!" called another guard, from some forty yards away. "Are you all right?"

"Yes!" he called.

But the man had apparently seen the movement of a spear among the workers.

He turned suddenly and, bolting, fled toward the platform and main buildings.

"A spear!" I said.

But by the time it was in my grasp the man was well out of its range.

"He will give the alarm," said the chief guard. "You are finished. Return to me my weapons and place yourselves again in chains. I will petition that your lives be spared."

"Well, Lads," said I, "let us now to work with a good

166

heart. I do not think we will have a great deal of time to spare."

With a will, then, they set themselves to the opening of the wall.

"You are insane!" said the chief guard. "You will all be trampled."

As soon as one log was tortured out of the earth and lifted away Imnak slipped through the opening, out among the tabuk.

"He at least will escape," said one of the men.

"He will be killed out there," said another.

I was disappointed that Imnak had fled. I had thought him made of sterner stuff.

"Quickly, Lads," I said. "Quickly!"

Another log was pulled out of the earth, levered up by bars and, by many hands, heaved to the side.

We could hear the alarm bar ringing now. Its sound carried clearly in the clear, cold air north of Torvaldsland.

"Quickly, Lads!" I encouraged them.

"You, too," I said, gesturing to the three guards who were conscious. "Work well and I may spare your lives."

Angrily, then, they, too, set themselves to the work of drawing logs out of that cruel turf.

Suddenly a tabuk, better than eleven hands at the shoulder, thrust through the opening, buffeting men aside.

"Hurry!" I said. "Back to work!"

"We will be killed!" cried the chief guard. "You do not know these beasts!"

"Guards are coming," moaned a man.

Hurrying toward us we could now see some forty or fifty guardsmen, weapons at the ready.

"Surrender!" said the chief guard.

"Work," I warned him.

He saw that I was ready to make an example of him. Earnestly he then bent sweating to his work.

"I surrender! I surrender!" cried a man, running toward the guards.

We saw him cut down.

I took again the spear which had earlier been pressed into my grasp.

I hurled it into the guards, some fifty yards now away. I saw a man fall.

The guards stopped, suddenly. They did not have shields. I took the other spear.

"Work!" I called to the men behind me.

"Heave!" I heard Ram call.

Two more tabuk bounded through the rupture in the wall. There would not be enough. They did not know the wall was open. Some four more tabuk, as though sensing freedom, trotted past.

There would not be enough.

I threatened the guards with the spear. They fanned out, now, wisely, warily.

Another log was rolled aside.

Two more tabuk bounded through.

"Kill him!" I heard the chief of those guardsmen say. Four more tabuk trotted past.

There would not be enough tabuk! The guards now crept more close, blades ready.

"Aja! Aja!" I heard, from behind the fence. "Aja! Hurry, my brothers! Aja!"

There was a cheer from those who labored at the destruction of the wall.

Forty or more tabuk suddenly, with startling rapidity, a tawny blur, trotted past me. They were led by a magnificent animal, a giant buck, fourteen hands at the shoulder, with swirling horn of ivory more than a yard in length. It was the leader of the herd of Tancred.

"Aja!" I heard from behind the fence.

Suddenly it was as though a dam had broken. I threw myself back against the logs. The guardsmen broke and fled.

Floodlike, like a tawny, thundering avalanche, blurred, snorting, tossing their heads and horns, the tabuk sped past me. I saw the leader, to one side, on a hillock, stamping and snorting, and lifting his head. He watched the tabuk streaming past him and then he bounded from the hillock, and, racing, made his way to the head of the herd. More tabuk now, a river better than sixty feet wide, thundered past me. I heard logs splintering, and saw them breaking and giving way. They fell and some, even, on the backs of the closely massed animals, were carried for dozens of yards, wood floating and churned, tossed on that tawny, storming river, that relentless torrent of hide and horn, turned toward the north. I moved to my left as more logs burst loose. In minutes the river of tabuk was more than two hundred yards wide. The ground shook beneath me. I could hardly see nor breathe for the dust.

I was aware of Imnak near me, grinning.

11 WHAT FURTHER EVENTS OCCURRED IN THE VICINITY OF THE WALL; I AGAIN TURN MY EYES NORTHWARD; I PAUSE ONLY TO REDUCE A WOMAN TO SLAVERY

I tied her wrists together. There was a great cheer from my men.

As I had anticipated there had been little actual fighting.

Once the wall had been broken, Drusus, of the Assassins, had departed with several men.

Several guardsmen, too, their discipline broken, had sought supplies and fled south. The wall broken there seemed little point to them to remain and die.

We had little difficulty with the guards and work crews east of the break in the wall. It had been a simple matter to don the uniforms of guards and seem to march a new chain of men east. The men in the chain, of course, were not locked within, save for those at the end of the chain who had been former guards, now clad in the rags of laborers. I was of the warriors, and Ram, as it turned out, was quite skillful with the sword. Confronted with us and the majority of the putatively chained laborers, suddenly throwing off their chains and encircling them, they offered little resistance. Soon they, like their colleagues, wore locked manacles and laborers' rags. At the eastern end of the wall a similar ruse surprised the camp of hunters. We lost some of these as they fled south but others we captured and chained, acquiring several longbows, which might be used at the latitude of the wall, and several hundred arrows. Some nine men among our forces were of the peasants. To these I gave the bows.

At the end of the wall Imnak wept, seeing the strewn fields of slaughtered tabuk. The fur and hide of the tabuk provides the red hunters not only with clothing, but it can also be used for blankets, sleeping bags and other articles. The hides can serve for harnesses for the snow sleen and their white-

169

skinned, female beasts. Too they may be used for buckets and tents, and for kayaks, the light, narrow hunting canoes of skin from which sea mammals may be sought. Lashings, harpoon lines, cords and threads can be fashioned from its sinews. Carved, the bone and horn of the animal can function as arrow points, needles, thimbles, chisels, wedges and knives. Its fat and bone marrow can be used as fuel. Too, almost all of the animal is edible. Even its eyes may be eaten and, from its stomach, the half-digested mosses on which it has been grazing.

Fluttering jards, covering many of the carcasses like gigantic flies, stirred, swarming upward as Imnak passed them, and then returned to their feasting.

He looked about, at the slaughtered animals. Only one in ten had been skinned.

The sinew had not been taken, nor the meat nor bones. Some hides had been taken, and some horn. But the mission of the hunters had not been to harvest from the herd of Tancred. Their mission had been to destroy it.

With a sudden cry he fell upon a bound hunter. I prevented him from killing the man.

"We must go," I said. I vomited. My stomach had been turned by the stench.

I used capture knots on her wrists. There was a great cheer from my men.

"I am your prisoner, Captain," she said.

I did not speak to her, but handed her, her wrists bound before her body, to one of my men.

"We shall hold you to your word," said Sorgus, the hide bandit, uneasily.

"It is good," I told him.

He, with his men, some forty, who had taken refuge in the wooden hall, that serving as the headquarters of the wall commander, filed tensely between the ranks of my men. I had permitted them their weapons. I had little interest in the slaughter of minions.

The men and guardsmen who had been at the wall's center, in the buildings there, and west along the wall, including the hunters at that termination of the structure, learning the breaking of the wall and the freeing and arming of many laborers, had for the most part fled. Others, however, under the command of Sorgus, had boldly rallied to turn the tides of victory in their favor. They had not at that time, however, realized that nine of our men, peasants, gripped bows of yellow

Ka-la-na wood. Behind each of these nine stood men bearing sheafs of arrows. Of the original force of Sorgus, some ninety-five men, fifty had succumbed to the fierce rain of steel-tipped arrows which had struck amongst them. Only five of his men had been able to reach the bowmen. These I slew. Sorgus, with some forty cohorts then, seeing me deploy bowmen to his rear, broke for the hall and barricaded himself within.

"He is waiting," said Ram, "for the return of the tarnsmen, those on patrol."

We would have little protection from attack from the air.

The arrow flighted from a diving tarn, allied with gravity and the momentum of the winged beast, can sink a foot into solid wood.

Such an attack would necessitate the scattering of my men, their seeking cover. Defensive archery, directed upward from the ground, fighting against the weights of gravity, is reduced in both range and effectiveness. The dispersal of my men, of course, would provide Sorgus and his men with their opportunity, under the covering fire of their tarnsmen aloft, to escape from the hall.

"When are the tarnsmen due to return from patrol?" I asked.

"I do not know," said Ram.

"Sorgus!" I had called, to he within the headquarters.

"I hear you," he responded.

"Surrender!" I called.

"I do not!" he said. Arrows were trained on the door through which he spoke.

"I do not wish to slay either you or your men," I called to him. "If you surrender now I will permit you to retain your weapons and withdraw in peace."

"Do you think me a fool?" he called.

"When do you expect your tarnsmen to return?" I asked.

"Soon!" said he.

"It could be days," said Ram.

"I hope, for your sake, Sorgus," I called, "that they return within the Ahn."

I positioned my archers at the openings to the hall, with armed men to defend them. I encircled the hall with my men. They carried stones and clubs.

"What do you mean?" called Sorgus.

"I am going to fire the hall," I said.

"Wait!" he said.

171

"You and your men may depart in peace now," I said, "or die within the Ahn."

More men joined me, still in their chains. They had come east from the farther portions of the wall. They had been abandoned by their guards. These wore even their chains as yet. We would remove them from them later with tools. These newcomers carried, many of them, the iron bars used for chipping at the permafrost, and picks, and shovels. Two carried axes.

Now there were some three hundred and seventy men encircling the hall, all armed in one way or another, some even with stones. They were not in a pleasant mood.

"Do not fire the ball!" called Sorgus.

I ordered fires lit. Rags, soaked in oil, were set at the tips of arrows.

"How do I know you will let us leave, if we leave now, in peace?" he asked.

"I have pledged it," I said. "And I am of the warriors."

"How do we know you are of the warriors?" he asked.

"Send forth your best swordsman," I said, "that my caste may be made clear to you."

I waited.

No one emerged from the hall.

"I shall wait one Ehn," I said. "Then I shall have the hall fired."

In a few moments I heard her screaming, from within the hall. "No, no," she cried. "Fight to the death! Fight to the death!"

I knew then I had won.

Sorgus emerged from the hall, his hands raised, his sword slung still at his hip.

I watched Sorgus and his men depart.

"I am a free prisoner," she said. "I demand all the rights and privileges of such a prisoner."

"Free these new men of their chains," I said, indicating those fellows who had recently joined us, from the western portions of the wall.

"Yes, Captain," said a man.

I turned to the fair captive.

"I am a free prisoner," she said, "and I—"

"Be silent, I said to her. Her own dagger was at her throat.

"You were once in command here," I said. "But that is now finished. You are now only a girl on Gor."

She looked at me, suddenly frightened.

"When are the tarnsmen due?" I asked.

"Soon," she said.

A man pulled back her head, by the hair. I laid the blade across her throat.

"Four days," she whispered. "They are due to return on the afternoon of the first day of the passage hand."

"Put her in the handle tie," I said. "Yes, Captain," said the man, grinning.

Her fur boots were pulled off and her ankles were linked by leather thongs; she had good ankles; the leather permitted them a separation of some twelve inches; the tether on her wrists then was taken between her legs and lifted up and behind her, where its loose end was tied about her neck. The linking of the ankles prevents the slipping of the handle tie, and controls the length of her stride when she is put in it. A given pressure on the handle tie, exerted through the strap at the back, permits it to function as a choke leash; a different pressure permits her to be hurried along on her toes. The handle tie is usually, of course, reserved for naked slave girls.

"Oh," she said.

The man had looped his fist twice in the strap, tightening it.

She looked at me. She was in the control of the man who held the strap.

"If the tarnsmen return before the afternoon of the first day of the passage hand," I said, handing the man who controlled her her dagger, "cut her throat."

"Yes, Captain," he said.

"Oh," she cried, being hurried from the presence of men. Did she not know she was now only a girl on Gor?

"We have much to do," I told my men. "The wall is to be destroyed. After that you may divide what supplies and treasures exist here and take your leave. Any who leave before the work is done, trailed and recaptured, are to be staked out among the fallen tabuk."

The men looked at one another, uneasily. They did not care to become feasting meat for the scavenging jards.

"We are hungry," said a man.

"Imnak," said I, "go to the platform. Keep watch. You shall be relieved in two Ahn."

He grunted and went to the platform.

"We are hungry," said men.

"I, too," said I. "Make a feast, but there is to be no drinking of paga. It is late now for commencing our labors. Morning for such work will be soon enough."

173

There was a cheer.

In the morning they would work with a hearty will. I did not think it would take long to destroy the wall, surely not more than the days to the first passage hand. We had more than three hundred and fifty men for work. In many places, too, the wall had been weakened by the buffeting ta-buk over the past weeks.

I heard the miserable cries of two girls. A man was coming from the cook shack, where Thimble and Thistle had hidden themselves. He now dragged them before us, bent over, a hand in the hair of each.

"What have we here!" cried a man cheerfully.

"Slaves!" cried others.

"Hold," said I. "We are honest men, and are not thieves. Release them."

The man loosed the hair of the girls. Swiftly they knelt, frightened.

"These girls," said I, "belong to Imnak."

"He is a red hunter," said a man.

"He is one with us," I said.

There was an angry cry.

I drew my blade. "None may use them without his permission," I said. "I shall maintain discipline, if need be, my comrades, by the blade."

I looked down at the kneeling girls. "There are many men here," I said. "Doubtless they are quite hungry. Perhaps you should consider scurrying to the cook shack, to be about your duties."

"Yes, Master!" they cried.

"Pull down your camisks," I warned them.

Weeping they fled to the cook shack, trying with their small hands to adjust their garments so that they would reveal less of their beauty. The men roared with laughter. I smiled. The brief, open-sided camisks they wore had not been designed to permit a girl much success in such a project.

"We are now alone," I told her.

It was early afternoon, on the first day of the passage hand.

"All alone?" she asked.

"Yes," I said.

"Completely?" she asked.

"Yes," I said.

"Where have the men gone?" she asked.

"The work is finished," I said. "The wall, burned and

174

uprooted, has been destroyed. Other buildings, too, with the exception of this hall, have been fired. The laborers, in various groups, laden with goods and gold, have filtered away, scattering, returning to the south."

"They have taken my gold?" she asked. She was sitting at the side of the hall, her back against its wall of horizontally fitted logs. Her ankles were drawn up. The same thongs which, looped about her stomach and threaded through a ring behind her, holding her to the wall, led to her ankles, drawing them back. The original thongs on her ankles, which had served as leather ankle shackles, I had had removed. She still wore, however, the tether on her wrists, the loose end of which had been taken up behind her and tied about her neck, the handle portion of the handle tie.

"Ten strongboxes were found," I said, "and forced open. Their contents were divided. Few men are discontent to have earned fees so rich for their services."

"I am now without economic resources," she said.

"You are pretty," I said, "perhaps men might be persuaded to let you live."

"You are a beast!" she said.

"Captured guardsmen and hunters," I said, "released, given supplies, have also taken their way south."

"You are generous," she said.

"Sometimes," I said. "—with men."

She shrank back in her bonds.

"They labored well with the others to destroy the wall," I said.

"What of the red hunter?" she asked.

"He alone, of all who worked at the wall," I said, "treks northward."

"What of the two girls?" she asked.

"He drives his pretty beasts before him," I said. Imnak had fashioned a sled, which would be of use in crossing Ax Glacier. Thimble and Thistle drew it now across the tundra toward the snows. Before he had left he had had them sew northern garments for themselves, under his instruction. From the furs and hides among the spoils at the wall they had cut and sewn for themselves stockings of lart skin, and shirts of hide, and a light and heavy parka, each hooded and rimmed with lart fur. Too, they had made the high fur boots of the northern woman and the brief panties of fur, to which the boots, extending to the crotch, reach. On the hide shirts and parkas he had made them sew a looped design of stitching at the left shoulder, which represented binding fiber.

175

This designated the garments as those of beasts. A similar design appeared on each of the other garments. About their throats now, too, they wore again the four looped strings, each differently knotted, by means of which a red hunter might, upon inspection, determine that their owner was Imnak. This morning Imnak, walking behind and to one side of the sled, had left the camp's area. Because it was warm he had not permitted the girls to wear their hide shirts or parkas. Northern women often do not do so in warm weather. When he had cracked his whip they had put their shoulders to the traces. The sled was heavily laden, but with little gold. More significant to Imnak had been sugars and Bazi tea, and furs and tools. Interestingly he had also placed much wood on the sled, both boards and poles, for it is of great value in the north. Wood can be used for sleds, and tent frames and the frames of kayaks and umiaks, the large, broad vessels which can hold several individuals, sometimes used in whaling. Trees do not flourish in the land of Imnak and their needs for wood must largely be satisfied by occasional finds at the shore, driftwood, from hundreds of pasangs south, dragged from the chilled water. Imnak's whip cracked and she who had been Barbara Benson, a middle-class girl, and she who had been the rich, upper-class Audrey Brewster, now Thimble and Thistle, cried out and began to draw their master's sled. I watched them leave. Both were now leveled women. Both would now have to compete in absolute equality, beginning at the same point, neither with an advantage, as pure females, and as slaves, for the favor of men. I did not know which might be more pleasing. In time I thought both might prove superb.

Sidney Anderson, tied sitting at the wall, looked up at me. "You, too," she said, "had better flee."

"The laborers," I said, "have not fled. They are simply returning to their homes."

"You have remained behind," she said.

"Of course," I said.

"I do not understand," she said. Then she said, "Do not touch me!"

I released her from the wall and removed the thongs, too, which had held her ankles. I pulled her to her feet. I slipped my fist into the handle of the tie she wore and, looping it about my fist twice, tightening it, thrust her before me toward the door of the hall.

"Where are you taking me?" she asked.

I tightened the tie more. "Oh!" she said. Then she was

quiet. She bit her trembling lip. Outside I scanned the skies. They were clear.

Sidney Anderson looked about. Buildings were burned. No one was in sight. The wall had been destroyed. The platform, too, had been pulled down, and had then been burned. Ashes were about, and debris, and turf cut by the feet of many men.

I thrust her before me, toward the whipping platform, which I had ordered remain intact.

"What are you going to do?" she asked.

"Tarnsmen," I said, "will soon be here, will they not?"

"Yes," she said, angrily. "What are you going to do?"

I thrust her up the steps, onto the platform. "You are going to serve Priest-Kings, my pretty little charmer," I told her.

I removed the tether from her throat and, bringing it between her legs and before her, tossed it through the ring on the crossbeam.

"Oh," she said.

I drew her from her feet, and hung her by her bound wrists from the ring.

I then crossed her ankles and, with a peice of rope, tied them together, and fastened them to the lower ring, that fastened in the floor of the whipping-frame platform.

I pulled back the hood from the furs she wore. The auburn hair took the sun beautifully.

I scanned the skies again. There was nothing in sight, save clouds.

"How am I to serve Priest-Kings?" she asked, wincing.

"As naked bait," I told her.

"No!" she said. I cut the furs from her. "You are quite beautiful," I told her.

"No, no!" she wept.

I regarded her. "You are even beautiful enough to be a Gorean slave girl," I said.

"No!" she cried.

"Those who brought you to Gor," I said, "doubtless had that fate eventually in mind for you."

"That is a lie!" she said.

"It would have been easy enough to find ugly women," I said.

"No," she said. "No!"

"You are too beautiful to be long left free," I said.

"No!" she said.

177

"It is my conjecture," I said, "that you were eventually to be given to Drusus."

"Given?" she said.

"Of course," I said, "as a slave."

"No!" she cried.

"You are indeed naive," I said. "Do you think a woman as beautiful as you on Gor could long keep out of the collar?"

She looked at me with horror. I gagged her, that she might not cry out.

The tarnsmen were wary. There were five of them. They circled the area several times.

They would have little difficulty, even from their distance aloft, in identifying the lovely captive suspended from the ring. There were few white girls this far north, above Torvaldsland, at the brink of Ax Glacier. Her auburn hair, too, would leave little doubt as to her identity. Such hair, as I have noted, is rare on Gor.

They would see the girl. They would see the destruction of the wall, and of the buildings, except for the hall.

Then one would land, to reconnoiter.

It was his tarn that would serve me.

I fitted an arrow, of black tem-wood, with a pile point, to the string of the yellow bow. The string was of hemp, whipped with silk. The arrow was winged with the feathers of the Vosk gull.

"Beware!" she cried, as soon as the gag was cut from her mouth. "One remains! One remains!" But I do not think he heard her. She screamed, and he spun back, falling from the platform to the turf. At the same time I, casting the bow aside, began the race for the tarn. I leaped into the saddle and dragged back fiercely on the one-strap. The winged monster screamed with rage and reared upward, wings cracking like whips at the air. I leaned to one side as the raking talons of a second tarn tore downward for me. I dragged back again on the one-strap, almost throwing the bird on its back, bringing its talons high. I almost lost the saddle as my bird, struck by the next tarn, reeled buffeted, twisting backward, some forty feet in the air. Then, both birds, screaming, talons interlocked, grappled in the air. The bolt of a crossbow sped past my head. Another tarn closed in from my left. I tore the shield from its saddle straps and blocked the raking talons that furrowed the leather. The fourth tarn was below us. I saw the man thrust up with his spear. It cut my leg. I wheeled the tarn to the left and it spun, still interlocked with

178

its foe. The tarnsman to my left drew back on the one-strap to avoid fouling straps with his ally. The fellow whose tarn was tearing at mine drew back, too, on his six-strap, and the bird swept upward and away, from my right. A bolt from a crossbow skidded ripping through the saddle to my left. Then he who had fired it swept past behind me. My tarn was then loose. The four of them, now grouped, in formation, ascended in an arc some hundred yards from me. I took my tarn higher, swiftly, to be above them. Then the sun was behind me and they were below me. They broke apart and began to circle, separately. They had no wish to meet me falling upon them from the tarn's ambush, the sun. I kept them generally below me. I fastened the safety strap now. I examined the shield. It was torn deeply but still serviceable. There was a spear at the saddle. I loosened it in its straps. A crossbow hung to my right. A sheaf of bolts was behind the saddle. I saw the girl, suspended from the ring, far below. Suddenly I laughed with elation. I pulled back on the one-strap again. I would wait for them in the clouds.

The moons of Gor were high when I returned to the sturdy platform.

The hunt had been long. It had carried for several pasangs. Two had been foolish enough to follow me into the clouds. The other two had fled. I had not managed to overtake them until late afternoon. They had fought desperately, and well.

"You have escaped," she said, in wonder. "There were four of them."

My tarn, now, was weak and bloodied. I did not know if it would live.

In the end they had struck at the bird. It was shortly after that that I had finished the hunt.

"You had best flee," she said, "before they return."

"Do you think they will rescue you?" I asked.

"Surely," she said.

I was weary. I put my hand on her body. It was the first time that I had touched her. She was really quite beautiful.

"Do not touch me!" she hissed.

"Do you still hope for succor?" I asked.

"Of course!" she said. Then she screamed as I threw the four heads to the turf. I was weary then, and I had lost blood, from the wound in my leg, so I turned away, descended the steps of the whipping platform, and made my way to the hall, where I would sleep.

"You are a barbarian! A barbarian!" she screamed.

I did not answer her but entered the hall, to rest, for I was weary.

In the morning I was much refreshed.

The sun was high and bright, and I had fed well, and had rigged a backpack, in which I had placed supplies and my things, when I again climbed the steps to the whipping platform.

The girl was unconscious. I slapped her awake.

"I am leaving now," I told her.

She looked at me, dully. I looked away from her, out over the tundra, the loneliness, the blackened remains of the scattered logs which had been the wall, the ruined buildings. I would fire the hall, too, before I left. There is a bleakness to the north which, in its harsh way, can be very beautiful. It was chilly. A dust of snow had fallen in the night. I saw a group of five tabuk, stragglers, cross the line that had been the wall. They would follow the herd north. They would be unaware that there had ever been an impediment to their journey. I watched them pick their way through burned logs and, in their characteristic gait, turn northward. One stopped to nuzzle at the turf, pushing back snow with its nose, to bite at moss.

"Are you going to leave me here, to die?" she asked.

I cut her down, and cut the bonds on her wrists and ankles. She sank to the wood of the platform. It was coated with crystals of snow. She clutched the furs there to her. I had yesterday cut them from her.

I then descended the steps of the platform. In a few moments I had set fire to the hall.

As I stood before the burning edifice I turned once to look at the platform. She knelt there, small, the furs clutched to her.

She was an enemy.

I turned away, northward. I, too, would follow the herd.

I did not look back.

Toward noon I stopped to make a camp. I ate dried meat. I watched the small figure some two hundred yards behind me slowly approach.

When she was some three or four yards from me she stopped. I regarded her.

She knelt. "Please," she said.

I threw some meat to the snow before her and, eagerly, she ate it.

The beauty was ravenous. "Please," she begged, "give me more."

"Crawl to me on your belly in the snow," I told her.

"Never," she said.

I continued to eat.

Then I reached down to where her head, as I sat cross-legged, lay in the snow by my knee. She was on her belly. "Please," she begged. "Please."

I thrust meat in her mouth. Gratefully she ate it. In time she looked up at me. "You made me crawl to you on my belly," she said, resentfully.

I stood up. I must be on my way.

"I never thought I would meet a man so strong," she said. She shuddered. I thought it must be from cold.

"The tarn?" she asked.

"It was weak," I said. "I freed it."

"You are going north," she said.

"I have business in the north," I said.

"You will go afoot?" she asked.

"Yes," I said.

"You will have little chance to survive," she said.

"I will live on the herd," I said. "The only danger, as I see it, will be the winter."

In such times even groups of the red hunters sometimes perished.

"Do not follow me further," I said.

"I cannot live alone in the north," she said. "I would surely fail to reach the south safely."

I thought her assessment of the situation accurate.

"Panther Girls," I said, "such as, here and there, frequent the northern forests, might survive."

"I am not a Panther Girl," she said.

I looked at her kneeling in the snow at my feet, her small, trim figure, her soft, sweet exquisite curves, her delicately beautiful throat and face, the pleading blue eyes, the lush wealth of auburn hair loose behind her naked shoulders.

"That is true," I said. I looked upon her. Her body, so helpless and exquisitely feminine, seemed made for rapacious seizure at the hands of a rude master. Her face, vulnerable and delicate, would be easy to read. Tears might swiftly be brought to her eyes by a word, or fear to those lovely features, by as little as an imperial gesture. I considered whether it would be worth while teaching her the collar.

"I am an Earth girl," she said.

I nodded. She knew nothing of woodcraft or of survival. She was alone on a harsh world.

"You are an enemy," I told her.

"Do not leave me," she begged. She swallowed hard. "Without a man to feed and protect me," she said, "I will die."

I recalled how she had responded when, before I had won my freedom, I had informed her that the red hunters might starve, if the tabuk were not permitted to continue their northward migration.

"It is not my concern," she had said.

"Please," she said, looking up at me.

"It is not my concern," I said.

"Oh, no!" she wept. "Please!"

"Do not attempt to follow me," I said. "If you persist, I shall bind you, hand and foot, and leave you in the snow."

"I am pretty," she said. "I know that I am pretty." She looked up at me, tears in her eyes. "Might not men be persuaded," she asked, "to let me live?"

I smiled, recalling what once I had suggested to her.

"Please," she begged.

"You do not know of what you speak," I laughed. "You are only an ignorant Earth girl."

"Teach me," she begged.

She put her arms to her sides and lifted her body before me.

"What a salacious tart you are," I said.

Tears formed in her eyes.

I considered to myself how she might look in a snatch of slave silk and a steel collar, one bearing a master's name. The prospect was not completely displeasing.

"Assume attitudes and postures," I said to her. "Try to interest me."

With a cry of misery she tried then to provoke my interest. She was clumsy but I learned, incontrovertibly, that which I had wished to determine. She who performed so desperately before me was a natural slave. I had thought this the first instant I had laid eyes on her. It was now confirmed beyond doubt. The insight, sensitivity, taste and lust of the Kur agents who had recruited her was surely to be commended.

"It is enough," I told her.

She lay at my feet in the snow, terrified.

"What do you feel like?" I asked.

"It is a strange feeling," she said. "I have never felt it before."

182

"It is the feeling of being a woman," I said.

She reached out to touch my ankle. "Please," she said, "take me with you."

I bent to her and began to tie together her ankles. "No!" she said. "Please! Please!"

Her ankles were tied.

"No!" she said.

"I do not wish the inconvenience in the north," I said, "of bothering with a free woman."

I knotted her hands behind her back.

"I do not ask to come with you as a free woman!" she cried.

"Oh?" I asked.

"No!" she said.

"Do you know the meaning of your words, foolish girl?" I asked.

"Yes," she wept.

"You would dare to be a slave?" I asked.

"Yes," she whispered. I wondered at her words. Did she not know the hopelessness, the completeness, of being a slave girl on Gor? If she did not, she would learn.

I rose to my feet.

She struggled to her knees, her ankles crossed and bound, her hands tied behind her. "I beg to be a slave," she wept.

I looked down upon her.

"I know," she said, "that with a man of your strength I could never be anything but a slave."

"To any Gorean male," I said.

"Yes, yes," she said.

I freed her ankles of the bonds and freed her hands, but then retied her hands before her body. I knelt her before me, knees wide, back on her heels, arms lifted and raised, her head down, between her bound arms.

"Are you familiar with any of the rituals of enslavement?" I asked.

"I, Sidney Anderson, of Earth," she said, "submit myself to Tarl Cabot, of Gor, as a slave, completely, his to do with as he pleases."

I saw that she had been curious as to what it would be like to be a slave. She had inquired into this matter. It was an excellent sign.

She was then a beautiful, little exquisite brute at my feet, a slave animal.

I took a length of binding fiber and knotted it, with capture knots, about her throat. It was her collar. Too, the capture knots, those of a warrior, would serve to identify her as mine in the north.

She looked up at me, frightened, a slave.

"Kiss my feet," I told her.

She bent her head to my feet and, through the fur of my boots, I felt her lips press against them. She then, timidly, tears in her eyes, lifted her head.

I put my hands in her hair. She must regard me. "You are Arlene," I told her.

She shook with emotion.

"Lift your wrists," I said.

She did so.

I freed her of the binding fiber on her wrists, and returned it to my pack.

"I have never had a girl's name before," she said.

"You are now only a girl," I told her.

"Yes," she whispered.

"Yes, what?" I asked.

"Yes," she whispered, "—Master."

I then threw her to her back in the snow, that I might begin to teach her the meaning of her collar.

12 I TENT WITH IMNAK AT THE GATHERING OF THE PEOPLE; I ADVANCE ARLENE A BIT IN HER TRAINING

"Put them on, Slave Girl," said Thimble, not pleasantly.

"Yes, Mistress," said Arlene. In the hide tent she slipped into the brief fur panties worn by the women of the north. She had been forced to sew them herself, under the direction of Thimble and Thistle. At the left hip they bore the sign of the looped binding fiber, sewn in them with red-dyed sinew, which identified them as the garment of one who was an owned beast.

Imnak and I sat across from one another, both crosslegged. He dropped a tiny bone to the fur mat between us.

Each player, in turn, drops a bone, one of several in his supply. The bone Imnak had dropped was carved in the shape of a small tabuk. Each of the bones is carved to resemble an animal, such as an arctic gant, a northern bosk, a lart, a tabuk or sleen, and so on. The bone which remains upright is the winner. If both bones do not remain upright there is no winner on that throw. Similarly, if both bones should remain upright, they are dropped again. A bone which does not remain upright, if its opposing bone does remain upright, is placed in the stock of him whose bone remained upright. The game is finished when one of the two players is cleaned out of bones.

"Pull on the stockings," said Thimble to Arlene. Arlene did so. The stockings were of lart fur. Each, in its side, wore the sign of the looped binding fiber. "Now," said Thimble, "the boots." In cold weather a layer of grass, for warmth, for insulation, changed daily, is placed in the bottom of the boots, between the inside sole of the boot and the foot of the stocking. Arlene now, of course, did not bother with this. The best harvests of grass for use in this way occur, naturally, at the foot of the bird cliffs. Arlene drew on the high boots. They reached to her crotch. It was a hot crotch, as I had determined, a superb crotch for a slave girl. The fur trim at their top touched the panties. She was stripped from the waist up. Many of the women of the red hunters, too, went about so, inside and outside the tents, in the warmer weather. They, of course, being free, did not have leather, like Arlene, or bondage strings, like Thimble and Thistle, at their throats. Similarly, their garments did not bear the slave marks of the looped binding fiber. Such marks, of course, were not necessary, in the north, for determining what Thimble, and Thistle and Arlene were. Even the leather or bondage strings at their throats were not necessary for that purpose. Their white skins alone, as they were females, identified them as slave beasts.

The tiny tabuk which Imnak had dropped remained standing upright.

I took my eyes from Arlene. What a lovely catch she had been!

I had not yet bothered to teach her complete slavery. I was in no hurry. Let her retain for a time a shred of her pride and dignity. I could always rip it from her when I wished, or when she herself should beg me to take it from her.

"Try on the shirt, Slave Girl," said Thimble.

Arlene drew on the hide shirt. At the left shoulder, prominently, it bore the sign of the looped binding fiber. I glanced at her and she straightened her body, but then tossed her

185

head and looked away, as though disdaining to take cognizance of my appraisal. The shirt fell nicely from her breasts, standing as she was. She was exquisitely figured. She stood as few Earth girls would have dared to, displaying her beauty, though she appeared to be completely disinterested in any such objective. I smiled to myself. She was discovering her sexuality. She looked at me, and then, quickly, looked away. I wondered if she knew she was being brought along slowly as a slave. Sometimes I read in her eyes a look that said, "I can resist you," and, at other times, a look that said, "I begin to sense and fear what you might do to me. Please be kind, Master." Once she had said to me, angrily, "You are dallying with me, aren't you, Master?" "Perhaps," I had told her. "Perhaps, Slave Girl."

I dropped the tiny carved tabuk I held. It, too, remained upright.

Imnak picked up his tiny carved tabuk and held it over the fur mat,

Arlene made a small noise. I sensed that she was angry that I no longer looked upon her.

Was she not sufficiently beautiful? She had a girl's vanity. Did she not yet know she was a slave, and that she might account herself fortunate should a free man so much as glance in her direction?

"Try on the first parka," said Thimble.

Arlene slipped it on, over the head, as such garments, like northern garments generally, are donned.

"Hood," said Thimble.

Arlene lifted the hood and placed it properly.

"Do I please you, Master?" asked Arlene. She wished attention.

I looked up. Her face was very beautiful, rimmed in the lart fur trimming the hood.

"It is very nice," I said.

"Thank you, Master," she said, acidly.

"Put on the second parka and its hood," said Thimble. Arlene complied. Both the parkas bore, at their left shoulder, the design of looped binding fiber, identifying them as the garments of slaves.

"Master?" asked Arlene.

"Excellent," I said. "The garments are superb, and you are very beautiful in them."

She flushed. "Thank you, Master," she said. Then she said, acidly, "A girl is pleased if her master is pleased."

"It is well," I said, soberly. She trembled, momentarily.

"Take them off," said Thimble, "all of them, everything, except the leather on your throat."

"Yes, Mistress," said Arlene.

Arlene stripped herself, to the leather collar, in Imnak's hide tent. Thimble and Thistle were also naked. All were girls, only slave beasts in the tent of their masters.

I dropped the tiny carved tabuk which was mine, that which was my piece in the game. It did not land upright.

"I have won," said Imnak.

"What are you gambling about?" asked Arlene. She was folding her garments.

"Put away the garments," I said, "drop to all fours, and come here."

Arlene put the folded garments to one side in the tent, and, in fury, on her hands and knees, crawled to where we had played.

I put my hand in her hair and pulled her to her stomach. "Here she is," I told Imnak.

"Master!" she cried.

Imnak took her and turned her over, pulling her on her back across his legs.

"Master!" cried Arlene.

"Imnak has won your use, until he chooses to leave the tent," I told her. "Obey him as though he were your own master."

"Please, no!" she cried.

"Obey him," I said, sternly, "as though he were your own master."

"Yes, Master," she said, miserably.

Imnak then dragged her to the side of the hide tent.

Perhaps I was struck most by the absence of trees.

Some five days after I had acquired the slave girl, Arlene, following the herd of Tancred, generally climbing, I came to the edge of Ax Glacier. There I found the camp of Imnak, and Thimble and Thistle.

"I have been waiting for you," had said Imnak. "I thought you would come."

"Why did you think this?" I had asked.

"I saw the furs and supplies you put aside for yourself when we were near the wall," he said. "You have business in the north."

"It is true," I said.

He did not ask me my business. He was a red hunter. If I wished to tell him, he knew that I would. I decided that I would speak to him later. In my pouch was the small carving, in bluish stone, of the head of a Kur, one with an ear half torn away.

"I had hoped you would wait for me," I said. "It might be difficult otherwise for one such as myself to cross the ice."

I knew that he had watched me prepare my pack.

Imnak grinned. "It was you," said he, "who freed the tabuk." Then he turned to his girls. "Break camp," he had told them. "I am anxious to go home."

With Imnak's help we would cross Ax Glacier and find the Innuit, as they called themselves, a word which, in their own tongue, means "the People." I recalled that in the message of Zarendargar he had referred to himself as a war general of the "People." He had meant, of course, I assumed, his own people, or kind. Various groups are inclined to so identify themselves. It is an arrogance which is culturally common. The Innuit do not have "war generals." War, in its full sense, is unknown to them. They live generally in scattered, isolated communities. It is as though two families lived separated in a vast remote area. There would be little point and little likelihood to their having a war. In the north one needs friends, not enemies. In good years, when the weather is favorable, there tends to be enough sleen and tabuk, with careful hunting, to meet their needs. One community is not likely to be much better or worse off than another. There is little loot to be acquired. What one needs one can generally hunt or make for oneself. There is little point in stealing from someone what one can as simply acquire for oneself. Within given groups, incidentally, theft is rare. The smallness of the groups provides a powerful social control. If one were to steal something where would one hide or sell it? Besides, if one wished something someone else owned and let this be known, the owner would quite possibly give it to you, expecting, of course, to receive as valuable a gift in return. Borrowing, too, is prevalent among the red hunters. The loan of furs, tools and women is common.

I looked downward, out across the ice of Ax Glacier. Beyond it lay the polar basin.

The north is a hard country. When one must apply oneself almost incessantly to the tasks of survival there is little time to indulge oneself in the luxury of conquest.

Thimble and Thistle dismantled the hides and poles of Imnak's tent, and began to load them on the sled.

Violence, of course, is not unknown among the Innuit. They are men.

188

Aside, however, from considerations such as the fewness, comparatively, of their numbers, and their geographical separation, and the pointlessness of an economics of war in their environment, the Innuit seem, also, culturally, or perhaps even genetically, disposed in ways which do not incline one to organized, systematic group violence. For example, they seem generally to be a kindly, genial folk. Hostility seems foreign to them. Strangers are welcomed. Hospitality is generous, honest, open-hearted and sincere. Some animals, doubtless, have better dispositions than others. The Innuit, on the whole, seem to be happy, pleasant fellows. Perhaps that is why they live where they do. They have been unable, or unwilling, to compete with more aggressive groups. Their gentleness has resulted, it seems, in their being driven to the world's end. Where no others have desired to live the Innuit, sociable and loving, have found their bleak refuge.

Imnak's whip cracked down across the bare back of Thimble, the blond, who had been Barbara Benson, and she cried out and wept, "I hurry, Master!" She busied herself with loading the sled. Thistle, the dark-haired girl, who had once been the rich Audrey Brewster, hurried, too, lest it would be her own back which next would feel the lash.

The red hunters, though a genial folk, keep their animals under a firm discipline.

"I see you, too, have a beast," he said, looking beyond me to the lovely Arlene.

She stood back, in the light snow, frightened of the red hunter. She wore a sleeveless jacket of fur, belted with binding fiber, which depended to her knees; fur leggings; and skins wrapped and tied on her feet. I had improvised these garments for her. I looked at her. She did not even know enough to kneel.

"Those garments," said Imnak, "will be insufficient in the north."

"Perhaps you could teach her," I suggested, "to sew herself more adequate clothing."

"I have showed my girls," he said. "They will teach her."

"Thank you," I said.

It was rather beneath the dignity of a man to show a girl how to sew. Imnak had done this with Thimble and Thistle and did not wish to repeat the task. It is enough for a girl to teach a girl to sew.

"I see you have leather on your throat," said Thimble to Arlene.

"I see your breasts are uncovered," said Arlene to Thimble.

189

"Remove your jacket," I told Arlene. Angrily, she did so. Imnak's pupils dilated. He would welcome this lovely she in our small herd.

"Into the traces," said Imnak.

Thimble and Thistle bent down and each looped the broad band of her trace across her body.

"You are animals, aren't you?" called Arlene to them.

"Can you rig another trace?" I asked Imnak.

"Of course," he said.

Soon Arlene, too, to her fury, stood in harness.

Imnak cracked his whip over their heads and they threw their weight against the traces and the long, narrow, freighted sled eased upward, over the rocks, and then slid down onto the ice of Ax Glacier. Imnak and I held the rear of the sled that it not move too rapidly downward. The ice of Ax Glacier, where we crossed it, had been cut by the countless hooves of the herd of Tancred, leaving a trial of marked ice more than one hundred and fifty yards wide. We would follow the herd.

It took ten days to cross Ax Glacier. There are many glacial lines among the rocks and mountains of the north, but Ax Glacier is easily the broadest and most famous. These glaciers, like frozen rivers or lakes of ice, or emptying seas, depend to the shores of Thassa, seeking her, flowing some few feet a year, imperceptibly like stone, to her chill waters. More than once we heard gigantic crashes as hundreds of feet or more of ice broke away from the glacial edge and tumbled roaring into the sea. It is thus, of course, that icebergs are formed. These great pieces and mountains of ice, shattering from the brinks of Ax Glacier and her smaller sisters, in time, drifting, carried by currents, would reach the northern sea, that eastward-reaching extension of Thassa rimming the polar basin. It was in that northern, or polar, sea that there was said to exist, if it were not myth or invention, the "mountain that did not move," that iceberg which, in defiance of tide, wind and current, stood immobilely fixed. Sometimes we could see, from where we stood, the sea, with these great pieces of ice within it. Some of these pieces of ice reared more than a thousand feet into the air. Sometimes they are even miles long. Their occasional vastnesses, and the might of the forces that have formed them, become even more impressive when it is understood that what one can see above the surface does little more than hint at what lies below. The fresh-water ice from which such blocks are formed

190

is less dense than the salt water in which they float, weighing only about seven eighths as much. Thus, in a given piece of such ice, there is some seven times more beneath the surface than appears visible above it. These pieces of ice, like moving, drifting reefs, can be hazardous to shipping. The smaller ones, especially at night, can be particularly dangerous. Gorean ships, however, seldom run afoul of them. They are, generally, very shallow-drafted, which permits them to come much closer to such ice without the danger that would threaten deeper-keeled craft; too, the Gorean ship, because of the shallow draft, can occasionally run up on such ice, sliding onto it, rather than breaking apart when it strikes it; too, the Gorean vessel, because it is usually light in weight, tends to be extremely responsive to its helm or helms, this permitting such obstacles to be avoided on shorter notice than would be possible with a heavier more sluggish vessel; too, Gorean vessels, except when manned by those of Torvaldsland and the northern islands, usually beach at night; thus, when visibility is poor, they are not abroad; if they do not beach they will sometimes lower their masts and yards and throw over their anchors; that most Gorean ships are oared vessels, too, gives the crewmen recourse in an emergency; they are not at the mercy of the wind and they can, if necessary, back the ship off the ice; lastly, few Gorean ships ply the northern waters in the months of darkness; sufficiently far north, of course, the sea freezes in the winter. A much greater danger to Gorean shipping than the iceberg is the sea itself, when it begins to freeze. A ship caught in the ice, if not constantly cut and chopped free, its men on the ice itself, can become solidly frozen, arrested, in the ice; then it is at the mercy of pressures and bucklings; the ice, grinding, shifting, can shatter a ship, breaking it apart like a lacing of frozen, brittle twigs.

"Har-ta!" said Imnak to the girls. "Har-ta!" The expression 'Har-ta' is Gorean. "Faster! Faster!" He spoke sometimes to them in his own tongue, and sometimes in Gorean. Imnak himself spoke fair Gorean. He had traded furs and skins south more than once. Many of the red hunters cannot speak Gorean.

Imnak and I, too, applied our strength to the haul, thrusting at the wooden uprights at the back of the sled.

Imnak wished Thimble and Thistle to know Gorean. Would a white trader not pay more to rent one if she could understand his commands?

The nose of the sled tipped upward and then fell to the

level on the glacial pebbles, and Ax Glacier, like the broad blade of a Torvaldsland ax, lay behind us.

"Har-ta!" called Imnak. Again we trekked.

There are tiers of mountains, interlaced chains of them, both east of Torvaldsland and north of her. Ax Glacier lies in one valley between two of these chains. These chains, together, are sometimes called the Hrimgar Mountains, which, in Gorean, means the Barrier Mountains. They are surely not a barrier, however, in the sense that the Voltai Mountains, or even the Thentis Mountains or Ta-Thassa Mountains, are barriers. The Hrimgar Mountains are not as rugged or formidable as any of these chains, and they are penetrated by numerous passes. One such pass, through which we trekked, is called the pass of Tancred, because it is the pass used annually by the migration of the herd of Tancred.

Four days after leaving the northern edge of Ax Glacier, we climbed to the height of the pass of Tancred, the mountains of the Hrimgar flanking us on either side. Below the height, the pass sloping downward, we could see the tundra of the polar plain. It is thousands of pasangs in width, and hundreds in depth; it extends, beyond horizons we could see, to the southern edge of the northern, or polar, sea.

I think this was a moving moment for Imnak. He stopped on the height of the pass, and stood there, for a long time, regarding the vastness of the cool tundra.

"I am home," he said.

Then we eased the sled downward.

I suppose I was not watching well where I was going. I was watching the fellow being tossed in the fur blanket. The leather ball struck my back.

That was not all that struck my back. In a moment a small woman, a girl of the red hunters, fiery and very angry, was striking it. She stopped striking my back primarily because I turned to face her. She was then, however, striking my chest. After a time she stopped and, looking up at me, began to scold me vociferously.

I am pleased in some respects that words are less dangerous than arrows and daggers, else there surely would have been little left of me.

She finally grew weary of berating me. I gather she had done a good job of this from the interest and occasional commendations of the onlookers.

She looked at me, angrily. She wore the high fur boots and panties of the woman of the north. As it was, from their point of view, a hot day, one which was above the freezing point, she, like most of the women of the red hunters, was stripped to the waist. About her neck she wore some necklaces. She seemed pretty, but her temper might have shamed that of a she-sleen. The fur she wore, interestingly, was rather shabby. Her carriage and the sharpness of her tongue, however, suggested she must be someone of importance. I would later learn that the unmated daughters of even important men, namely, good hunters, were often kept in the poorest of furs. It is up to the mate, or husband, if you wish, to bring them good furs. This perhaps is intended as an encouragement to the girls to be a bit fetching, that they may attract a man and, subsequently, have something nice to wear. If this were the plan, however, clearly it had not yet worked in the case of my pretty critic. I was not surprised. It would be a bold fellow indeed who would dare to make her a present of fine feasting clothes.

She tossed her head and turned away. Her hair was worn knotted in a bun on the top of her head, like that generally of the women of the red hunters. Their hair is worn loose, interestingly, out of doors, only during their menstrual period. In a culture where the gracious exchange of mates is commonly practiced this device, a civilized courtesy, provides the husband's friends with information that may be pertinent to the timing of their visits. This culture signal, incidentally, is not applicable to a man's slaves in the north. Animals do not dress their hair and slaves, generally, do not either. Imnak sometimes did give Thimble and Thistle a red string to tie back their hair, but often he did not; he did with them what he pleased, and they did for him what they were told. He usually gave them the red string when he took them out with him, as a way of showing them off. Imnak had his vanities. I had not bothered to place Arlene under any strictures in these regards. Sometimes she wore her hair up, and sometimes let it fall loosely about her shoulders.

"You spoiled her kick," said a man to me, in Gorean.

"I am sorry," I said.

The girl, with other youths, had been playing a soccerlike game with the leather ball, with goals drawn in the turf. I had not realized, until too late, that I had been traversing the field of play.

"I am sorry," I said.

"She has a very loud mouth," said the man.

"Yes," I granted. "Who is she?"

"Poalu," he said, "the daughter of Kadluk." Red hunters,

193

though they are reticent to speak their own names, have little reservation about speaking the names of others. This makes sense, as it is not their name, and it is not as if, in their speaking it, the name might somehow escape them. This is also fortunate. It is sometimes difficult, if not impossible, to get one of these fellows to tell you his own name. Often one man will tell you the name of his friend, and his friend will tell you his name. This way you learn the name of both, but from neither himself. The names of the red hunters, incidentally, have meaning, but, generally, I content myself with reporting the name in their own language. 'Imnak,' for example, means "Steep Mountain"; 'Poalu' means "Mitten"; 'Kadluk' means "Thunder". I have spoken of "Thimble" and "Thistle." More strictly, their names were 'Pudjortok' and 'Kakidlarnerk'. However, since these names, respectively, would be 'Thimble' and 'Thistle', and Imnak often referred to them in Gorean as "Thimble" and "Thistle" I have felt it would be acceptable to use those latter expressions, they being simpler from the point of view of one who does not natively speak the tongue of the People, or Innuit.

"She is a beauty, is she not?" asked the man.

"Yes," I said. "Is it your intention to offer her bright feasting clothes?"

"I am not insane," he said. "Kadluk will never unload her."

I thought his assessment of the situation was perhaps true.

"Have you a friend who might know your name?" I asked.

He called to a fellow who was nearby. "Someone would like to know the name of someone," he said.

"He is Akko," said the man. He then left.

"I can speak my own name," I said to him. "I am from the south. Our names do not go away when we speak them."

"How do you know?" asked Akko.

"I will show you," I said. "My name is Tarl. Now listen." I waited a moment. "Tarl," I said. "See?"

"Interesting," granted Akko.

"My name did not go away," I said.

"Perhaps it came back quickly," he suggested.

"Perhaps," I said.

"In the north," he said, "we do not think one should take unnecessary risks."

"That is doubtless wise," I granted.

"Good hunting," he said.

"Good hunting," I said. He left. Akko, or Shirt Tail, was a good fellow.

I smelled roast tabuk.

The great hunt had been successful. I did not know if it were morning, or afternoon, or night. In these days the sun, low on the horizon, circles, it seems endlessly, in the sky.

Six days ago Imnak and I, and our girls, had descended from the height of the pass of Tancred. The great hunt had been already in progress. Hundreds of the women and children of the red hunters, fanned out for pasangs, shouting, beating on pans, had turned the herd toward the great alley of stone cairns. These cairns, of piled stone, each some four or five feet high, each topped with black dirt, form a long funnel, more than two pasangs in depth. The herd, which in the grazing on the tundra, has scattered is reformed to some extent by the drivers. It, or thousands of its animals, fleeing the drivers, pour toward the large, open end of the funnel. The stone cairns, which are perhaps supposed to resemble men, serve, perhaps psychologically, to fence in and guide the herd. The animals seem generally unwilling to break the imaginary boundary which might be projected between cairns. For example, the human seeing three dots spaced one way "sees" a line; seeing three dots spaced another way, he "sees" a triangle, and so on. One may fear to transgress a boundary which, in fact, exists only in one's mind. It is not an unusual human being who finds himself a prisoner in a cell which, if he but knew it, lacks walls. Whatever the explanation the tabuk, generally, will postpone breaking the "wall" as long as possible. They flee along the alley of cairns. At the end of the cairns, of course, they turn about, milling, and many are slain, until some, wiser or more panic-stricken than others, break loose and, nostrils wide, snorting, trot to freedom and the moss of the open tundra.

I watched two men wrestling.

I had not yet spoken to Imnak about the carving of bluish stone among my belongings, the carving of a Kur, with an ear half torn away.

I could see the blue line of the Hrimgar Mountains in the distance to the south. To the north the tundra stretched forth to the horizon.

Many people do not understand the nature of the polar north. For one thing, it is very dry. Less snow falls there generally than falls in most lower latitudes. Snow that does fall, of course, is less likely to melt. Most of the land is tundra, a cool, generally level or slightly wavy, treeless plain. In the summer this tundra, covered with mosses, shrubs and lichens, because of the melted surface ice and the permafrost beneath, preventing complete drainage, is soft and spongy. In the winter, of course, and in the early spring and late fall, desolate, bleak and frozen, wind-swept, it presents the aspect of a barren, alien landscape. At such times the red hunters will dwell by the sea, in the spring and fall by its shores, and, in the winter, going out on the ice itself.

I stepped aside to let a young girl pass, who carried two baskets of eggs, those of the migratory arctic gant. They nest in the mountains of the Hrimgar and in steep, rocky outcroppings, called bird cliffs, found here and there jutting out of the tundra. The bird cliffs doubtless bear some geological relation to the Hrimgar chains. When such eggs are frozen they are eaten like apples.

I saw a woman putting out a pan for a domestic snow sleen to lick clean.

In another place several women sat on a fur blanket playing a cat's cradle game. They were quite skilled. This game is generally popular in the Gorean north. It is played not only by the red hunters, but in Hunjer and Skjern, and in Torvaldsland, and as far south as the villages in the valley of the Laurius.

The tundra at this time of year belies its reputation for bleakness. In many places it bursts into bloom with small flowers. Almost all of the plants of this nature are perennials, as the growing season is too short to permit most annuals to complete their growing cycle. In the winter buds of many of these plants lie dormant in a fluffy sheath which protects them from cold. Some two hundred and forty different types of plants grow in the Gorean arctic within five hundred pasangs of the pole. None of these, interestingly, is poisonous, and none possesses thorns. During the summer plants and flowers will grow almost anywhere in the arctic except on or near the glacial ice.

At certain times in the summer even insects will appear, black, long-winged flies, in great swarms, coating the sides of tents and the faces of men.

Two children raced past me, playing tag.

I looked to the north. It was there that Zarendargar waited.

"Greetings, Master," said Thimble.

"Greetings," I said to her. She was dressed, save for her bondage strings, in much the same way as most of the women of the red hunters, bare-breasted, with high boots and panties. Thistle, however, behind her, was naked, in a northern yoke and on a leather leash. The northern yoke is either of wood or bone, and is drilled in three places. The

196

one Thistle wore was of wood. It was not heavy. It passed behind her neck at which point one of the drilled holes occurred. The other two holes occurred at the terminations of the yoke. A leather strap is knotted about the girl's wrist, passed through the drilled hole at one end of the yoke, usually that on her left, taken up through the hole behind the neck, looped twice about her neck, threaded back down through the center hole, taken up through the other hole at the end, usually the one at her right, and tied about her right wrist. She is thus fastened in the yoke. From each end of the yoke hung a large sack.

"We are going to pick moss and grass," she said. Moss is used as wicks for the lamps. Grass, dried, is used for insulation between the inner soles of the boots and the bottom of the fur stockings in the winter.

"That is good," I said. "Why is Thistle yoked?"

"It pleased me, Master," said Thimble, first girl. There was little love lost between the girls.

"Was she insubordinate?" I asked.

"She said a sharp word to me," said Thimble.

"Did you switch her, too?" I asked.

"Of course, Master," said Thimble.

"Excellent," I said. Discipline must be kept in the tent.

I looked at Thistle. She met my eyes, briefly, and then looked down. She was quite attractive. I had not as yet had either Thimble or Thistle.

"Is Imnak finished yet with the new slave girl?" I asked, referring to Arlene.

"I think so, Master," said Thimble, smiling. "At least he has tied her to a pole behind the tent."

"Why is that?" I asked.

"I do not think she is much good, Master," said Thimble, one slave girl appraising another.

"Do not let me detain you from your labors," I said.

Thistle, suddenly, knelt down before me, yoked, and put her lips to my boot. Her head was jerked up by the leash in the hand of Thimble. Her eyes were moist. "Master!" she begged.

"Come, Slave!" snapped Thimble, and pulled her to her feet and dragged her away, behind her. Thistle looked over her shoulder, at me. I gave no sign of response. She stumbled away, on Thimble's leash. I smiled to myself. Thistle, as I had expected, was the first of the girls to begin to understand and feel her slavery.

"Help us, Tarl," said Akko, whom I had met earlier in the day.

"He is a big fellow," said a man.

"Yes," said another.

I followed Akko and his friends to a place where two teams of men waited, a heavy, braided rope of twisted sleen-hide stretched between them.

They put me at the end of the rope. Soon, to the enthusiastic shouts of observers, we began the contest. Four times the rope grew taut, and four times our team won. I was much congratulated, and slapped on the back.

I was, accordingly, in a good mood when I returned to Imnak's tent.

"Greetings, my friend," I said. I had noted that Arlene, her wrists crossed and over her head, bound, was fastened to the horizontal pole of a meat rack, supported by its two tripods of inclined poles.

"Have you had a good day?" inquired Imnak, politely.

"Yes," I said.

"That is good," he said.

I waited a while. Then I said, "Have you had a good day?"

"Perhaps someone has not had a good day," said Imnak.

"I am sorry to hear that," I said.

"Perhaps someone who won a wager," he said, "is not well repaid for his having won."

"Oh?" I said.

"Sometimes," he said, "it is hardly worth winning." He shrugged.

"I will return in a moment," I said.

I went back of the tent to Arlene.

"I want to talk to you," she said. "I will have no more of this treatment on your part. You cannot simply give me to anyone you please."

"I did not hear you say, 'Master'," I said.

"Master," she said.

"You are never again," she said, "to give me to another man." Her eyes flashed.

"I gather Imnak was not pleased," I said.

"Imnak!" she cried.

"Yes, Imnak," I said. I reached up and cut her loose. I, with my left hand, then took her by the hair.

"Please, stop!" she said.

I turned her face to look at me. With my right hand I jerked the leather at her throat. "What is this?" I asked.

"A collar," she said.

198

"You are a slave," I said.

"Yes," she whispered, "Master," frightened.

I threw her to my feet and she looked up at me. "You will now crawl to Imnak," I said, "and beg to try and please him again. If he is not pleased, do you understand, I will feed you to the sleen."

"No, no!" she whispered.

"It is up to you, Slave Girl," I said. "For what do you think you are kept and fed?"

"No," she whispered.

I looked down at her.

"You would not," she whispered.

"I should have left you at the remains of the wall," I said.

"No," she whispered. Then she looked up at me, and reached out her hand. "Sometimes I feel so slave," she said. She touched my thigh with her finger tips. "Sometimes I feel I want your touch, and as a slave girl." I could scarcely hear her. "Your touch," she said, "not his."

"What you want is unimportant," I said. "If Imnak is not pleased," I said, "you will be fed to the sleen."

She looked up at me, in horror. "Would you do that?" she asked.

"Yes," I said.

"I do not even know how to please a man!" she wept.

"You are an intelligent woman," I said. "I suggest, if you wish to live, that you apply your intelligence to the task."

Her tears, her head down, shaking, fell into the turf.

"Do you obey your master?" I asked.

"Yes," she whispered. "I obey my master."

"On your belly," I told her.

On her belly she crawled to Imnak. No longer was she a commander among the agents of Kurii. She was now a naked slave girl obeying her master.

"Have you had a good day?" I later asked Imnak.

"Yes," he said, "I have had a good day."

"How is the auburn-haired slave beast?" I asked him.

"Splendid," he said. "But Thimble and Thistle are better."

I did not doubt but that this was true. But then they had been slaves longer, too.

"Make us tea, Arlene," I said.

"Yes, Master," she said. She was very pretty. I wondered what she would look like in a snatch of a slave silk, and a true collar.

Imnak, and Thimble and Thistle were asleep. Outside the low sun, as it did in the summer, circled the sky, not setting.

"Master," whispered Arlene.

"Yes," I said.

"May I share your sleeping bag?" she asked.

"Do you beg it?" I asked.

"Yes, Master," she said.

I permitted her to creep into the bag, beside me. I put my arm about her small body. Her head was on my chest.

"Today, you much increased your slavery over me, did you not?" she asked.

"Perhaps," I said.

"You forced me to crawl to a man and serve him," she said. "How strong you are," she said, wonderingly. She kissed me. "I did not know what it was like to be a slave," she said.

"You still do not know," I told her.

"But you are teaching me, aren't you?" she asked.

"Perhaps," I said.

"It is a strange feeling," she said, "being a slave."

"Does it frighten you?" I asked.

"Yes," she said, "it frightens me, terribly." I felt her hair on my chest. "One is so helpless," she said.

"You are not yet a true slave," I told her.

"Sometimes I sense," she said, "what it might be, to be a true slave."

"Oh?" I asked.

"Yes," she said.

"And it frightens you?" I asked.

"Yes," she said, "but, too, and this is frightening, too, I—" She was silent.

"Go on," I told her.

"Must I speak?" she asked.

"Yes," I told her.

"Too," she wept, "I—I find myself desiring it, intensely." I felt her tears. "How terrible I am!" she said.

"Such feelings are normal in feminine women," I told her. "Sometimes it takes courage to yield to them."

"I must try to fight these feelings," she said.

"As you wish," I said, "but in the end you will yield to them, either because you wish to do so or because I force you to do so."

"Oh?" she asked.

"Yes," I said, "in the end you will become a true slave."
She was silent.

"You were brought to Gor to be a slave," I said. "When

200

your tasks were finished at the wall, you would have been put in silk, collared and placed at a man's feet."

"Do you truly think so, Master?" she asked.

"Of course," I said. "Consider your beauty, and the nature of the men of Gor."

She shuddered. "I fear slavery, and myself," she said.

"You are a true slave," I told her.

"No," she said.

"Only you do not yet know it," I said.

"No," she said.

"Fight your feelings," I said.

"I will," she said.

"In the end it will do you no good," I said.

She was silent.

"You have been counter-instinctually conditioned," I said. "You have been programmed with value sets developed for competitive, territorial males. There are complex historical and economic reasons for this. Your society is not interested in the psycho-biological needs of human females. The machine is designed with its own best interests in mind, not those of its human components."

"I do not want to be a component in a machine," she said.

"Then," said I, "listen in the quiet for the beating of your own heart."

"It is hard to hear in the noise of the machine," she whispered.

"But it beats," I said. "Listen."

She kissed me, softly.

"You have been taught to function," I said, "not to be alive."

"How wrong it is to be alive!" she wept.

"Perhaps not," I suggested.

"I dare not be true to myself," she said.

"Why not?" I asked.

"Because I think," she whispered, "deep within me, there lies a slave."

"One day you will be awakened," I said, "and will discover that it is you yourself who are that slave."

"Oh, no," she said.

"Surely you have been curious about her," I said, "about that girl, your deep and true self."

"No, no!" she said. Then for a long time she was quiet. Then she said, "Yes, I have wondered about her."

I put my hand gently on her head.

"Even as a girl," she said, "lying alone in bed, I wondered

201

what it might be like to lie soft and small, perfumed, helpless, in the arms of a strong man, knowing that he would treat me as he wished, doing with me whatever he wanted."

"It is uncompromising manhood which thrills you," I said. "It is found but rarely on your native world."

"It is not useful to the machine," she said.

"No," I said, "but note, interestingly, in spite of the fact that you perhaps never in your life on Earth encountered such manhood, yet you were capable of understanding and conceiving it, and longing for its manifestation."

"How can that be?" she asked, frightened.

"It is a genetic expectation," I told her, "more ancient than the caves, a whisper in your brain bespeaking a lost world of nature, a world in which the human being, both male and female, were bred. You were fitted to one world; you found yourself in another. You were a stranger in a country not of your own choosing, a troubled guest, uneasy in a house you knew was not yours."

"I fear my feelings," she said.

"They hint to you of nature's world," I told her. "They are inimical to the machine."

"I must fight them," she said.

"They are a reminiscence," I said, "of a vanished reality. They whisper of old songs. The machine has not yet been able to eradicate them from your brain. Such feelings, in their genetic foundations, lie at the root of women, and of men. They antedate the taming of fire. They were ancient when the first stone knife was lifted to the sun."

"I must fight them," she wept.

"Fight yourself then," I said, "for it is your deepest self of which they speak."

"It is wrong to be true to oneself!" she said.

"Perhaps," I said. "I do not know."

"One must always pretend to be other than what one is," she said.

"Why?" I asked.

"I do not know," she said.

"Gorean men," I said, "you will learn are less tolerant of pretense than the men of Earth."

"They would force me to be what I truly am, and in my heart long to be?" she asked.

"Yes," I said.

"I'm frightened," she whispered. We did not speak for a time. "Why are there no true men on Earth?" she asked.

"I am sure there are many true men on Earth," I said. "But it is much more difficult for them."

"I do not think there are any men on Earth," she said, angrily.

"I am sure they exist," I said.

"What of the others?" she asked.

"Perhaps someday," I said, "they will cease to fear their manhood."

"Is there much hope for those of Earth?" she asked.

"Very little," I said. "A reversal of the pathology of centuries would be required." I smiled. "The wheels are heavy, and the momentum great," I said.

"The machine will tear itself apart," she said.

"I sense that, too," I said. "How long can it continue to spread, to grow and devour? Stalemate will be achieved upon the ashes of civilizations."

"It is horrible," she said.

"Perhaps it will not occur," I said.

"Perhaps the lies of civilization are preferable to the truths of barbarism," she said.

"Perhaps," I said. "It is hard to know."

"Cannot there be a civilization that makes room for the realities of men and women?" she asked.

"A civilization that makes room for life?" I asked.

"Yes," she said.

"I do not know," I said. "Perhaps."

"You are kind to talk to me," she said.

"Once we were both of Earth," I said.

"How can you talk to me like this and yet keep me a slave?" she asked.

"I do not detect the difficulty," I said.

"Oh," she said.

"One of the pleasant things about owning a slave," I said, "is the opportunity to converse with her, to listen to her, to hear her express herself, her feelings and ideas. One can learn much from a slave. Many slaves, like yourself, are highly intelligent. They can express themselves articulately, clearly, trenchantly and lyrically. It is a great pleasure to talk with them."

"I see," she said.

"Then, when one wishes," I said, "one puts them again on their knees."

"You are cruel," she said.

"Kiss me, Slave," I said.

"Yes, Master," she said, and kissed me, softly.

We were then silent for a time.

"Master," she whispered.

"Yes," I said.

"I begin to sense," said she, "what it might be like to be a true slave."

"You are an ignorant girl," I said.

"I have learned some things," she said.

"Very little," I said.

"I have learned to obey," she said, "and to call free men, 'Master.' "

"What else have you learned?" I asked.

"Something which you have taught me," she whispered.

"What is that?" I asked.

"I have learned to need the touch of a man," she said.

"I will sleep now," I said.

"Please do not sleep now," she said. I felt her fingers tips at my shoulder.

"Touch me," she begged. "Touch me—as a slave girl."

"Do you beg it?" I asked.

"Yes, Master," she whispered.

"Very well," I said.

She looked up at me. "Are you going to make me a full slave?" she asked.

"No," I said. "I am only going to satisfy your slave needs as they exist at your present level."

"Yes, Master," she said.

Later she wept and squirmed in my arms lost in the sensations and ecstasies which she could at that time reach. Then she lay at my thigh. "Can there be more?" she asked. "Can there be more?"

"You have not yet begun to learn your slavery," I told her.

I almost cried out as her teeth bit into my side and her fingernails tore at my thigh in her frustration. She seemed almost fastened on me like an animal. With my hand in her hair I pulled her head upward. She lay then with her head just below my chest. Her eyes were wide. Her small hands held me tightly. She was breathing heavily. "Master, Master," she whispered.

"Be silent, Slave," I said. "It is now time to rest."

"Yes, Master," she whispered.

13 IMNAK BROACHES TO ME A TOPIC OF SOME IMPORTANCE; WE ENCOUNTER POALU

One of the problems in approaching tabuk on the tundra is the lack of cover.

I followed Imnak's example, crawling on my belly, after him, the horn bow in my hand, an arrow loose at the string. I was very cold, and was soaked through. The tundra is cold, and much of it is boglike in nature.

Some eleven tabuk were grazing on the mosses some one hundred yards from us.

The horn bow, unfortunately, formed of pieces of split tabuk horn, bound with sinew, is not effective beyond some thirty yards, One must, thus, be almost upon the animal before loosing the shaft. Wood is scarce in the north and the peasant bow, or longbow, is not known there. More importantly, in the colder weather, the long bow would freeze and snap, unable to bear the stress of being drawn to its customary extent. I had brought a longbow north with me but I wished to accustom myself to the horn bow, for the larger weapon, I knew, would be useless for most of the year in these latitudes. It is difficult to convey the nature of a world subject to great cold. A nail struck by a hammer can shiver into fragments. Urine can freeze before striking the ground. The squeal of a sleen may be heard for ten to twelve miles. A common conversation can be heard half a pasang away. A mountain which seems very close, given the sharpness of visibility in the clear air, may actually be forty pasangs in the distance. The cold air, touching the body of a sleen, forms a steam which can almost obscure the animal. A running tabuk can leave a trail of such steam drifting behind it. One's breath can freeze in a beard, leaving it a mask of ice.

I cursed inwardly, as the tabuk trotted a few yards farther away, grazing.

I had suggested to Imnak that we come hunting. I wished to speak to him alone, without the girls being present. A hunt had seemed at the time a convenient way in which to accomplish that objective. Now I wished we had simply sent them off packing to gather moss.

Hot Bazi tea I wanted. This is an important trade item in the north. I now knew why. The southern sugars are also popular. I had originally supposed this was because of their sweetness, there being few sweet items, save some berries, in the north. I now began to suspect that the calories of the sugars also played their role in their popularity. The red hunters think little of eating half a pound of sugar at a sitting.

We were trying to move close to a large bull tabuk. He moved away from us again.

I resisted the desire to rise to my feet and run screaming at the animal, bow drawn.

I followed Imnak. He almost seemed a part of the tundra itself. When the bull tabuk would turn, lifting its head, ears high, we would stop, remaining immobile.

We inched closer. We had been on our bellies for more than an Ahn trying to approach the animals.

Imnak gestured that I should crawl beside him. I did so.

"Are you cold?" he whispered.

"Oh, no," I said.

"That is strange," he said. "I am very cold."

"I am glad to hear that," I said. "I am very cold, too."

"It is hard not to be cold," he said, "when one is soaked with icy water crawling on the tundra."

"That is it," I said.

"You do not seem in a good mood," he said. "Was Arlene not pleasant in the sleeping bag?"

"She was very nice," I said. "How was Thimble?"

"She squeaks a lot," he said.

"Some girls are noisier than others," I said.

"It is true," he said.

"Perhaps you are not in a good mood because you are cold," suggested Imnak.

"I wager that is it," I said. "Why are you in a good mood," I asked, "if you are cold?"

"It is bad enough to be cold," he said, "without being in a bad mood, too."

"I see," I said. For some reason, ridiculous as it was, I felt cheered up.

"I wanted to come hunting with you," said Imnak, "because I have something serious to discuss with you."

"That is strange," I said, "I wanted to discuss something with you."

"My business is serious," he said.

"So, too, is mine," I said.

"Men of the south must be approached so cautiously," said Imnak. "They are so touchy and strange. Else I would have mentioned my business to you long ago."

"Oh," I said. It had been for much the same reason that I had delayed broaching to Imnak the nature of my mission in the north.

"My business," said Imnak, "concerns Poalu, the daughter of Kadluk."

"Your business is more serious than mine," I said. "Mine pertains only to the saving of the world." I well remembered Poalu, the coppery spitfire whose kicked leather ball I had unwisely permitted to strike me.

"I do not understand," said Imnak.

"It does not matter," I said. "What of Poalu?"

"I love her," said Imnak.

"That is unfortunate," I said.

"Do you love her, too?" he asked.

"No," I said. "I thought that it was unfortunate for you."

"Oh," he said. Then he said, "That is not unlikely, but it is difficult to help matters of that sort."

"True," I said.

"And Poalu loves me, too," he said.

"Are you sure?" I asked.

"Yes," he said, "once when I took feasting clothes to her father's house she threw the urine pot at me."

"That is a hopeful sign," I said.

"Another time," he said, cheerfully, "she beat me with a stick, calling me a good-for-nothing."

"It is clear she is very interested in you," I said.

"It is strange that so beautiful a girl has so few suitors," he said.

"Yes, it is quite strange," I admitted.

"Akko, who is my friend," said Imnak, "says that to take such a woman would be to leap naked into a pit of starving snow sleen. Do you think so?"

"I think so," I said. Actually I thought Akko's appraisal of the potentialities of the situation was overly hopeful, it being colored by his native good humor and optimism, vices endemic among red hunters.

"But I am shy," he said.

"I find that hard to believe," I said. "You seem to me a bold fellow."

"Not with women," he said.

"You are certainly fierce enough with Thimble and Thistle," I said. "They live in terror of displeasing you in the least."

"They are not women," he said.

"Oh?" I asked.

"Oh, they are women of a sort," he said, "but they are not of the People. They are nothing, only pretty, white-skinned slave beasts. They do not count."

"That is true," I said. They did not count. They were only slaves.

"Poalu is different," he said.

"That is for certain," I granted him.

"I will have Poalu!" he said, suddenly. He climbed to his feet. "Yes!" he said. "I will have Poalu!"

The tabuk trotted away.

"The tabuk have gone," I said.

"But I am shy," he said. "You must help me."

"The tabuk have gone." I said.

"You must help me," he said.

"Very well," I said. "The tabuk have gone," I added.

"I knew I could count on you," he said.

"The tabuk have gone," I said.

"Yes, I know," he said.

"What do you want me to do?" I asked.

"I am too shy to do it," he said.

"You are too shy to do what?" I asked.

"I am too shy to carry her off," he said.

"You want me to carry her off?" I asked.

"Of course," he said. "Do not worry. No one will mind."

"What about Poalu?" I asked.

He frowned. "Well, I do not know about Poalu," he admitted. "Sometimes she is moody."

"Perhaps you should carry her off yourself," I suggested.

"I am too shy to do this," he said, miserably.

"I suppose it might be done," I mused, "under the cover of darkness."

"But then you could not well see what you are doing," said Imnak. "Besides it will not be dark for several weeks."

"I know," I said. "We could wait."

"No, no, no, no, no," said Imnak.

"You want her carried off in full daylight?" I asked.

"Of course," he said. "That is the time for carrying girls off."

"I did not know that," I said. "I am new in the north." I looked at him. "Do you not occasionally run into problems," I asked, "like being speared in the back by her brothers?"

"Poalu has no brothers," said Imnak.

"That is lucky," I said. "What of her father? He is inept and weak, I trust."

"He is a great hunter, Kadluk," said Imnak. "He can throw a harpoon into the eye of a sea sleen from a tossing kayak."

"What if Kadluk does not approve of my carrying off his daughter?" I asked.

"Why should he disapprove?" asked Imnak.

"Oh, I do not know," I said. "It was just a thought."

"Do not fear," said Imnak, reassuringly. "All the arrangements have been made."

"Arrangements?" I asked.

"Yes," he said.

"Kadluk, then, knows that I am to carry off his daughter?"

"Of course," said Imnak. "Surely one would not wish to carry off Kadluk's daughter without his permission."

"No," I said, "from what I have heard of Kadluk, I think not."

"That would not be polite," said Imnak.

"True," I granted him. Also I did not want a harpoon in my head. The thought of the steely-eyed Kadluk drawing a bead on me with his harpoon was unnerving. I could not get the sea sleen out of my mind.

"Does Poalu know she is supposed to be carried off?" I asked.

"Of course," said Imnak. "how else could she be ready on time?"

"I just was not thinking," I said.

"That is all right," said Imnak, generously.

"Well," I said, "let us return to the tent. The tabuk are gone and I am soaked and freezing. I will well relish a hot cup of Bazi tea."

"Ah, my friend," said Imnak, sadly, "I am sorry there is no Bazi tea."

"Recently," I said, "there was a great deal of it."

"True," said Imnak, "but now there is not."

"You used the tea to buy Poalu?" I asked.

Imnak looked at me, horrified. "I made a gift to Kadluk," he said.

209

"Oh," I said.

"Also," said Imnak, "there is no sugar left, and few furs."

"What of the gold pieces you took for trading?" I asked.

"I gave them to Kadluk, too," said Imnak. "and most of the wood."

"At least we have the tabuk slices from the kills we made earlier," I said, glumly.

"Kadluk likes tabuk," said Imnak.

"Oh," I said.

We trudged back, wet and miserable, to the encampments of the People.

As luck would have it we encountered Poalu.

"Ah," she said, "you have been hunting."

"Yes," said Imnak.

"I see that your shoulders are heavy with game," she said.

"No," said Imnak.

"I see," she said. "You made many kills in the fields and have marked the meat. You will later send out your girls to cut steaks for all of us."

Imnak hung his head.

"You surely do not mean to tell me that you have returned to the camp with no meat," she said, disbelievingly.

"Yes," said Imnak.

"I cannot believe that," she said. "A great hunter like Imnak comes back without meat! It is just too hard to believe!"

Imnak looked down, shuffling.

"Can my father be wrong?" she asked.

Imnak looked up, puzzled.

"He says Imnak is a great hunter! I think it is true. It is only that Imnak is not too smart and leaves all the meat out in the fields for the jards."

Imnak looked down again.

"It is fortunate," she said, "that you are only a miserable fellow with no wife. Think how embarrassed she would be. She speaks to her guests, "Oh, no, Imnak has forgotten to bring back the meat again." "Not again," they say. "Yes," she says. "He is a great hunter. Only he always forgets to bring the meat home. He is not too smart. He leaves it in the fields for the jards." "

"Are you sure she expects to be carried off?" I asked Imnak.

"Of course," said Imnak. "Can you not see she loves me?"

"Yes," I said, "it is certainly clear."

Then Poalu looked at me. She whipped a knife out from

210

her furs. "Do not think you are going to carry me off," she said. "I will cut you to ribbons!"

I stepped back, in order not to be slashed with the knife. Imnak, too, leaped backward.

Poalu then turned about and walked away.

"She is moody sometimes," said Imnak.

"Yes," I admitted.

"But she loves me," he said, happily.

"Are you sure?" I asked.

"Yes," said Imnak. "She cannot hide her true feelings." He nudged me. "Did you not notice that she did not stick the knife into us?" he asked, secretively.

"Yes," I said, "she missed."

"Did Poalu not love me," he said, smiling, "she would not have missed."

"I hope that you are right," I said.

"She did not miss Naartok," he said.

"Oh," I said.

"He was in his tent for six weeks," he said.

"Who is Naartok?" I asked.

"He is my rival," said Imnak. "He still loves her. He may try to kill you."

"I hope he is not good at throwing harpoons into the eyes of sleen," I said.

"No," said Imnak. "He is not so good a shot as Kadluk."

"That is good," I said.

"Yes," said Imnak.

14 THE COURTSHIP OF POALU; WHAT FOLLOWED THE COURTSHIP OF POALU

It is not easy to knock at a tent.

"Greetings, Kadluk," I called.

A coppery face poked itself outside the tent. It was a very broad face, with high cheekbones, and very dark, bright eyes, a face framed in cut, blue-black hair, with bangs across the forehead.

"Ah," beamed Kadluk. "You must be the young man who has come to carry off my daughter."

"Yes," I said. He seemed in a good mood. He had, perhaps, waited years for this moment.

"She is not yet ready," said Kadluk, shrugging apologetically. "You know how girls are."

"Yes," I said. I looked back a few yards to where Imnak stood, lending me moral support. He smiled and waved encouragingly. Reassured I stood waiting outside the tent.

I waited for several minutes.

Another figure emerged from the tent, a woman, Tatkut, or Wick-Trimmer, the woman of Kadluk, the mother of Poalu. She smiled up at me and bowed slightly, and handed me a cup of tea.

"Thank you," I said, and drank the tea.

After a time she returned and I handed her back the cup. "Thank you again," I said.

She smiled, and nodded, and returned to the tent.

Imnak sidled up to me. He was looking worried. "It should not take this long to carry a girl off," he whispered. I nodded.

"It should not take this long to carry a girl off," I called. Imnak backed away, expectantly.

Inside the tent then we heard an argument in course. There was much expostulation. I could make out Poalu's voice, and that of Kadluk and Tatkut. They spoke in their own tongue and I could pick up but few of the words. I did hear the expression for Bazi tea a few times. I gathered that Kadluk had little intention, or desire at any rate, to return Imnak's quantities of Bazi tea, or other gifts, to him.

After a time Kadluk's head reappeared. "She does not want to be carried off," he said.

"Well, that is that," I shrugged. I turned to Imnak. "She does not want to be carried off," I said. "Let us return to our tent."

"No, no!" cried Imnak. "You must now rush into the tent and carry her off by force."

"Is Kadluk armed?" I asked.

"What possible difference could that make?" asked Imnak.

"I thought it might make a difference," I said. I still remembered the harpoon and the sleen.

"No," said Imnak. "Kadluk!" he called.

Kadluk came outside the tent.

"It seems your daughter must be carried away by force," said Imnak.

"Yes," agreed Kadluk. This reassured me.

"Go ahead," said Imnak. "Go in and get her."

"Very well," I said.

"She has a knife," said Kadluk.

"Go ahead," urged Imnak.

"We need not make haste in this matter," I observed. "Are you sure you really want to have Poalu in your tent? Perhaps you should subject the matter to further consideration."

"But we love one another," said Imnak.

"Why do you not go in and get her yourself?" I asked.

"I am too shy," said Imnak, hanging his head.

"Perhaps she will listen to reason," I said, hopefully.

Kadluk turned about, holding his sides. In a moment he was rolling on the ground. Red hunters are often demonstrative in the matter of their emotions. In a few moments he had regained his composure, wiping the tears from his eyes.

I lifted aside the tent flap, cautiously, Inside was Poalu. She was dressed in feasting clothes. Near her was her mother, Tatkut, beaming her pride in her daughter.

I dodged as the knife sailed past my head, narrowly missing Imnak outside.

"You will never carry me off by force!" she cried.

"I grant you the likelihood of that," I said.

She seized a heavy iron pan, of the sort used out of doors across stones for cooking.

It would not be pleasant to have that utensil beating on my head.

"Look," I said, "I am supposed to carry you off."

"Don't touch me," she said.

"The arrangements have all been made," I pointed out.

"I did not make them," she said.

That seemed to me a good point. "She says she did not make the arrangements," I called out to Imnak.

"That does not matter," called Imnak in to me.

"That does not matter," I told her.

"It does matter," she said.

"It does matter, she says," I relayed to Imnak, outside.

"No, it does not matter," he said.

"It does not matter," I relayed to Poalu, from Imnak outside.

"She is only a woman," pointed out Imnak.

"You are only a woman," I told her, relaying Imnak's point. It seemed to me a good one.

She then rushed forward, striking down at me with the

213

heavy, flat pan. I removed it from her. I did this that I not be killed.

She then fled to the back of the tent. She looked about, but found nothing else which seemed suitable as a weapon. Kadluk, I then understood, had wisely removed his gear, such as knives and arrows, from the tent before Imnak and I had arrived.

His daughter was as well known to him as others, of course.

"Would you please hand me the blubber hammer behind you," asked Poalu.

Obligingly I handed her the hammer. I thought I could probably avoid or fend its blows. The object, wooden-handled, with a stone head, is used for pounding blubber to loosen the oil in the blubber, which is used in the flat, oval lamps.

"Thank you," said Poalu.

"You're welcome," I said.

She then faced me, holding the hammer.

"If you do not wish to be carried off," I said, "why are you wearing your feasting clothes?"

"Isn't she pretty?" asked Tatkut, smiling.

"Yes," I admitted.

Poalu looked at me, shrewdly. "I am not your ordinary girl," she said, "whom you may simply carry off."

"That seems certain," I granted her.

"Where is Imnak?" she asked.

Surely she knew he was just outside the tent. "He is just outside the tent," I said.

"Why does he not carry me off?" she asked.

"I wish that he would," I said. "He is shy."

"Well," she said, "I am not going."

"She says she is not going," I called out to Imnak.

There was a pause. Then I heard Imnak say, "That is all right with me."

Poalu seemed startled. I was relieved. I turned about to take my departure.

"Wait," she said. "Aren't you going to carry me off?"

"I would be content," I said, "if it were up to me, to leave you in your father's tent forever."

I heard Imnak outside. "Yes," he said, "it is all right with me if she does not come."

"I will give you back your gifts, Imnak," said Kadluk, rather more loudly than was necessary.

"You may keep them," said Imnak, expansively.

214

"No, I could not do that," said Kadluk. I found myself hoping that he would indeed return Imnak's gifts. We in Imnak's tent could use that Bazi tea, those furs and the tabuk steaks.

"It will be amusing to hear the songs they will sing in the feasting house about Poalu," said Imnak, loudly, "how no one wants her."

"How can you carry me off?" called Poalu. "You have no sled."

"There is no snow," I said to her.

"There is a proper way and an improper way to do things," said Poalu to me.

"Oh, look," said Imnak, "here is a sled."

Poalu, still clutching the blubber hammer, poked her head outside.

There was indeed a sled there, that which Imnak had built at the wall, and which the girls had drawn, that sled by means of which his supplies and gear had been transported across Ax Glacier.

Harnessed to the sled, in their full furs, were Thimble, Thistle and Arlene.

"Ho! Ho!" called Poalu, derisively. "You would expect to carry a girl off in a sled drawn by white-skinned slave beasts! What a scoundrel you are! How insulting!"

"I will borrow a snow sleen," said Imnak. "Will that be sufficient?"

I thought a snow sleen, one of those long, vicious animals, would surely be puzzled to find itself attached to a sled where there was no snow.

"Perhaps," called Poalu.

Imnak unhitched Thimble, Thistle and Arlene. They stood about, puzzled. He then turned and left the vicinity of the tent. "Would you like more tea?" asked Tatkut.

"Yes, thank you," I said. I was at least getting some of the tea back which Imnak had given to Kadluk.

In a few minutes Imnak returned with a snow sleen on a stout leash. Soon it was hitched to the sled. It was Akko's animal, and he, in the fashion of the red hunters, had cheerfully volunteered its services.

"Someone has a snow sleen hitched to a sled outside of the tent of someone," called Imnak.

"It is a poor beast," said Poalu. "Find a better."

"Someone has not even looked at it," said Imnak.

Poalu stuck her head out the tent. "It is a poor beast." said Poalu. "Find a better."

Imnak, for no reason that was clear to me, scouted about and located another snow sleen.

"That is worse than the other," said Poalu.

Imnak angrily unhitched the second animal, and rehitched the first one, that which belonged to Akko.

"Surely you do not expect me to ride behind so poor a beast?" inquired Poalu.

"Of course not," said Imnak. He made ready to leave.

"What are you doing?" asked Poalu.

"I am going away," said Imnak. "I am going to my tent."

"I suppose it will have to do," said Poalu.

"You could strike her heavily along the side of the head," said Kadluk to me. "That is what I did with Tatkut." Tatkut nodded, beaming.

"It is a thought," I said.

"Will no one protect a girl from being carried off!" cried Poalu.

She still carried the blubber hammer. If struck properly with it one might be brained.

"Is there no one who will save me?" wailed Poalu.

Kadluk looked about, anxious should anyone interfere. There were by now several bystanders about.

"Naartok," cried Poalu, "will you not save me?"

A heavy fellow nearby shook his head vigorously. He still carried his right arm high and close to his body, his shoulder hunched somewhat. I recalled that Poalu had in the past driven her blade into his body somewhere in that vicinity. Imnak had warned me that Naartok, his rival, might try to kill me, to prevent my carrying Poalu off. Naartok, however, seemed competely willing that I should undertake that task. It was clear that I had his best wishes for success in this endeavor. Naartok, like many of the red hunters, was not a fellow to be bitter about such things.

"Come along," I said to Poalu. "It will soon be dark." That was true. In a few weeks the Arctic night would descend.

She hurled the blubber hammer at my head and I slipped to the side. It sped past me and struck Naartok a cruel blow on the forehead.

She fled back into the tent and I nimbly pursued her. In the tent I scooped her up and threw her over my shoulder. Her small fists beat rapidly on my back.

"Will you stop that?" I asked.

"I do not want to go," she said.

"Oh," I said.

I put her to her feet and turned about, leaving the tent. "She says she does not want to go," I told Imnak.

"Go back," urged Imnak.

"Nonsense," I said. "Look, Imnak," I said, "I value your friendship but I have really had enough of this. I frankly do not think Poalu wants to be carried off by me."

Imnak looked at me, miserable.

"That is my considered opinion," I told him, confirming his fears.

"You will just have to carry her off yourself," I said.

"I am too shy," he wailed.

"Well, let us go home then," I said, "for I have drunk enough tea at the tent of Kadluk and evaded enough missiles to last me for several years."

"It is true," said Imnak, glumly. "You have endured more than one could rightfully ask of a friend."

"Too," I pointed out, "I was of aid in freeing the tabuk at the wall."

"Yes," said Imnak. "Forgive me, my friend, for imposing on you."

"It was no imposition," I said. "I would cheerfully carry off a girl for you, but it is one thing to carry off a girl and quite another to carry off Poalu."

"Poalu is a girl," said Imnak.

"I am not at all sure of that," I said.

"Do you think she may be a she-sleen?" asked Imnak, concerned. His metaphysics allowed this possibility. Sometimes men took the form of animals, and animals the form of men.

"Quite possibly," I said gravely.

"That would explain much," mused Imnak. "No," he said, seriously. "That cannot be true. I have known Poalu for years. When we were children we would gather eggs together at the bird cliffs, and hold hands, and, together, fight the coming of sleep." He looked at me, intently. "Too," he said, "she is the daughter of Kadluk."

"I guess you are right," I said. "She is not really a she-sleen."

"But she acts much like one," said Imnak.

"Yes," I said.

"Some girls are like that," said Imnak.

"Have you ever known anyone like Poalu?" I asked.

"Not exactly," he admitted.

"Where are you lazy men going?" asked Poalu.

"Home," said Imnak.

We began to trudge back toward Imnak's tent. It was some

two hundred yards away. Imnak led the snow sleen, drawing the sled on the tundra, and I walked beside him. Thimble, Thistle and Arlene walked beside the sled.

"Imnak is a lazy fellow!" called Poalu. "Imnak cannot sing in the feasting house! Imnak cannot paddle a kayak! Imnak is a poor hunter!"

"I am getting angry," said Imnak to me.

"Red hunters do not get angry," I told him.

"Sometimes red hunters get angry," said Imnak.

"I did not know that," I said.

"Yes," said Imnak.

"Imnak is a lazy fellow! Imnak is a terrible hunter! I am fortunate not to be Imnak's woman. Pity the poor woman who goes to Imnak's tent! I am pleased that I am not going to his tent! I would not go to his tent for anything!"

"I have had enough," said Imnak suddenly.

"A man does have his pride," I said.

"It is unfortunate that I am so shy," said Imnak between gritted teeth.

"Yes," I said, "that is unfortunate."

Suddenly Imnak threw back his head and howled at the sky. He made a wild animal noise and, wheeling about, in his fur boots, sped rapidly back toward the tent of Kadluk.

"Let us continue on," I said to the girls. We continued on, toward Imnak's tent, not looking back. The snow sleen padded along behind us, drawing the sled over the trodden turf.

Behind us we heard cheering.

We did not look back until we came to the threshold of Imnak's tent.

A large crowd was approaching, yet in such a way as to give Imnak room. Leading the crowd, but seeming half in the midst of it, came Imnak. He was pulling a bent over, stumbling, screaming, fighting figure behind him, his hand in her hair. She wore feasting clothes.

At the opening to his tent he threw her over his shoulder. Her feet were then off the ground, and she was helpless. She could be carried wherever he chose, and placed wherever he chose to place her. He carried her inside the tent, and threw her to the furs at his feet.

She looked up at him in fury. She tried to get up, but he pushed her back down.

"You are wearing feasting clothes," he said. "Do you think you are going to a feast?"

She looked up at him.

218

"No," he said, "you are not going to a feast. You do not need to wear feasting clothes."

"Imnak," she said.

"Take them off, everything!" he said.

"Imnak," she cried.

"Now!" he said.

Frightened, she stripped herself, and crouched on the fur in his tent. Nudity is not unusual among the red hunters. But even for them it is a treat to see a girl as pretty as Poalu stripped naked. I suspected that we would have numerous guests in the house of Imnak.

Imnak then bound her wrists together before her body and pulled her to her feet. "Imnak!" she cried. He pulled her from the tent, stumbling, to the pole behind the tent, that from which tabuk meat was sometimes hung to dry. A few days ago Arlene had been tied to the pole. Imnak fastened Poalu's hands over her head and to the pole.

"Imnak!" she cried. "What are you going to do?"

Imnak, who had returned to the tent after fastening her in place, returned to the pole. He carried a sleen whip.

"Imnak," she cried, "what are you going to do?"

"Only one can be first," cried Imnak.

"Imnak!" she cried, struck.

The hunters and the women gathered about cheered Imnak on. He put the leather to her well.

Then she cried out, "It is Imnak who is first in his tent!" She shuddered in the straps that bound her. Then she was struck again. "Imnak is first!" she cried. "Imnak! Imnak!"

He thrust the whip in his belt.

He went before her, where she could see him. "You are first, Imnak," she wept. "I am your woman. Your woman will obey you. Your woman will do what you tell her."

"No, Imnak!" she cried.

"Aiii," cried a man in the crowd.

He tied bondage strings on her throat.

The men and women in the crowd roared their approval. They stomped on the turf. Some began to sing.

None, I think, had thought to see so rare and delicious a sight as bondage strings on the throat of the arrogant, fiery Poalu.

Her temper and sharp tongue, I think, had made many enemies among the red hunters and their women. There were few there I think who did not relish seeing her in bondage strings. She might now be beaten with impunity, and must obey free men and women.

219

"Now," said Kadluk, her father, "you will not come running home to the tent."

He rubbed his nose affectionately on the side of her face, patted her on the head and turned away.

"Father!" she cried.

"Do I hear the wind?" he asked, his back to her.

"Father!" she cried.

"Yes," he said, "I hear the wind." Then he left.

Indeed, she could not now go running home to the tent of her father. Imnak, if he wished, could slay her for such an act. She wore bondage strings.

The crowd began to dissipate, leaving Imnak and Poalu much alone.

"Why have you done this to me, Imnak?" asked Poalu.

"I wanted to own you," he said.

"I did not know a man could want a woman so much that he would want to own her," said Poalu.

"Yes," said Imnak.

"I did not know you would be strong enough to own me," she said.

"I am strong enough to own you," he said.

"Yes," she said, "it is true. I see in your eyes that it is true."

He said nothing.

"And you will own me?" she asked.

"Yes," he said.

"It is a strange feeling, being owned," she said.

Imnak shrugged.

"I have loved you since we were children, Imnak," she whispered. "I have thought for years that I would someday be your woman. But I did not think, ever, that I would be your beast." She looked at him. "Will you truly make me obey you, Imnak?" she asked.

"Yes," he said.

She smiled. "Your beast is not discontent," she said.

He touched her softly with his nose about the cheek and throat. It is a thing red hunters do. It is a very gentle thing, like smelling and nuzzling.

Then his hands were hard on her waist.

She looked up at him. "The lamp must be lit," she said, "and the water heated, that I may boil meat for supper."

"Supper may wait," he said.

He began to caress her, with tender, powerful caresses, gentle yet strong, possessive and commanding, as one may touch something which one owns and loves.

220

She began to breathe more swiftly. "Imnak," she whispered, "you may do what you want with a beast, and a beast must do, fully, what you want."

"That is known to me," he said.

"Oh, Imnak!" she cried. "Please! Please!"

Then her hands were untied from the pole, and freed, and she knelt at his feet. At his gesture, she, frightened, pressed her lips to his boots, and then looked up at him, waiting to be commanded.

He indicated that she should crawl to the tent. She did so, and he walked behind her, the whip now loose in his hand. I saw him thrust it, crossways, between her teeth and throw her back to the furs. She looked up at him, the whip clenched in her teeth. This is a device which helps to keep a slave girl quiet in her ecstasies. She can then do little more than gasp and squirm.

Imnak looked about, and drew shut the flaps of the tent.

I gather that, later, he had, mercifully, removed the whip from her mouth, for I heard from the tent's interior the delicious ear-shattering scream of a slave girl yielding to her master.

Thimble and Thistle looked at one another. I saw in their eyes, though doubtless neither would have confessed it to the other, that they wished, each of them, that it was they, and not the new girl, in the arms of the male.

Arlene timidly reached forth to touch me. "Master," she said.

"Do you beg it?" I asked.

"Yes, Master," she said, "Arlene begs it. Arlene, who is your slave, begs it with all her heart."

"Very well," I said.

I took the slave girl in my arms. How delicious it is to do such a thing. How pleased I was to own her!

Thimble looked away. I saw Thistle, who had been the rich girl, Audrey Brewster, lips parted, look at me. Then she bit her lip and, too, looked away. I smiled to myself. Thistle, I thought, or Audrey, as I sometimes thought of her to myself, using that name now as a slave name, would probably be the first of the three girls to come to a full slavery. I recalled when she had, once, almost inadvertently, when wearing the yoke Thimble had put on her, when they had been going out to gather moss and grass, knelt to me. She, I had conjectured, would be the first of the three girls to come to a full slavery, or, as the Goreans sometimes put it, she would probably be the first to lick her chains.

"Master," whispered Arlene.

I began to kiss her about the face and throat and shoulders.

She clutched me. It was good to own her. She was beautiful, and intelligent, and hot, and mine. I suppose those who have not owned a woman cannot understand what a pleasure it is.

"Oh, Master, Master!" she whispered.

"Be quiet, Slave," I whispered to her.

"Yes, Master," she whispered.

15 AUDREY

There is something nice about having a girl lying naked in your arms, who wears bondage strings on her throat.

"I have waited long for your touch, Master," whispered Thistle, who had once been the rich Audrey Brewster. I caressed the side of her face. She looked up at me. She was worth having.

I had won her use in the bone gambling, her use as complete slave, until I chose to leave the tent.

The hunt had gone well. Imnak and I had brought down four tabuk. Poalu, whom Imnak, with my consent, had made first girl, and the other girls, had followed us. Poalu had showed them how to cut the meat and lay it out on stones to dry.

All now slept in the tent, save Thistle and myself. "You were once Audrey Brewster," I said.

"Yes, Master," she said.

"For purposes of my use of you," I said, "for I have full rights over you, I shall name you, for the tenure of my ownership of you, Audrey."

"Thank you, Master," she said.

"But you wear the name now," I said, "not as a free name, but as a slave name I choose to put on you."

"Oh," she said.

"Do you object?" I asked.

"No, Master," she said. "I am Audrey, your slave." She

222

clutched me. "Why have you made me wait so long?" she asked.

"It pleased me," I said.

"Yes, Master," she said.

I had wanted her to be well ready.

Two sleeps ago I had had to whip Arlene and Audrey apart. "Stay away from him!" had cried Arlene.

"I do not know what you are talking about," had protested Audrey.

"Do you think I cannot see you putting yourself before him, smiling, brushing his arm!" cried Arlene.

"Liar!" had cried Audrey.

"Do you deny it?" exclaimed Arlene.

"Of course!" cried Audrey.

Arlene had leapt upon her and, in an instant, both girls, scratching and tearing, biting, rolled on the tundra.

"He is my master, Slave!" screamed Arlene. She knelt over Audrey.

"If Imnak gives my use to him I must serve him!" cried Audrey.

"He has not given your use to him!" said Arlene. "Stay away from him!"

"Do not strike me!" cried Audrey.

"He is my master, not yours," said Arlene, her small fist raised. "Stay away from him!"

"I am a slave girl," said Audrey. "I must be pleasing to all free men!"

Arlene struck down at her and, suddenly, they again were locked together, tearing and scratching at one another on the trodden turf.

"Do not hurt me!" suddenly cried Arlene, she now on the bottom, Audrey kneeling over her.

"I am a slave. I will be pleasing to any free man I want," said Audrey.

"Slave!" screamed Arlene up at her.

"Slave!" screamed Audrey at Arlene.

Arlene squirmed free and again, together, they fought. I thought them extremely well matched slave beauties. Arlene might have been a little stronger. Either of them could have been severely bested by blond Thimble.

At last I, with a switch, fell upon them. "Oh," they cried. I took them, one hand in the hair of each, and threw them to their knees under the pole. "Strip and stand," I told them, "hands over head, wrists crossed, beneath the pole." They did so, and I fastened them in position, side by side.

"Now you are going to have us whipped," said Audrey to Arlene.

"Be quiet, Slave Girl," snapped Arlene.

Audrey began to cry.

I handed the switch to Thimble, who once had been Barbara Benson. "Discipline them," I said to her. "Twenty strokes to each."

"Yes, Master," had said Thimble.

I had then walked away. Arlene received the first stroke, Audrey the last.

I now looked into the eyes of Audrey, naked in my arms. "I have waited long for your touch, Master," she whispered. "I wait lovingly and eagerly to serve you."

"It is well," I said.

She kissed me delicately on the arm. Arlene could not now attack her. She must serve me, and serve me to the best of her abilities, superbly and obediently. Her use was now mine.

"You have won in the bone gambling before," she said. "Why did you wait so long to select me to serve you? Am I not pleasing to a master?"

"You are acceptable, Slave Girl," I said.

"I will try to be pleasing," she said.

Before, when I had won in the bone gambling, the dropping of the tiny figures of bone and ivory, I had, of intent, selected blond Thimble, whom I would, in the tenure of her service to me, name 'Barbara', putting that name on her, though then of course as a slave name.

"I wanted to let the little pudding named Audrey simmer," I told her.

"You were cruel," she said.

Imnak, since he had acquired Poalu, had scarcely glanced at his two white-skinned slave beasts. It was not that he had meant to be cruel. It was rather that he was simply otherwise occupied. And even had he thought of it, their deprivation would not have been of concern to him, for they were only animals.

Both girls would kneel to one side, stripped, awaiting the outcome of the bone gambling. Sometimes I won, and sometimes Imnak won. When Imnak won he might have the use of Arlene, if he chose, or a tabuk steak. Not unoften, to my amusement and Arlene's outrage, Imnak would select the steak. As I explained to her this was not because there was anything intrinsically lacking in her but because Imnak had eyes only, or generally, for Poalu. He was usually anxious to get his little red slave into the furs. His little slave was forced to compensate him well, indeed, a thousandfold and more, for the frustrating years of her freedom and arrogance. Interestingly, too, she did not seem to mind.

Both Barbara and Audrey had knelt to the side, awaiting the outcome of the sport.

Since the coming of Poalu to the tent life had become hard for them. It was not that Poalu, though she was first girl, and firm, was cruel to them, but rather simply that Imnak now had little time for them and paid them scant attention.

Unfortunately, before the coming of Poalu to the tent, both girls had been brought to the second stage of slavery. The first stage is knowing they must obey, the second stage is needing the touch of a man.

Imnak now seldom touched them.

Their needs, accordingly, were much on them.

Freedom permits a woman to live without men. Slavery makes a woman need a man's touch. The sexuality of a free woman is largely inert; the sexuality of a slave girl, on the other hand, has been deliberately and seriously activated. Men, as it has pleased them, have done this to her. They have, as masters, careless of the consequences of their actions, awakened the poor girl's sexuality; it can never then, regardless of the torment and misery it may inflict upon her, return to sleep. It has been made hot and alive. She is no longer free; her freedom is gone; she is now only an ignited slave. Sexuality is a glory in a slave girl which sets her apart from free women, but it is also a force within her which she must fear, for it puts her so helplessly at the mercy of masters. The aroused sexuality of the slave girl is surely the strongest of the chains with which she is bound. Some slave girls, lovely fugitives, have been recaptured simply because they have thrown themselves whimpering at the feet of a man on a road, begging his touch, One of the most humiliating things that can occur to a slave girl is to find herself on her belly, unbidden, moaning, crawling to the feet of a hated master. She puts her lips to his feet. "I beg your touch, Master," she says.

The sexuality of the aroused slave girl is incomprehensible to the free woman. It is nothing she will ever understand. It is a color she cannot see, a sound she cannot hear.

I glanced at the two girls, kneeling to the side. Their sexuality, in the weeks of their slavery, had well begun to be aroused. Sparks had been kindled within them. Already they needed the touch of men.

They did not yet, of course, as slaves still relatively fresh

225

to bondage, suspect the torments and wonders that might lie before them. They did not yet understand how a woman screaming in a cell might break her body against the bars trying to touch a guard.

"You have won," had said Imnak, cheerfully.

"Yes," I said.

I had glanced at the two beauties. Both straightened themselves before me. Both now seemed far from the simple Earth girls they had been. I let my eyes move casually from one to the other.

"Please pick me, Master," said Audrey.

"I am more beautiful, Master," had said Barbara.

"Please, Master," begged Audrey.

I glanced at Barbara. Before, when I had won, I had always chosen her. She lifted her body before me. She was a quite lovely slave. How far from Earth she seemed.

No longer was she a blond tease, dressing to excite boys, yet fearing her sexuality.

She was now a slave girl.

I looked at Barbara. Then I pointed to Audrey. "This one," I said.

"Master!" breathed Audrey.

Barbara looked away, angrily.

Imnak got up and seized Poalu by the arm. He threw her to his furs.

I went to my furs and threw off my garments, and lay down on my furs, reclining, on one elbow.

Audrey remained kneeling, where she had been, though she watched me.

I indicated a place beside me on my furs. She crawled to the furs, head down, and lay timidly beside me.

"On your back," I told her.

She lay on her back, and I put my left arm under her, that I might lift, turn or control her as I wished, leaving my right hand free to caress her body.

I looked at the line of her body.

"You are a pretty slave," I told her.

"Thank you, Master," she said.

There is something nice about having a girl lying naked in your arms, who wears bondage strings on her throat.

"I have waited long for your touch, Master," whispered Thistle, who had once been the rich Audrey Brewster. I caressed the side of her face. She looked up at me. She was worth having.

"I am pleased that you won my use in the gambling," she said.

"Are you any good?" I asked.

"Master will use me and tell me," she said. "I will try to be good."

I looked down at her.

"Will master use me only briefly?" she asked. Imnak was seldom patient with his white-skinned slave beasts. Not only were they slaves, but they were white.

"You are pretty," I said. "It is my intention, in these hours of my ownership of you, to use you several times."

"Several times?" she asked.

"Yes," I said. I smiled at her. "We shall sleep from time to time," I said.

"But what if we are not awake at the same time?" she asked.

"What a naive slave you are," I said.

"Oh," she said, a bit archly.

"Yes," I said, "you will awaken as you are entered or seized, or slapped awake."

"Oh," she said.

"It is very simple," I assured her.

"You may, of course, do with me whatever you wish, and when you wish," she said, a little resentfully.

"I shall," I said.

"I am certain of that," she said.

"Do you object?" I asked.

"I may not object," she said. She smiled. "I am a slave," she said.

"Are you a pert, intemperate slave?" I asked.

"No," she said.

"Will it be necessary to whip you?" I asked.

"No," she said, quickly.

"You will try to be a good slave?" I asked.

"Yes, Master," she said.

"Please me," I said.

"Master!" she said.

"Please me," I said.

"But I am the female," she said.

I looked at her.

"I will try to please you," she said quickly. She began, clumsily, to kiss and caress me. I laughed at the ineptness of her efforts.

"Why do you laugh?" she asked, tears in her eyes.

"I was thinking," I said, "that if I had bought you in the

Sardar and thrown you to my men you would have been slain by now."

"Teach me to survive as a slave girl," she begged.

"I will show you some simple things," I said. "But girls usually learn from other girls, or from their slave trainers in the pens."

"Pens?" gasped Audrey.

"Of course," I said. "Sometimes," I admitted, "trainers are brought to the compartments, with their whips, but that is more expensive."

She turned white.

"You are a slave, and you are going to continue to be a slave," I told her, "so you had better learn how to be a good one."

She looked at me.

"Do you want to live?" I asked.

"Yes," she said.

"Then learn," I said.

"Yes, Master," she said.

"Here," I said, "hold your lips to my thigh. Put your lips thusly."

"Yes, Master," she whispered.

"It is strange," she said, looking up at me. "I longed for your touch, but now it is I who must touch you."

"Do not fear, little slave beauty," I said, "you, too, will be touched in your turn."

Her eyes were moist. She pressed her lips to my belly. "Thank you, Master," she whispered.

"What is slavery like in the south?" asked Audrey.

"It is the same as here," I said. "You would be in the absolute power of a man."

"I know that, Master," she said. "But how would I be dressed? What would I have to do?"

"You would be dressed, if at all, as your master pleased," I said, "and you would have to do whatever you were told."

"Oh, I know that, Master," she said, laughing, kissing me. Then she lay with her head on my shoulder.

"Would I be branded?" she asked.

"Doubtless," I said. "It is easier to keep track of a slave that way."

"Does that hurt much?" she asked.

"At the time," I said, "not later."

228

"Where are we branded?" she asked.

"A girl is commonly branded on the left or right thigh," I said, "sometimes on the lower left abdomen."

"I am afraid to be branded," she said.

"It does not hurt afterwards," I said. "It is only a mark to help keep track of you."

"Really, Master?" she asked.

"Well," I said, "if the truth must be told, it does, considerably, enhance your beauty. Also it is sometimes not without its psychological effect."

"I can well imagine its psychological effect," she said. She shuddered.

"It can help to impress upon a girl that she is a slave," I admitted.

I touched her on the thigh.

"There?" she asked.

"Quite possibly," I said.

Suddenly she clutched me. "Oh, oh," she cried. "It is the thought of being branded," she whispered, intensely. "Please, Master, hold me, hold me!"

Her thighs were clenched fiercely. "I am going into orgasm," she cried out, frightened. I held her, as she gasped and wept in my arms. I had not even entered her, or touched her intimately. She looked up at me, tears in her eyes. Angrily I thrust apart her legs. "Forgive me, Master," she wept. "It was the thought of being branded."

"So, Slave," I said, "you want the iron?"

"Yes, Master," she wept.

"If I should have you in the south," I said, "I would have you soon marked."

"Yes, Master," she wept. "Yes, Master!"

"Serve me now, Slave," I said.

"Yes, Master," she cried. "Yes, Master!" she cried.

"Serve me again," I said.

"Yes, Master," she said. "Audrey will now serve her master again."

"Does Audrey like serving her master?" I asked.

"Audrey loves serving her master," she whispered.

"Why is that?" I asked.

"Audrey is a slave," she whispered.

"It is true," I said.

"Yes, Master," she said. Then she began to cry out with helpless pleasure.

229

"In the south," I said, "there are many cities. Many of these cities consist largely of high cylinders, joined by traceries of high bridges."

"It sounds very beautiful," she said.

"It is," I said.

"Are there many slave girls in these cities?" she asked.

"Yes, many," I said.

"Tell me of them," she said.

"They are commonly kept barefoot," I said, "and are clad in brief tunics. Their hair is usually worn long and loosely. Their throats are normally encircled by collars, which identify their masters."

"Are such girls treated kindly?" she asked.

"It depends on the will of the master," I said. "They are slaves."

"Of course," she said.

"Most girls are treated kindly," I said, "provided they are absolutely pleasing in all ways."

She was silent.

"That is little enough to expect from a slave," I pointed out.

"Yes, Master," she said.

"Do you object?" I asked.

"No," she said. "It is only that the domination to which the Gorean slave girl is subject is so uncompromising, so complete."

"It is absolutely uncompromising and complete," I told her. "Goreans are not men of Earth," I said. "They will have what they truly want from a woman, everything."

"Though I am destined to be the helpless victim of their will, their power and their lust," she said, "yet I cannot help but admire and fear such men."

"They will make you be a woman, their woman," I said.

"In my most secret dreams," she said, "I longed for such a man. I did not know they could exist."

"Something in your heart," I said, "whispered to you that there must be somewhere such men."

"It was only a longing dream," she whispered, "the yearning of a girl for a true man, one proud and free and strong, one not dishonest, one not broken, one not robbed of himself, one who could by his might and strength make me as much a woman as he was a man."

"And then?" I asked.

"And then, one day, on a platform in the Sardar, I learned

230

that it was not a simple dream, but that it had been a dream to which there corresponded a fearful reality."

"You, wench of Earth," I said to her, "now lie naked on Gor, a slave girl."

"Yes," she whispered.

"Are you frightened?" I asked.

"Yes," she whispered. "I am terribly frightened." She clutched my arms. "Should those of Earth not be told that there truly is a Gor?" she asked.

"No," I said. "It is better that they do not know."

"How many girls, this very night on Earth," she asked, "are being brought to Gor?"

"I do not know," I said. "Perhaps none. I do not know the schedule of the slave runs."

"The horror, and the joy, of it," she said.

"Joy," I asked, "Slave?"

"Yes, joy," she whispered. "Master?" she asked.

"Yes," I said.

"Would you please stand over me?" she asked.

I did so.

"Yes," she said, "that is how I imagined him, the man in my dreams, he for whom I longed, he who would come for me and place me, regardless of my will, resolutely in his total bondage."

"And what did you do?" I asked.

"I knelt before him, like this," she said, "and put my head to his feet." She looked up at me. "You see," she said, "I knew, in seeing him, that he was my master."

"And what did he do?" I asked.

"He did not let me speak," she said, "but took me by the shoulders and gently, but powerfully, pressed me back."

"Like this?" I asked.

"Yes," she said. "Oh, I wanted to protest, and speak, and question him, but I saw in his eyes that I must not do so."

"And then?" I asked.

"He told me that he would try me out," she said, "and see if I pleased him. If I did not he would leave me alone, and unharmed, and I should not see him again. But to beware, for if he was pleased with me, he would take me away with him, to a far world, one very different from my own, where he could keep me as he wished, and would do so, as a slave." She smiled at me. "He encouraged me to try to resist him, that I might keep my pride and freedom." She looked up at me. "You see, he only wanted me if I truly was a slave," she said.

231

"What did you do then?" I asked.

"I opened my body to him like a flower," she said. "I said to him, 'Do not leave me, Master. Take me with you. I am truly a slave as you have suspected. You are the first man to discern this. Thus you are the first man to whom I belong.'" She smiled. "'Yes,' he said, 'I see that you are a slave, but I do not know if you will please me.'"

"And then?" I asked.

"Then," she said, "I was very afraid, for I sensed that if he should so much as touch his lips to mine I could never again be anything but a man's slave. What if I should not please him? Would he not then simply abandon me, leaving me behind, a masterless girl, a lonely, forlorn slave on a world empty of men strong enough to be a woman's master?"

I supposed it was hard for one who was a slave to be in a world in which there were no masters. Perhaps there were masters on such a world, but she had not yet found them. The slave seeks her master, the master his slave. When they find one another they will know it. She will kneel to him, and he will accept her as his.

"Did he permit you to speak further?" I asked.

"Yes," she said. I opened my arms to him. I said to him, 'I will try with all my heart to please you, my master, that I may be found worthy to be taken with you as your slave.'"

"What then did he say?" I asked.

"He said nothing," she said. "He only held me by the arms, and I could not move. Then he laughed. Then he used me for his pleasure."

"His domination was ruthless?" I asked.

"Yes," she smiled, "lovingly ruthless."

"He treated you as a slave?" I asked.

"Completely," she said.

"As was proper," I said.

"Of course," she smiled. "I was his slave. Should a slave not be treated as a slave?"

"Of course," I said.

"When he finished with me," she said, "I said to him, 'Have I pleased you, Master?' He did not respond but, from a bottle, poured a tiny bit of fluid into a cloth. 'Did I please you, Master?' I again begged. Then he placed the damp cloth over my mouth and nose, holding it tightly. 'Yes,' he said, 'you have pleased me, Slave.' I looked up at him. I could sense the fumes in the cloth. 'You are a pretty slave,' he said. 'You will bring a good price in the market.' I realized then that he would only keep me for a time, and would then sell me. I realized then that I would have many masters. I struggled, but I could not escape. Then I lost consciousness."

"An interesting dream," I said.

"Then one day," she said, "I awakened, chained on Gor." She kissed me. "Master," she said.

"Yes," I said.

"The girls who are kept slave in the cities," she asked, "are they happy?"

"Many are blissfully happy," I said. "Strange," I mused, "that that should be so, and yet the facts are incontrovertible. Many of them, collared, subject to the whip, are yet blissfully happy. It makes little sense to me. I do not profess to understand it."

"I sense how it could be, Master," she said.

"A girl, of course," I said, "in having many masters learns how to please men. She must, of course."

"I am sure that is part of it, Master," said Audrey. "May I speak?"

"Yes," I said. "I sense," she said, "what my true master would be like."

"Any man who owns you is your true master," I said.

"That is true," she laughed. "But I have a dream of a perfect master, to whom I could be but a perfect slave."

"I see," I said.

"Other girls, too," she said, "must sense this sort of thing."

"Perhaps," I said.

"Do not men have some sense of what sort of girl would be their perfect slave?" she asked.

"Some girls are surely more attractive and desirable than others," I said, "and clearly this is not a simple function of physical appearance. Indeed, some rather plain girls are, for no reason that is clear to me, tormentingly attractive, intensely desirable."

"There is no simple answer," she said.

"No," I said, "I do not think so."

"Is it not true," she laughed, "that all men want a woman who will bring them their slippers in her teeth?"

"Sandals," I corrected her.

"Sandals," she laughed.

"Yes," I said, "every man wants such a woman."

"And a slave girl must," she said.

"If the master so instructs her," I said. "Of course."

"All men want," she laughed, "is a girl panting in their arms."

"Surely more than that," I said. "Any girl can be made to pant in a man's arms," I pointed out.

"That is true," she said, bitterly. She was slave. She knew she could be forced to yield to any man.

"What is it that you are trying to say?" I asked.

"You could not easily delineate for me your criteria for the perfect slave," she said, "nor I to you my criteria for the perfect master. Indeed, one might be a perfect slave to one master and not to another, as one might be the perfect master to one slave and not to another."

"Go on," I told her.

"But we both sense," she said, "that there would be a rightness, or rightnesses, about such matters."

"Perhaps," I said.

"I think I would know my perfect master as soon as his eyes met mine," she said.

"I doubt it," I said.

"I would certainly know," she said, "that it might well be he."

"Perhaps," I granted.

"Too," she said, "I suspect that you generally have little difficulty in picking from a line of chained girls those who are of the most interest to you."

"That is true," I smiled. "But such difficulties, even should they occur, are, of course, not intolerable."

"Beast," she said. "But my point, Master, if I may be permitted to continue to speak, is that both of us would sense rightnesses, fittingnesses, matches, agreeabilities. complementarities, in such matters."

"Of course," I said. Then I said, "Ah, yes, your point is an interesting one."

"Yes," she said. "Suppose that a woman is, as I am, a natural slave."

"Yes," I said, "the buying and the selling."

"A girl will often have many masters, will she not?" she asked.

"Yes," I said. "A comely girl may change hands many times."

"And a master, of course," she said, "is likely to own, from month to month, or year to year, several different girls."

"Yes," I said. Most Gorean masters could not afford more than one girl. The price obtained on one, of course, can be applied to the purchase of the next. In this sense, after the initial investment, provided one both sells and buys, girls are cheap.

"A man, too," she said, "buys women who are attractive to him. It is harder for the woman, but she, too, at times, is in a position to influence her sale. She will try to appear more beautiful and pleasing to the man she wishes to buy her than to one she does not wish to buy her."

"The slaver will take her hide off with the whip if he catches her at it," I said. "Too," I said, "at a public auction that sort of thing is difficult or impossible."

"Yes," said Audrey, "in a public auction, as I understand it, a woman is completely at the mercy of the men."

"Your point is an excellent one," I said. "If women are true slaves, and men are true masters, and slave exchanges are frequent, there is a resonable chance that a man may find his choice slave, and a girl her choice master."

"Or perfect slave and master," she whispered.

"Yes," I said.

The bliss of many slave girls now seemed less puzzling to me. First, as girls, natural slaves, they were in a relationship to which, in effect, they were bred by nature, that of the submitting organism in an ancient biological complementarity of male and female; female slavery is but the cultural institutionalization, the expression and perfection, to be expected in conscious, intelligent organisms, intent upon remaining true to nature, rather than violating it, of the male's control and ownership of his female. Man owns woman by nature; in a complex society, and in a world with property rights and laws, female slavery, as a legalized fact, is to be expected; it will occur in any society in which touch is kept with the truths of nature. Gorean law, of course, is complex and latitudinous on these matters. For example, many women are free, whether wisely or desirably or not, and slavery is not always permanent for a slave girl. Sometimes a girl, winning love, is freed, perhaps to bear the children of a former master. But the freedom of a former slave girl is always a somewhat tenuous thing. Her thigh still bears the brand. And, should her ears be pierced, it is almost certain she will, sooner or later, be re-enslaved. It is hard for men to leave a woman who can be a good slave girl free. She will always dread that in the night men will come again for her, hooding her, carrying her to a distant city, to be again put on the block of a steaming market, that once again her throat will be encircled by a steel collar and that she will kneel at the feet of a new master. Slavery also, of course, encompasses the ownership of male slaves, for which there is less precedent in nature. Where males are concerned the institution is primarily economic. The labor of male slaves is useful and cheap. It is applied in such places as the quarries, the roads, the great farms, in certain types of cargo galleys, on the wharves, at the walls of cities and in the forests. Male slaves are usually debtors or criminals; sometimes they are captives, taken in actions against enemy cities or facilities; sometimes they have merely accrued the displeasure of powerful men or families; some slavers, working in gangs, specialize in the capture of free men for work projects; they obtain a fee per head on a contractual basis.

The second reason for the bliss of many slave girls, that sequent upon the appropriateness of bondage for the beautiful woman itself, her female joy in being made to be true to herself, slave, was that, given the flesh transactions in a given city, sooner or later, masters tended to find girls who were, from their point of view, superb slaves, and girls tended to find men who were, from their point of view, marvels as masters. It is a beautiful moment when the woman realizes that the man who owns her is her love master, and the man realizes that the girl he bought, looking up at him, tears in her eyes, is his love slave.

Then the only danger is that he will weaken. One must be strong with a love slave. If one truly loves her, he will be that strong. The slavery in which a love slave is kept is an unusually deep slavery. She must serve him with a perfection which would stun and startle other girls; if she should fail in any way, even in so small a way that the lapse would be overlooked in the case of another wench, or bring perhaps a mild word of reprimand, she is likely to be tied at the slave ring and whipped; there is a good reason for this; she is, you see, a love slave; no woman can be more in a man's power; and with no woman must he be stronger.

Too, of course, if a relationship should weaken, or not prove enduringly satisfactory, the girl is simply put in cuffs and taken to a market.

The relationship which does not prove satisfactory is soon terminated. This termination is completely in the power of the master.

"Enough discussion," I said. "Let us have you."

"Yes, have me, Master," she whispered. Her lips met mine, eagerly.

"You are a highly intelligent slave," I said, "Audrey."

"Thank you, Master," she said.

"You have been instructive to me," I said. "I am pleased by this."

"Men of Earth," she said, "will not listen to a woman."

"Some men will," I said. "But what you intimate is true. Generally men of Earth will not listen to women. Their minds are closed on the matter. Being men they think all human beings are the same as themselves. It is a natural fallacy. Masculine women, those unfortunate creatures, in their frustration, exploit this weakness in the men of Earth. They tell them what they want to hear. This they then take as evidence confirming their preconceptions. It is sad that the true needs of women must then be sacrificed to the ignorance of men and the political and economic ambitions of hirsute frustrates."

"You speak cruelly," she said.

"I am sorry," I said. "Doubtless the matter is more complex than these simplicities suggest."

"I pity women who are not women," she said.

"On Earth," I said, "they proclaim themselves the true women."

"That is natural," she said. "What do you expect them to say?"

"I suppose you are right," I said.

"I think so," she said.

"What counts on Earth as the liberation of women," I said, "is conformance to a certain stereotype, an aggressive, manlike, Lesbian image, one alien to, and offensive to, most normal women. Most women do not truly wish to be men. They find it difficult to believe that they cannot be true women until they are like men. A true liberation of women might be desirable, one which would permit them to be themselves, whatever they might be, a liberation that would free a woman to be feminine rather than constrict her to the imitation of manhood, a liberation without preset images and goals, which would permit her to find herself, wherever and however she might be, honestly, a liberation that would not be a gibberish of political prescriptions, a facsimile of the most sordid side of alien, malelike egoisms, a liberation that would free women in all their latent richness, their diversities and glories, that would be open enough to accept gratefully and, yes, celebrate such currently denigrated properties as softness, tenderness and love. A liberation of a woman, too, which does not permit her to be wild and free and sensuous, and true to her true needs, is not a liberation but a new imprisonment."

237

"I do not want to be liberated," she whispered to me.

"Do not fear," I told her. "You will not be."

She looked up at me, and kissed me.

"A woman as beautiful as you will be kept as a slave." I said. "You are too beautiful to be free."

"I will be kept as a slave?" she asked.

"Yes, because men want you as a slave," I said.

"My will means nothing?" she asked.

"Nothing," I told her.

'She looked up at me. "I am content, Master," she said.

"You are a slave," I said.

"I am a woman," she said.

"And a slave," I said.

"Yes, a slave," she said. Her eyes were moist. "Do you know why I am content?" she asked.

"No, Slave," I said.

"Because I am a slave," she said. "It is strange," she said, "we have talked of freedom, of liberation. And yet I feel that somehow, though I am slave, I am the most liberated, the most free of women, For the first time in my life I am free to obey, to love and be pleasing."

"You are not simply free to do such things," I said, "you must do them."

"Yes," she said, "and I have found myself, with bondage strings on my throat, in a barbarian's tent, on a strange world."

"It is here," I said, "that you are forced to be true to your own nature. Nothing else is permitted."

"True freedom," she said, "is to follow one's own nature."

"All else," I said, "is rhetoric, and the dictates of others."

"Then I am free!" she cried.

"Be quiet," I said, "or I will take you outside, tie you to the pole and whip you."

She looked at me, frightened. "Yes, Master," she whispered.

"Do you think you are free now?" I asked.

"No, Master," she said.

"You are not free," I said. "You are a slave. You are in total bondage."

"Yes, Master," she said.

"Do not forget it," I said.

"No, Master," she whispered, frightened.

"Perhaps I should whip you," I said.

"Rather let me try to please you," she begged. She was frightened.

"Very well," I said. The slave girl then fell to kissing me, eager to placate the master.

It is well not to let a girl grow too enamoured of her bondage. It is well not to let her forget that she is only a slave.

Later Audrey lay in my arms. "I am happy, Master," she whispered.

"Let us sleep now," I said.

"Yes, Master," she whispered. "Master," she said.

"Yes," I said.

"I am pleased that you won my use in the gambling. I have been pleased to serve you."

"Let us sleep now," I said.

"Yes, Master," she whispered.

"Master," she said. She spoke very softly, that she not awaken me, should I be asleep.

"Yes," I said.

"Do you think Imnak will keep me a slave forever," she asked.

"No," I said, "I do not think so."

"Will he free me?" she asked.

"Of course not," I said.

"Will I be killed?" she asked.

"I do not think it likely," I said, "if you are sufficiently pleasing."

"I will be sufficiently pleasing," she said, earnestly. "What do you think will be done with me?" she asked.

"Imnak now has Poalu," I said.

"He does not need me any longer," she said.

"No," I said, "nor Thimble, though you are both pretty things to have in the tent."

"What will he do with us?" she asked.

"It is my guess," I said, "that both Thimble and yourself will be traded south next spring for tea and sugar."

"Traded! For tea and sugar!" she said.

"Yes," I said.

"Audrey Brewster sold for tea and sugar!" she said.

"Thistle, the slave," I said.

"But I am she" she said.

"Be pleased that panther girls are not selling you for arrow points and a handful of candy," I said.

"Who are panther girls?" she asked.

"Strong women, huntresses who frequent the northern forests," I said. "They enjoy selling feminine women like yourself."

"Oh," she said.

"You are a slave," I said. "Do you think you would like to be a woman's slave?"

"No," she said, shuddering. She kissed me. "I am a man's slave," she said.

"It is true," I said.

"Are panther girls truly so strong?" she asked.

"Not really," I said. "Once captured and conquered, collared and silked, their thigh burned by the iron, thrown to a man's feet, they are as quick to kiss and lick as any woman. Indeed, they make superb slaves. They bring high prices in the markets. They are only girls desperate to fight their femininity. When they are no longer permitted to do this they have no choice but to become marvelous women and slaves. A conquered panther girl is one of the most abject and delicious, and joyful, of slaves."

"I see, Master " she said.

"How would I be taken south?" she asked.

"Afoot, your neck tied to a sled," I said.

"I do not want to remain a slave of red hunters indefinitely," she said. "I think I would like to be taken south."

"What you like is of no interest," I said.

"I know," she said.

"If I were to be taken south," she said, "would I be sold there?"

"Doubtless," I said.

"Publicly?" she asked.

"Presumably," I said.

"Naked?" she asked.

"You might wear chains," I said. "I do not know."

"Only a fool buys a woman clothed," she said.

"That is a Gorean saying," I said.

"Imnak taught it to me," she laughed.

"Surely you see the sense of it?" I asked.

"Of course," she said, "if I were a man I would buy a woman only if she were naked. I would want to see what I was getting, completely."

"Precisely," I said.

"I would even want to try her out," she said, boldly.

"That is done in certain sorts of sales," I said, "such as purple booth sales in the courtyard of a slaver's house."

"If there were a handsome buyer, I would try hard to please him," she said.

"You would try hard to please any potential buyer," I said,

"or your owner, the slaver, would express his dissatisfaction to you."

"I see," she said.

A slaver normally expresses his dissatisfaction to his girls with a whip.

"But what of large sales, public sales?" she asked.

"Even in most private sales," I said, "the prospective buyer is not permitted to use the girl, fully."

"Fully?"

"He might be permitted to feel her a bit," I said. "A great deal can be told by simply getting your hands on a girl," I said. "What does her arm feel like above the elbow? How does she turn when you take her by the shoulders and face her away from you? What of the delights of her thigh, the sweetness behind her knees, the turn of her calves? You lift a foot. Does she have a high instep. A girl with a high instep is often a fine dancer. You turn her again to face you. The eyes are very important. Much can be learned there of her intelligence. You kiss her breasts softly, you brush her lips with yours. You study her eyes, her expressions. Then, unexpectedly perhaps, or perhaps first warning her, you touch her. Again attend to the eyes. You continue to touch her. You watch the eyes. Then she screams for mercy, writhing in her chains or in the grasp of the slaver, his hand in her hair. You then know about all you can, without putting her through slave paces or forcing her to perform on the furs."

"Then slavers seldom permit their girls to be fully used?" she asked.

"Not for free," I said. "A common arrangement, however, is to charge a prospective buyer, if he wishes it, a rent fee, which fee may then be, should he want the girl, applied to her purchase price."

"That seems sound business " she said.

"I think so," I said. "Why should a slaver give away the use of his properties?" I asked. "After all that is how he makes his living, buying and selling, and leasing and renting women."

"Of course," she said. "But there are the purple booth sales," she said.

"Those are usually for a well-fixed clientele, known to the slaver," I said. "They are known to him as serious, bonafide buyers. If they do not buy one girl, they will probably buy another."

"Oh," she said.

"But what of large, public sales?" she pressed.

241

"In which, say, an auction block would be used?" I asked.

She shuddered. "Yes," she said.

"Such sales are common on Gor," I said.

"Common?" she gasped.

"Certainly," I said. "Many women are auctioned from the block in a given year in a given city," I said. "Do you remember the large blue and yellow pavillion near the platforms where Imnak bought you?"

"Yes " she said.

"Women were being auctioned there," I said.

"Oh," she said. "I was not," she said.

"You were not regarded as being sufficiently interesting at that time to be put on the block," I said. "The platforms were good enough for your sort."

"But I am beautiful," she said.

"On Gor," I said, "beautiful women are plentiful, and cheap."

"Am I more interesting now, Master?" she wheedled.

"Yes," I said, "You are perhaps worthy now to grace the block—"

"Thank you, Master," she said.

"—in a minor sale in a small city," I added.

"Oh, Master!" she laughed.

"I jest," I said, "but, too, I am serious. You will grow in slavery and beauty. Who knows what a woman's potential is for love?"

She looked at me.

"You have far to go, my lovely little tart," I said. "But in the end I think you might be worthy of the central block, at the Curulean in Ar."

She kissed me, frightened. "What a fearful thing it is to be a slave girl, and what a wonderful thing," she said.

I said nothing.

"How does one know, on the block," she asked, suddenly, "if a girl is any good?"

"A certification of a girl's heat, in certain cities," I said, "is sometimes furnished, with the slaver's guarantee, among the documents of sale. Her degree of heat, in such a situation would also be listed of course, among her other properties, on her sales sheet, posted in the vicinity of the exhibition cages, available twenty Ahn before her sale. It would also be proclaimed, of course, in such a situation, along with her weight and collar size, and such things, from the block, during her sale."

"Is that sort of thing done in many cities?" she asked.

242

"In very few," I said, "and for a very good reason."

"Out of respect for the girls?" she asked.

"Of course not," I said. "It is rather done in few cities because of the possibility of fraud on the part of the buyer. He might use the girl for a month and then claim a refund in virtue of the guarantee. Slavers prefer for their sales to be final. Too, other problems exist. For example, a free woman who, before her sale, is cold may become, after her sale, knowing herself then as a vended slave, helpless and torrid in the arms of a master. Similarly a girl who is only average, generally, so to speak, may, at the very glance of a given master, one who is special to her for no reason that is clear, become so weak and paga hot that she can scarcely stand."

"Generally, then," she said, "the buyer would not know, from the block information, whether the girl would be any good or not?"

"He will certainly know if he, personally, finds her attractive. Too, even a frigid woman, in the arms of a Gorean master, can be made to sweat and cry."

"Frigidity is not permitted to the slave girl?" she asked.

"No," I said. "The master will not accept it."

"Poor girl," she laughed.

"Frigidity is a neurotic luxury," I told her. "It is allowed only to free women, probably because no one cares that much about them. Indeed, frigidity is one of the titles and permissions implicated in the lofty status of a free woman. For many it is, in effect, their proudest possession. It distinguishes them from the lowly slave girl. It proves to themselves and others that they are free. Should they be enslaved, of course, it is, for better or for worse, taken from them, like their property and their clothing."

"Not all free women are frigid," she said.

"Of course not," I said, "but there is actually a scale, so to speak, in such matters. But just as some free women are insufficiently inert, or cold, to qualify, strictly, as frigid, perhaps to their chagrin, so none of them, I think, are sufficiently ignited to qualify in the ranges of "slave-girl hot," so to speak. A free woman's sexuality may generally be thought of in terms of degrees of inertness, or coolness; a slave girl's sexuality, on the other hand, may generally be thought of in terms of degrees of responsive passion, or heat. Some slave girls are hotter than others, of course, just as some free women are less cold than others, whether this pleases them or not. Whereas the free woman normally maintains a plateau of frigidity, however, the slave girl will usually increase in

243

degrees of heat, this a function of her master, his strength, her training, and such. The slave girl grows in passion; the free woman languishes in her frigidity, congratulating herself on the starvation of her needs."

"Do free women know what they are missing?" she asked.

"I think, on some level, they do," I said. "Else the resentment and hatred they bear the slave girl would be inexplicable."

"I see," she said.

"Beware the free woman," I said.

"Yes, Master," she said.

"On the block, of course," I said, "the girl is under the control of the auctioneer, who functions as her master while she is being sold. He will often exhibit her skillfully. A good auctioneer is very valuable to a slaver's house. He will guide her with his voice, and touches, or strokes, of his whip. He may put her through slave paces on the block, forcing her to assume postures and attitudes. If she is a dancer, she may be forced to dance. She may be, if he sees fit, publicly caressed on the block."

"Before the buyers!" she said.

"Of course," I said. "It does not matter. She is a slave."

"Of course," she whispered. "She is only a slave."

"It is not unusual," I said, "to even send a girl aroused onto the block, that the nature of her movements may make clear her needs to the audience."

"And should such a girl be caressed?" she asked.

"She might enter orgasm on the very block," I said. "Sometimes it is necessary to whip such a woman from the feet of the auctioneer. At the very least she will beg to serve a master within the very Ahn, either a buyer or one of the slaver's men, to achieve closure on the arousal which has been inflicted upon her."

"How cruel Goreans are!" she said.

"Is this more cruel than making clear the color of her hair and eyes?" I asked. "The Goreans are buying the whole girl."

She looked down.

"Do not fear," I said. "Normally there is no time for a lengthy sale. One must take a few bids and then thrust the wench from the block, to make room for the next girl. A sale often takes no more time than one or two Ehn. Sometimes four hundred girls or more must be sold from a single block in a given night."

"One might be exhibited and sold before one scarcely knew what was occurring," she said.

"I suppose so," I said. "I am not a woman."

"But I am," she said.

"It is thus likely to be your problem and not mine," I told her.

"How you tease one who is only a slave," she said.

"One does what one pleases with them," I told her.

"Of course," she said. "We are only slaves."

"Master," she said.

"Yes," I said.

"Is there no cure for a free woman's frigidity?" she asked.

"Of course," I said.

"Total enslavement?" she asked.

"Yes," I said.

She said nothing.

"Every woman has a need to submit herself to a master," I said. "When she finds herself at the feet of her master her body will no longer permit her to be frigid. There is no longer any reason. She is now where nature places her, at his feet and in his power. She kisses his feet and, weeping, feeling the heat and oils between her lovely legs, cannot wait to be thrown to the furs."

She did not speak.

"But I do not speak here merely of the simplicities and negativities of a cure," I said. "I speak rather of the beginning of a career, a helpless, flowering biography of service, love and passion."

"You speak of a woman being made a slave girl," she said.

"Yes," I said.

"I wonder if I will be pleasing to a master," she said.

"Any slave girl," I said, "with the proper management, and master, can become a wonder of sexuality and love."

"I think I will love being a slave girl," she said.

I shrugged. What did it matter, what her feelings were? She was a slave.

"No wonder the free women hate us so," she said.

"Of course," I said. "You are everything that they desire to be and are not."

She bit her lip. She looked at me. "Are free women permitted to watch us being sold?" she asked.

"Of course," I said. "Why not? They are free."

She looked at me, miserably.

"Ah, yes," I said. "I see. It would be quite humiliating, one woman, a slave, being sold, while another woman, a free woman, observes."

"Yes," she said.

"Let us hope that the free woman is not one of powerful family," I said, "who has had the other captured, and put upon the block."

"That would be dreadful," she said.

"Women are capable of such things," I said.

She put down her head.

"Perhaps it is well that they are not dominant," I said. "Perhaps they should all be controlled, and kept in collars."

"Or bondage strings," she laughed.

"Yes, or bondage strings, like you, my pretty slave," I said.

"Men want us as their abject slaves, don't they?" she asked.

"Yes, like you, my dear," I told her. "Any man who tells you differently is lying."

"Are most Gorean women slaves?" she asked.

"No," I said. "Indeed, statistically, in those parts of Gor with which I am familiar, very few. Commonly only one woman in, say, forty or fifty is a slave. This varies somewhat of course, from city to city. The major exception to these ratios is the city of Tharna, in which almost every woman is a slave." I looked at her. "There are special historical reasons for that," I said.

"But over a large population," she said, "there would be literally thousands."

"Of course," I said.

"Are the most beautiful and desirable women those who, generally, are the slaves?" she asked.

"Yes," I said, "the most beautiful and desirable women on the planet seem generally to be the slaves."

"Such women would be the prime target for the strike of slavers," she said.

"Yes," I said. "A girl of low caste, of a poor family, who is truly beautiful, a girl who cannot afford shelter in a protected area, is almost certain, sooner or later, to find her neck ringed with a collar. As far as that goes, a girl of wealth and high caste, who is beautiful, is not out of danger. It is regarded as great sport to take them."

"A sport of men," she said.

"Yes, to make beautiful women slaves," I said.

"A delicious sport," she said.

"I think so," I said.

"Beast," she said.

"Perhaps," I said. "I think it is true," I said, "that it is generally the most beautiful and desirable women who are the slaves, but I will tell you something you may find of interest."

"What is that?" she asked.

"Slavery itself," I said, "often makes a woman more beautiful and desirable. It removes tensions. It removes inhibitions. It makes women happy. It is hard, I think, sometimes, for a woman who is happy not to be beautiful. Sometimes Goreans ask, is she a slave because she is beautiful, or beautiful because she is a slave?"

She kissed me, gently.

"Are many Gorean slave girls of Earth origin?" she asked.

"I assume all human Goreans are of Earth origin," I said.

"I mean," she said, "like me, a girl born and raised on Earth, and then brought to Gor as a slave."

"Statistically," I said, "surely few. How many I would not know."

"Ten," she asked, "twenty?"

"Perhaps some four or five thousand," I said. "I would not know." Such a number, I conjectured, would not even be missed in a population which teemed like that of Earth.

"We are brought here as slaves," she said.

"Of course," I said.

"And the slaving continues," she said.

"I suppose so," I said. "On Gor there is a market for beautiful Earth girls. They make excellent slaves."

"I am glad to hear that," she said.

"Please me," I said.

"Yes, Master," she said, obediently, this time without surprise or demur. And then she well pleased me. She was becoming skillful.

"Please tell me more of the south," she said.

"Please me," I said.

"Yes, Master," she said. Yes, she was becoming quite skillful.

"Please tell me more of the south," she said.

"Curiosity is not becoming in a Kajira," I said.

"Oh, Master," she said.

"That is a Gorean saying," I said.

"I know," she said. "Imnak taught it to me."

"You now know two Gorean sayings," I said.

"Yes," she said. " 'Only a fool buys a woman clothed' and 'Curisoity is not becoming in a Kajira.' "

"Yes," I said.

"Please, Master," she said.

"You have them down well," I said.

"Oh, please, please, Master," she begged.

It was natural that she should be desperately eager to learn the nature of a slave girl's lot.

"Perhaps," I said.

"Oh, thank you, thank you, Master," she said.

"What would you like to know?" I asked.

She was at my side, on her stomach and elbows. Her eyes were excited. "In the south," she asked, "would a master put me in a collar?"

"It is quite likely," I said.

"I might like a pretty collar," she said.

"Do not think of the collar as a simple piece of jewelry," I said, "though it can serve that purpose. Its primary objective is to identify he to whom you belong."

"What if I take it off?" she asked.

"It locks on your throat. You cannot take it off," I said.

"Oh," she said. She looked at me. "Will I be given pretty things to wear," she asked, "and cosmetics, perfumes?"

"It is quite likely," I said. "Masters like their girls to make themselves beautiful."

"I hope that I will please my master in the furs," she said.

"You will do so or be lengthily and severely punished," I said. "If you fail, you could even be slain,"

She shuddered. "I will try to be pleasing to him," she said.

"Most masters," I said, "own only one girl. Do not think you are likely to spend all your time squirming at the slave ring."

"I do not understand," she said.

"There is much for a girl to do," I pointed out. "She keeps his compartments. She dusts and cleans. When they do not use the public kitchens she must cook for him. If he does not wish to take advantage of the public laundries, she must do his washing and ironing. She shops for him, and bargains in the markets, and so on. There is much for her to do."

"Does it take long to clean compartments?" she asked.

"Only a few moments," I admitted. "Goreans live simply, and do not much approve of cumbersome furniture."

"It does not sound to me like the slave girl is overburdened with domestic labors," she said.

"I suppose, objectively, she is not," I said. "Still, there are things for her to do."

"Is she as occupied as the wife of Earth?" asked the girl.

"Of course not," I said. "That would be foolish. The wife of Earth is, from the Gorean point of view, much over-worked. When the husband returns home she is often, actually, engaged in labors. How can she greet him properly? At night, so numerous and excessive have been her labors, she is often exhausted. That would be preposterous from the Gorean point of view. The Gorean master does not buy a girl with the primary objective of obtaining a domestic servant but with the intention of acquiring a marvelous slave. He wants the girl to be a wonder to him. He is quite cheerful about the sacrifice of domestic servitude in order to obtain what is far more important to him. When he returns to his compartments he does not want to find a worn chore woman there but a lovely slave, fresh, vital, eager and fully alive, kneeling before him, waiting to be commanded."

"What does the girl do in her free time?" asked Audrey.

"Much what she pleases," I said. "She will have friends among other slaves. She walks, she visits. She exercises, she reads. Within limits she does what she wants to do."

"Can she work outside the compartments?" asked Audrey.

"If it is permitted by the master," I said, "and it does not in any way compromise her slavery." I smiled. "Some women," I said, "wear to their work the garments of a free woman but, when they return to their compartments, don as they must the silk of a slave, which is their true condition."

"Is such a thing often permitted by a master?" asked Audrey.

"Commonly not," I said. "Such a thing is often thought to compromise a girl's slavery. It is usually not permitted to her. Usually she is kept as full and absolute slave, not so much as permitted to touch the garment of a free woman."

"I would like my master to be like that," said Audrey.

"Most masters are," I said.

"If I am a slave, I would want to be a full slave," she said.

"I think you have little to fear, pretty Audrey," I said. "Any master who so much as looks at you would know that you should be kept only as a full slave."

"Yes," she said, kissing me, "that is right for me."

"Sometimes, Masters, as a discipline, rent their girls out to employers to perform repetitious, trivial tasks."

"How horrid," she said.

"See that you please your master well," I said.

"I will certainly try," she said.

"There are, of course, many slaveries in the south," I said. "I have described only the most common to you."

"Tell me of others," she begged. "For I might be sold into them."

"There are paga slaves," I said, "who must please their master's customers in his tavern. There are the girls who staff

249

the public kitchens and laundries. There are rent slaves, who may be rented to anyone for any purpose, short of their injury or mutilation, unless compensation be rendered to the master. There are state slaves who maintain public compartments, and work in offices and warehouses. There are girls in peasant villages, and girls on great farms, who cook and carry water to the slave gangs. There are beauties who are purchased for a man's pleasure gardens. There are other girls who work in the mills, chained to their looms."

She looked at me, frightened.

"Any of these slaveries, or any of many others," I said, "could be yours. It depends entirely, pretty Audrey, on who buys you, and what he wants."

"How helpless I feel," she whispered.

"You are helpless, absolutely helpless," I told her.

"Surely," she whispered, "I can attempt to influence the nature of my slavery."

"Of course," I said. "But the decision is never yours. In that sense you are absolutely helpless."

"Yes, Master," she said, trembling.

"The mills and the public kitchens, and such, are not pleasant." I said.

"I do not want to go to such slaveries as the mills or public kitchens," she said. "I will try to be a pleasing slave."

"Excellent, Audrey, Slave Girl," I said.

"Do masters much talk with their girls, or take them with them?" she asked.

"Certainly," I said. "It is extremely pleasurable to talk with a girl one owns. Also, one takes her many places, she heeling him, to concerts, contests, song dramas and so on, both to show her off and because he finds her a joy to be with."

"I think I could well serve such a master," she said.

"You would," I said, "or you, being a slave, would be promptly and efficiently disciplined, most likely whipped."

"Whipped?" she asked. "Could such a man whip a girl?"

"Of course," I said. "Do not think that the pleasure he finds in you will be permitted in the least to compromise his mastery of you."

"I would thrill to be owned by such a man," she said.

I smiled to myself. Girls sometimes fought one another viciously, merely to be the first to display themselves naked before a Gorean master.

I lay there on my back.

"Master," she said.

"Yes," I said.

"The others, soon, will be awake," she said.

"Yes?" I said.

"Please, Master," she said. "Once more, before they awaken, have your slave."

"Have you?" I asked.

"Yes, have me," she whispered.

"Does Audrey beg?" I asked.

"Yes, Master," she said.

"How shall I have you?" I asked. "Gently, tenderly, politely, courteously, respectfully, accomodatingly, solicitously, as would a man of Earth?"

"No, no," she begged. "Take me as what I am, a slave!"

I touched her, gently, timidly.

"Oh!" she cried, miserably. "No, that is like a man of Earth! How cruel you are! Do not insult the helpless womanhood of a poor slave. Do not play with my needs as a man of Earth, oh, Master; fulfill them as a man of Gor! I beg it of you, Master."

I laughed.

"You teased a slave," she said, reproachfully. "How helpless I am as a slave."

"Spread your legs, Slave," I said.

"Yes, Master," she said. "My Gorean master has spoken," she said.

"Wider," I said.

"Yes, Master," she said.

She watched my hand. Her teeth were clenched. Her eyes were wide.

"Aiii!" she started to cry, but my left hand closed her mouth. She squirmed helplessly. Her thighs were clenched on my hand. She looked at me, over my hand on her mouth.

"You are a pretty slave," I told her.

With my knee I thrust apart her legs.

Then her body clasped me. Her eyes were closed. I removed my hand from her mouth. She opened her eyes. "Thank you," she whispered, "for covering my mouth, that I not be heard to scream."

"You did not wish to awaken the others," I said.

"I could not bear to have them know how I yielded to you," she whispered. "It would be humiliating."

"It is nearly time for them to awaken," I said.

"Master?" she asked. "Master, no!" she cried. "What are you doing?"

"I am going to induce in you," I said, "the first of your slave orgasms."

"No," she wept. "Please, no! There are others in the tent! I do not want the other girls to know what a slave I am! Please, no, Master!"

But I did not choose to show her mercy.

"Cover my mouth!" she begged. "Oh, oh!"

I held her arms pinned to her sides. Then she half reared up under me, squirming and struggling, and then threw back her head, screaming, and I pressed her down on the furs. Imnak lifted his head quickly, and then, understanding the nature of the noise, shook his head and reached over and seized Poalu. She was drawn to him, tightly, and began to kiss him. "I submit," screamed Audrey. "I submit to you, oh, my Master!" Arlene and Thimble, sullenly, angrily, regarded her.

"Slave!" said Arlene.

"Yes, slave, slave!" sobbed Audrey, then covered my face with tears and kisses. I later held her quiet in my arms while she, with her small, soft tongue, licked clean the stubble of my beard.

16   IMNAK CARVES

Imnak sat in the corner of the tent, aimlessly whittling at a piece of tabuk horn.

Once in a while he would stop and turn the ivory, and look at it. Sometimes he would whisper, "Who hides in there? Who are you?" Then he would begin to carve again. Then, suddenly, he said, "Ah, sleen!"

I watched him flake and trim ivory from the horn. Slowly, as I watched, I saw the shape of a sleen emerging, almost as though it had been hidden in the ivory, the snout and legs, and the long, sinuous shape. Its ears were flat back against its head.

Often the red hunter does not set out to carve something, but rather to carve, patiently waiting to see if there is something there, waiting to be released. It is a little like hunting. He is open to what may be found. Sometimes there is a shape in the ivory or bone, or stone. Sometimes there is not. He removes the excess ivory and there, where it had lain hidden before, now revealed, is the shape.

Imnak's knife had a wooden handle, some fourteen inches long. Its point was some three inches in length. He braced it on his leg in carving, his fingers near the blade end where they might delicately control the movement of the metal. Bracing the knife permits force from the leg to be applied, whereas balance and control are not sacrificed, because the point is subtly guided by the movement of the fingers.

Imnak held up the sleen.

In the language of the Innuit there is no word for art or artist.

"It is a handsome animal," I said.

They need no such words. Why should there be special words for men who find beauty in the world. Is this not a concern of all men?

"It is your sleen," said Imnak, giving it to me.

"I am grateful," I said. I looked at it. It was a snow sleen, easily identified by the thickness of the coat, the narrowness of the ears, the breadth of the paws.

"I am very grateful," I said.

"It is nothing," he said.

17 I FIRST HEAR OF KARJUK; I MUST MEET HIM

"But I have never seen it before," said Imnak.

He examined the carving.

It was the head of a Kur, in bluish stone, the ear at the left side of its head half torn away. I had brought it with me from Port Kar. I had originally obtained it at the Sardar Fair, at the booth of the curio dealer.

"I thought you had sold it to the dealer at the fair," I said.

"I sold carvings at the fair," said Imnak, "yes, but I did not sell this."

"I had thought you did," I said.

"No," said Imnak.

"Then he must have obtained the carving from some other," I said.

Imnak shrugged. "It would seem so," he said.

"Who other than you of the Innuit," I asked, "journeyed this year to the fair?"

"Only I," said Imnak.

"Can you be sure?" I asked.

"Reasonably so," said Imnak. "It is a long journey to go to the fair. If some other had gone I think I would have heard of this. It makes good telling in the tents."

"Where then," I asked, "might the dealer have obtained this carving?"

"I do not know," said Imnak. "I am sorry, Tarl, who hunts with me."

"Forgive me, Imnak, who hunts with me," I said, "it was not my intent to impugn your honesty." I had pressed the matter too much with him. He had told me he had not seen the carving before. For a red hunter that was sufficient.

"Can you tell from the styling or toolwork," I asked, "who might have made this carving."

The art of the Innuit is often similar, from object to object. Yet to a subtle eye there are slight differences. One man will release from bone or ivory, or stone, a figure in a way which is slightly different from the way in which another will release it.

Imnak examined the carving carefully, turning it about in his hand.

I felt sick. That carving had, in effect, brought me to the north. Now it seemed it had led me only to a dead end. Miserably in my mind I contemplated the vastness of the polar basin. The summer, too, was already advanced.

"Imnak," I asked, "have you heard of a mountain that does not move?"

He looked at me.

"A mountain of ice," I said, "in the polar sea."

"No," said Imnak.

"Have you not even heard the story of such a mountain?" I asked.

"No," said Imnak.

I looked down at the mat. "Imnak," I said, "have you ever seen such a beast as is represented in that carving?"

"Yes," he said.

I looked up at him, quickly.

"North of Torvaldsland," he said, "I saw one once, some

254

years ago. I threatened it with my harpoon, and it went away."

"Was its ear thusly torn?" I asked.

"It was night," he said. "I did not see it well. I do not think so."

"Was it a large animal?" I asked.

"Not too large," he said.

"What do you call such animals?" I asked.

He shrugged. "Beasts," he said.

I sighed. Some years ago Imnak had seen a Kur north of Torvaldsland. It had probably been a young beast, an off-spring of ship Kurii, stranded long ago on Gor. Such animals are found occasionally, usually in remote areas.

"But it was not an ice beast," he said.

I did not understand him.

"It was not white," he said.

"Oh," I said. "Are there such beasts in the north?"

"Yes," he said, "here and there, on the ice."

These too, I assumed would be native Kurii, the survivors of stranded ship Kurii, perhaps crashed, brought down or marooned generations ago. There were different races of Kurii, I knew, though from my point of view there did not seem much point in discriminating among them. It was speculated that it had been fratricidal wars among such various forms of Kur which had resulted in the destruction of their native world.

Imnak handed the carving back to me.

I was at a loss. I had no clues. My northward journey had brought me to an impasse. There was now nothing to do, nowhere to go.

I was now alone in the north, an isolated, meaningless fool.

"After I sleep," I said, "I am going to return to the south."

"All right," said Imnak.

I placed the carving in the fur wrapper in which I kept it, and then put the carving, in this wrapper, in my pouch.

"That is the work of Karjuk," he said.

I looked up, suddenly.

"You asked me who did the carving, I thought," he said.

"Yes!" I said.

"Karjuk did it," he said.

I embraced him. "You are marvelous, Imnak!" I cried.

"Once, in one day, I slew six sleen," he admitted. "But I am really a poor hunter," he insisted.

"Where is this Karjuk?" I asked. "I would speak with him."

"He is not here," said Imnak.

"Where is he?" I asked.

"In the north," said Imnak.

"Where in the north?" I asked.

"In the far north," said Imnak. "No man lives north of Karjuk," he added.

"Who is Karjuk?" I asked.

"He is the guard," said Imnak.

"The guard?" I asked.

"Yes," said Imnak, "he guards the People against the ice beasts."

"We must find him," I said.

"Karjuk is a strange man," he said. "If the ice beasts cannot find him how can we?"

"I am leaving as soon as I have slept," I told Imnak.

"You are going south?" he asked.

"No," I laughed, "I am now going north."

"You have business in the north?" inquired Imnak politely.

"Yes," I said.

"But the tabuk are not yet fat," he said, "and their coats are not yet thick and glossy."

"I do not understand," I said.

"It is not yet time to go north," he said. "There is a right time and a wrong time to do things. This is the time to hunt tabuk."

"I must go north," I told him. "I can dally here no longer."

"It is not yet time to go north," he said. "The tabuk are not yet fat."

"Nonetheless, I must go north," I told him.

"Your business seems pressing," said he.

"It is," I said.

He looked at me.

"I seek an enemy," I said.

"In the north one needs friends, not enemies," he said.

I smiled at him.

He looked at me. "The beast?" he asked. "You seek the beast with the torn ear? He is your enemy?"

"Yes," I said.

"Let us hope the tabuk grow fat slowly," he said. He grinned.

"After I sleep," I said, "I will leave for the north."

"I will accompany you," he said.

"But the tabuk are not yet fat," I said.

"It is not my fault they came late to the tundra," said Imnak. He stuck his head outside of the tent.

"Poalu," he called. "After we sleep, we are going north."

"It is not time to go north," she cried, horrified.

"I know it is crazy," said Imnak, "but we are going to do it."

"Yes, Imnak," she said, "my master."

Imnak returned to where I sat.

"Where will we find Karjuk?" I asked.

Imnak shrugged. "If Karjuk does not want to be found, he will not be found," he said. "No man knows the ice like Karjuk. We will go to the permanent camp and wait for him there. Sometimes he comes to the permanent camp."

"Where is that camp?" I asked.

"It is by the shore of the sea," he said.

"But what if he does not come to that camp?" I asked.

"Then we will not be able to find him," said Imnak. "If the ice beasts cannot find Karjuk, how can we expect to do so?"

18 WE HUNT IN THE VICINITY OF THE PERMANENT CAMP

I studied the waters carefully.

"It will be soon now," said Imnak. It was not that he had been consciously counting, but rather that he had, doubtless from his experiences in such matters, a sensitivity to the rhythms involved, and the increase in their intensity, given the stress of the beast.

The chill waters seemed very quiet. Here and there pieces of ice drifted in them.

The pebbled shore lay some half pasang away, behind us.

I could see smoke from the permanent camp.

Five men, besides myself, waited in the large skin boat, the umiak. It was some twenty feet in length, and some five feet in its beam. The skins which were sewn over its frame, interestingly, were those of tabuk and not sea sleen. The skins were stretched over a framework, lashed together with sinew cord, of driftwood and long bows of bone.

The waters did not stir.

Usually such a boat is paddled by women, but no women were now within it. One would not risk a woman in our current work, even a slave beast.

"It is nearly time now," said Imnak.

Many times the umiaks, or the light, one-man vessels, the kayaks, do not return.

"Be ready," said Imnak.

The waters seemed very still.

I grasped the long harpoon. It was some eight feet in length, some two and a half inches in diameter. Its major shaft was of wood, but it had a foreshaft of bone. In this foreshaft was set the head of the harpoon, of bone, drilled, with a point of sharpened slate. Through the drilled hole in the bone, some four inches below the slate point and some four inches above the base of the head, was passed a rawhide line, which lay coiled in the bottom of the boat. As the hole is drilled the line, when it snaps taut, will turn the head of the harpoon in the wound, anchoring it.

Suddenly, not more than a dozen feet from the boat, driving upward, rearing vertically, surging, expelling air in a great burst of noise, shedding icy water, in a tangle of lines and blood, burst the towering, cylindrical tonnage of the black Hunjer whale.

I hurled the harpoon.

"Now!" cried Imnak.

Four feet of the shaft disappeared into the side of the vast mammal.

The line, uncoiling, snapping, hurtled past me, upward. The monster, as though it stood on its flukes, towered forty feet above us, the line like a tiny thread, billowing, leading downward to the boat.

"Look out!" cried Imnak.

The beast, grunting, expelling air, fell downward into the water. There was a great crash, that might have been heard for pasangs. The line was now horizontal. The boat was half awash. We were drenched. My parka began to freeze on my body. With leather buckets four men began to hurl water from the boat. The air was thick with vapor, like smoke, the condensing moisture in the monster's warm breath, like a fog, or cloud, on the water. I saw the small eye of the monster, that on the left side of its head, observing us.

"It is going to dive," said Imnak. As he pointed ice broke from his parka.

Imnak and another man began to draw on the line, to pull us to the very side of the monster.

The other hunters in the boat, discarding their buckets, seized up their lances, slender hunting tools, with fixed heads, commonly used not in throwing but in thrusting.

I reached out with my hand and pushed against the side of the mammal. The Hunjer whale is a toothed whale.

Beside me now Imnak and the other hunters, all with lances, began to drive them, like needles, into the side of the animal, again and again.

Its flesh shook, scattering water. I feared the side of the umiak would be stove in.

It grunted.

"Hold the line!" cried Imnak.

I held the line, keeping the umiak at the beast's side, so that the hunters could thrust into it at point-blank range.

Then the animal's eye disappeared under the water. I saw the flukes rearing up.

"Give it line!" cried Imnak.

I threw line over the side.

The flukes were now high above us, and the animal's body almost vertical. The line disappeared under the water.

It was gone.

"Now we will wait," said Imnak. "And then it will begin again."

I looked down at the placid waters. We would wait, until it began again.

The waters seemed very calm. It was hard to believe that we were attached, by a thin line, to that great form somewhere below us. There was some ice in the water about us. The wind scattered the breath of the monster, dispelling the cloud of vapor.

On the pebbled shore, some half pasang away, behind us, I could see smoke from the permanent camp.

I was very cold. I would like some tea when we returned to camp.

19   I DISCIPLINE ARLENE

I looked at Arlene. She, naked, was chewing the ice from my boots. She held the boot with two hands and bit and chewed carefully.

She looked up at me, the fur of the boot in her mouth.

"Continue your work," I told her.

She continued to free the fur of the tiny bits of ice, biting and chewing. How marvelous are the mouths of women, so delicate, with their small teeth, their sweet lips, their soft, warm tongues. When she had broken the ice from a place on the boot, she would place her mouth over that place, breathing upon it, softening and melting the residue of ice there. Then, with her tongue, she would lick the fur smooth.

When she had finished with both boots she placed them on the drying rack.

I sat in Imnak's hut, cross-legged. She returned to a place before me, and knelt.

It is pleasant to have a slave girl kneeling before you.

"May I have permission to speak, Master?" she asked.

"Yes," I said.

"Why have you come north?" she asked.

"It pleases me," I said.

"Must I be content with that?" she asked.

"Yes," I said.

"Why?" she asked.

"Because it pleases me," I said.

"Yes, Master," she said.

"Spread the furs," I told her. "Your insolence requires discipline."

"Yes, Master," she said.

20 THE FEASTING HOUSE; WE RETURN TO THE FEASTING HOUSE

"Aja! Aja!" sang the woman.

I bit into the steak. Beside me, cross-legged, sat Imnak, grease from the raw blubber he chewed at the side of his mouth. He wiped his face with his sleeve.

The feasting house was full. There were some forty individuals, men and women, crowded into the structure.

Imnak and I, and the girls, had come north in the summer, early. For weeks we had waited at the empty permanent camp. Finally, in the early fall, several families had arrived to occupy their seasonally abandoned dwellings. As it had turned out we could have taken our way north with the People, the various groups scattering to their diverse permanent camps. No time had been saved by my haste. We had hunted and fished, and sported with our slaves, and had waited.

"I did not think Karjuk would come to an empty camp," said Imnak, "but I did not know. So I came north with you."

"The camp is not now empty," I had told Imnak.

Imnak had shrugged. "That is true," he said.

"Where is Karjuk?" I asked.

"Perhaps he will come," had said Imnak.

"But what if he does not?" I asked.

"Then," said Imnak, "he does not."

As the weeks had passed I had grown more fretful and anxious.

"Let us hunt for Karjuk," I had urged Imnak.

"If the ice beasts cannot find Karjuk," said Imnak, "how can we find him?"

"What can we do?" I asked.

"We can wait," he said.

We had waited.

The drum of the red hunters is large and heavy. It has a

handle and is disklike. It requires strength to manage it. It is held in one hand and beaten with a stick held in the other. Its frame is generally of wood and its cover, of hide, usually tabuk hide, is fixed on the frame by sinew. Interestingly the drum is not struck on the head, or hide cover, but on the frame. It has an odd resonance. That drum in the hand of the hunter standing now in the midst of the group was some two and one half feet in diameter. He was now striking on it and singing. I could not make out the song, but it had to do with the mild winds which blow in the summer. These songs, incidentally, are rather like tools or carvings. They tend to be regarded as the singer's property. It is unusual for one man or woman to sing another's songs. One is expected to make up one's own songs. It is expected that every man will be able to make up songs and sing them, just as every man is supposed to be able to carve and hunt. These songs are usually very simple, but some of them are quite beautiful, and some are quite touching. Both men and women sing, of course. Men, interestingly, usually do the carving. The ulo, or woman's knife, with its semicircular blade, customarily fixed in a wooden handle, is not well suited to carving. It is better at cutting meat and slicing sinew. Also, carving ivory and bone requires strength. But women sing as well as men. Sometimes they sing of feasting clothes, and lovers, and their skill in quartering tabuk.

Another man now took the drum and began to sing. He sang a kayak-making song, customarily sung to the leather, wood and sinew, with which he worked, that it not betray him in the polar sea. A fellow after him sang a sleen song, usually sung on the water, encouraging the sleen to swim to where he might strike them. The next song dealt with a rascal who, supposedly hunting for tabuk, lay down and rubbed his boots on a rock, later returning to his companions with a report of luckless hunting, indicating his worn boots as evidence of his lengthy trekking. From the looks cast about the room I gathered the rascal might even be present. One fellow, at least, seemed quite embarrassed. He soon leaped up, however, and sang a song about the first fellow, something about a fellow who could not make good arrows. Two women sang after this, the first one about gathering birds' eggs when she was a little girl, and the other one about her joy in seeing the face of a relative whom she had not seen in more than two years.

It is rather commendable, I think, that the red hunters make up songs. They are not as critical as many other people. To them it is often more important that one whom they love sings than it is that his song is a good song. If it is a "true" song, and comes from the heart, they are pleased to hear it. Perhaps then it is a "good song," after all. Songs, even simple ones, are regarded by the red hunters as being precious and rather mysterious. They are pleased that there are songs. As it is said, "No one knows from where songs come."

"Sing, Imnak!" called Akko.

"Sing, Imnak!" called Kadluk.

Imnak shook his head vigorously. "No, no," he said.

"Imnak never sings," said Poalu, helpfully volunteering this information, forgetful apparently of the bondage strings knotted on her throat.

"Come, Imnak," said Akko, his friend. "Sing us a song."

"I cannot sing," said Imnak.

"Come, come, sing!" called others.

To my surprise Imnak rose to his feet and, hastily, left the feasting house.

I followed him outside. So, too, concerned, did Poalu.

"I cannot sing," said Imnak. He stood by the shore. "Songs do not come to my mouth. I am without songs. I am like the ice in the glacier on which flowers will not bloom. No song will ever fly to me. No song ever has been born in my heart."

"You can sing, Imnak," said Poalu.

"No," said Imnak, "I cannot sing."

"Someday," said Poalu, "you will sing in the feasting house."

"No," said Imnak, "I will not sing. I cannot sing."

"Imnak," she protested.

"Go back to the feasting house," he said.

She turned about, and returned to the feasting house. The feasting house, except for being larger, was much like the other dwellings in the permanent camp. It was half underground and double walled. These two walls were of stone. Between them there were layers of peat, for insulation, which had been cut from the boglike tundra. Hides, too, were tied on the inside, from tabuk tents, affording additional protection from the cold. There was a smoke hole in the top of the house. One bent over to enter the low doorway. The ceiling, supported by numerous poles, consisted of layers of grass and mud. There was the feasting house, and some ten or eleven dwellings in the camp. Although there were some fifteen hundred red hunters they generally lived in widely scattered small groups. In the summer there was a gathering for the great tabuk hunt, when the herd of Tancred crossed Ax Glacier and came to the tundra, but, even in the summer, later, the smaller groups, still pursuing tabuk, would scatter in their hunts, following the casual dispersal of the tabuk in their extended grazings. At the end of the summer these groups, loosely linked save in the spring or early summer, would make their ways back to their own camps. There were some forty of these camps, sometimes separated by journeys of several days. Imnak's camp was one of the more centrally located of the camps. In these camps the red hunters lived most of the year. They would leave them sometimes in the winter, when they needed more food, families individually going out on the pack ice to hunt sleen. Sleen were infrequent in the winter and there would not, often, be enough to sustain ten or twelve families in a given location. When game is scarce compensation can be sometimes achieved by reducing the size of the hunting group and extending the range of the hunt. In the winter, in particular, it is important for a family to have a good hunter.

Imnak looked out, over the water.

"Once, I thought I would make up a song," he said. "I wanted to sing. I wanted very much to sing. I thought I would make up a song. I wanted to sing about the world, and how beautiful it is. I wanted to sing about the great sea, the mountains, the lovely stars, the broad sky."

"Why did you not make up a song?" I asked.

"A voice," said Imnak, "seemed to say to me, 'How dare you make up a song? How dare you sing? I am the world. I am the great sea. I am the mountains, the lovely stars, the great sky! Do you think you can put us in your little song?' Then I was afraid, and fell down."

I looked at him.

"Since that day I have never tried to sing," said Imnak.

"It is not wrong to sing," I said.

"Who am I to make up a song?" asked Imnak. "I am only a little man. I am unimportant. I am no one. I am nothing."

I did not attempt to respond to him.

"All my songs would fail," he said.

"Perhaps not," I said. "At any rate, it is better to try to make a song and fail, than not to try to make a song. It is better to make a song and fail, than not to sing."

"I am too small," said Imnak. "I cannot sing. No song will sit on my shoulder. No little song comes to me and asks me to sing it."

"No song," I said, "can catch the sky. No song can encompass the mountains. Songs do not catch the world. They are beside the world, like lovers, telling it how beautiful it is."

"I am unworthy," said Imnak. "I am nothing."

"Perhaps one day," I said, "you will hear a voice say inside you, 'I am the world. I am the great sea, I am the mountains, the lovely stars, the great sky. And I am Imnak, too! Tell me your song, Imnak, for I cannot sing without you. It is only through you, tiny insignificant Imnak, and others like you, that I can see myself and know how beautiful I am. It is only through you, my tiny, frail precious Imnak, and others like you, that I can lift my voice in song."

Imnak turned away from me. "I cannot sing," he said.

We heard laughter from the feasting house. I could see the stars now above the polar sea. It was thus already the polar dusk.

The remains of the great Hunjer whale lay beached on the shore, much of it already cut away, many bones, too, taken from it.

"The meat racks are full," I said, referring to the high racks here and there in the camp.

"Yes," said Imnak.

Two weeks ago, some ten to fifteen sleeps ago, by rare fortune, we had managed to harpoon a baleen whale, a bluish, white-spotted blunt fin. That two whales had been taken in one season was rare hunting, indeed. Sometimes two or three years pass without a whale being taken.

"It is good," said Imnak, looking at the meat racks. "It may be that this winter the families will not have to go out on the ice."

Ice hunting can be dangerous, of course. The terrain beneath you, in wind and tides, can shift and buckle, breaking apart.

The sun was low on the horizon. We heard more laughter from the feasting house.

The polar night is not absolutely dark, of course. The Gorean moons, and even the stars, provide some light, which light reflecting from the expanses of the snow and ice is more than adequate to make one's way about. Should cloud cover occur, of course, or there be a storm, this light is negated and one, remaining indoors, must content oneself with the sounds of wind in the darkness, and the occasional scratching of animals on the ice outside.

"I cannot remember the racks being so heavy with meat in my lifetime," said Imnak.

"It is little wonder the people are so pleased in the feasting house," I said.

Besides the whales many sleen and fish had been taken. Too, the families, coming north, had dragged and carried what dried tabuk meat they could with them. Even the children carried meat. With them, too, they had brought eggs and berries, and many other things, spoils from the summer, though not all for the larder, such as horn and sinew, and bones and hides. They did not carry with them much grass for the boots or mosses for the wicks of lamps as these materials could be obtained readily somewhat inland of the permanent camps.

When the sun dipped beneath the horizon it would not be seen again for half a year. I would miss it.

"I think we have enough food for the winter," said Imnak. "When night falls we will have enough to eat."

I looked at the high meat racks, some with tiers, some twenty feet or more in height, to protect the meat from sleen, both those domesticated and the wild sleen that might prowl to the shores as the hunting, the leems hibernating, grew sparse inland. Wild snow sleen, particularly when hunger drives them to run in packs, can be quite dangerous.

"Even if we have enough food for the winter," I said, "if Karjuk does not come soon, I must hunt for him, even if it means going out on the ice in the darkness."

"Remain in the camp," said Imnak.

"You need not come with me, my friend," I said.

"Do not be foolish, Tarl, who hunts with me," he said.

"You may stay with your friends," I said, "who now so please themselves in the feasting house."

"Do not think lightly of my people," he said, "that they are pleased to laugh and to look upon one another and tell stories and sing. Life is not always pleasant for them."

"Forgive me," I said.

"There is no one in the feasting house who is of my people, who is not a child," he said, "who has not lived through a season of bad hunting. The children do not yet know about bad hunting, we do not tell them."

I did know the red hunters were extremely permissive with their children, even among Goreans. They very seldom scolded them and would almost never strike a child. They protected them as they could. Soon enough the children would learn. Until that time let them be children.

"There is no one in the feasting house who is of my people, who is not a child," he said, "who has not seen people

266

starve to death. Many times, too, it is not the fault of the people. There is sickness, or there is bad weather. Sometimes there is a storm and the snow hides the breathing holes of the sleen." He spoke very quietly. "Sometimes," he said, "there is an accident. Sometimes one's kayak is rent. Sometimes one falls. Sometimes the ice breaks." He looked at me. "No," he said, "do not think too lightly of my people. Let them laugh and be happy. Do not despise them that they are joyful that for once their meat racks are heavy."

"Forgive me, my friend," I said.

"It is done," he said.

"You are a great hunter," I said.

"I am a terrible hunter," he said. "But once I did slay six sleen in one day," he said. He grinned.

"Let us return to the feasting house," I said.

Together we returned to the feasting house.

21 ARLENE

"Let us put the lights out!" suggested Akko, happily.

This suggestion met with enthusiastic acclaim.

"What are they doing?" asked Thimble, or Barbara, who had been serving boiled meat to the hunters and their women.

"You will learn," I told her.

I, like the others, slipped from my garments. The slave beasts in the feasting house, Poalu, Arlene, Thimble, or Barbara, and Thistle, or Audrey, were already naked. The feasting house, because of its structure, the lamps and the heat of the many bodies within it, is quite warm. I have no way of knowing precisely what its temperature often was but I would have conjectured it would often have been in the eighties. The huts, and even the houses of ice sometimes built by the hunters in their journeys and hunts, can be quite comfortable, even when the weather outside may be dozens of degrees below zero. Often, however, in the night and near morning, the lamps extinguished, and the guests departed, it can become quite cold in such dwellings, often falling below the freezing point. Often, in the morning, one must break through a layer

267

of ice in the drinking bucket. When the houses are cold, of course, the hunters are generally sleeping in their furs, together with their women. Because of the body heat of the companion it is much warmer to sleep with someone than to sleep alone. The furs, being impervious to the passage of air, of course, tend to trap the generated body heat. It is thus possible to sleep quite comfortably in a dwelling whose objective interior temperature may be well below freezing. Also, sleeping is usually done on a sleeping platform. This is raised above the floor level. The platform is warmer than the floor level of the dwelling, of course, because of the tendency of warm air to rise. A yard of height can make a difference of several degrees of temperature inside a typical dwelling of the red hunters. Althogh the red hunters can and do experience intense cold their lives, generally, are not made miserable by their climate. They have intelligently adapted to it and are usually quite comfortable both indoors and outdoors. Also, it seems to me objectively true that they are less sensitive to cold than many other types of individual. For one thing they are generally short and heavy, a body configuration which tends to conserve heat; for another there are serological differences between them and even other red races of Gor; these serological differences, presumably selected for in the course of generations, doubtless play some role in their adaptation to cold. I think it is probably true, though it is difficult to tell, that a given degree of severe cold will not be as unpleasant to one who is a red hunter as it would be to someone who is not of that background or stock. Red hunters, for example, will often go about cheerfully stripped to the waist in weather in which many individuals of the south would find both a tunic and a cloak comfortable.

There were six lamps in the feasting house.

One after the other began to be extinguished. Imnak had his eye on Poalu. Arlene, Barbara and Audrey looked at one another, uneasily. "What is going on?" asked Barbara. "If they put out the last lamp, the room will be dark."

The last lamp was extinguished. I saw hide pulled over the smoke hole.

"Walk around!" called Akko, cheerfully. "Do not touch anyone! Change your places!"

I moved about. It was, after all, the culture of the red hunters.

Outside, objectively, it was rather dark. Also, the feasting house had no windows. It is harder to heat a building with windows, of course. Too, hides, from tents, were hung about the inside of the feasting house, supplying additional insulation and warmth. Light in the feasting house was supplied generally from lamps. These were now extinguished, and the smoke hole covered. It was quite dark within.

No one spoke while they moved around.

I heard Barbara whimper. She was frightened. There was nothing to be frightened about. It was only that someone, she would not know who, would find her, catch her and have her.

"Now" cried Akko. "Who can you catch?"

I heard women laugh, and move swiftly. Men groped about.

I felt my way around, as I could. I heard a woman cry out with pleasure, caught.

"Be quiet!" called Akko.

I heard a pair, struggling, near me. Then the woman was, as I determined by putting forth my hand, put down on her back, on the floor of the feasting house. She squirmed in the dirt, pushing futilely up against the aggressive male who pinioned her beneath him for his pleasure. He was surprised at her resistance, so he struck her, and then she was quiet, until, in a few minutes, she began to cry out with pleasure. I felt bondage strings on her throat. I did not know if it was Thimble or Thistle. In touching the hair I knew it was not Poalu, whose hair was bound high on her head, in the usual fashion of her people.

I heard more women caught. One brushed past me but I missed her in the darkness.

Suddenly a nude girl, fleeing, struck against me. "Oh," she cried. And my arms had closed about her. She was caught. She was helpless. I put her to the floor. She squirmed. I did not permit her struggles to be successful.

In a few moments her belly and haunches were writhing with pleasure which I had enforced upon her.

Then, helpless, she yielded.

When the lamp was relit I looked down into the face of Barbara.

I had known it was she, from the bondage strings on her throat, and the responses of her body.

"You make a slave yield well, Master," she said. "You make her yield totally, leaving her no dignity."

"Did you know it was I?" I asked.

She looked up at me. She lifted her lips to mine and kissed me. "I knew it the moment your arms closed on me, Master," she said.

I shrugged.

"I have been many times in your arms, Master," she said. "And no two men, I suspect, will seize and rape a slave identically."

"I suppose not," I said. I looked about. Many of the women were laughing, and the men, too. Poalu, I saw, was beside Imnak. I suspected they had cheated. Thistle, or Audrey, and Arlene looked at me, still held by the men who had caught them.

"Let us feast!" called Akko.

The lamps were relit. The women who had been caught by given men must now serve them.

In the hours that followed this game was played again, and again, five times in all, interrupted by feasting.

In the second and third round I caught women of the red hunters. In the fourth round I got my hand on Audrey's neck and threw her down to the floor. She was quite good. I spent a long time with her. In the fifth round, when the lamps were relit, it was Arlene who looked up at me from my arms.

"Greetings," I said to her, "former agent of my enemies."

"Greetings, Master," she said to me.

"Did you know it was I?" I asked.

"Must a girl tell the truth?" she smiled.

"Yes," I said.

"Yes," she said. "I knew it was you, instantly."

"How could you know?" I asked.

"Do you think a girl does not know the touch of her master?" she smiled.

"I suppose so," I smiled. I supposed a girl had better know the touch of her master.

"But did you know it was I?" she asked, archly.

"Of course," I said.

"From the strap on my throat?" she said.

"I would have known without that," I said.

"How?" she asked.

"From the feel of you," I told her.

"The master knows the feel of his slave," she said.

"Certainly," I said.

"I would have thought all slaves, all miserable girls in bondage, would be alike," she said.

"No," I said. "Each girl wears her bondage differently. Each girl is unique and excitingly different."

"How can that be?" she asked.

"I do not know," I said. "Perhaps bondage releases a woman's uniqueness and individuality. It releases her from the constrictions of verbalisms and stereotypes and permits

270

her to be truly herself, within of course the latitudes of her nature, that of slave."

"Do you think women are truly slaves?" she asked.

"Ultimately and profoundly," I said. "That does not agree with the principles you have been taught, principles developed to facilitate a certain sort of society, or perhaps even with your immediate intuitions on the matter, a function of your conditioning to accept these principles, but it stands up to the test of life experiences."

"I sense that it is so," she whispered.

"Why else," I asked, "would women dream of chains and the collar?"

"I do not know," she said.

"Why else do you think," I asked, "that many highly intelligent women, functioning brilliantly in their world, are yet in the privacy of their own homes the secret slaves of their husbands?"

"I do not know," she said.

"But you are not a secret slave," I said.

"No," she smiled, "I am openly and publicly a slave, yours or any other man's, to whom you might give or sell me."

"Absolute power is held over you," I said.

"Yes, Master," she said. "I am in your absolute power."

"Or in that of any other who should own you," I said.

"Yes, Master," she said.

"How do you feel about this?" I asked.

"It frightens me," she said.

"Anything else?" I asked.

"It thrills me," she whispered.

"Of course," I said.

"Is this a sign that I am truly a slave?" she asked.

"Yes," I said.

"I feared it might be," she said. She looked up at me, chidingly. "You are bringing me along slowly, aren't you?" she asked. "You are liberating my slavery slowly, aren't you?"

"Yes," I said.

"Why do you not have done with it," she asked, "and make me a complete slave?"

"Perhaps, in time," I said.

"The girl must wait upon the will of the master?" she asked.

"Of course," I said.

"Of course," she said. "What a slave you make me!" she exclaimed, bitterly.

"Of course," I said.

"Yes, of course," she said.

People were getting up around us, but I did not let her up.

"You caught me," she said. "It is now time for the captured women to serve their captors boiled meat."

"I will choose how you will serve me," I told her.

"Of course," she smiled. "It is you who will choose. You are the master."

I lifted her up in my arms.

"Do you think I think only of food?" I asked her.

"I have never been under that delusion, Master," she said.

I took her to the side of the feasting house, out of the way, and put her on her back again in the dirt. She held my arms. "Before me," she said, "you caught Thimble in the dark."

"Yes," I said.

"Did she and you know one another?" she asked.

"Yes," I said.

"You caught Thistle, too," she said. "Did she, the little vixen, and you, too, know one another?"

"Yes," I told her. Thistle and I, or Audrey and I, as I usually thought of her, using her former name as a slave name, had, too, recognized one another immediately, even in the darkness.

"I would like to switch her!" said Arlene.

"Why?" I asked.

"What a little slave she is," said Arlene.

"She will indeed prove to be a superb slave," I said. "But so, too, will you."

"I would like to beat her," said Arlene.

"You and she," I said, "are quite evenly matched. Perhaps you are a little stronger. I do not know."

"I can beat her," said Arlene.

"I do not know," I said. "Perhaps she could now beat you."

"That would be terrible," said Arlene. "I could not stand to call her 'Mistress.'" When one slave girl is beaten by another the loser commonly finds herself forced to call the winner 'Mistress'. In slave kennels and pleasure gardens the beaten girl is often expected to obey and serve the stronger girl. Such cruel devices help to keep order among female slaves.

"You and Thistle," I said, "are extremely well matched. Perhaps that is why you hate her so."

"She wants your hands on her!" said Arlene.

"Are you jealous?" I asked.

"You are my master, not hers," she said.

"You and Thistle had better watch your step," I warned her, "or I will have Thimble thrash you both."

"Yes, Master," smiled Arlene. She feared Thimble, whom she knew could easily best her.

I looked about. I saw Thimble, or Barbara, serving a hunter, and Thistle, or Audrey, bringing meat to another. Poalu served Imnak.

"I note," I said, "that Poalu is bringing meat to Imnak."

"That makes five times in a row," smiled Arlene, looking up at me.

"Yes," I said.

"It is possible he has not played the game fairly," she smiled.

"Yes," I said, "I think that is possible."

"I think he is a scoundrel, like all men," said Arlene.

"Beware how you speak of men, Slave Girl," said I.

"Is a slave not expected to tell the truth?"

"Yes," I said, irritably.

"Surely then you have no objection to a girl's recognizing the objective truth that all men are scoundrels."

"I suppose not," I granted.

"How outrageous that such lovely creatures as I must come into the power of such scoundrels," she said.

"I do not regard it as all that outrageous," I said.

"But that is because you are a scoundrel," she pointed out.

"Perhaps," I admitted.

"But you are sometimes a nice scoundrel," she said.

"We all have our weaker moments," I admitted.

"I am not the first slave girl you have owned, am I?" she asked.

"No," I said.

"Doubtless you have forced many girls to submit to your lust," she said.

"Of course," I said.

"Bold scoundrel," she said, "how I admire you doing what you want with us."

"That is a bold admission for an Earth girl," I said.

"I am no longer an Earth girl," she said. "I am a Gorean slave."

"That is true," I said. It was true.

I put my hand in her hair and turned her head to the side, to see the beauty of her profile.

"Strength in men, not weakness," she said, "excites me. You are the strongest man I have ever known."

"I am sure there are many men stronger than I," I said.

273

"Physical strength," she said, "is only a small part of what I mean, though it is not unimportant. I mean strength of will. Many men who are strong physically are spineless weaklings, tortured and dominated by women, and ideas. Women, despite what they may feel obligated to proclaim publicly, detest such men, for they betray their dominance, their genetic heritage as male primates, thus cheating not only themselves of the fulfillment of their nature but precluding the woman from also fulfilling hers. It is no wonder that women, in their helplessness and frustration, their own confusions, turn upon such men, hurting them and making them miserable. This, of course, causes such men, who do not understand the problem, to redouble their efforts to be accommodating and pleasing to the females, to give them whatever they want, and to reassure them of anything and everything they wish to hear. A vicious cycle is thus generated."

"There is an escape from this cycle, of course," I pointed out. "Not all human beings are idiots."

"Yes," she said.

"It is called manhood, and womanhood, and nature."

"It is a long time since those of Earth recollected the many names of nature."

"It is time again, perhaps," I said, "to seek for her forgotten faces."

"It will never be done on Earth," she said.

"I do not know," I said. "I think, perhaps, that some human beings, here and there, even in the midst of the suffering, even in the very countries of confusion and pathology, will create for themselves small islands of reality and truth."

I turned her head again to face me.

"Perhaps," she smiled. Her eyes were moist.

I removed my hand from her hair.

She looked up at me, and shook her head, and laughed. She touched the leather strap on her throat with her small fingers.

"Do you find me of interest, Master?" she asked.

"Yes," I said.

"How can a girl who is only a slave be of interest?" she asked.

"Your question is foolish," I said. "All men desire a slave, or slaves. It is their nature. Thus, that a woman is a slave, even in itself, makes her extraordinarily interesting. Her slavery in itself, apart from her intelligence or beauty, is found extremely provocative and exciting to the male, because of his nature."

"But aren't free women more interesting?" she asked.

"All women are interesting," I said. "But consider the matter objectively. Anything that was interesting about you when you were free remains interesting about you now. But now you are additionally interesting because you are in helpless bondage. Too, slavery, because of its relation to a female's genetic predispositions, tends to free her to be herself, rather than an imitator of male-type values. It frees her individuality by liberating her from the necessities of pretense. Too, slavery, by removing certain inhibitions and demands alien to a female's deepest nature generally results in an increase in her beauty and energy; she is no longer as constricted and miserable, and needs no longer spend energy fighting to suppress herself and her natural desires, surely a grotesque and pathological misapplication of effort, a tragic waste of time and energy. That the girl, thus, becomes more beautiful and energetic does not, of course, diminish her interest. Indeed, similarity, routine, identity, boredom, those things which tend to make a woman less interesting, tend often to be functions of widespread conformances to externally imposed demands and images. It is thus that the free woman, though interesting, being female, is usually, sadly, a bound prisoner of her own prejudices, a rigid, constricted, ideologically restrained organism, an imitator of images and stereotypes alien to her own nature, a puppet obedient to principles foreign to herself. How can a woman be free until she obeys the laws of her own nature?"

"I do not know," said Arlene.

"Interest, of course, is somewhat subjective," I admitted. "Some men may prefer neurotic, frustrated, rigid, imitative, conforming free women, mouthing the correct slogans and adopting the correct views on all matters, and eager to slander all who disagree with her, but other men, perhaps naive types, would just as soon own an intelligent, beautiful, reflective, loving slave, a girl who thinks for herself, but must nonetheless obey him, regardless of her will, in all things. The matter seems a simple one. Let men choose between such women. Let men choose between them, between the stereotype and the truth, between the pain and the pleasure, between the unhappy and the happy, between the tasteless and the delicious, between sickness and health, between suffering and joy."

She looked up at me.

"But regardless of the truth in these matters," I said, "you are objectively my slave. Thus, whether you are or are not of interest is not really much to the point. Whether you are of more or less interest than your duller sisters in their intellectual cages congratulating themselves on how free they are is not important. What is important is that I own you. From my point of view I find you, and girls like you, far more interesting than your smug sisters. They seem generally much alike, even in their mode of dress, and tend in their thinking and conversation, because of their conditioning, to be repetitiously similar. Free women, though they need not be, are often boring. Who does not know, for example, what a female 'intellectual' will think on a given topic, provided it is a topic on which agreement is expected?"

"I am, then, of interest?" she asked.

"Yes," I said.

"A girl is pleased," she said.

"I found you of interest when you were free," I said, "and I find you of much greater interest now."

"Yes, Master," she said.

"Part of this," I said, "is doubtless that I now can, and will, do with you exactly as I please."

"Oh, Master?" she asked.

"There is a sense, of course," I said, "in which you are supposedly of less interest than a free woman."

"What is that," she asked, "Master."

"Suppose," I said, "that I was, in my compartments, entertaining a free woman. In such a situation you would be expected to efface yourself, and humbly serve. You would not speak unless you were spoken to, and then presumably only to respond deferentially to commands. You would remain in the background, a mere instrument to serve us. In no way would you in the slightest be permitted to detract from the impression or effect the free woman desires to create or compete with her in any way. You would be nothing in the room but an almost invisible convenience."

"I see," she said.

"And yet this is all on the surface," I said, "and largely a matter of theory."

"Oh, Master?" she asked.

"Yes," I said, "for in the depth of the situation your presence is felt profoundly by the free woman. Indeed, she will hate you with a ferocity which is difficult for you to understand. For you are a reproach, in the depths of your womanhood, to her superficiality. There is more excitement she knows in your slightest movement, the turning of your head, the tiny movement of a wrist or finger, that of a girl in bondage, than in her entire, tight, proud, righteous body. She can never touch you in the profundity of your existence and reality unless sometime she, too, should learn what it is to be only a collared slave. She knows that you have found your womanhood and she has not. Thus she hates you. She knows the free man is anxious for her to leave, that he may hurry you, his slave, to the furs. Thus she hates you. It is you whom he has put in his collar, not her. It is you he rapes in his arms, not her. It is thus that she despises and hates you. She must rise and leave. You will remain, and serve. She hates you, and, with a depth and intensity which is difficult for you to understand, envies you."

"But why?" she asked.

"Because you are a slave," I said.

"I see," she said.

"Thus," I said, "that is a situation in which a free woman is theoretically of more interest than a slave, but, upon closer analysis, the center of interest, even in such a situation, because of her latency, her womanhood, her helplessness, what can be done with her, is the slave."

"I see," she said.

"Beware of free women," I smiled.

"Yes," she said, "I think I would be very afraid of them."

"And you should be," I said. "They can often be terribly cruel to slave girls."

"I do fear them," she said.

"Speaking of who is of interest and who is not," I said, "what of you, lovely slave, and men?"

"I do not understand," she said.

"Do you find men now that you are a slave more or less interesting than when you were free?" I asked.

She looked at me, startled. "I find them now a thousand times more interesting," she said, surprised.

"Of course," I said.

"I look at them," she said, "and I wonder what it would be like to be owned by them, or touched by them. I never looked at men so deeply or closely, or fearfully, before. I am now so sensitive to my slavery, and my vulnerability to men. Now, for the first time in my life, they seem to me of profound importance and interest. You see, they can own me, and I might have to serve them."

"Does your slavery make men more sexually interesting to you?" I asked.

"Of course," she said, "a million times more so than when I was free. I know I might have to serve their pleasure. Too, now, with many men, I find myself wanting to serve their pleasure. When I was free I could never kneel to a man and beg him for his touch. Now that I am a slave I could do so. I would need fear only whether or not you would permit it, for you are my master."

I looked down at her. She was very beautiful.

"My sexuality has been liberated by my slavery," she said. "It is now a force within me." She looked at me, chidingly, reproachfully. "You freed it," she said. "What am I now to do? It is a joy and a torment." She clutched my arms. "It makes me helpless," she said. She looked up at me, angrily. "You have made me so I now need the touch of men," she said. "I hate you!" Then, her nails digging into my arms, she said, "Touch me!"

I looked down at her.

"You did this to me," she said. "You made me a slave girl. You made me a slave girl!"

"Of course," I said.

"Touch me, Master," she whimpered.

"Do you beg it?" I asked.

"Yes, Master," she said, "Arlene, your girl, Arlene, your slave, begs your touch!"

"Oh," she sobbed. "Thank you, Master."

"It is probably time for you to get up and serve me boiled meat," I said.

"No, no, no, no," she whimpered.

"But it can wait, I suppose," I said.

"Yes, yes, yes, yes, yes," she said.

"Yes, what?" I asked.

"Yes, Master," she said.

"You are a hot slave," I said.

"Please do not so speak of me," she begged. Then she said, "Oh, no, please do not stop touching me. Please do not stop touching me." Then she said, "Yes, yes, Master."

"Are you a hot slave?" I asked.

She opened her eyes, writhing under my touch. She looked at me, angrily, defiantly. "Yes," she gasped, "I am a hot slave!"

"I thought so," I said.

"How you shame me!" she wept.

"A slave should be proud of her heat," I said. "You are not a free woman, permitted to be smug in the icy conceit of her frigidity."

She looked up at me.

278

"Writhe freely, Slave," I said. "Yield to the sensations, or be whipped."

"Would you truly whip me?" she asked.

"Yes," I said.

"I do not want to be whipped," she said.

"Yield then to the sensations, as a slave girl," I said.

"I dare not," she cried.

"Yield, or die," I said to her.

"Oh, oh," she cried.

"Yield, as a slave girl, or die," I said to her.

"Aiii," she cried, throwing her head back in the dirt, her finger nails tearing at my arm. "Aiii!" she screamed wildly to the poles and the leather and the grass and dirt of the roof of that feasting house in the polar basin of Gor's far north.

She began to sob uncontrollably. She looked up at me, her eyes filled with tears.

"You are a monster, a beast," she said.

I said nothing to her.

"You made me yield," she said, "—as a slave girl."

"Yes," I said, "you have yielded as a slave girl."

"Make me yield again as a slave girl, Master," she begged.

"There are yieldings beyond those which you have as yet experienced," I said.

"Can there be more?" she asked.

"You have not yet begun to learn your slavery," I said.

She looked up at me. "Your girl awaits your pleasure, Master," she said.

"Do you desire to serve me?" I asked.

"Yes, Master," she said, "very much."

I lay beside her and she bent over me, her lips and mouth to my body. I felt her small, warm tongue.

She stopped, and looked up at me. "Surely I am now a complete slave," she said.

"You have not yet begun to learn your slavery," I said.

"Yes, Master," she said, bending her head down again. I felt her tongue, and that lovely auburn hair, on my body.

"Arlene," I said.

"Yes, Master," she said.

"Is it a slave girl's first duty to be interesting?" I asked.

"No," she said. "That is a concern of free women."

"What is the first duty of a slave girl?" I asked.

"To be pleasing to the master," she said.

"Let that be your concern," I said.

"Yes, Master," she said.

Then the lovely slave bent again to her sweet task.

22 IMNAK AND I HUNT SLEEN; WE CONSIDER THE NATURE OF THE WORLD

"Over there," said Imnak, indicating the place in the water.

"Yes," I said.

I laid the two-headed paddle on the leather of the kayak behind me. I pulled off the mitten on my right hand and held it in my teeth. I picked up the beaded throwing board and the light harpoon, and fitted the harpoon shaft into the notch on the throwing board. The harpoon had a foreshaft of bone, with a bone head and point. A light rawhide line, of twisted tabuk sinew, ran to the head. In a flat, rounded tray directly before me, on the leather, there were coiled several feet of this line. At my right, alongside the outer edge of the circular wooden frame, bound with sinew, within which I sat, lay the long lance.

"There," whispered Imnak, in his own kayak, a few feet from that which I was using, which belonged to Akko.

The head of a sleen, glistening, smooth, emerged from the water. It was a medium-sized, adult sea sleen, some eight feet in length, some three to four hundred pounds in weight.

I had missed four sleen in a row and I was not too pleased with my performance.

I looped some of the line loosely over the palm of the mitten on my left hand.

I tried to keep the stem of the kayak pointing roughly toward the beast in the water. One does this, when not using the paddle, by moving one's legs and body inside the frame.

The head of the sleen disappeared beneath the water. I put down the harpoon and throwing board; I took the mitten which I had held between my teeth and pulled it back on. It had two thumbs, like the one on my left hand. They were paddle mittens. When they are worn on one side they may be turned to the other.

"You are too slow, Tarl, who hunts with me," said Imnak.

"Last time," I said, "I was too hasty."

"Yes," Imnak agreed, "last time you were too hasty."

"The kayak moved," I said.

"You should keep it steady," said Imnak.

"Thank you, Imnak," I said. "That would not have occurred to me."

"What are friends for?" asked Imnak.

"Imnak!" I cried. His kayak had suddenly flipped over and was bottom side up in the chilled water. In an instant, however, it was right side up again. Water was running from the kayak and Imnak's gutskin jacket. "It is too dark to see under the water," he said.

"You did that on purpose," I said.

"Yes, someone is a big show-off," he said, grinning. He was in a good mood. He had taken two sleen which now lay near us in the water. With a tube he had blown air under the skin of the sleen and, with wooden plugs, closed their wounds. This served to keep the animals afloat. When he returned to shore he would tow them behind his kayak.

"It is difficult to throw from a sitting position," I said, "and I am not used to the throwing board."

"It is lucky for the sleen that you are here," said Imnak. "Otherwise it might be dangerous for them."

"With encouragement such as you afford," I said, "doubtless I shall soon become a great hunter of sea sleen."

"Perhaps you are not friendly enough to the sea sleen," said Imnak. "Perhaps they think you do not like them."

It had not hitherto occurred to me that one might like sea sleen.

"Perhaps that is the trouble," I admitted.

"Talk to them, be friendly," said Imnak. "Coax them. They like to be coaxed."

"They would cheerfully permit themselves to be harpooned by someone who is friendly to them?" I asked.

"Would you like to be harpooned by someone who was an enemy?" asked Imnak.

"No," I said, "but I would not like to be harpooned by someone who was a friend either."

"But you are not a sea sleen," said Imnak.

"That is true," I admitted.

"Come now," said Imnak, "would you not prefer to be harpooned by a friend rather than an enemy?"

"I suppose so," I said, "if I had my choice."

"There you are!" said Imnak triumphantly.

281

"But I would not like to be harpooned by either," I reminded him.

"But," Imnak reminded me, "you are not a sea sleen, are you?"

"No," I granted him. That seemed incontestable. It was sometimes difficult to enter into disputation with Imnak.

"Be friendly," said Imnak. "Do not be a sour fellow. Do not be morose. Be outgoing!"

"Hello, Sleen!" I called.

"Good," said Imnak. "That is a start."

"How do you do this?" I asked.

"Listen," said Imnak. He spoke out, over the icy waters. "Tal," said he, "my lovely brothers, my dangerous brethren. How beautiful and strong you are. How fast you swim. And your meat is so good in soups. I am Imnak, only a poor hunter. I would like very much to harpoon you. I have a little harpoon here who would like to see you. I would take it as a great honor if you would let me harpoon you. I would be very grateful."

"That is the silliest thing I have ever heard," I told Imnak.

"How many sleen have you harpooned today?" asked Imnak.

"I have harpooned no sleen today," I said.

"I have harpooned two," said Imnak. "Try it."

"Very well," I said. I wondered if I had been on the water too long. Sometimes there is an affliction which affects those in kayaks though it is usually the case when it is clearly daylight and the rocking, the endless waiting, the reflections off the water, make one suddenly lose all sense of time and place, and one seems lost in nothingness, and then one must sing or scream, and strike the water with the paddle, or go mad and die, sometimes cutting one's own kayak to pieces.

I looked out over the water. "Greetings, lovely sleen," I said. "I have been out here a long time waiting for you. I would certainly like to harpoon one of you. If you could see your way clear to coming over and being harpooned, I would certainly appreciate it."

"Not bad," said Imnak.

"Arlene would like to have something for a soup," I said. "Do you think you could help me out?"

"Now you are catching on," said Imnak.

"I admire you very much, you long, sleek swimmers," I said. "You are very beautiful and strong, and you swim like lightning." I looked at Imnak. "How was that?" I asked.

"Splendid," said Imnak. "Look out!" he cried.

282

The sleen had risen up under the kayak and it lifted a yard from the water and tumbled from the surfacing back of the glistening, wet mammal. I and the craft, one functional unit, slipped from the animal's back and fell sideways into the water. I wrenched myself to the side and righted the light, narrow vessel. The sleen shook itself in the water and then snapped away some yards from the kayak. My face felt frozen from the sea water freezing on it. I jerked a mitten off and rubbed my eyes. I still held the paddle but the harpoon and lance were in the water.

"You see," said Imnak, "you are catching on."

I spat out some water.

"There is the sleen," said Imnak, pointing.

I looked out across the icy water, where he had pointed. To be sure, there was the head of the sleen, about a quarter emerged, the eyes and nose flat with the water. What I could see of the head seemed very large. It was eighteen inches or more in breadth. I pulled the mitten back on. My hand was cold.

"I think he likes you," said Imnak.

I drew the harpoon toward me by the line fastened to the kayak.

"Do not move too swiftly," said Imnak, "lest he charge and kill you."

"It is well he does not dislike me," I said. "Otherwise I might be in real danger."

"Oh, oh," said Imnak.

"What is wrong?" I asked.

"Perhaps you should not have talked to that sleen," said Imnak.

"Why not?" I asked.

"That, I think, is a rogue sleen," said Imnak. "It is a broad-head, and they are rare in these waters in the fall. Too, see the gray on the muzzle and the scarring on the right side of the head, where the fur is gone?"

"Yes," I said.

"I think it is a rogue," he said. "Also, see the way he is watching you."

"Yes," I said.

"I think it has been hunted before," he said.

"Perhaps," I said. Generally a sleen watches you warily and then, as you approach, submerges. Normally, though it is swift to attack an object moving about in the water, like a swimmer, it will not attack a vessel. Its attack instincts are apparently not triggered by that configuration, or perhaps

283

there is no stimulating smell or familiar pressure patterns, such as it would commonly associate with its prey or a vulnerable object, in the water, from the passage of the craft and the stroke of the paddle. This sleen, however, did not seem to be watching us warily. Rather there was something rather menacing in its attitude.

"Hello, Sleen," I said.

"Do not be silly," said Imnak. "That is a very dangerous animal."

"Am I not supposed to talk to it?" I asked. I thought I might give Imnak back a bit of his own medicine.

"One must be careful what sleen one talks to," said Imnak. "There is a time to talk and coax, and a time to be quiet."

"I see," I said, smiling.

"You may talk to it if you wish," said Imnak, "but I would not do so if I were you."

"Why not?" I asked.

"It might listen," he said.

"Is that not the point?" I asked, chuckling.

"That is one sleen you would just as soon not have listen to you," said Imnak. "That is a rogue broad-head, and I think he has been hunted before."

"One must be careful what sleen one takes up with," I said.

"Precisely," said Imnak.

I fished the lance out of the water. I now had both the lance and the harpoon beside me.

"Arlene would like something for a soup," I said to the sleen. "Can you help me out?"

"Be silent," whispered Imnak, horrified.

"I thought you said he liked me," I said.

"He may be only pretending," said Imnak.

"I think he is really a good fellow," I said.

"Let us not take the chance," said Imnak. "Do not turn your back on him. We will wait quietly until he goes away, and then we will go back to camp."

"No," I said.

"We have two sleen," said Imnak.

"You have two sleen," I said.

"Do not be foolish, Tarl, who hunts with me," said Imnak.

"I am sure he is really a nice sleen," I said.

"Look out!" cried Imnak. "He is coming!"

I dropped the harpoon for it would be an extremely difficult cast to strike the animal head on. The bone point of the harpoon, thrown, would probably not penetrate the skull and it would be difficult to strike the submerged, narrow forepart of the body knifing toward the kayak. I thrust the lance point into the rushing, extended, double-fanged jaws and it penetrated through the side of the mouth, tearing, the animal's face a yard up the shaft. It reared six feet out of the water vertically beside the slender hide vessel. With two hands on the shaft I forced the twisting body to fall away from the craft. One of the large flippers struck me, buffeting me, spinning me and the vessel about, the animal then slipping free of the shaft of the lance. It circled the craft its mouth hot with blood flowing into the cold water. It was then I retrieved the harpoon again from the water by its line, for it had been once more struck away from me. I set the light harpoon into the notch on the throwing board and, even mittened, an instant before the beast turned toward me, grunted, snapping the throwing board forward and downward, speeding the shaft toward the enraged animal. The bone head, vanishing, sunk into its withers and it snapped downward, diving, bubbles breaking up to the surface, and swift blood. The line snapped out from its tray darting under the water. In moments the harpoon shaft and foreshaft bobbed to the surface, but the bone harpoon head, its line taut, turning the head in the wound, held fast. I played the line as I could. The animal was an adult, large-sized broad-head. It was some eighteen to twenty feet in length and perhaps a thousand pounds in weight. At the length of the line I feared the kayak and myself would be drawn under the water. Imnak, too, came to the line, and, straining, together we held it. The two kayaks dipped, stems downward. "He is running," said Imnak. He released the line. The kayak spun and then nosed forward. I held the line being towed by the beast somewhere below the water. "Loose the line!" called Imnak. "He is running to the ice!" I saw a pan of ice ahead. "Loose the line!" called Imnak. But I did not loose the line. I was determined not to lose the beast. I held the line in my left hand, wrapped about my wrist. With the lance in my right hand I thrust against the pan of ice. Then the lance slipped on the ice and the line slipped to the side and I in the kayak was dragged up on the ice skidding across it and then slipped loose of it and slid into the water to the side. "It is running to the sea!" called Imnak, following me as he could in his own vessel. Then the line went slack. "It is turning," said Imnak. "Beware!" But in a few moments I saw the body of the sleen rise to the surface, rolling, buoyant. It was some sixty feet from the kayak. "It is not dead," said Imnak. "I know," I said. It was easy to see

285

the breath from its nostrils, like a spreading fog on the cold water. The water had a glistening, greasy appearance, for it had begun to freeze. It was dark about the animal, from the blood. We brought our kayaks in close, to finish the animal with our lances. "Beware," said Imnak. "It is not dead." "It has lost much blood," I said. "It is still alive," he said. "Beware."

We nosed our kayaks on each side of the beast, approaching it from the rear.

"It is not breathing now," I said.

"It has been hunted before," said Imnak, "and lived."

"It is dead," I said. "It is not breathing."

"It has been hunted before, and lived," said Imnak. "Let us wait."

We waited for a time. "Let us tow it home," I said. "It is dead."

I poked the beast with the tip of my lance. It did not respond, but moved inertly in the water.

"It is dead," I said. "Let us draw it home now behind us."

"I would not be eager to turn my back on him," said Imnak.

"Why not?" I asked.

"He is not dead," said Imnak.

"How can you be sure?" I asked.

"He is still bleeding," said Imnak.

The hair rose on the back of my neck. Somewhere in that great body, apparently lifeless in the water, there still beat its heart.

"It is a broad-head," said Imnak. "It is pretending."

"It is losing blood," I said. "Too, it must soon breathe."

"Yes," said Imnak. "It will soon make its move. Be ready."

"We could go in with lances now," I said.

"It is waiting for our closer approach," said Imnak. "Do not think its senses are not keen."

"We shall wait?" I asked.

"Yes," said Imnak. "Of course. It is bleeding. Time is on our side."

We waited in the polar dusk.

After a time Imnak said, "Be ready. I have been counting. It must soon breathe."

We readied our lances, one of us on each side of the beast. Suddenly with a great, exploding noise, expelling air, the sleen leaped upward. At the height of its leap we struck it with our lances. It pulled free of the lances and, sucking in air, spun and dove. Again the harpoon line darted downward.

"We struck it fairly!" said Imnak. "Watch out!" he cried. The line had grown slack. I peered downward into the water. Then I felt the swell of the water beneath me, clearly through the taut hide of the kayak. I thrust downward with the lance and was half pulled from the kayak, myself and the vessel lifted upward, as the sleen's impaled body reared up almost beneath the craft. Imnak struck again at it from the side. It fell back in the water and I, jerking free the lance, thrust it again into the wet, bloody pelt. It attacked again, laterally in the water, fangs snapping, and I pressed it away with the lance. Imnak struck it again. It thrashed, bloody in the icy water. It turned on Imnak and I thrust my lance deeply into its side, behind the right foreflipper, seeking, hunting, the great, dark heart. It expelled air again. I pulled the lance free to drive it in again. The beast regarded me. Then it rolled in the water.

"It is dead," said Imnak.

"How do you know?" I asked.

"The nature of your stroke, and its depth," said Imnak. "You have penetrated to the heart."

"Its heart is centered," I said.

"Consider the blood on your lance," he said.

I noted it. New blood was splashed more than twenty-eight inches along the shaft.

"You have great strength," said Imnak.

He took his kayak to the side of the beast. With wooden plugs he began to stop up the wounds. He did not wish to lose what blood might be left in the animal. Frozen blood is nutritious.

"Will you blow air under its skin?" I asked.

"Not unless it becomes heavy in the water," said Imnak. "We are going in now."

"It is going to sink," I said.

"Here," said Imnak, "support it between the kayaks. We will use them as floats."

We tied the great beast between the two kayaks and then, one vessel on each side of the huge sea mammal, began to paddle toward camp. There is an ivory ring below each place where the paddle is gripped, between the hand and the paddle blade. Thus, when the paddle is lifted the water, falling from its blade, does not run back down the lever and into one's sleeve.

"I told you earlier I thought the sleen was really a good fellow," I said.

"I was not sure of it for a time," said Imnak.

"You doubted him," I said.

"It was wrong of me," granted Imnak. "But he is good at pretending. He had me fooled for a time."

"That is the way sleen are," I said.

"They are playful fellows," admitted Imnak.

"You are the one who first noted that he liked me," I said.

Imnak looked at me, and grinned. "You see," he said, "I was right."

"I was not sure of it for a while," I said.

"When you are longer in the north," said Imnak, "these things will become clearer to you."

"Perhaps," I admitted.

"You should thank the sleen for letting himself be harpooned by you," said Imnak. "Not every sleen will do that."

"Thank you, Sleen," I said.

"Good," said Imnak. "That is a simple courtesy. You surely cannot expect sleen to come over to be harpooned if you are not even going to be civil to them."

"I guess you are right, Imnak," I said.

"Of course I am right," said Imnak. "Sleen have their pride."

We had then arrived at the two sleen he had left floating in the water, beneath whose hides he had blown air. He deferentially thanked the two sleen for having permitted themselves to be slain by him. Then he tied them behind his kayak and, together, paddling, we headed back toward the pebbled shore.

"When the sleen are dead, how can you expect them to know they are thanked?" I asked.

"That is an interesting and difficult question," said Imnak. "I do not really know how the sleen manage it."

"It seems it would be hard to do," I said.

"It is a belief of the People," said Imnak, "that the sleen does not really die but, after a time, will be reborn again."

"The sleen is immortal?" I asked.

"Yes," said Imnak. "And when he comes again he will hopefully be more willing to let himself be harpooned again if he has been well treated."

"Are men, too, thought to be immortal?" I asked.

"Yes," said Imnak.

"I know a place," I said, "where some people would think that men are immortal but animals are not."

"They do not like animals?" asked Imnak.

"I do not know," I said. "Perhaps they think they are immortal because they are smart and sleen are not."

"Some sleen are pretty smart," said Imnak. He thought for

288

a bit. "If sleen were to talk these things over," he said, "they would probably say that they were immortal and men were not, because they were better at swimming."

"Perhaps," I said.

"Who knows what life is all about?" asked Imnak.

"I do not know," I said. "Perhaps it is not about anything."

"That is interesting," said Imnak. "But then the world would be lonely."

"Perhaps the world is lonely," I said.

"No," said Imnak.

"You do not think so?" I asked.

"No," said Imnak, drawing his kayak up on the shore, "the world cannot be lonely where there are two people who are friends."

I looked up at the stars. "You are right, Imnak," I said. "Where there is beauty and friendship what more could one ask of a world. How grand and significant is such a place. What more justification could it require?"

"Help me pull the meat up on shore," said Imnak.

I helped him. Others came down to the shore and helped, too.

I did not know what sort of place the world was, but sometimes it seemed to me to be very wonderful.

23   ONE COMES TO THE FEASTING HOUSE

"Night has fallen," I said to Imnak. "I do not think Karjuk is coming."

"Perhaps not," said Imnak.

Snow had fallen several times, though lightly. Temperatures had dropped considerably.

Some three weeks ago, more than twenty sleeps past, Imnak and I had taken three sleen in kayak fishing. But then kayak fishing had been over for the year. The very night of our catch the sea had begun to freeze. It had first taken on a slick greasy appearance. In time tiny columns of crystals had formed within it, and then tiny pieces of ice. Then the water, in a few hours, had become slushy and heavy, and had contained, here and there, larger chunks of ice. Then, a few hours later, these reaches of ice, forming and extending themselves, had touched, and struck one another, and ground against one another, and slid some upon the others, forming irregular plates and surfaces, and then the sea, still and frozen, was locked in white, bleak serenity.

"There are other villages," I said. "Let us travel to them, to see if Karjuk has been there."

"There are many villages," said Imnak. "The farthest is many sleeps away."

"I wish to visit them all," I said. "Then, if we cannot find news of Karjuk, I must go out on the ice in search of him."

"You might as well look for one sleen in all the sea," said Imnak. "It is hopeless."

"I have waited long enough," I said. "I must try."

"I will put ice on the runners," said Imnak. "Akko has a snow sleen, Naartok another."

"Good," I said. A running snow sleen can draw a sled far faster than a human being. They are very dangerous but useful animals.

"Listen," said Imnak.

I was quiet and listened. Far off, in the clear, cold air I heard the squeal of a sleen.

"Perhaps Karjuk is coming!" I cried.

"No, it is not Karjuk," said Imnak. "It is coming from the south."

"Imnak! Imnak!" called Poalu, from outside, running up to the door of the hut. "Someone is coming!" She had been dressing skins, with the other girls, and other women, in the feasting house.

"Who is it?" he asked.

"I do not know," she said.

"Well, climb up on the meat rack and look, lazy girl," he said.

"Yes, Imnak," she cried.

Imnak and I drew on our mittens and parkas and emerged from the lamp-warmed, half-underground hut. It was clear and still outside, and sounds, even slight ones, were very obvious. The snow was loud beneath our boots, crackling. Moonlight bathed the village and the snow on the tundra, and the ice on the sea. I could hear other villagers, quite clearly, as they conversed with one another. Everyone in the village seemed now to be outside of their dwellings. Several were on the meat racks, in the moonlight, trying to see out across the snow. It was not cold for the arctic night, though this sort of thing is relative. It was very calm. I suspect the temperature would have been objectively something like forty below zero. One was not really aware of the cold until one's face became numb. There was no wind.

"What do you see?" asked Imnak.

"It is one sled and one man!" called down Poalu.

We heard the sleen again in the distance. The sound, of course, in the clear, cold air, carried extremely well. The sleen may have been ten pasangs away or more. Sometimes one can hear them from as far away as fifteen pasangs.

"Light lamps, boil meat!" called Kadluk, who was the chief man in the village. "We must make a feast to welcome our visitor!"

Women scurried about, to obey. I saw Arlene, and Barbara and Audrey, slaves, glance at one another. If the visitor fancied white-skinned females, they knew the village, in its riches, had such delicacies, themselves, for his sexual taste. Then, under Poalu's sharp tongue, she perched still on the meat rack, they fled to heat water for the boiling of meat.

"It is one sled and one man!" called down Poalu.

"Let us go out to meet him," said Kadluk.

"Who from the south would come in the winter?" I asked Imnak.

"It must be a trader," said Imnak. "But that is strange, for they do not come in the winter."

"I know who it must be!" I said. "He may have news! Let us hurry to meet him!"

"Yes," said Imnak. "Of course!"

"Let us hurry to meet our visitor," called out Kadluk cheerily.

The men hurried to their huts to gather weapons. There are upon occasion wild snow sleen in the tundra, half starved and maddened by hunger. They constitute one of the dangers of traveling in the winter. Such sleen, together with the cold and the darkness, tend to close the arctic in the winter. No simple trader ventures north in that time.

Kadluk in the lead, Imnak and I following, with Akko and Naartok, and the others, too, behind him, harpoons and lances in our hands, tramped out of the village, heading toward the sound of the sleen.

A pasang outside of the village, Kadluk lifted his hand for silence.

We were suddenly quiet.

291

"Away!" we heard, "Away!" The sound, far off, drifted toward us.

"Hurry!" cried Kadluk.

We ran up, over a small hillock, the snow about our ankles.

A pasang or so away, in the sloping plain between low hillocks, under the moonlight, small, we saw the long sled, with its hitched sleen. Too, we saw two figures in the vicinity of the sled. One was that of a man.

"An ice beast!" cried Akko.

The other figure was that, clearly, shambling, long-armed, of a white-pelted Kur.

The man was trying to thrust it away with a lance. The animal was aggressive.

It drew back, wounded, I believe, but not grievously. It crouched down, watching the man, sucking at its arm. Then it stood on its short hind legs and lifted its two long arms into the air, lifting them and screaming with rage. It then crouched down, fangs bared, to again attack.

I was running down the hillock, slipping and sliding in the snow, my lance in my hand.

The other men, behind me, lifting their weapons and shouting, hurried after me.

The beast turned to look at us, hurrying toward him, shouting, weapons brandished.

I had the feeling, and it startled me, as I ran towards it, that it was considering our distance from it, and the time it would take us to traverse that distance.

I sensed then it was not a simple beast, the degenerate and irrational descendant of survivors of a Kurii ship perhaps crashed generations ago, descendants to whom the discipline and loyalty of the ship codes were meaningless, descendants who had for most practical purposes, save their cunning, reverted to a simplistic animal savagery. The Kur who is only a beast is less dangerous in most situations than the Kur who is more than a beast. The first is only terribly dangerous; the second is an incomparable foe.

In the moment that the Kur had turned to regard us the man had hastened to unhitch the snow sleen at the sled. When the Kur turned back suddenly to regard him the snow sleen was free and leaping for its throat.

I was now within a few hundred yards of the Kur.

I saw it fling the dead, bloodied snow sleen, torn and half bitten through, from it.

The man had struck it again when it had seized the snow

sleen but the blow, again, had not proved mortal. There was blood about its neck where the blade had cut at the side of the throat.

It seized the lance from the man and broke it in two. The man then began to run towards us.

The Kur flung the pieces of the broken lance to the side. The sleen, fresh-killed meat, lay behind in the snow. The sled, too, was now abandoned. Its supplies of meat and sugar, or whatever edibles it might carry, were now free to the depredations of the Kur.

It did not concern itself with the sleen or the sled, however. It looked at the man.

I knew then it was not an ordinary beast. A simple Kur, hungry, predatory, aggressive, would have presumably seized up the body of the sleen or perhaps meat from the sled and, in the face of the charging red hunters, made away, feeding as it retreated.

It dropped to all fours and began to pursue the man. I knew then it must be a ship Kur.

It was not after meat, but after the man.

He sped past me, and I braced myself, my arm drawn back, lance ready.

"Ho, Beast!" I cried. "I am ready for you!"

The Kur pulled up short, some twenty yards from me, baring its fangs.

"Come now, and taste my lance!" I cried.

A common Kur then, I think, would have charged. It did not. Behind me I could hear the red hunters, some hundred yards away, and running toward me.

I took another step toward the Kur, threatening it with the lance.

In moments the Kur would be surrounded by a swarm of men, screaming, striking at it, hurling their weapons into its body.

With a last enraged snarl the Kur, not taking its eyes from us, moving sideways and back, moving on all fours, slipped diagonally away from us to our left. We ran toward it but it turned suddenly and reached the body of the sleen first and, dragging it by a hind paw, hunched over, moved swiftly away over the snow-covered tundra.

Before it had turned I had seen that it had worn in its ears two golden rings.

We watched it disappear over the tundra.

"You have saved my life, all of you," said Ram.

"Are you hurt?" I asked.

"No," he said.

We clasped hands.

"I thought I would find you in the village of Kadluk and Imnak," he said.

Imnak had been with us at the wall. Too, I had not gone south.

"Do you have Bazi tea?" asked Akko. "Do you have sugar?" asked Naartok. The word 'Naartok' in the language of the Innuit means 'Fat Belly'. In many cases there is no particular correspondence between the name and the individual. In Naartok's case, however, the name was not inappropriate. He was a plump, jolly fellow with a weakness for sweets prodigious even among red hunters.

"Yes," said Ram, "I have tea and sugars. And I have mirrors, and beads and knives, and many other trade goods."

This news was welcome indeed. No traders, because of the wall, had come to the north for months.

"We will make a feast for our friend!" cried Kadluk.

"Oh," moaned Akko, "it is unfortunate that there is so little meat in the camp, and so our feast will be such a poor one."

"Also," said another fellow, "the women did not know anyone was coming, so they will not have any water boiling."

It takes some time to get water boiling over an oil lamp, though, to be sure, the flame can be elongated and enlarged by manipulating and trimming the wick moss.

"That is all right," said Ram.

Actually, of course, the camp was heavy with meat. There had not been so much meat in the camp for years and the women, even now, were busy preparing a splendid feast.

"We are sorry," said Kadluk, looking down.

"That is all right," said Ram, cheerfully. "Even a little piece of meat with friends makes a great feast."

The red hunters looked at one another slyly.

We turned about and, some men drawing the sled, began to trek back to the camp. Ram, of course, a trader for years, was familiar with the tricks and jokes of red hunters. It had not escaped his notice, for example, that he had been met by almost every male in the village better than two pasangs from the permanent camp. He thus knew both that he was expected and, from the number of men available to meet him, that there must be much food in the camp. Otherwise many men would be out on the ice with their families.

"The beast was after you," I said.

"It was hungry," he said.

"It was not after the snow sleen, or the food you were carrying," I said. "It was after you, specifically."

"I find that hard to believe," said Ram. "You speak as though it were intelligent."

"I believe it to be so," I said. "Did you not notice the rings in its ears."

"Of course," said Ram.

"Surely they are ornaments," I said.

"It escaped from a master," speculated Ram. "Doubtless he placed such ornaments in its ears."

"It was by its own will, I believe," I said, "that those rings were put in its ears."

"That seems to me unlikely," said Ram. "Did you not see how like a beast it was?"

"Do you think," I said, "because something does not look like a man that it cannot be intelligent?"

Ram turned white. "But intelligence," he said, "if coupled with such ferocity—"

"It is called a Kur," I said.

Ablaze with light was the feasting house.

Arlene, naked, the strap of bondage on her throat, head down, knelt before Ram, lifting a plate of boiled meat to him.

He thrust a thumb under her chin and roughly pushed up her chin.

"Who is this pretty little slave?" he asked. "She looks familiar."

She looked at him, in terror.

"Oh, yes," he said. "She is the one who commanded us at the wall."

"Yes," I said.

"You made her your slave," he said.

"Yes," I said.

"Is she any good?" he asked.

"You will soon find out," I told him.

He laughed.

"Remain kneeling here before us, Girl," I told Arlene.

"Yes, Master," she said.

Ram and I took meat from her plate, and she remained where she was, kneeling back on her heels.

"I am sure the beast was hunting you," I said.

"Perhaps," said Ram.

"How do you like our poor feast?" asked Kadluk, coming by.

"It is the greatest feast I have ever eaten," said Ram. "It is glorious."

"Maybe it is not bad," said Kadluk, putting his head down, grinning, and sliding over to his place.

"But did it follow you for a long time?" I asked.

"I do not know," said Ram.

"I speculate, though I do not know," I said, "that it intercepted you, that it had been waiting for you."

"How would it know where to wait?" he asked.

"I fear," I said, "my presence in this village is known. When I did not return south, it would be speculated I would go north. Only one red hunter was at the wall, Imnak. Surely it would be thought that I might then go to his village. Too, I may have been spied on here. I do not know."

Ram regarded me. "I understand little of this," he said.

"I think it was known," I said, "that I would be, or was, in the village of Kadluk. In Lydius, we had been seen together, too. Thus, when you came north it might be thought that you were seeking me."

"I made no secret of this," said Ram.

"Thus, if the enemy, if we may speak of them so, knew my location and your intent, to contact me, it would be simple to lay an ambush for you outside of the village."

"Yes," he said.

"What did not occur to them, I suspect," I said, "is that the sound of your sleen would carry as far as it did, and that the hunters would come forth to greet you."

"There is another possibility, a fearful one," said Ram.

"What is that?" I asked.

"In following me," he said, "I may have led foes to your location."

"That is possible," I said. "But if it is true, it is acceptable."

"How is that?" asked Ram.

"I think it is the desire of at least one other that I participate in an interview. I have come north, in a sense, responding to an invitation. If it is known where I am, the enemy may attempt to contact me here."

"Or kill you," he said.

"Yes," I said.

"Why would the Kur attempt to kill me?" asked Ram.

"Perhaps you are carrying information it did not wish me to receive," I said.

"In Lydius," he said, "Sarpedon, the tavern keeper, and several others, like myself, newly arrived from the wall, suddenly and without warning, fell upon Sarpelius and his henchmen." Sarpelius, I recalled, had been the heavy, paunchy fellow who had taken over the tavern from Sarpedon. He had worked with several others, who had functioned to impress workers for the wall.

"Sarpedon now has his tavern back?" I inquired.

"Of course," said Ram. "Sarpelius and his men, before we sold them from the wharves as naked slaves, were persuaded to speak."

"Doubtless that was wise of them," I speculated.

"Their information was not so precious to them that they preferred to retain it in the face of death by torture," said Ram. "Sarpelius, for example, did not wish to be thrust feet first, bit by bit, into a cage of hungry sleen."

"It would not be pleasant," I admitted.

"But it seems, unfortunately, as minions, they knew little."

"What did you gather?" I asked.

"The one called Drusus, whom we knew at the wall," he said, "paid their fees and issued their instructions. Tarnsmen transported the workers, drugged, to the wall."

"What of the girls?" I asked. I remembered Tina and Constance. "They were not at the wall."

"We learned from Sarpelius, from what he had learned from Drusus, that there was a headquarters farther north, one which could be reached only in the late spring, summer or early fall."

"Perhaps it is at sea," I said. The sea, being frozen, would be impassable to shipping in the winter.

"Perhaps," he said.

"But, too," I said, "tarns, like most birds, will fly in the arctic only during those seasons."

"That is true," he said.

"I think the headquarters, however," I said, "must be at sea."

"Why is that?" asked Ram.

"If it were on the land," I said, "I think the red hunters, of one village or another, in their hunting, would have come across it. It would be, I assume, a large installation."

"I do not know," said Ram.

"Did you learn more?" I asked.

"We learned that it was to this mysterious headquarters that Drusus reported. Too, it is to that headquarters that, from time to time, choice slave beauties were taken."

"Such as Tina and Constance," I said.

297

"Yes," he said. "You see, I thought you might have known this and thus had come north to find Constance."

"You have come north then primarily," I said, "seeking Tina."

"Yes," he said.

"But she is only a slave," I smiled.

He reddened. "But she is my slave," he said, angrily. "She was taken from me, and I do not like that." He struck himself on the chest. "No one takes a slave from Ram of Teletus!" he said. "I will fetch her back, and then, if I wish, I will give her away, or beat and sell her."

"Of course," I said.

"Do not misunderstand me," he said, irritably. "It is not the girl who is important, for she is only a slave. It is the principle of the thing."

"Of course," I granted him. "Yet there seems much time and risk involved in recovering someone who is probably only a silver-tarsk girl."

"It is the principle of the thing," he said.

"Of course," I said.

"You seem very agreeable," he said.

"I am," I said.

"I think Tina is my perfect slave," he said, grinning. "I must have her at my feet, kneeling, in the shadow of my whip." He then looked, seriously, at me. "I hoped to join you in the north," said he. "Together we might seek out Tina and Constance."

"Who is Constance, Master?" asked Arlene.

"One who, like yourself, was once free," I said. "She is now a lovely slave. She might teach you much about being a woman."

"Yes, Master," said Arlene, putting her head down.

I was bringing her along slowly in her slavery.

"You, Slave," I said to Arlene, sharply. She lifted her head, quickly.

"Yes, Master," she said, frightened.

"Meat," I said.

She lifted the plate of boiled meat to us. Ram and I helped ourselves.

"What do you know about a headquarters in the north, Girl?" I asked her.

"Nothing," she whispered, "Master."

I took another piece of meat. I regarded her. I put the meat in my mouth, and chewed it.

"I did not say to take back the plate, Girl," I said.

298

"Forgive me, Master," she said, holding it as she had. I continued to regard her. "I really know nothing, Master," she said. "Drusus brought moneys. He was my contact. I know nothing!"

I took another piece of meat.

"I supervised work at the wall. I thought myself then the superior of Drusus. I do not know where he came from or where he obtained what moneys he brought. I supposed, in truth, there were other operations or facilities on this world, but I did not know their location." Tears sprang into her eyes. "Believe me, I beg you," she said. "If there is a head-quarters somewhere I know nothing of it. I beg you to believe me, Master!"

"Perhaps I believe you," I said.

She half fainted. I thought it true what she had said, not only from her asseverations and the fact that I had come to be able to read with facility her face and body in the months I had owned her, but from the general circumstances of the situation. When she had been free she had not, I was sure, recognized the carving of the head of a Kur for what it had been. I recalled her puzzlement, which I think was genuine, in the hall to the south, that which had formed her own headquarters near the now-broken wall. Too, I did not think that the Kurii would permit minor minions, such as she had been, though not understanding herself so, to know more than was absolutely necessary to perform their parts in their complex plans. Too, interestingly, it is difficult for a woman who is naked before a man to lie to him. Clothing makes it easier to lie. Naked, a woman is exposed not only physically to a man but, in a sense, psychologically, as well. She fears, psychologically, exposed as she is, that she can hide nothing, that he will see all, and detect all, that she is utterly open and vulnerable to him in all ways. This, for subtle and subjective reasons, having to do with psychology, makes it hard for her, when she is fully exposed to his scrutiny, to lie convincingly. She fears, somehow, he will know. And, actually, of course, there is something to her fear, indeed, a great deal. When she tries to lie there is a fear involved and this fear, in subtle ways, in subtle drawings back, in tenseness, is manifested in her beautiful body, proclaiming it that of a liar. Many times a girl does not know how the master knows she is lying. At the slave ring, struck, she cries out in her misery. How could he have known? The answer is simple. Her body betrayed her. It told him. Too, slave girls seldom lie, for the punishments connected with lying can be extremely severe. A girl

299

may be thrown alive to sleen for having lied. The severity of the possible punishments attendant upon falsehood in a slave tend, too, of course, to increase the fear of falsehood, and this fear then, felt deeply in the body, is all the more difficult to conceal. I would suppose that slave girls are among the most truthful of intelligent organisms, at least when stripped and confronted seriously by the master. They must be. Lying, serious lying, is not permitted to them. This is not to deny, however, that petty lying, pilfering and such, where the master is not directly concerned or affected, is often tolerated, if not encouraged. That sort of thing is expected of slave girls. They are, after all, slaves. For example, when a former free woman, now enslaved, steals her first pastry from another girl, this is often smiled upon, and punished, if at all, quite lightly. The master is not displeased. It is taken as evidence that the girl is now learning to be a slave. Slaves do that sort of thing. The petty jealousies and resentments that build up among girls make them easier to control. The master, to whom they belong, though he will normally refrain from interfering in their squabbles, is, of course, if need be, the ultimate arbiter for all their disputes. He owns them.

I looked at Arlene, and she shuddered. I thought it likely that she had told the truth.

"Audrey!" I called, summoning the former rich young woman by the name by which I often commanded her.

"Yes, Master," she said, and came to us, and knelt.

"Take the boiled meat from Arlene," I said, "and serve it about."

"Yes, Master," she said. She took the meat and rose to her feet, lifting herself and turning her body in such a way as to expose her beauty insolently to Ram. Then she sauntered away, glancing once over her shoulder at him, with a tiny smile.

"She has nice flanks," said Ram.

"Yes," I said.

"An excellent catch," he said.

"She is Imnak's," I said. "He bought her at the fair."

"A splendid purchase," said Ram, congratulating Imnak.

"I bought the other one there, too," said Imnak, indicating Barbara, who was serving across the room.

"Another splendid purchase," said Ram. "She is quite attractive."

Barbara looked over her shoulder. Ram had not spoken softly. She knew herself the object of our conversation. She

300

straightened herself. She was proud that she was beautiful, and of interest to strong men.

"I had them both for the pelt of a snow lart and the pelts of four leems," said Imnak, rather pleased with himself.

Barbara looked angry.

"To secure such a brace of beauties for such a price is indeed marvelous," said Ram.

"The market was slow," admitted Imnak.

"But you are, too, a skillful bargainer," pointed out Ram.

Imnak shrugged modestly. "They did cost me five pelts," he said.

"Five pelts is nothing for such beauties," insisted Ram.

"Perhaps you are right," said Imnak. "At any rate they are now both in my bondage strings."

Barbara came to us and knelt before us. She looked at Ram. She carried a bowl of dried berries. Their eyes met over the bowl as she lifted it to him. He, without taking his eyes from her, thrust his hand into the bowl and scooped out a large handful of berries. She then rose lightly, sinuously, before him, and, turning her back, left. Ram watched her. She walked slowly, gracefully, away. She was intensely conscious of his eyes upon her. When she dared, she turned once and looked at him, then put her head down, smiling.

"They are good at pulling sleds," said Imnak.

"They have other utilities, too," I said.

"You may use either, of course," said Imnak, putting Thimble and Thistle, both, at Ram's disposal.

"Thank you," said Ram. "But neither of them commanded me at the wall."

He looked at Arlene, who knelt before us, a bit to the left. She shrank back.

"Meat," he said to her.

"I will fetch some," she said, starting to rise.

"Do not be a little fool," I said. "He means you."

"Oh," she said, frightened.

"Are you any good?" asked Ram.

"I do not know," she whispered. "Master will tell me."

Ram rose to his feet and walked over to the wall of the feasting house. There he threw off the lart-skin shirt he wore.

"With your permission, Imnak," said Ram, "I will try the others later."

"Use them whenever you wish," said Imnak. "Their use is yours."

Ram stood, waiting by the wall.

Arlene looked at me, frightened.

301

"Please him," I told her.

"Yes, Master," she said. She made as though to rise.

"No," I said. "Crawl to him on your hands and knees."

"Yes, Master," she said.

"And please him well," I said.

"Yes, Master," she said.

I turned my attention to the clearing in the feasting house. There there was miming going on. The hunters and the women clapped their hands and cried out with pleasure at the skill of the various mimers. Naartok was being a whale. This was the occasion of additional jests from the audience.

"Tarl, who hunts with me," said Imnak, seriously, "I am afraid."

"What are you afraid of?" I asked.

"The animal we saw," said Imnak, "was surely an ice beast."

"So?" I said.

"I fear Karjuk is dead," he said.

"Why do you say this?" I asked.

"Karjuk is the guard," he said. "He stands between the People and the ice beasts."

"I see," I said.

White-pelted Kurii are called ice beasts by the red hunters. These animals usually hunt from ice floes in the summer, generally far out at sea. Unlike most Kurii, they have an affinity for water, and are fond of it. In the winter, when the sea freezes, they occasionally rove inland. There are different races of Kur. Not much was known of the mysterious Karjuk, even among the red hunters, save that he was one of them. He was a strange man, who lived alone. He had no woman. He had no friends. He lived alone on the ice. He roved in the darkness, silent, with his lance. He stood between the People and the ice beasts. The Kur that I had seen outside the village, which had escaped with the slain snow sleen, had been white-pelted. I was confident, however, that it had been a ship Kur, and not a common ice beast. On the other hand, I was confident, too, that it must have come from the northern sea or the northern ice. Thus, presumably, it would have penetrated and passed through the territory in which Karjuk maintained his lonely outpost. That it had appeared this near the village suggested that it had either slipped by Karjuk or that it had found him, of all those Kurii which may have hunted him, and killed him.

"Perhaps the beast slipped past Karjuk," I suggested.

"I do not think an ice beast could slip past Karjuk," said Imnak. "I think Karjuk is dead."

A man was now being a sea sleen, swimming, before the group. He was quite skillful.

"I am sorry," I said.

Imnak and I sat together for a long time, not speaking.

Akko and Kadluk were then before the group. Akko was an iceberg, floating, drifting about, and Kadluk, pressing near and withdrawing, was the west wind. Akko, the iceberg, responded to the wind, heavily, sluggishly, turning slowly in the water.

Both were skillful.

There was much laughter and pleasure, and delight, taken in their performance.

Suddenly, as they finished their performance, there was a breath of chill air that coursed through the feasting house. All heads turned toward the door. But no one spoke. A man stood there, a red hunter, dark-visaged and lean, thin and silent. At his back there was a horn bow and a quiver of arrows; in his hand there was a lance and, held by cords, a heavy sack. He turned about and swung shut the door, and pulled down the hide across it. There was snow on his parka, for, apparently, snow had begun to fall outside during the feast. When he had closed the feasting house, he turned again to look upon the feasters.

Imnak's hand was hard upon my arm.

The man then put his weapons near the rear wall of the feasting house and walked, carrying the sack he had brought with him, to the clearing on the dirt floor. There, not speaking, he shook loose from the sack, causing it to fall to the dirt, the head of a large, white-pelted Kur, an ice beast. In its ears were golden rings.

I looked at Imnak.

"It is Karjuk," he said.

24 WE HOLD CONVERSE IN THE HUT OF IMNAK; A DECISION IS REACHED; I PERMIT ARLENE TO SHARE MY FURS

"It is fortunate for me, perhaps," said Ram, to Karjuk, in Imnak's hut, "that you were trailing the ice beast and managed to kill it." He looked at the severed head in the corner of the hut. "I would hate to meet it again."

Karjuk nodded, but did not speak.

He had cut the rings from the ears of the beast, and had given them, with Imnak's permission, to Poalu, who now wore them on her left wrist, as bracelets.

Before she had put them on her wrist I had held them, looking at them closely, and weighing them in my hand.

"Are you sure," I asked Ram, "that this is the head of the beast who attacked you?"

"Could there be more than one such beast," he asked, "with rings in its ears?"

"It does not seem likely," I admitted. I had examined the head with great care, the ears and the mouth in particular.

"I had followed the beast for days," said Karjuk. "I trailed it to where I encountered sled tracks, and blood in the snow, and the trampling of the snow by many feet."

"That would be where it had attacked my sleen and sled," said Ram, "and where the men from the village came to rescue me."

"I then trailed the beast further, some pasangs across the snow. It had been wounded twice, and was found feeding on the carcass of a snow sleen with harness marks in its fur."

"That then is the same beast," said Ram, "assuredly."

"I then slew it," said Karjuk.

I sipped my Bazi tea, and looked at him, over the rim of the bowl. He, too, looked at me, and sipped his tea.

The girls, Poalu, too, remained in the background, in case the men should need aught. The white-skinned girls did not

304

go close to the severed head. Poalu, a woman of red hunters, had no fear or repulsion concerning the object. Bones, and blood and hide, and such things, were a part of her world.

"Have you heard aught, Karjuk," I asked, "of a mountain of ice, an ice mountain in the sea, which does not move?"

"In the winter," said Karjuk, "the mountains in the water do not move, for then the sea is frozen."

"Have you heard of such a mountain which does not move, even when the sea flows?" I asked.

"I have not heard of such a mountain," he said.

"I told him there could be no such thing," said Imnak.

"But I have seen it," said Karjuk. He had spoken with the literalness of the red hunter.

We were all silent.

"There is such a thing?" said Imnak.

"Yes," said Karjuk. "It is far out to sea, but once, in sleen fishing, I paddled my kayak about it."

"Is it large?" I asked.

"Very large," he said.

"How can there be such a thing?" asked Imnak.

"I do not know," said Karjuk, "but I know it exists, for I have seen it."

"Have others, too, seen it?" I asked.

"Perhaps," said Karjuk, "I do not know."

"Could you take me to it?" I asked.

"It is far out on the ice now," he said.

"Could you take me to it?" I asked.

"Yes, if you wish," he said.

I put aside my tea. "Fetch my pouch," I said to Arlene. She hurried and brought the pouch to me.

I drew forth from the interior of the pouch the carved head of a Kur, wrought in bluish stone, that savage head with one ear half torn away.

"Is this your work?" I asked.

"Yes," said Karjuk, "I made that."

"Did you ever see such a beast?" I asked.

"Yes," he said.

"Where?" I asked.

"Near the mountain that did not move," he said.

"Is it the head of an ice beast?" I asked.

"No," he said. "It was too darkly pelted to be an ice beast."

"Could you lead me soon to the mountain that does not move?" I asked.

"It is the night now," said Karjuk, "and the time of

darkness. The ice is dangerous. It is at this time that the ice beasts sometimes come inland."

"Yet you will lead me there, will you not?" I asked. I smiled.

"Yes," said Karjuk, "if you wish."

"That is my wish," I said.

"Very well," said Karjuk.

"There will be little danger if Karjuk is with us," said Poalu. "He is the guard."

"I will come with you," said Imnak.

"You need not do that," I said.

Imnak looked at the severed head of the white-pelted Kur. It was difficult to read his face. "No," he said, "I will come with you."

Karjuk sipped his tea.

"I, too, of course, will accompany you," said Ram.

"Will you trade Bazi tea to the ice beasts?" I asked.

"I am coming," said Ram.

"Very well, my friend," I said. I looked at Karjuk. "When shall we leave?" I asked Karjuk.

"I must finish my tea," he said, "and then sleep. We may then leave."

"Would you like the use of any of my women?" asked Imnak of Karjuk, indicating Poalu, and Thimble and Thistle.

"Or the use of my pretty slave?" I asked, indicating Arlene.

Arlene drew back. She was frightened of the thin, dour Karjuk. Yet she knew that at my slightest word, should I speak it, she would have to serve him, fully, for she was slave.

Karjuk looked at Poalu, in the two golden bracelets, which had been rings in the ears of the slain Kur. The rings, as bracelets, were pretty on her small red wrist. She was a lovely red slave.

She drew back a bit.

"No," said Karjuk.

He finished his tea and then crawled into furs on the sleeping platform. The others, too, prepared to retire.

"Let us not bring the girls with us," I suggested to Imnak.

"No," said Imnak. "We will bring them. Who else will chew the ice from our boots, and sew for us, and boil meat and tend the lamps, and keep us warm in the furs?" He rolled over in the furs. "We will take snow sleen and women," he said.

"Very well," I said. I did not think, objectively, there

would be great danger for the women. If what I suspected was true, uses would be found for them. They were all beautiful.

"Master," whispered Arlene.

"Yes," I said.

"May I crawl into your furs?" she asked.

"Are you cold?" I asked. She had her own furs. Sometimes she had to sleep alone, as when I was sleeping with Audrey or Barbara.

"No, Master," she whispered.

"Your need to serve a man is hot on you, Slave?" I asked.

"I am frightened," she said.

I held open the furs and let her creep into them, beside me. I held her, under the furs, in my arms. She trembled, small, against me.

"I'm frightened," she whispered, her face, so soft, against my chest.

"Of what are you frightened?" I asked.

"Of Karjuk," she said, "and of going out on the ice." She held me, closely. "What will you find there?" she asked.

"I do not know," I said.

"You search for the headquarters of those who were my superiors, do you not?" she asked.

"Yes," I said, "Slave."

"They must assuredly be dangerous," she said.

"Perhaps," I said.

"Avoid them then at all costs," she said. "Flee to the south," she whispered.

"Do you beg it?" I asked.

"Yes, Master," she said.

"No," I said. "Your will means nothing."

She sobbed.

"Do you know the nature of those who were your superiors," I asked.

"No," she said.

"Look," I said to her, taking her head and turning it, so that she might see, in the dim light of the lamp, the head of the Kur. "They are much like that," I said.

She half choked with horror. "No," she said.

"It was such as they whom you, when free, served, my lovely slave beauty," I said.

"No, no," she whispered.

"But, yes," I smiled. "It is true."

"What will be done with you, if you fall into their hands?" she asked.

307

"I do not know," I said. "I suspect it would not be pleasant."

"What would they do with me, if I fell into their hands?" she asked.

"Perhaps you would be restored to all your rights and privileges," I said, "and would again become an operative for them."

"I failed them," she whispered.

"That is true," I said. "Perhaps they would find some other tasks for you to perform."

"Like what?" she asked.

"You would look well," I said, "in a wisp of slave silk and a steel collar."

"They would keep me as a slave?" she asked.

"I am sure you were brought to Gor, ultimately, to be a slave," I said. "You are too beautiful to be indefinitely left free."

She held me.

"Your beauty, you see," I said, "has a cost on this world. Its price is your freedom. Beauty, and exquisite femininity, such as yours, buys for itself on this world chains and a master."

"I am going to say something to you," she said, "which I had never thought I would say to a man."

"What is that?" I asked.

"I would love to wear your chains, Master," she whispered. Then she sobbed, shaken with the horror of this confession.

"Do not weep," I said. "It is only that you are a slave." I kissed her. "Would you lick and kiss your chains?" I asked.

"Do not make me do that," she begged, turning her head aside, weeping.

"It is not my intention to make you do that," I said.

"I do not know what I would do if you were to throw your chains to my feet," she said.

"I know what Audrey would do," I said.

"Yes," said Arlene, bitterly, "so do I, the little slut. She would kneel, and lift them, and lick and kiss them."

"I think so," I said.

"What a slave she is," said Arlene.

"Her intelligence," I said, "is fully comparable to yours, and may be superior," I said.

"That is what I cannot understand," said Arlene. "How can a woman of her intelligence be such a slave?"

"Perhaps her intelligence frees her to be more quickly and honestly responsive to her deepest needs," I said. "Perhaps she is quicker to recognize her deepest feelings, and more willing to accept them, than a duller woman, or perhaps only a more constricted woman. Often the superior woman searches, lonely and frustrated, for a man superior to herself, who can be a full man to the hidden woman in her. Unfortunately many who could be a man to the woman in such a female do not, because of their training and conditioning, become so. When the superior woman does meet a man superior to herself, who will also, simply because he is a true man, put her in the authentic biological male/female relationship where she belongs, at his feet, she will generally, unless there are mitigating psychological reservations, functions of her own conditionings, submit herself joyfully to him as what is, for all practical purposes, his slave. On Gor, of course, men have not been conditioned against the authentic biological male/female relationship, at least where female slaves are concerned. Similarly, on Gor, a woman, collared, is not permitted psychological reservations or that sort of thing. Her will is nothing. Also, the society backs the master. The girl has absolutely no one to call. She has absolutely nowhere to run. She has no recourse. She is an owned slave."

"It is very frightening," she said.

"And for many women," I said, "very thrilling."

"Yes," she whispered, softly, "it is very thrilling. I do not know why it should be, but it is very thrilling."

"In your heart," I said, "You know you are a woman. Thus, when you find you simply will be given no alternative other than being a true woman, in the full sense of the word, designed by nature as a love slave for males strong enough to master you, you cannot help but be thrilled. You are forced to be yourself, your true self. There is a joy in this, and a liberating honesty, and openness; it is natural that this be felt as exciting, as genuine, as authentic, as real, as significant, as true, indeed, as profoundly and thrillingly true. Gone are the politically and economically motivated lies; gone is the cant and hypocrisy. Present then is the sweet thrilling truth, at last freed, no longer suppressed and hidden, and love."

"Please kiss me, Master," she said.

I kissed her.

"Are you going to keep me, Master?" she asked.

"I do not know," I said. "But do not fear, lovely slave. On this world there are hundreds of thousands of men fully capable of mastering you. You will someday, doubtless, given the sellings and exchanges, and your growth in skills and beauty, find love."

"A woman desires love," she whispered.

"Love is found more often among slave girls than free women," I said. "If you would learn love, learn slavery."

"Yes, Master," she said. She kissed me.

"Please me," I said.

"Yes, Master," she said.

The lamp went out softly in the darkness. This frightened her. "Must you go out on the ice?" she whispered.

"Yes," I said.

"Are you going to take me with you?" she asked.

"Yes," I said.

"I am afraid," she said.

"Do not be afraid," I said to her.

"I cannot help it," she said.

"Please me in the darkness, in the furs, Slave," I said.

"Yes, my master," she said.

In a few minutes I took her in my arms and threw her to her back. She gasped. "I thought I was to please you," she said.

"You are pleasing me," I said.

"You are making me yield," she said, intensely.

"That pleases me," I said.

Then she began to buck and writhe and was soon lost in the throes of the slave orgasm, helplessly yielded to her master. She came silently, intensely, clutching me, this not known to the others asleep in the hut. That a slave girl had been conquered in the darkness need not be known to them.

Afterwards I held her, naked, closely, warmly.

After a time she whispered, "I want to be touched again."

"Do you beg it?" I asked.

"Yes, Master," she said.

"Your will means nothing," I said.

"I know," she said.

"But I will touch you," I said.

"Thank you, Master," she said. Soon again she squirmed in silence, taken, in the furs in the hut of Imnak.

"Thank you, Master," she whispered, afterwards. "You give a girl much pleasure."

"Sleep now, Slave," I said.

"Yes, Master," she said.

I do not know how long we slept, but it was perhaps no more than two or three Ahn. I awakened, conscious of her holding me. Her head lay on my belly. She was not asleep. "Master," she whispered.

"Yes," I said.

She knelt beside me. "Please, Master," she said.

"Is your need to serve a man hot upon you?" I asked. I could tell that it was from her breathing.

"Yes, Master," she said.

"You are a slave," I said.

"Yes, I am a slave, Master," she said.

"Very well, Slave," I said. "You may serve me."

"Thank you, Master," she said.

Soon I marveled at her skill. It was all I could do to keep from crying out with pleasure and delight, and my pride in the skill of the slave I owned. How proud I was of her! She was for most practical purposes untrained and new to the collar and yet many girls whom I had had, even in paga taverns, I suspect, could not have equaled her performance.

"What is going on with you?" I asked.

"I do not understand," she said.

"What has happened?" I asked. "What has gone on in your head, pretty slave?"

"I do not understand," she said.

"I went to sleep with a pot wench," I said, "and I awaken with a pleasure slave."

She laughed. Then she said, soberly, "I love being a slave, Master."

"That is well," I said, "for on this world you are a slave, and you are going to continue to be a slave."

"Yes, Master," she said, trembling. Then she said, "I am content, Master."

"Continue your work, Slave Girl," I said.

"Yes, Master," she said.

I then let her pleasure me, fully, not so much as touching her, that she might learn to please completely, without being so much as granted the least kiss or caress of the male beast. Slave girls are forced thus, sometimes, to serve, totally, unilaterally; it helps to impress their slavery on them.

She then lay beside me.

"Do you still love being a slave girl?" I asked.

"Yes, Master," she said.

"But I did not so much as touch you," I said.

"Oh, sex is terribly important," she said, "and you may use it as you do, you beasts, to conquer and discipline us, and make us your sex slaves, but, too, there are other things in slavery which are perhaps harder for you to understand, for you are not the woman."

"What can there be," I asked, "other than chains and the whip, the kiss and the collar?"

"You men are so simple, so naive," she laughed. "You do not even understand the fullness of the power you hold over us. Slavery is not a mere condition; it is a kind of life. The woman is not simply a slave when you seize her and throw her to your feet. She is a slave, too, before this, and after this, subject to your will, and knowing it. There is a wholeness, a fullness, a beauty in a woman's being a slave, of which I fear you may be unaware."

"Perhaps," I said.

"Do you think women would make you such marvelous slaves if there was not something in them which wanted to be enslaved?"

"Perhaps not," I said.

"A slave girl is not a slave only, you see, when she is commanded or taken in the arms of the master. She is a slave wholly, fully, all the time. It is what she is. I think it is this wholeness, this fullness, this beauty, this totality of bondage which you men do not understand. It is hard to speak of it. When a girl is a slave all of her is a slave. It is what she is. Oh, I could speak to you of a woman's need for emotional fulfillment, security, excitement, romance, discipline; her need to relate, to be happy, to a strong male figure, one before whom she knows herself, truly, in the intimacy of herself to be a female, and his; the bankruptcy of egoism, ambition and greed for many women; their need to love, their desire to please and be of service; their intrinsic yearning to submit to an uncompromising, dominant organism; their deep-seated desire to be found so beautiful and attractive that men will want them, and want them so much that they will own them and make them give them everything, but are not all these things only futile words peripheral to the speechless emotional reality felt by the girl when she kneels before the master, and he then touches her as his own?"

I did not speak.

"There is something about being owned, and belonging to another, which is very meaningful to a woman," she said. "It is also, in a way that is hard to make clear to a man, profoundly satisfying."

"It has to do with nature," I suggested.

"I suppose, in some way," she said.

It seemed likely to me that there would be a genetic base for feelings so deep, and widely spread.

"Are you going to free me?" she asked.

"No," I said.

"That pleases me," she said.

312

She lay beside me. I did not touch her.

"It is hard to make clear to a man," she said.

"What?" I asked.

"The ecstasy of being a slave girl," she said. "You see, Master," she said, "the joy of being a slave girl is a very deep and continuous thing. Its emotional fulfillments extend far beyond the masterly depredations and disciplines you inflict, as you please, upon me."

"Surely they are not unimportant," I said.

"No," she said, "they are important. Indeed, it was your touch which first made me a slave."

I sensed her turn toward me in the darkness. "But, you see," she said, "I must serve you whether I am touched or not. And that, too, in a way you may have difficulty understanding, I find very meaningful, very thrilling."

"You respond then, not only to my touch but also to the very condition of slavery itself?" I asked.

"Yes," she said, "but I would prefer to think of it as responding not so much to the condition of being a slave as to the clear and incontrovertible fact that I am a slave. I think that is it, that that is my reality, that I am a slave."

"That you find thrilling in itself?" I asked.

"Yes," she said, "to be will-lessly at the mercy of another, his helpless slave."

"I see," I said.

"Too, sometimes," she said, "being a slave I feel very free and happy."

"Perhaps that has something to do with the repudiation and abandonment of egoism, the enemy of love," I speculated.

"Perhaps," she said, "I do not know. I suspect it involves many things and is very deep."

"Only fools have simple explanations for complex phenomena," I said. "Nothing human is simple."

"I lie vulnerably beside you," she said, "yours to do with as you please. I am a slave."

I took her in my arms, and began her slow, patient rape.

"Release me," she said.

"No," I said.

She squirmed, futilely, impaled.

"Let me go," she said.

"No," I said.

"I demand to be released," she said.

I laughed, softly, holding her. She tried to free herself, and could not.

She stopped struggling. "Ai, Ai!" she said, clutching me.

I, holding her right arm with my left hand, thrust my right hand over her mouth, tightly, that she not disturb the others in the hut. My right hand felt wet and hot, from the heat and moisture of her breath. I felt her teeth under her lips. She tried to twist her head, and then yielded.

It was pleasant having her in that way.

"Why did you resist?" I asked.

"To see if my resistance would be acceptable to you," she said.

"It was not," I said.

"Of course not," she said. "I am a slave." There was a pause. "Are you going to whip me," she asked, "for being troublesome?"

"I did not find you troublesome," I said.

"Oh," she said. We lay together, quietly, for a time. "You took me against my will," she said.

"Yes," I said.

"I wondered if you would do that," she said.

"I take you when and as I please," I said.

"Of course," she said. "I am a slave." In time she put her lips to me, tenderly. "Oh," she said. She drew back. "You are strong, Master," she laughed.

"You are a sweet-lipped and beautiful slave," I said. It was true. With a girl like Arlene what man would not be driven half mad with lust? How marvelous she was. How easy it was to desire her.

"I did not know a man could be so strong," she said, wonderingly.

"Do you think you have nothing to do with it, you pretty idiot?" I asked.

"Oh?" she asked.

"You have a great deal to do with it," I said.

"You cannot even see me in the dark," she said.

"I know what you look like," I said, "and I can feel you, your closeness, your body, your touch. It has an interesting modality in the darkness, in the furs." I reached to her, and, by the strap on her throat, pulled her down beside me. "Also," I said, "you are a naked slave. No woman can be more interesting than a naked slave."

"Oh," she said. I held her by the strap.

"That you are a slave makes you additionally stimulating to the male," I said, "aside from your mere beauty and intelligence."

"Yes," Master," she said.

"So do not be surprised, in your servitude," I said, "that you find men strong. Simply to look upon you, a beautiful slave, will commonly be enough to stimulate their lust. You are no longer a free woman, filled with her rigidities and negativities, for whom it is permissible to be irritating and boring. No. You are a lovely slave. Looking upon you men will want you. They will want to buy you. They will want to own you."

"Yes, Master," she said.

"Men even kill to possess women such as you," I told her. "You are that desirable."

"Yes, Master," she said.

"So do not prate in awe of male power," I said. "It is you, and your beauty, and your slavery, and your intelligence, which provides so powerful an incentive to their strengths and aggressions. Whether this pleases you or not, you are such that men, looking upon you, will want you, and will want you so much that they will be willing to pay for you, or even fight for you. Do you begin to understand the meaning now of being a beautiful slave?"

"Yes, Master," she whispered, frightened.

"You are property," I said.

"Yes, Master," she said.

"A treasure," I said.

"Your treasure," she said.

"Yes," I said.

"How strange it is to be helplessly owned," she marveled, "to be subject to sale or exchange."

"Do you find it thrilling?" I asked.

"Yes, Master," she said.

"Who owns you?" I asked.

"You do, Master," she said.

"Whose are you?" I asked.

"I am yours," she said, "literally."

"Yes," I said.

"Take your girl, Master," she said. "She begs you."

"Very well," I said.

"This is what it is to be a slave," she whispered. "Slavery is more than your touch, but without your touch it would be nothing."

I kissed her, softly.

"It is your touch," she said, intensely, "which makes a girl a slave!"

"The touch of any master," I said, "can turn a girl into a slave."

"Do you leave me no pride?" she wept.

"None," I said, "for you are a slave."

Her breathing became more intense.

"Do not disturb the others in the hut," I cautioned her.

"Yes, Master," she whispered. Then she again yielded, intensely, helplessly.

Afterwards she lay against me, soft and warm, and small and lovely. "Do you know what I would do now," she asked, "if you were to throw your chains before me?"

"No," I said, kissing her.

"I would kneel," she said, "and I would lift them in my hands, and—"

"Yes?" I asked.

"And then I would kiss and lick them," she whispered.

"Of course," I said, "you are a slave."

"Yes, I am a slave, Master," she said.

"Sleep now," I said.

"Master," she said.

"Yes," I said.

"I am not afraid now," she said, "to go out on the ice."

"Why not?" I asked.

"You will be with me," she said.

"It will be dangerous," I said.

"I am not afraid. You will be with me," she said. Then she said, "Thank you for letting a frightened girl enter your furs tonight."

"That is all right," I said. I rolled over.

"You are kind," she said.

"Beware," I said.

"Forgive me, Master," she said, suddenly frightened. "I meant no harm. It was a small slip. I did not mean to insult you. Please do not whip me for it."

"Very well," I said. I was tired. Too, it did not seem to me that her remark, inadvertent and perilous as it may have been, impaired the discipline in which I held her. Kindness is not always a weakness you must understand. Indeed, it, and its withdrawal, may be used to better control the girl. To be sure, the master who is harder to please gets more from his girl than the master who is easy to please, but, nonetheless, I think kindness is not out of place upon occasion toward a bond girl. Indeed, in a certain context a kind word can almost cause such a wench, collared and at your mercy, to faint with love. I do not think I am a particularly kind or unkind master. I think I am in the normal range where such matters are concerned. Kindness is acceptable, in my opinion, provided the girl knows that she is kept within the strictest of disciplines. I want no more from a girl than everything. If I own her, then, like any other Gorean master, I will simply see that I get it. Beyond that, I may be kind to her or not, as I see fit. Sometimes, of course, kindness is cruelty, and a certain harshness may be kind. One must know the girl. The truly kind master, I think, is he who treats the girl in such a way that she is forced to fulfill her needs in their radical depth and diversity; he gives her no choice but to be a woman, in the full meaning of this word, which is the only thing that can truly, ultimately, make her happy. If a woman were a man perhaps the way to make her happy would be to treat her like a man. If she is not a man perhaps treating her like a man is not the way to make her happy. It may seem hard to understand but the man who truly cares for his slave is often rather strict with her; he cares for her enough to be strong; sometimes she may resent or hate him but, too, she is inordinately proud of him, for what he makes her do, and be, and she loves him for his strength and his will; in her heart she knows she is the slave of such a man; how can she not love the man who proves himself to be her master? But the natures of men and women are doubtlessly complex and mysterious. Perhaps women, after all, are not women, but only small, incomplete men, as many women and men, espousing the current political and economic orthodoxies on the matter, the required, expected views on the matter, would insist. I do not know. And yet how peculiar and surprising would such a perversion appear against the expanse of history.

"Sleep now, sweet slave," I said.

"Yes, Master," she said.

I lay awake for a time, wondering on the natures of women and men, and then I was pleased that I was on Gor, and not on Earth. I kissed the lovely slave beside me, but she did not know I kissed her, for she was asleep. I thought of Karjuk, and the ice. The word 'Karjuk', incidentally, in the language of the Innuit, means 'Arrow'. The wind began to rise outside. I did not care to hear the wind. I hoped it did not presage a storm. Then I fell asleep.

25 WE GO OUT UPON THE ICE; WE FOLLOW KARJUK

It was bitterly cold. I did not know how far out on the ice we were.

"Shove!" called Imnak. Imnak and I, and the girls, tipped the sled over a slope of pack ice, it tilting and then sliding downward.

"Wait!" called Imnak to Karjuk.

Karjuk stepped off the runners of his sled and called to his snow sleen, dragging back on the tabuk-horn uprights at the rear of the sled, by means of which he guided the snow vessel.

There were three sleds in our party. Karjuk had his own, and his own snow sleen. The second sled was Imnak's, and the third was Ram's, brought with him from the south, which the men of the permanent camp had drawn to the camp for him. Imnak's sled was drawn by a snow sleen borrowed from his friend, Akko, and Ram's sled was drawn by another snow sleen, replacing the one the Kur had slain outside the camp. He had purchased it from Naartok for Bazi tea. Karjuk sledded alone; so, too, did Ram; Imnak and I brought up the rear with Imnak's sled, fashioned long ago at the remains of the wall. The four girls traveled with us, usually running as we did, with the sled. Sometimes, as they grew exhausted, we would permit one or another of them to ride upon the sled.

Karjuk lifted his hand, to again commence our journey.

"No, wait!" called Imnak. He was looking up at the sky. No storm had yet struck, but the sky was growing overcast. We had been five days now upon the ice. A storm, for days, had foreboded, but it had not yet materialized. In this we had been fortunate. As I may have mentioned the arctic night is seldom completely dark. Indeed, the visibility is often quite good, for the light of the moons, and even the stars, is reflected from the vastness of the ice and snow. I looked about at the irregular and jagged shapes, wierd and mighty, which loomed about us, of the pack ice, eerie in the deep shadows, and bright, strange light of the moons and snow. We stood small in the midst of incredible and fearful geometries. There was a beauty and a menace in these gigantic structures, fashioned by the bitter gnawing of the wind and the upheavals of the sea stirring beneath us. Sometimes we could feel the ice move. Sometimes we bridged, carefully, leads of open water, broken open by the groaning, shifting ice, soon to close again, almost beneath our feet.

Imnak pointed upward, back toward the south. We could not see the stars there. Cloud cover obscured them.

"Let us make camp here," called Imnak to Karjuk.

Karjuk did not respond, but looked ahead, onward. Again he lifted his arm.

Ram came up to us. "There is going to be a storm," said Imnak. "We must camp."

Karjuk again lifted his arm.

"I must check the runners on my sled," called Imnak.

Karjuk stood still, waiting.

The runners of our sleds were of wood. At the beginning of the season, usually in the late fall, a paste, a muck, formed of earth, and grass and moss, for solidity, is shaped and placed on the wood, some five to six inches to thickness. Ice will adhere to this coating, which is plastered thickly on the wood, as it will not to the wood alone. The ice is extremely important. At low temperatures snow becomes granular and has a texture somewhat like sand. A coating of ice on the earthen plaster, fixed on the runners, reduces friction. The coating, or plaster, will normally suffice, with patching, for a season. The layer of ice, of course, is renewed often, sometimes many times a day. Urine, which freezes instantly, is often used for the ice coating. But, too, a skin bag, filled with snow, placed within the clothing, next to the body, which causes the snow to melt, may also be used. At night, when the sled is not being used, it is overturned, so that the runners will not freeze to the ice. Sleen harnesses and traces are hung on a pole, thrust upright in the snow, to protect them from being eaten by the sleen.

Imnak relieved himself, icing the runners. He also used water from the skin bag he carried about his waist. One may also take snow in one's mouth, melt it and spit it on the runners, but this takes time. When one eats snow, incidentally, one melts it first, thoroughly, in the mouth, before swallowing it. This helps to preserve body heat and prevent shock to the system.

"Let us continue on," called Karjuk.

"A storm is coming," said Imnak, pointing to the southern sky. "Let us camp."

"We will camp later," said Karjuk.

"Very well," said Imnak.

"Is it wise to continue on now?" asked Ram of Imnak.

"No," said Imnak.

We righted our sled.

"Tie the slaves to the sled," said Imnak.

The wind was rising.

I took a length of binding fiber and tied it about Arlene's neck, knotting it tightly. It was about fifteen feet long.

"Master," protested Arlene.

"Oh!" she cried, struck brutally to the snow. She looked up at me, blood about her mouth, the tether on her neck.

Audrey hurried to me, to be fastened by me to the sled. I tied another piece of binding fiber, smiling to that with which I had secured Arlene, about her neck. Audrey then stood before me, tethered. I threw her to her knees in the snow before me, beside Arlene. Let Audrey not think she was privileged, or better, than Arlene. Both were only slave girls at my feet. I then tied the two loose ends of the tethers about the base of the tabuk-horn upright at the rear, right-hand side of the sled. Meanwhile Imnak had similarly secured Barbara and Poalu to the left-hand, rear upright on the sled.

"Do you want your wrists, too, bound behind your backs?" I asked Audrey and Arlene.

"No, Master," they said.

"On your feet, pretty beasts," I said.

They leaped to their feet, obeying me.

Karjuk stepped on the runners of his sled, and cracked his whip over the head of his snow sleen.

Ram's sled fell into line behind him.

"On!" called Imnak, taking his place behind his sled, and cracking the long-bladed sleen whip over the snow sleen, Akko's beast, which was in his traces. The animal, with its back hunched, and its wide, furred paws, claws extended, scratching, threw itself against the harness, making taut the trace and linkage, and the sled moved. From the side I gave it an additional shove, to help it gain momentum. Imnak did not now ride the runners of the sled, but ran between them. I moved at the side of the sled, on its right. The girls, now on their tethers, ran, too. Sometimes a man or woman runs before the sled, to hasten the sleen, which will normally match the guide pace. Now, however, that was not necessary, as we had before us two sleds to set our pace, that of Karjuk, in the lead, and that of Ram, behind him.

From time to time, then standing on the runners, Imnak would turn to regard the jagged terrain behind him. This is a habit of red hunters. It gives a check on what may be behind one, and, too, it shows him what the country will look like on his return. This is a procedure which helps to prevent the red hunter from becoming lost. It makes it easier to find his way back because he has already, in effect, seen what the return journey will look like. He has, so to speak, already filed its appearance in his memory. This habit, of course, tends to be less fruitful in a terrain of sea ice, such as that in which we now found ourselves, because of the bizarre, twisted sameness of much of the ice scape. There remain, of course, the stars and the winds. Winds are extremely important in direction finding to the red hunter, for at certain seasons they prevail in different directions. Indeed, even in the darkness, the total darkness of an overcast sky in the arctic night, when the winds do not blow, he may often find his way simply by feeling with his mittened hands the alignment of ice crystals on slopes and blocks, which are a residue of the earlier passage of such winds. This is not to say that red hunters cannot become lost. They can. On the other hand an experienced trekker usually has a good idea of his whereabouts. The lay of the land, the winds, the stars, help him with directions, as well as, of course, his own keenly developed sense of orientation, probably selected for in the harsh environment. Distance he tends to measure in terms of sleeps. Interestingly, in his descriptions and rude maps of terrain, scratched in the snow, he shows little awareness of or interest in land masses or shapes. His interest tends to lie in given geographical points and landmarks. The shape of a peninsula on which he may have a permanent camp, for example, is of less interest to him than is the direction and distance to the next nearest camp. I suppose this makes sense. If one had to choose between cartographical fidelity and arriving alive in the next camp perhaps one would sooner sacrifice the former excellence to the latter desideratum. And even if a red hunter should become lost it is normally possible for him, at least for a time, to live off the land. He generally carries such things as hooks, fish line, knives, snare strings and harpoons with him. Sometimes, when one does become lost, as on a trading journey south, it takes months to find his way back to his camp. "Where have you been?" he is asked. "Oh, I have been hunting," he says. Sled sleen, too, of course, may be killed for food. It is important, of course, to be the first to kill in such a situation. A sufficiently hungry snow sleen will turn and attack its driver. There is much danger in the north, and much to know. I was very pleased to be in the company of Imnak. Though I thought him strange I admired him greatly. I did not delude myself that I did not owe him much. It was fortunate we were friends, for between friends there can be no debts.

I, too, from time to time, looked back. This was not only to consider the terrain as it might appear on a return journey, something I had learned from Imnak, but for another reason as well, one held in common by warriors and red hunters. It is well to see what might come behind one.

I fell back a bit, jogging beside Imnak.

"Did you see it?" I asked.

"It has been with us for four days," he said.

"Do you think Karjuk knows it is there?" I asked.

"How could he not know?" asked Imnak.

"Do you have any recommendations?" I asked.

"Let us continue to press on," said Imnak. "I think it would elude us in the ice. And I do not wish to turn my back on Karjuk."

"But he is the guard," I said.

"Did you see the head of the ice beast which he brought to camp?" asked Imnak.

"Yes," I said.

"Did you examine it closely?" he asked.

"Yes," I said. "But Karjuk is the guard," I said.

"Yes," said Imnak. "But whom does he guard?"

26   IMNAK MAKES A CAMP; POALU BOILS MEAT

The wind howled about us, and I could hardly keep my footing.

"We must stop!" I called to Imnak, over the storm. I do not know if he could even hear me, and yet he was little more than a yard away. It was utterly dark. The moons, the stars, were obscured. Winds struck against the hides I wore, almost tearing them from me. I kept my left hand, mittened, on the supplies on the sled. It then began to snow, the crystals whipping against our faces, driven almost horizontally over the level and among the pinnacles and turrents of the jumbled, bleak terrain. I pulled down my hood. The lart fur, with which it was trimmed, snapped against my face on the left, and was almost torn from the hood on the right. I felt my face might freeze. I could see nothing. I stumbled on, holding the sled. I could not see the girls but I knew they were fastened to the sled. Imnak had had us tether them thusly, that they might not be swept away from us and lost in the storm.

"We cannot see where we are going!" I cried out to Imnak. "We must stop!"

I heard the sleen in the traces squeal ahead of us, the noise torn in the fierce snow and wind. I sensed Imnak turning about, and then again he was at the tabuk-horn uprights at the sled, glimpsed momentarily in a break in the clouds. I saw the girls then, too, their hands on their neck tethers, small, pelted, coated with snow, pathetic in the storm, weary, with us. Then again it was dark. Ahead I had seen Ram's sled for a moment. I had not seen Karjuk's sled.

"It is madness to continue!" I cried to Imnak.

The sled stopped, wedged between two ice blocks. Imnak and I tilted it and it slid on one runner and then righted itself and again moved on.

"Let us stop!" I called out to Imnak.

323

I thought I heard a scream but I could not be sure, in the howling wind.

Imnak threw his weight back on the uprights. I held back, too, on the sled. The sled stopped. I fumbled for the tethers of Audrey and Arlene and pulled them to the sled. Then I went toward the head of the sled. The sleen was there, already curled in the driving snow. Its pelt shook under my touch. It would be asleep in moments. Snow was almost to my knees. I felt my way back about the sled to the uprights. Imnak was shouting to me, but I could not hear him. Audrey and Arlene, as I could tell by putting forth my hands, were crouched beside the sled. I went about the back of the sled. I could see nothing. The wind howled fiercely. On the other side of the sled, extending my hand, I felt Poalu. She, like the other girls, was crouched beside the sled. Imnak was at my side. He pressed a strap into my hand. I drew it to me. Barbara was gone. The end of the strap had been cut. I made to move out into the snow, to search for her, but Imnak, bodily, obstructed me. He pushed me back. I did not resist. Imnak, of course, was right. It would be madness to go forth into the howling darkness, the snow and wind, to search for her. In moments one's trail would be obliterated and, shortly, wandering foolishly in the darkness, the storm, one might find oneself lost, and dangerously separated from the sled and its supplies.

I do not think the other girls even realized, at that time, that Barbara was gone. Poalu, exhausted, fell asleep almost immediately, beside the sled. The other girls, too, were soon asleep.

"What are we going to do?" I shouted at Imnak, putting my face near the side of his head.

"One will sleep, one will watch," called Imnak.

I found it hard to respond. I found it hard to believe he had said what he had.

"Are you sleepy?" asked Imnak.

"No!" I shouted.

"You watch first," shouted Imnak. "I will sleep."

I stood beside the sled. Imnak then lay down by the sled. It was hard for me to believe, under the circumstances, that he could sleep. Yet, in moments, I think he was asleep.

After a while I crouched beside the sled, and peered into the darkness.

The wind howled about the sled. I wondered how far Ram had continued on. I had not seen Karjuk when the clouds had parted for a moment earlier. I wondered where Barbara was. I did not think she was lost. The strap which had held her had been cleanly cut. The lovely blond slave had been taken prisoner, but by whom, or what, I did not know.

After a time Imnak awoke. "Sleep now," he said. "I will watch."

I then slept.

I awakened, Imnak's hand on my shoulder.

"Observe the sleen," said Imnak.

The animal, some nine feet in length, twisting, was awake, and restless. Its ears were lifted, its nostrils distended. The claws in the wide, soft paws emerged, and then retracted. It did not seem to be angry.

It lifted its snout to the wind.

"It has taken the scent of something," I said.

"It is excited, but not disturbed," said Imnak.

"What does this mean?" I asked.

"That we are in great danger," said Imnak. "There are sleen in the vicinity."

"But we are far out on the ice," I said.

"The danger is thus much greater," said Imnak.

"Yes," I said, understanding him. If the snow sleen had taken the scent of sleen in this area it might well be one or more sleen wandering on the ice, sleen driven by hunger from the inland areas. Such animals would be extremely dangerous.

"Perhaps Karjuk or Ram are in the vicinity," I said.

"The sleen knows the animals of Karjuk and Ram" he said. "If it were they he would not be as excited as he is."

"What can we do?" I asked.

"We must hasten to build a shelter," said Imnak, getting to his feet. The girls were still sleeping. The storm had passed, and the light of the three moons was bright on the snow and ice. "There is little time," he said.

"What can I do?" I asked.

Imnak, with his heel, traced a circle, some ten feet in diameter, in the snow near the sled. "Trample down the snow inside the circle," he said. "Then unload the sled and place our supplies within the circle."

I did as I was told, and Imnak, with a large, curved, bone, saw-toothed knife, a snow knife, began to cut at a nearby drift of snow.

The sleen grew more restless, and it began to make noises.

"Listen," said Imnak. I listened, in the cold, still air. In the cold air I did not know how far away it was.

325

"They are on a scent?" I asked.

"Yes," said Imnak.

"Ours?" I asked.

"That seems quite likely," he speculated.

He had begun to take snow blocks from the drift and place them in a circle, within the edge of the area I was trampling down. The first block was the most difficult block to extract from the bank. The first row of blocks were about two feet in length, and a foot in breadth and height.

I started, suddenly, Audrey screaming. Imnak ran toward her, snow knife in hand.

"Where is Barbara!" screamed Audrey. "She is gone!" There was horror on her face. In her hand she held the severed strap, that which had tethered Barbara before it had been cut. She had awakened, crawled to the strap, understood its import, and screamed.

I saw Imnak strike her to the snow. She fell, twisting, to his feet, her own neck tether, seeming to emerge from her furs, still fastening her to the sled.

Imnak stood over her, his head lifted, listening. There was a distinct modulation in the hunting cries of the distant sleen pack. It was almost as though the sound began afresh, energized and renewed.

Imnak tore back Audrey's hood. His hand was in her hair, pulling her head cruelly back. Her throat was fully exposed. She was on her knees. The blade of the saw-toothed snow knife was at her throat. Then Imnak threw her angrily to her stomach in the snow.

There was no doubt now that the sleen pack was turning in our direction.

The scent it had been following was doubtless a difficult and fragmented one, carried on the air, suggesting little more than a direction. The storm had obliterated sled tracks and the customary trail signs of an afoot passage. This difficult trail to follow, little more than a waft of scent in the air, carrying over the ice, had now, however, because of Audrey's scream, been supplemented with a clear auditory cue, one supplying both an approximate distance and location to the pursuing pack. Its meaningfulness to the sleen was reflected in the sudden alteration in the nature of the pack's hunting cries. They had now, for most practical purposes, targeted their quarry. An analogy would be the hunter's pleasure when first he actually catches sight of the prey.

Audrey wept in the snow.

I listened to the sleen in the distance.

Imnak placed the first block of the second row of blocks across two blocks in the first row. The blocks of the second row, those forming the second ring of the circular shelter, were slightly smaller than those of the first row.

"Barbara is gone," said Arlene to me. She stood near me, the tether on her throat fastening her to the sled.

"Yes," I said.

"Where is she?" said Arlene.

"The strap was cut," I said. "She was taken."

"Where?" asked Arlene.

"I do not know," I said.

"Let us turn back," begged Arlene.

I took her in my arms, and looked down into her eyes. How beautiful she was. For a moment I felt tenderness for her.

"Please turn back," begged Arlene.

Then I recalled she was a slave.

Swiftly she knelt. "Forgive me, Master," she said.

I listened. The hunting cries of the sleen carried to us.

"Even if we wished to turn back," I told Arlene, at my feet in the snow, "it does not seem we could do so."

"I hear sleen," she said.

"Yes," I said.

"Oh, no!" she said.

"Yes," I said.

I looked down at her. She was quite beautiful. It would be tragic indeed for that lovely body to be torn to pieces by the teeth of the hunger-crazed sleen.

She shuddered.

I listened to the sleen. The sound was now quite clear. "How much time is there?" I asked Imnak.

He did not answer me, but continued, swiftly, not pausing, to cut blocks of snow.

"Imnak," called Poalu, "you will need the knife and the ice."

I did not understand this.

"Free Poalu, and the others," said Imnak.

I untied the girls.

"Help me load the supplies into the ring," I said to Arlene.

Crouching inside the ring, among supplies, Poalu began working near the lamp. Striking iron pyrites together she showered sparks into tinder, dried grass from the summer. The lamp was lit.

Imnak completed the low, second row of snow blocks.

"Thistle," said Poalu, to Audrey, "bring the cooking rack

and the water kettle." One of the first things that is done, following the lighting of the lamp, which serves as light, heat and cook stove in the tiny shelters, is to melt snow for drinking water, and heat water for boiling meat.

Our sleen suddenly threw back his head and emitted a long, high-pitched, hideous, shrill squeal.

"It will revert," said Imnak.

"Shall I kill it while there is still time?" I asked Imnak.

"Tie its jaws, and bind it," said Imnak. "The madness will pass."

I took the binding fiber with which the girls had been tethered.

"I see them now!" cried Arlene. "There! There!"

The sleen squirmed but I, forcing it to its side in the snow, lashed shut its jaws. I then tied together its three sets of paws.

"Put it in the shelter," said Imnak.

I unhitched the sleen's harness from the sled and, by the harness, still on the animal, dragged it into the shelter.

"Its struggles will break the wall, or put out the lamp," I said.

"Do not permit that to happen," said Imnak.

I tied the forepaws of the sleen to its rearmost hind paws, the power, or spring, paws. Its struggles would now be considerably circumscribed and the mighty leverage it could exert would largely be dissipated in the circle of its bonds.

"They are coming closer!" cried Arlene.

"Get into the shelter," I told her. Imnak had managed only to build two rows, and part of a third, in the shelter. He did not cease, however, to cut blocks from the drift. One uses a drift, when possible, which has been formed in a single storm. The structure of the drift, thus, is less likely to contain faults, strata and cleavages, which would result in the blocks being weaker and more likely to break apart.

Arlene joined me inside the low, circular wall. The hunting cries of the sleen were now fierce and distinct. I did not think them more than a half of a pasang away.

"There is little time, Imnak," I said. "Return to the shelter."

He continued to cut blocks of snow, though he now made no effort to place them in the walls. One normally places such blocks from the inside. When the domed shelter is completed, as ours was not, the last block is placed on the outside and the builder then goes within, and, with the snow knife, trimming and shaping, slips it into place. A hole is left for the passage of air and smoke. Imnak's walls were rough, and

328

not too well shaped. The snow knife suffices, when there is time, to shape the dwelling. Chinks between blocks are filled with snow, as though it were mortar.

"Prepare to strike sleen from the walls," said Imnak to me.

I stood within the low walls, lance in hand. "Return with me, to fight within," I told him.

"I shall," he said. Then he called out to Poalu, "Is the water boiling?"

"No," she said, "but it is warm."

"Hurry, Imnak!" I called. I could not understand why he still cut blocks, which he had no time to place in the walls. Too, I did not understand why Poalu should be busying herself with melting snow over the flat, oval lamp. This seemed a strange time to engage in such domestic chores.

The sleen were now, like a black cloud, breaking apart in the wind, and then rejoining, flooding toward us over the ice. The cloud was no more now than a quarter of a pasang away.

"Is this the end, Master?" asked Arlene.

"It would seem so," I said. "For my part, it will be a good fight. I am sorry, however, that you are here."

"Will you not free me?" she asked.

"No," I said.

If we were to die beneath the fangs of the sleen I would be torn apart as a free man, and she as a slave. It was what we were.

"Yes, Master," she said.

The hideous crying of the sleen was now piercing to our ears. We could hear, too, in the cold air, even the panting of the animals, their gasping, the scratching of their claws, scattering snow and ice behind them, on the ice.

Imnak now, with a knife, cut down at the ice some twenty feet from the partially erected shelter.

The sleen were now some two hundred yards away, swift, frenzied.

Imnak hurried to the low wall of the half-erected shelter. There, instead of joining us, he took from Poalu a slice of meat and, in the other hand, the handle of the water kettle. He hurried to the hole he had cut in the ice. He thrust the meat on the blade of the knife and then thrust the handle of the knife down into the hole he had cut in the ice. He poured the water then into the hole in the ice, about the handle of the knife. He waited only a moment, for the water, poured into the icy hole in the subzero temperatures, froze almost instantly, anchoring the knife with the solidity of a spike in cement.

"Hurry!" I cried.

A sleen was on Imnak. He fell rolling with the animal. I leaped over the low wall and ran to him, driving the lance into the animal, then holding it down on the ice, it snapping at the lance, while Imnak, his furs torn, leaped up. He kicked at a sleen which was leaping toward me, striking it in the snout. I pulled the lance free of the wounded animal which scrambled up, fangs wide, and, with the butt of the lance, struck back another sleen. Imnak was shouting in my ear. With the point of the lance I fended back the jaws of the wounded sleen. Then there were other sleen about us, twisting, circling. Imnak, shouting, kicking, dragged me back toward the shelter. Another sleen brushed past me. I felt another tear at the fur on my boot. Then Imnak and I stood within that small, low rampart, each armed with a lance. The full flood of sleen, the pack at large, not the lead animals, then swept about the small, circular shelter, hissing and squealing. Their eyes blazed in the moonlight. I thrust one back from the wall with the lance. Imnak, too, thrust animals away. Our own sleen was frenzied at our feet, struggling. An animal leaped into the snow circle and I, bodily, under it, lifted it over the wall and hurled it among others. Audrey screamed. Poalu threw oil from the lamp, burning, into the face of another animal. Arlene, screaming, reeled back from another animal, half over the wall, her sleeve torn open. I caught the animal under the throat with one hand and, getting another hand on its left foreleg, thrust it back over the wall among the others. Imnak thrust back another sleen. I again seized up the lance which I had carried. I thrust it into the face of another sleen, its head up, crouching to spring at the wall. It twisted away, hissing and snarling.

Then the sleen were outside, some twenty or thirty feet away, dark on the ice, though they were snow sleen. Some circled the shelter.

One sped toward the shelter and leaped upward but I managed to meet its charge with the lance point and it, its face bloodied, twisted, the lance through the side of the mouth, and I managed to deflect its charge to the side and it fell, snarling, slipping free of the lance, to the side of the shelter. Imnak thrust two others back.

Then it was quiet for a time.

"There are so many," said Arlene.

"It is a large pack," I said.

I could not well count the animals in the uncertain light and shadows, and with their dark minglings and changings of position, but it was clear that there were a large number of beasts there, probably more than fifty. Some sleen packs run as high as one hundred and twenty animals.

"I wish you well, Imnak," I said.

"Are you going somewhere?" he asked. "This is not a good time to do so."

"There are a great many sleen out there," I said.

"That is true," said Imnak.

"Are you not ready to die?" I asked him.

"Not me," he said. "Red hunters do not expect to die," he said. "They may die, but it always comes as a surprise to them."

I threw back my head and laughed like an idiot.

"Why do you laugh, Tarl, who hunts with me?" he asked.

"In the strait circumstances in which we now find ourselves immeshed, I gather," I said, "that you have no intention of dying."

"That is exactly it," he said. "You have hit it. That is not something I have planned on."

"Imnak," said Poalu, "does not fear the sleen of death."

"If he comes around me," said Imnak, "I will hitch him to my sled."

"I would be proud to die beside you, Imnak," I said.

"I am an even better fellow to live beside," said Imnak. "This is my view of the matter."

"I will accept that," I said.

I looked down into the eyes of Arlene.

"Is there no hope?" she asked.

"All is lost, I fear," I said. "I wish you were not here."

She put her head against my arm. She looked up at me. "I would rather be nowhere else than here," she said.

"I would rather be in the feasting house," said Imnak.

"All is not lost," said Poalu.

"Look," said Imnak.

I looked out, several feet across the ice. "No," I said, in repulsion.

"Do you wish to live?" asked Imnak.

"Yes," I said.

"Then we must do what is necessary to achieve that aim," he said.

I looked out, across the ice, understanding then the effectiveness, the hideous efficiency, of the sleen trap which Imnak

331

had so swiftly constructed, the sleen pack nearing the shelter as he had worked.

One of the larger animals circled the meat on the knife twice and then, suddenly, bit at it, to tear it from the blade. He ripped the meat from the blade, making away with it, his jaws cut by the knife's edge. There was then hot fresh blood on the knife. Another sleen, frenzied with the smell, ribs protruding from its fur, racked with hunger, hurried to the knife, licking at the blood. As it did so, of course, the blade, anchored fixedly in the ice, cut its mouth, its lips and tongue. In the frenzy of its hunger the sleen, further stimulated by the newly shed blood, redoubled its efforts to lap it up. Another animal, larger, bit at it, and shouldered it from the blade, it then licking at the blood, unwittingly cutting itself, its mouth and tongue, as well. There was dark blood, frozen about the stained, exposed blade. One sleen attacked the first animal, which was profusely bleeding at the mouth. In a raging, vicious tangle of whirling fur and snapping jaws the two animals fought. One's throat was ripped open and, instantly, four or five dark shapes on the ice attacked the fallen animal, thrusting their heads, fangs tearing, feeding, into its belly. It squealed hideously. Other sleen tried to thrust into the orgy. Two or three scrambled literally onto the backs of the feeders, trying to push down between them. Other sleen ran to the knife. The blood on it, in the moment it had been left alone, had frozen on the steel. Two sleen fought to lick the frozen blood from the blade. Instantly as the blade cut their lips and tongue there was again hot, fresh blood on the steel. A sleen can kill itself in this manner, licking at the blade until it bleeds to death.

Arlene and Audrey looked away.

But no sleen that night bled to death, a victim of the simple, cruel trap, for there were too many animals present with too great a hunger to permit this to occur.

As a sleen weakened, or the stimulus of the blood became too great, other animals, tortured by their own hunger, attacked it.

In less than an Ahn Imnak, to my amazement, left the half-constructed shelter, and, walking among gorged sleen, and feeding sleen, and dead sleen, went to the drift and began to carry blocks back to the shelter.

In a moment I went to help him. We passed, literally, within feet of savage snow sleen, and scarcely did they notice us.

Some fifteen or twenty sleen had been killed, all by other

sleen in the pack. The remaining sleen had fed on these. Some still fed, pulling and tearing at the bones and exposed ventral cavities and limbs of the fallen sleen.

Several of the animals, gorged with meat, curled in the snow, in a white coil, and slept.

Imnak added the new blocks to the snow shelter and, with his snow knife, cut those blocks he needed to finish the low, domed structure. It does not take long to construct such a shelter, if the snow is appropriate. I do not think he had worked longer, altogether, than some forty or fifty minutes on it. With the snow knife, on the outside, he trimmed and shaped the dwelling, and filled in the chinks with snow. Inside Poalu had relit the lamp and was already melting snow for drinking water and setting a pot to boil, hanging from the cooking rack, for meat.

27 THE FACE IN THE SKY; THE CODES; IMNAK WILL TAKE FIRST WATCH

We pressed on, further northward.

It had been four sleeps now since we had left the first snow shelter, where we had been threatened by the sleen pack. Each sleep we had again constructed such a shelter.

The reversion frenzy of our sleen had passed quickly, even by the time the first shelter had been constructed, but we had left it tied, loosening its jaws only to feed it, because of the presence of the wild sleen in the vicinity. After our sleep in the first shelter we had reconnoitered. The majority of the sleen pack had departed, filled with meat. Imnak had retrieved his knife, it having claimed no more victims. Some five sleen had lingered in the vicinity, nosing about the fur and gnawed bones of the fallen members of the pack. From a distance they had eyed us, balefully.

We had left the shelter and trekked northward, our sleen again in its traces. The five sleen had drifted with us, some half pasang or so away. We saw them from time to time.

Their presence no longer excited our own sleen, as it had now passed through its reversion frenzy.

"What lazy animals those sleen are," said Imnak. "They are not even really hungry, but they are keeping us in mind. They should be out hunting snow bosk, or basking sea sleen, or burrowing and scratching inland for hibernating leems."

"I suppose you are right," I said.

"But look at them," he said, righteously. "There they are, right there. They should be ashamed of themselves."

"Yes," I said, "they certainly should."

"No self-respecting sleen follows a man like that," he said.

"You are quite possibly correct," I granted him. Though sleen were not fastidious, men were surely not their preferred prey.

"But there they are," said Imnak.

"They certainly are," I said.

"We must teach those lazy, greedy fellows a lesson," he said.

"I doubt if we could get close enough to them to harm them," I said. "When they become sufficiently hungry, then they will come in."

"But then they will be extremely dangerous," said Imnak. "And there are five of them."

"True," I said. It did not seem likely that we could sustain the attack of five snow sleen without a shelter. Instinctively such animals, when in packs, tend to circle and attack simultaneously from different directions. The shelter, incidentally, tends to confuse them. It is not a shape which releases their normal attack behaviors. The best that we could do, presumably, if caught in the open, would be to fight back to back, the girls, low, at our feet. Even then they might be dragged away from us. Our best chance, presumably, would be to have pack ice behind us.

Before we had slept that night, and after Imnak had constructed our shelter, he removed from the supplies several strips of supple baleen, whale bone, taken from the baleen whale, the bluish blunt fin, which we had killed before taking the black Hunjer whale. He had brought this with him from the permanent camp. Why I had not understood.

"What are you doing?" I asked him.

He worked in the light of the lamp.

"Watch," he said.

He took a long strip of baleen, about fifteen inches in length, and, with his knife, sharpened both ends, wickedly sharp. He then, carefully, folded the baleen together, with S-type folds. Its suppleness permitted this, but it was under great tension, of course, to spring straight again, resuming its original shape. He then tied the baleen, tensed as it was, together with some stout tabuk sinew. The sinew, of course, held the baleen together, in effect fastening a stout spring into a powerfully compressed position. If the sinew should break I would not have wished to be near that fierce, compressed, stout strip of sharpened baleen.

"Put it away," I said to Imnak.

Imnak made several of these objects. He then inserted them into several pieces of meat, one in each piece of meat.

He threw one of these pieces of meat, containing the compressed baleen, outside the shelter.

"Now, let us sleep," he said.

"It is a horrifying thing you are doing, Imnak," I said to him.

"Do you wish to live?" he asked.

"Yes," I said.

"Then do not object," he said. "It is us or it is the sleen."

I lay awake for a long time. Then, suddenly, piercing, horrifying, I heard the cry of the animal. The sinew had dissolved in its stomach.

"What is it?" cried Arlene.

"It is nothing," I told her.

I then slept.

We pressed on, further northward.

No sleen now followed us. The first of the five sleen had been killed two sleeps ago, outside one of the shelters as it had prowled about. It had been eaten by the other four. Two of those animals, apparently satisfied with the meat, had then left our trail, turning their attention elsewhere. Two others had continued to follow us. Yesterday, one sleep ago, when we had begun to trek, Imnak had cast behind the sled, in our tracks, another of his pieces of meat, containing the compressed baleen. The more aggressive of the two animals which had been following us was the first upon the meat. It died an Ahn later, while still following us. The other animal, more timid, crouched beside it. It waited until the first animal no longer moved, before it began to feed. After we had awakened after our most recent sleep and hitched the sleen to the sled Imnak had thrown out yet another of the cruel pieces of meat. Some hours later, when we heard the startled pain squeal of the mortally wounded beast, Imnak turned about in his tracks.

"Hurry!" he said. "It is meat!"

When we reached the animal it lay on the ice, its eyes open, not moving. Its pain must have been excruciating. It did not resist our lances.

"We will now make a shelter," said Imnak.

Once again, as he had before, he found a suitable drift of snow and began to cut blocks. We may call this type of shelter an igloo, or iglu, I suppose, for that is the word, an Innuit word actually, by which we would think of it. Yet in the language of the Innuit, or of the People, the word 'igloo' or 'iglu' designates more generally a dwelling or house. For example, it is not necessary for an igloo to be made from snow or ice. Imnak's half-underground hut, or house, at the permanent camp, for example, was also called an igloo.

Soon Imnak had completed the shelter and he had then come outside, to stand with me. Within the girls were preparing supper.

"We are now free of sleen," I told him.

"It is unlikely that sleen, new sleen, would come this far out on the ice," he said.

"We have then little to fear from them," I said.

"This is, however," said Imnak, "the country of the ice beasts."

"I have not seen any," I said, "not for several sleeps."

Imnak and I had both, several sleeps ago, caught glimpses of an ice beast. We had not seen it, however, since the great storm.

"Let us go inside," said Imnak. "The night is going to be cool."

I smiled to myself. Surely the temperature was at least sixty below zero.

I looked up at the sky, at streaks and curtains of light, mostly yellowish green, hundreds of miles in height. This is an atmospheric phenomenon, caused by electrically charged particles from the sun bombarding the upper atmosphere. It was unusual for it to occur at this time of year. The autumnal and vernal equinox times are the most frequent times of occurrence. In different light conditions these curtains and streaks can appear violet or red or orange depending on their height. This silent storm of charged particles, flung from millions of miles across space, raining upon an atmosphere, was very beautiful. On Earth this type of phenomenon is sometimes referred to as the Northern Lights or the Aurora Borealis. It occurs also, of course, in the south, in the vicinity of the southern polar circle.

I called Arlene out, and she came out, followed by Audrey. We stood for a time, quietly, watching the lights. Then I indicated that they should return inside the shelter.

Later, some Ahn later, Arlene lay within my arms. "It was very beautiful," she said.

"Yes," I said.

"The night is so still outside," she said. "How beautiful the north can be."

"Yes," I said. It was very quiet, very still, very calm, very peaceful.

"What is that?" she asked, suddenly.

"Imnak," I said, calling him.

"I hear it," he said.

We listened, carefully. For a time we heard nothing. Then, after a time, we heard the snow and ice crunch outside. Something was outside.

"Is it a sleen?" I asked.

"Listen," he said.

After a time Arlene asked, "Is it a sleen?"

"No," I said. "It is walking on two feet."

Then, after a time, the noise was gone. I heard Imnak replace the knife in its sheath. I then returned my own blade, too, to its sheath.

"I am going out," I said.

I drew on furs. The outer parka I retrieved from the long, low entrance way to the shelter. This entrance, contrived as it was, made it impossible for the direct blast of an outside wind to get inside. It is generally better for the fur of the heavy parka to be left in the entrance way, where it is colder. One brushes snow from the parka before leaning down and moving through the tunnel to the interior of the shelter, but, in the shelter, the residue of snow would melt, wetting the garment. Later, when the lamp goes out, the garment could stiffen and freeze. It is better for the fur not to be constantly put through this cycle of dampening and freezing; also, the heavy parka is rather large for the drying frame, which is generally used for smaller articles, like boots and mittens. Also, of course, the garment is more comfortable to put on if it is not cramped and frozen.

Crouching down I edged toward the opening. The roof of the exit tunnel was about a yard high, at the inner end. Usually a hide tent is hung inside the snow shelter, which provides additional insulation. It is fastened by pegs within the

337

shelter, which are anchored outside, on the rounded outer roof. We had not set the tent within the shelter this sleeping period, however. I had brushed aside a hide flap, though, which was hung over the inner entrance. At the outer end of the tunnel, where one emerged to the outside, the ceiling of the tunnel was about four and one half feet in height. The general reason for the tunnel dimensions is to prevent wear and tear on mittens and clothing, which can be a very serious matter in subzero temperatures; a needle and thread in the arctic can be as important as a knife and a harpoon. Another value of the tunnel dimensions, of course, is that one may emerge from the shelter with a weapon at the ready. This can be of value in a country where there may be dangerous animals.

I began to move down the tunnel. I heard Imnak behind me.

At the outer end of the tunnel, gently, I edged out the snow blocks which, for most practical purposes, closed the opening. One does not seal the shelter, of course; that can be extremely dangerous; it must be adequately ventilated, particularly when the lamp is lit. Air from the entrance, or another aperture, moving into or through the shelter and, warmed, rising, escaping at the smoke hole in the roof, supplies the required ventilation.

When I emerged from the opening I, knife in hand, looked cautiously about. A moment later Imnak, knife, too, in hand, straightening up, emerged beside me.

It seemed very calm.

The girls, too, Poalu first, and then Arlene and Audrey, crept out.

It was very quiet, and desolate, and cold.

The Northern Lights still spun and played in the sky.

Imnak and I, knives ready, the girls remaining at the hut, scouted the terrain in the immediate vicinity.

"I have found nothing," I told Imnak.

"Nor I," he said.

"There was something here," I said, "for we heard it outside."

"Did you find tracks?" asked Arlene.

"No," I said.

"The ice is hard," said Imnak.

"But it was here, something," I said.

"Yes," said Imnak.

"There seems to be nothing here now," I said.

"No," said Imnak.

I looked about again. "It is gone," I said. We sheathed our knives.

"Perhaps there was nothing here," said Arlene. "Perhaps it was only the ice and the wind."

"No," I said. "Something was here."

"Aiii!" cried Imnak, suddenly, pointing upward. Arlene screamed.

In the lights in the sky, in those shimmering, subtle, shifting streaks and curtains of light, mostly yellowish green, some hundreds of miles in height, clearly portrayed, though it was for a moment only, was the gigantic, hideous visage of a Kur.

Imnak stood in silence, looking at it, and I, too. Poalu did not speak. Audrey screamed, and turned away. Arlene stood beside me, clutching my arm.

There was no mistaking that towering face etched in the lights and the darkness. It was clearly that of a Kur. Its outline was shaggy. Its eyes seemed to blaze, as though fires burned behind them. Its nostrils were distended. Its mouth was fanged. Then its lips drew back, in the Kur's sign of anticipation, of pleasure, of amusement. Then its ears lay back against the side of its head. Then the visage faded and disappeared, the eyes last, as soon as it had come. Before the ears had lain back against the side of its head I had seen that one of them, the left, had been half torn away. Then the lights themselves were gone, and we saw only the stars and the polar night over the desolate horizon.

"What was it?" asked Arlene.

"It was that which you had served," I told her.

"No, no!" she said.

"Surely it is a sign that we should turn back," said Poalu.

"No," said Imnak.

"Do you not think it is a sign?" she asked.

"I think it is a sign," he said.

"Then we must turn back!" she said.

"No," said Imnak.

"Is it not a sign that we must turn back?" she asked.

"I do not think so," he said.

"Then what is its meaning?" asked Poalu.

"Its meaning, I think," said Imnak, "is that it is too late to turn back."

"I think you are right, Imnak," I said.

I looked up at the sky. It was too late, indeed, to turn back. I smiled to myself. I had come, after long trekking, to the country of Zarendargar, to the brink of the camp of my enemy, to the brink of the camp of Half-Ear.

339

"I think, Imnak," I said, "that I am close to finding him whom I have sought."

"Perhaps, already, he has found you," said Imnak.

"Perhaps," I said. "It is hard to know."

"Let us flee, Master," wept Arlene.

"I am of the Warriors," I told her.

"But such things," she said, "control even the forces of nature."

"Perhaps so, perhaps not," I said. "I do not know."

"Flee!" she said.

"I am of the Warriors," I said.

"But you may die," she said.

"That is acknowledged in the codes," I said.

"What are the codes?" she asked.

"They are nothing, and everything," I said. "They are a bit of noise, and the steel of the heart. They are meaningless, and all significant. They are the difference. Without the codes men would be Kurii."

"Kurii?" she asked.

"Beasts, such as ice beasts, and worse," I said. "Beasts such as the face you saw in the sky."

"You need not keep the codes," she said.

"I once betrayed my codes," I said. "It is not my intention to do so again." I looked at her. "One does not know, truly, what it is to stand, until one has fallen. Once one has fallen, then one knows, you see, what it is to stand."

"None would know if you betrayed the codes," she said.

"I would know," I said, "and I am of the Warriors."

"What is it to be a warrior?" she asked.

"It is to keep the codes," I said. "You may think that to be a warrior is to be large, or strong, and to be skilled with weapons, to have a blade at your hip, to know the grasp of the spear, to wear the scarlet, to know the fitting of the iron helm upon one's countenance, but these things are not truly needful; they are not, truly, what makes one man a warrior and another not. Many men are strong, and large, and skilled with weapons. Any man might, if he dared, don the scarlet and gird himself with weapons. Any man might place upon his brow the helm of iron. But it is not the scarlet, not the steel, not the helm of iron which makes the warrior."

She looked up at me.

"It is the codes," I said.

"Abandon your codes," she said.

"One does not speak to a slave of the codes," I said.

"Abandon them," she said.

340

"Kneel, Slave Girl," I said.

She looked at me, frightened, and swiftly knelt in the snow, in the moonlight, before me. She looked up at me. "Forgive me, Master," she said. "Please do not kill me!" She put her head to my feet, holding my booted ankles. "Please do not kill me," she said. "Forgive me! Let me placate you! Let me placate you!"

"Crawl to the shelter," I told her. She did so, head down, trembling, a terrified slave, one who had displeased her master.

I looked after her.

"Please do not kill her," begged Audrey, kneeling before me.

Imnak struck her to her side in the snow. "He will do what he pleases with her," he said.

"Yes, Master," said Audrey, his lovely, white-skinned slave beast.

Audrey entered the hut after Arlene. Then Poalu, followed by Imnak, entered the hut.

I looked once more at the sky, at the long, shifting lights, and then went into the hut.

Inside, Arlene had already removed her furs and knelt obediently, her head down, near where I would sleep.

"A girl begs to please her master," she said.

"Very well," I said.

Soon my wrath towards her had dissipated. I simply could not sustain it. What a sweet and clever slave she was. Even had it been my intention to punish her, which it had not been, I think she might well have won her freedom from punishment by the diligent and incredible merits of her helpless slave service. A beautiful slave girl, of course, has no official or legal power. Yet it would be naive to underestimate the weight and influence of her beauty, her vulnerability and service. Her display and submission behaviors, and performances, surely influence to a considerable extent the treatment she is likely to receive at the hands of a master. The sexual placation of the dominant male by the submitting female is universal among primates. It is, thus, presumably genetically determined, or a function of genetic determinations. In the end, of course, the slave girl is ultimately without power. It is the master, in the end, who will decide what is to be done with her.

Later Arlene lay in my arms. "Did I please you, Master?" she asked.

"Yes," I said.

341

"A girl is pleased," she said.

Near us we heard Poalu moaning. Then I heard Imnak leaving her side.

"Where are you going?" I asked.

"There may be danger about," said Imnak. "I think maybe we should have a guard."

"That is a good idea," I said.

"I will take the first watch," said Imnak. I heard him nuzzle Poalu, and heard her tiny cries, and then he had soon drawn on his furs and went outside the shelter.

Poalu was soon asleep, and so, too, was Arlene.

I heard Audrey whimper from the side of the hut. "No one has touched me," she said.

"Go to sleep," I said.

"Yes, Master," she said. I heard her sob, unheld, unravished.

I was weary. I was pleased that Imnak had elected to take the first watch. I would sleep well, fearing nothing.

28   I MUST CONSERVE MY STRENGTH

I felt her small, soft hands on my body. "Master, Master," she said.

"He is awakening," said a girl's voice.

I was drowsy. It was not easy to come to consciousness. I shook my head. Then again I dreampt.

I had had good dreams, in my own chambers feasting and sporting with slaves in pleasure silk, luscious, hot-eyed Gorean sluts, collared and perfumed, serving me and touching me. Their mouths, their fingers, their lips and tongues, were pleasant. Some danced well, the caress of others told me of their training.

"Master," said one, and I drank of the wine she proffered. I tied the goblet in her hair and sent her back for more.

"I do not know how to dance," cried one, and I looked

upon her and she tore away her silk and, trembling, danced, and well.

How beautiful are women. How little wonder it is that strong men make them slaves.

I struggled to awaken.

"He is awakening," said a girl, she who had first spoken to me.

I was vaguely aware that I was warm, and lay upon furs. I did not understand this. Beneath the furs I sensed an obdurate surface.

I opened my eyes, lying on my back. The ceiling above me swam momentarily, and then I focused. It was red.

Arlene knelt beside me. "Master," she said. I looked at her. I had never seen her before in the beautiful, subtle cosmetics of the Gorean slave girl. My strap was no longer on her throat. In its place there resided a slender steel band, locked, a Gorean slave collar. Her body was clad, if one may so speak of her garment, in a brief, obscenely luscious snatch of transparent, scarlet slave silk.

"How beautiful you are," I said.

"Master," she said.

It seemed she well belonged in my dreams. Had I brought her back to Port Kar with me it was thus that I would sometimes have attired her for my pleasure. One dresses one's girls for one's own pleasure, of course.

I looked across the furs and the floors to the other girl. "Master," she whispered. I shook my head, to clear it. She was blond. She wore a curla and chatka of yellow silk. The curla was a rope of twisted, yellow silk tied snugly about her belly and knotted, loosely, at the left hip. The chatka, about four feet in length, folded narrowly, to a width of some six inches, was thrust over the curla in front, taken between her legs and thrust behind and over the curla in back. It was drawn snugly tight. It was all she wore, save for a slave collar, like Arlene, and some beads, an armlet, and a barbaric anklet. Both girls were perfumed. How soft and exciting they were. The blond came to my side, crawling, and, putting down her head, kissed me on the belly. "Master," she wept.

"Constance," I said. I had not seen her since I had been impressed in Lydius into the service of Kurii, and taken northward to labor at the wall. She had once been free. I had made her my slave in the fields south of the Laura.

"What are you doing here?" I asked.

"Master," she wept, kissing me.

I looked up at the ceiling, which was red. I saw it clearly

343

now. It was a deep red, and covered with fur. The floor of the room, too, was covered with fur.

I cried out with rage, and leaped to my feet. I threw my weight against the heavy bars.

I could not budge them. I tore back the furs on the floor, and there encountered steel plates, riveted together. I put my hands over my head and tested the ceiling. It, too, seemed of steel. I tore down the overhead furs. The ceiling, uniformly, as did the floor, consisted of steel. In fury I tore away the fur at the walls. The cell was a cubic rectangle, some twelve feet by twelve feet, and eight feet in height. It was closed on five sides by steel walls, and the open side was barred.

Again I tore at the bars. They were some two and one half inches in thickness. The cell would have held a Kur and, indeed, perhaps it had been originally designed with that in mind.

I spun to look at the girls, who, frightened of my fury, cowered together in the center of the cell.

"We were brought here, somehow," said Arlene. "I awakened in slave silk, collared, in a kennel. I was brought to this cell this morning."

"Where is Imnak, Poalu, Audrey!" I said.

"I do not know," she wept.

"Constance," I said. "Where are we?"

"I do not know," she said. "I was hooded long ago in Lydius, when we were captured. I was brought northward by tarn and then sled. For months I have been here. I have never seen the outside."

"Who are our jailers?" I asked Arlene.

"I have seen only men," she said.

"There are others," said Constance, shuddering. "I have seen them, large but agile beasts."

"Neither of you know where we are?" I asked.

"No," they said.

I turned to look outside the bars. Beyond them there lay a larger room, also plated with steel. There was a door in the larger room, with a small, barred window in it.

"Do you know much of this place, Constance?" I asked.

"No," she said. "But it is large. I have not been in this part of it before."

"Speak to me further," I said.

"There is little to tell," she said. "I was brought here from Lydius. There are several other girls here, too."

"Slaves?" I asked.

"Yes," she said, "all that I know of, all collared slaves."

344

"You are kept here to serve and entertain the garrison?" I asked.

"Yes," she said.

"Fully?" asked Arlene.

"Of course," said Constance. "We are slaves. And so, too, are you."

Arlene trembled in the pleasure silk. She tried to pull it down a bit, about her thigh.

"How large is the garrison?" I asked.

"I do not know," she said. "I, and five other girls, serve twenty men, in one portion of this place. Our movements are restricted, by overhead neck chains and a guide track. A chain is fastened about our necks with a swivel and ball at one end. The swivel and ball is locked into one of two overhead tracks. Two tracks are used, that one girl may pass another in the hall. The smallest ball on the chain permits the slave to reach any area accessible to the full track, though only, of course, an area accessible to the track. The next smallest ball, because of baffles set in the track overhead, will permit the slave to reach only a more restricted set of areas. This principle is then used successively. My own movements have been considerably restricted. The ball on my own neck chain permits me only a very limited use of the track, since it is of the largest size in the arrangement, indeed, the most limited use possible. Originally I wanted to explore, but my neck chain was almost constantly caught in baffles. In the halls I can move only between the quarters of work and the quarters of pleasure."

"Surely you are released from this to work and serve?" I asked.

"Of course," she said, "but then we are locked within the quarters of work or those of pleasure."

"How many quarters of work or quarters of pleasure are there?" I asked.

"I do not know," she said, "but there are more than those in which I specifically serve."

"You cannot conjecture the size of the garrison then?" I asked.

"It might be a hundred, it might be a thousand," she said. "I, and my five sisters in bondage, serve twenty men."

"Are they easy to please?" asked Arlene.

"No," said Constance.

"I hope I am not put with you," she said.

Constance shrugged. "Those to whom you will be assigned will doubtless be no easier to please," she said.

Arlene shuddered.

"Do not fear, my dear," said Constance, "you will learn the whip well."

Arlene looked at me with horror.

I paid her no attention. What did she expect? She was a slave.

Arlene put down her head. She touched her silk. She moaned.

"What of beasts?" I asked Constance.

"I do not know their number either," said Constance. "But I think they are considerably fewer in number than the men."

"You are not now on a neck chain," I said.

"Nor was I this morning," she said. "I was brought here directly from my kennel. I was thrown into this cell. You were still unconscious." She looked at Arlene, not pleasantly. "This slave," she said, emphasizing the word, "was already here. The gate was then locked."

"I do not understand why this slave," said Arlene, also emphasizing the word, "was put in with us."

"I own you both," I told her.

"Oh," said Arlene. "She is very pretty," said Arlene. "Do you find her attractive?"

"Be quiet," I said to Arlene.

"Yes, Master," she said, looking away.

"I have missed the touch of my master," said Constance.

Arlene looked at her with fury.

"You said you were brought here this morning," I said. "Is it morning?"

"This complex, in its way," she said, "is its own world. It operates on a day of twelve divisions. I do not know how long the division is. I think it is well over an Ahn."

I remembered the timing devices in the crashed ship encountered in the Tahari desert, devices set to control the detonation of the fearsome explosives housed within its steel hull. They had been calibrated into twelvefold divisions. I speculated that they might be indexed to the periods of revolution and rotation of the Kurii's original world. Also, I suppose the twelvefold division may have some remote relation to the base-twelve mathematics utilized by the Kurii, itself perhaps a function of the six-digited paw. The complex, then, that in which I was prisoner, I conjectured, might well have a clock similar to those used on Kur ships, and in the distant steel worlds, a clock doubtless once developed for use on their former world, doubtless long since destroyed in their internecine wars.

"We can tell the morning from the night by the illumination in the complex," said Constance. "It seems to be controlled by some sort of device which regulates its intensity."

I supposed that it would not be difficult to arrange a rheostatic mechanism to control the degree of illumination. The mechanism, I conjectured, would be analogized to the waxing and waning of light on a native world.

"The beasts," she said, "move mostly at night. I sometimes hear their claws on the plates outside my kennel. There must be some light for them. But it is too dark for the human eye to see."

I nodded, understanding. The Kur, though its activities are not limited to the darkness, tends, on the whole, in most of its varieties, to be a predominantly nocturnal animal. Its hunt, and its day, commonly begins with the fall of darkness.

I grasped the bars of the cell. I shook them. They did not yield.

I heard the movement of a key in a lock, from some yards away, in the door in the larger room within which our cell lay.

I backed away from the bars. This might encourage someone to approach them more closely. I could move to them swiftly. Arlene and Constance knelt to one side and behind me. This was proper. They were slaves.

"Drusus," I said.

The man stood in the doorway, in the somber garb of his caste.

"I see you wear the scarlet of the warrior," he said. It was true. I had awakened in the tunic of my caste. The furs had been taken from me.

"And you, my friend," said I, "are clothed now in the proper habiliments of your caste." He wore now, brazenly, the black of the Assassin. Over his left shoulder, looped on a ringed strap, he wore a blade, the short sword.

"May I welcome to our humble headquarters," said he, "my colleagues in the arts of steel."

I inclined my head, in courtesy.

"It pleases us to have you in our power," he said. "You were a fool to come north."

"I come visiting," I said.

"You are welcome," said he, smiling. Then he snapped his fingers. Through the door, bearing a tray, came a small, exquisite, brunet female slave. She was naked except for her collar and a leather-and-metal lock gag. Her mouth was closed. I saw the curved metal bars, rounded, about a quarter

347

of an inch in diameter, emerging from the sides of her mouth. By means of a ratchet and pawl arrangement the device is fitted to the individual girl. It locks behind the back of the neck. It cannot be removed, even though the girl's hands are free. She knelt before the gate of the cell and put her head to the steel floor. Two flasks on the tray she placed through the bars. She then slipped the tray through an opening, some four inches in height, in the bottom of the cell door. She then again put her head to the floor, and then stood up and withdrew, backing away, her head down. She looked at Drusus, who indicated she should leave the room. She slipped swiftly out, obedient, barefoot on the steel plates.

"A pretty little slave," I said. "Why is she in lock gag?"

"It pleases me," he said.

"Of course," I said.

He turned to leave.

"Drusus," said Arlene. "You must help us!" She had once commanded him.

He looked at her, and she shrank back. "There is a pretty little slave, too," he said.

She, terrified, tried to cover her body with her hands, half naked in the pleasure silk. How vulnerable pleasure silk makes a woman.

"I own her," I told him.

"I shall have her," he said.

"Oh?" I asked.

"Yes," he said, "she was originally brought to Gor with the eventual object of being at my feet. I picked her out from several future slaves."

"I see," I said.

"Perhaps you should join forces with us," said Drusus. "The Kurii are generous with women."

"I am of the Warriors," I said. "I will take by the sword what women please me."

"Of course," he said. He continued to look at Arlene, who put her head down, trembling.

"Too," I said, "it is my intention to keep by the sword what women should please me." I gestured to Arlene. "This one," I said, "at the moment pleases me."

She looked at me, frightened.

"We shall see," said Drusus.

I watched him, from behind the bars.

"Join us," he said.

"No," I said.

"Your friend, Imnak, has joined us," he said.

348

"I do not believe you," I said.

Drusus shrugged.

"The Kurii are generous with women," he said, "—and gold."

He turned to leave.

"I would see Zarendargar," I said. "Half-Ear."

"None sees him," said Drusus. Then he turned away again. The heavy metal door closed.

I grasped the bars, angrily.

Then I turned to face the girls. I strode to Arlene. "You called out to Drusus," I said.

"Yes," she said.

"You called a free man by his name," I said, "and you spoke, too, without petitioning permission."

"Forgive me, Master," she said.

I struck her down to the furs and steel.

"Master," said Constance, "there is food." She served me the hot bosk meat, the yellow bread, warm and fresh, and the wine. Later, when she had served me she mixed the water and gruel which, too, had been brought by the brunet slave. With their mouths and fingers then, kneeling, in my sight, the two girls fed upon their gruel. Arlene looked at me over the rim of her bowl. There were tears in her eyes. There was blood at her lip. When she had finished, she came near to me, to where I sat, cross-legged, feeding. She lay on the steel, her face near my knee.

"You struck me," she said.

I looked at her. I did not speak to her. I continued feeding.

"I am sorry I displeased you, Master," she said. She then knelt beside me. She took her hair in her right hand and, gently, wiped the grease from my mouth. "I am sorry, Master," she said. Our lips were quite close. With the tip of my tongue I touched her lips. Some slave cosmetics are flavored. "Does Master enjoy my taste?" she asked. "The lipstick is flavored," I said. "I know," she said. "It reminds me of the cherries of Tyros," I said. "I do not know what the flavor is," she said, "but it is lovely, is it not?" "Yes," I said. "Taste your slave again," she begged. I kissed her. My hands were hard on her arms. "Kiss it from my mouth, ruthlessly, owning me, Master!" she begged. "Oh," she cried, my hands so hard on her arms. But then I put her from me.

"Master?" she asked.

"I must save my strength," I said. "I must think."

She crept away from me. I sat in the middle of the cell, cross-legged, in the position of the warrior.

29   THE CAGE CART

The men on either side of the cage cart carried some sort of projectile weapon. It fired, I conjectured, judging from the breech, a long, conical, gas-impelled dart. The principles of the weapon, I assumed, were similar to those of a rifle, except that the missile would not be a slug of metal but something more in the nature of a tiny quarrel, some six inches in length. The weapons had carved wooden stocks, reminiscent of a time in which rifles were the work of craftsmen. Eccentric designs surmounted these stocks. The actual firing of the weapon was apparently by means of a button in the forepart of the stock. Although this button could be depressed quickly it could not be jerked, as a trigger might be, either on a rifle or crossbow, an action which sometimes, in moving the weapon, ruins or impairs the aim. Each man carried a bag at his left hip. It contained, I supposed, among other accouterments, the missiles, or darts, for the weapon.

I grasped the bars of the cage cart.

It was wheeled through the halls by two men, leaning on handles from behind. Bringing up the rear, also with a dart weapon, was Drusus.

A comely slave girl, naked, carrying a roped bag of wine flasks over her shoulder, knelt to one side as we passed. Her head was down. Besides her collar there was a neck chain fastened on her throat. This dangled downward from one of two overhead tracks in the ceiling. The guard on my left lifted the chain over his head and held it to the side, that the cart might pass. He then let it fall behind us. I saw the girl, when we had passed, rise to her feet and hurry, barefoot, along the steel hall. She did not look back. If she had been caught looking back, I supposed she might be beaten. From what I could gather the girls were kept under close discipline in the complex. That is, of course, as it should be, in a master's house. I was puzzled, though, at the overhead track system. That seemed a security unwarranted by the minimal damage or mischief which, presumably, might be wrought by a lightly clad or naked slave. What harm might one woman or man wreak in such a formidable complex?

"Hold!" said Karjuk.

The cart stopped.

"Greetings, someone from the south," he said.

"Greetings," I said to him.

Karjuk had emerged from a door at the side of the hall. He wore fur trousers and boots, and some necklaces. He was stripped to the waist. There was a headband about his brow. "It seems we have you in a cage," he said. "That is where wild animals belong."

I grasped the bars. The cart was on eight wheels, some four inches in diameter, rimmed with rubber. It was some four feet by four feet, by some seven feet in height. It was barred on four sides, and closed at the top and bottom by steel.

"You were easily tricked," said Karjuk.

"Perhaps not so easily," I said.

In the doorway, to one side, that through which Karjuk had emerged, there loomed a white-pelted Kur, a large one. In its ears were golden rings. Its lips drew back from its fangs, a Kur's sign of amusement or pleasure.

"Behold the Kur, my ally," said Karjuk. "It was he who attacked Ram, your friend, but was prevented from finishing him by the interference of yourself and the men of the village. You thought I slew him."

"No," I said, "I did not."

"No?" said Karjuk.

"No," I said. "I examined the head which you brought to the camp. The rings of gold in the ears of that ice beast were smaller and lighter, I think, than those in the ears of this beast. Further, they had been newly set in the ears, as might have been determined by the condition of the ear. Beyond this the head of the ice beast was such that it had not been recently killed, but had been dead for some two or three southern days, at least. Too, the ice beast which had attacked Ram had eaten of the sleen which drew his sled. There was no trace of blood on the tongue, or in the mouth or jaws, or on the lips or fur of the head you brought to camp. Lastly, it was simply not the same animal."

Karjuk looked at me.

"Do you think I cannot tell one Kur from another?" I asked. Warriors are trained in acute observation and retention. The recognition and comprehension of a detail, some-

351

times subtle, can sometimes make a difference between life and death.

"You are right," said Karjuk. "It was the head of an ice beast, earlier slain, in whose ears we had placed the golden rings."

"From what I have heard of your skills in the ice," I said, "too, it did not seem likely that a beast would have slipped past you, or, if it did, that you, trailing it, would have taken so long to apprehend it."

"You honor me," said Karjuk.

"Considering all these things, and the obvious fraud of the severed head, which you purported was that of the infiltrating ice beast, it seemed clear that you were in league with Kurii, and that, indeed, you and the first beast had presumably been traveling together. You arrived almost at the same time in the vicinity of the camp."

"You are clever," said Karjuk.

"Too, in the journey, from time to time, Imnak and I found sign, and occasionally even glimpsed this beast," I said, indicating the white Kur, "paralleling or following our trail."

Karjuk looked at me.

"He was clumsy," I said. I was curious as to what the Kur could understand. I saw its eyes flash and its ears lay back against its head. That told me he could follow Gorean. He was then a ship Kur, trained in the apprehension of a human mode of speech. He could probably, too, make some sounds recognizable to humans. He and Karjuk would have had to have some way to communicate. I saw no translation device in the vicinity. I did not know if Kur technology had attained to this sophistication.

"He was unused to the ice," said Karjuk, excusing him. "He is, as you have doubtless conjectured by now, not a wary ice beast, but a different sort of Kur, one from faraway."

"He is a ship Kur," I said.

Karjuk looked puzzled. I gathered he did not know of the remote, orbiting steel worlds.

"From worlds in the sky," I said.

"Are there worlds in the sky?" he asked.

"Yes," I said.

"Are they far off?" he asked.

"Not as far as many would like to think," I said.

"If you are so clever, why did you follow me north?" he asked.

"I have business in the north," I said. "I have an appointment with one called Zarendargar, Half-Ear."

352

"None sees him," said Karjuk.

"You were the guard," I said.

"I am the guard," he said.

"You betrayed your post," I told him.

"I keep my post in my own way," he said.

"Where is Imnak?" I asked.

"He, too, is one with us," said Karjuk.

"You are a liar," I said.

"How do you think you were taken?" he asked.

"Liar!" I cried. I reached out to seize his throat, through the bars, but he stepped back. "Liar!" I cried. "Liar!"

Then the cart was again being wheeled down the hall. "Traitor!" I cried, turning in the cart, looking back at the thin, dour Karjuk, in his necklaces, standing behind me in the hall, the Kur at his side. "Liar! Traitor! Liar! Traitor!" I cried.

Then they turned and withdrew into the room whence they had earlier emerged.

"If I am not mistaken," said Drusus, walking behind the cart, behind the two men who wheeled it along, "your friend, Imnak, approaches."

I spun about, to look down the hall, in the direction in which the cart was moving.

Down the hall came Imnak. He lifted his hand in greeting, fifty yards away.

"Imnak!" I cried.

He, like Karjuk, was clad in boots and trousers. He, too, was stripped to the waist. He, too, wore a headband, tying back his blue-black hair. Several heavy gold necklaces were looped about his throat. He was chewing on a leg of roast vulo. Behind him, in pleasure silk, came three girls. Poalu was in brief yellow pleasure silk, and Audrey and Barbara in brief red pleasure silk. They were barefoot, and collared; they wore cosmetics; their right wrists wore bracelets; each, on her left arm, had a golden armlet; each, on her left ankle, had a golden anklet.

"Greetings, Tarl, who hunts with me," said Imnak, grinning widely.

"You, too, have been captured," I said.

"No," said Imnak. "I have not been captured. You have been captured."

"I do not understand," I said.

"It is too warm in here," said Imnak, biting on the vulo leg.

"How is it that you are free?" I asked.

"Why do you think they keep it so warm in here?" he asked.

"You were on watch," I said.

"I was watching for Karjuk," he said.

"Why are you not in a cage, as I am?" I asked.

"Maybe I am smarter than you," said Imnak.

I looked at him.

"Why should I be in a cage?" asked Imnak. "I do not understand."

"You have been captured," I said.

"No," he said, "it is you who have been captured." He turned to Poalu. "Isn't Poalu pretty?" he asked.

"Yes," I said.

"These garments are not practical for the ice," said Poalu.

"Maybe that is why they keep it so warm in here," speculated Imnak.

"They would have me believe that you have betrayed me, Imnak," I said.

"And you do not believe them?" he asked.

"Of course not," I said.

"If I were you," said Imnak, "I would give the matter serious consideration."

"No," I said. "No!"

"I hope that you will not permit this to interfere with our friendship," said Imnak, concerned.

"Of course not," I said.

"That is good," said Imnak.

"It is strange, Imnak," I said. "With some other man in your position, I would doubtless wish to kill him, and yet I find it hard to even be angry with you."

"That is because I am such a friendly, genial fellow," said Imnak. "You can ask anyone in the camp. I am very popular. It is only that I cannot sing."

"But you are not loyal," I said.

"Of course, I am loyal," said Imnak. "It is only a question as to whom I am loyal."

"I never looked at it just that way before," I said. "I suppose you are loyal to Imnak."

"He is a good fellow to be loyal to," said Imnak. "He is friendly and genial, and he is popular in the camp. It is only that he cannot sing."

"I hope you are proud of yourself," I said.

Imnak shrugged. "It is true that I am pretty good at many things," he said.

"Among them, treachery," I said.

354

"Do not be bitter, Tarl, who hunts with me," said Imnak. "I talked with Karjuk. It is all for the best."

"I trusted you," I said.

"If you had not, things would have been more difficult for me," admitted Imnak.

I looked at Barbara, in the red silk. "We were worried about you," I said.

"Not me," said Imnak.

"I was captured by an ice beast, or something like an ice beast," she said. "It had rings in its ears. It seems in league with Karjuk. I was brought here. When Imnak arrived, I was returned to him."

"You are very beautiful," I said.

"Thank you, Master," she said.

"You, too, Audrey," I said, looking at her.

"A girl is grateful if she is found pleasing by a free man," she said, tears in her eyes.

"We must be on our way," said Drusus.

"I wish you well, Tarl, who hunts with me," said Imnak, lifting the roast vulo leg in salute.

I did not speak further with him. The cart was pushed past the four individuals. I did not look back.

"Gold buys any man," said Drusus, walking behind the cart, behind the two men who wheeled it along. His sword was at his hip. In his right hand was the light, tubular, stocked, dart-firing weapon. "Any man," he said. I did not respond to him. Bitterly, I clutched the bars of the confining cage, moving slowly down the long, steel hall.

30   THE SMALL ARENA

There were two, small, rounded platforms. On each of them, in long, flowing, classic white, there stood a girl. Neither was collared. Each, though, was necklaced and bejeweled. Each wore a coronet. Their raiment, though simple, was rich. They might have been Ubaras. I could tell, however, from the fall of the garment, that each was naked beneath it. There was an upright iron post, about a yard in height, on each platform, behind each girl. Their small wrists, by means of slave bracelets and a ring at the top of the post, were fastened behind them and to the post. At the feet of each was an opened slave collar, with a bit of silk twisted about it.

One of these girls was the former Lady Tina of Lydius, whom Ram had once enslaved. The other was Arlene.

One of the men of the Kurii stepped down from the tiers into the sand, between and before the two platforms. He was armed with the Gorean short sword.

Opposite my cage there was another cage, in which Ram, whom I had not seen in days, since we were separated in the storm, was confined.

I was pleased muchly to see that he lived. Perhaps he had been spared for this sport.

Ram's cage was opened and he stepped down and into the sand. A short sword was placed in his grasp.

He cut the air twice with the sword, and then stepped back. A fellow in brown and black, which seemed to be the livery of the men of the Kurii in this place, stepped to the center of the sand.

Ram glanced at me.

"I wish you fortune," I said. He grinned.

I looked about the small amphitheater. There were some hundred men present in it. Bets were being taken.

I knew Ram was skillful. How skillful I did not know.

Behind my cage, and in the wall, some twenty feet in height, there was a mirror. I saw no reason for a mirror in such a place.

Behind it, I supposed, Kurii watched. It was, I assumed, one-way glass.

The man at the center of the sand spoke to the two combatants, who stood near to him.

He did not speak long.

The rules for the sport are simple. They are those of war.

Having a female at stake, or a bit of gold, adds spice to the contest. The reason why men do such things, I think, however, is not because of the women, or the gold, but because they enjoy it.

The two combatants then separated.

"Place each of you your right heel on the wooden rim of the sand oval," then said the man in the center of the sand.

Both Ram and the other fellow did this. They stood, then,

356

opposite to one another, facing one another across some twenty feet of sand.

The man in the center of the sand then withdrew. "Fight," he said.

"Excellent," I breathed to myself. I found myself admiring the skill of Ram. The other fellow was quite good, but there was little contest. In moments Ram was wiping his blade on the tunic of the man at his feet. I was faster than Ram but his quickness was unusual, even among warriors. I would have been pleased to have had him serve with me. There was now no doubt in my mind but what, before his exile in Teletus, despite his asseverations to the contrary, his tunic had been of scarlet.

"Well done, Warrior," I called to him. He lifted his blade to me, in salute.

Tina was released from the post, and fled to him, but stopped short, the point of his blade at her belly. She looked at him, startled. He would not permit her to touch him in the garb of a free woman. With his sword he gestured to her gown, the jewels, the coronet. Swiftly she stripped herself naked before him and knelt. He threw her the bit of silk which had been wrapped about the opened slave collar which had been at her feet on the platform. She slipped it on, that luscious mockery of a garment. He then, as she knelt, roughly locked the collar on her throat. He then took her in his arms as what she was, his slave girl. How she melted to him, his, crying out, owned. But then he saw the lowered dart-projectile weapons circling him. Laughing he put her to the side, and flung his sword down, blade first, to the hilt in the sand. He was placed again in the cage, and locked within. Tina was dragged in her collar and slave silk to the post. She was forced to kneel there, for she was now collared, a slave wench. Her hands were lifted, and again placed in the slave bracelets, which were again closed. She was again fastened at the iron post, this time kneeling beside it, her hands lifted above her face. Her hair came half way down her back.

The gate of my cage was opened, and a short sword was placed in my hands.

It had good balance. It was not a poor weapon.

Drusus himself, I was pleased to see, stepped forth into the sand.

"I have been waiting a long time to meet you in this fashion," said he.

I measured him, his movements, the cast of his eyes. I could gather little.

357

He seemed slow. But I knew he did not come to his somber garb by any tardiness of action or hesitancy in deed. The training of the assassin is thorough and cruel. He who wears the black of that caste has not won it easily. Candidates for the caste are chosen with great care, and only one in ten, it is said, completes the course of instruction to the satisfaction of the caste masters. It is assumed that failed candidates are slain, if not in the training, for secrets they may have learned. Withdrawal from the caste is not permitted. Training proceeds in pairs, each pair against others. Friendship is encouraged. Then, in the final training, each member of the pair must hunt the other. When one has killed one's friend one is then likely to better understand the meaning of the black. When one has killed one's friend one is then unlikely to find mercy in his heart for another. One is then alone, with gold and steel.

I looked at Drusus.

The assassins take in lads who are perhaps characterized by little but unusual swiftness, and cunning, and strength and skill, and perhaps a selfishness and greed, and, in time, transform this raw material into efficient, proud, merciless men, practitioners of a dark trade, men loyal to secret codes the content of which is something at which most men dare not guess.

Drusus was looking at me.

I kept in mind he had survived the training of the assassin.

We stood in the center of the sand, with the other man, listening.

Suddenly the blade of Drusus leapt toward me. I deflected it. I had been waiting for the blow.

The third man on the sand seemed startled. Ram, in his cage, cried out in fury. The girls gasped. Most sat, stunned. One or two of the men in the tiers cried out approval.

"You are skilled," I told Drusus.

"You, too, are skilled," he said.

The man in the center of the sand backed uneasily away from us.

"Place each of you your right heel on the wooden rim of the sand oval," he said. His voice faltered.

We did so.

"How will you manage," I asked Drusus, "without a dark doorway from which to emerge?"

He did not speak to me.

"Perhaps a confederate in the audience will strike me when my back is turned?" I suggested.

The face of Drusus showed no emotion.

"There is perhaps poison on your blade?" I said.

"My caste does not make use of poison," he said.

I then decided that it would not be easy to agitate him, perhaps impairing his timing, or making him behave in a hasty manner, too zealous for a quick kill.

"Fight," said the man at the side of the ring.

We met in the center of the ring. Our blades touched and parried.

"I received my early training in the city of Ko-ro-ba," I said.

Our blades touched one another.

"What is your Home Stone?" I asked.

"Do you think I am fool enough to talk with you?" he snarled.

"Assassins, as I recall," I said, "have no Home Stones. I suppose that is a drawback to caste membership, but if you did have Home Stones, it might be difficult to take fees on one whose Home Stone you shared."

I moved his blade aside.

"You are faster than I thought," I said.

Our blades swiftly met, a moment of testing. Then we stepped back, retaining our guard position.

"Some think the caste of assassins performs a service," I said, "but I find this difficult to take seriously. I suppose they could be hired in the service of justice, but it seems they could be as easily hired in the service of anything." I looked at him. "Do you fellows have any principles?" I asked.

He moved in, swiftly, too swiftly. I did not take advantage of it.

"Apparently staying alive is not one of them" I said.

He stepped back, startled.

"You were open there for a moment," I said. He knew it and I knew it, but I was not sure those in the tiers knew it. It is sometimes difficult to see these things from certain angles.

There were jeers from the tiered benches. They did not believe what I said.

I now stalked Drusus. He kept a close guard, covering himself well. It is hard to strike a man who elects defense. He limits himself, of course, in adopting this strategem.

Now jeers against Drusus came from the benches. He began to sweat.

"Is it true," I asked, "that you, in attaining the black of your caste, once slew your friend?"

I pressed the attack, but in a courteous fashion. He defended himself well.

"What was his name?" I asked.

"Kurnock!" he suddenly cried out, angrily, and rushed toward me.

I sprawled him into the sand at my feet, and my blade was at the back of his neck.

I stepped back.

"Get up," I said. "Now let us fight seriously."

He leaped to his feet. I then administered to him, and to those in the tiers, a lesson in the use of the Gorean blade.

They sat in silence.

Then, bloodied, Drusus, unsteadily, his sword arm down, wavered before me. He had been cut several times, as I had pleased.

He could no longer lift the blade. Blood ran down his arm, staining the sand.

I looked up to the mirror in the wall, that which I was confident was in actuality a one-way glass. I lifted my sword to that invisible window, in the salute of a Gorean warrior. I then turned again to face Drusus.

"Kill me," he said. "It is twice I have failed my caste."

I lifted the blade to strike him. "I will be swift," I told him.

I poised the steel.

"Let it be thus that an old debt owed to one named Kurnock is repaid," I said.

"That is the first time I failed my caste," said Drusus.

I regarded him.

"Strike," he said.

"I do not understand," I said.

"I did not kill Kurnock," he said. "He was no match for me. I could not bring myself to kill him."

I handed the sword to the third man on the sand.

"Kill me!" cried Drusus.

"Do you think a warrior can show less mercy than an Assassin?" I asked.

"Kill me," wept Drusus, and then, from the loss of blood, fell into the sand.

"He is too weak to be an assassin," I said. "Remove him."

Drusus was drawn from the sand. The man who had been in charge of the combat then released Arlene from the iron post.

Proudly she stepped down from the platform and stood before me.

She said nothing, but removed her jewels and necklaces, and the coronet she wore, dropping them into the sand. She then slipped the gown from her body. She then stood before me, proud and beautiful, and absolutely naked. She then turned and went to the foot of the small, round platform, picked up the opened slave collar, with the bit of silk wrapped about it, and returned to the place on the sand before me. She then knelt before me and lifted the collar and silk. "Collar your slave, Master," she said.

I locked the slave collar on her throat, not gently. I then took the bit of pleasure silk and, rather than throw it on her, tied it on her collar, at the side.

She would, by my will, wear only her collar on the sand. She turned, still kneeling, to the tiers. "He is my master!" she cried, proudly.

I was then ringed with the dart-firing weapons.

"Return to the cage," said the man who had controlled the combats.

"Wait!" said a man on the tiers. "Look!"

We looked up, and saw a light, red, flash once below the mirror.

"Excellent," said the judge, or controller of the combats.

Ram's cage was opened and a sword was again placed in his hand. My sword, too, was returned to me.

Ram threw down his sword. "He is my friend," he said. "I will not fight him!"

"Pick up your sword," I told Ram. I looked about the tiers.

"I will not fight you," he said. "They must kill me first."

"I am sure they would be willing to do that," I said. "Pick up your sword."

Ram, too, looked about the tiers. "I see they wish to see more bloodshed," he said.

"Let us not, then, disappoint them," I said.

Ram looked at me, and then, to the pleasure of the crowd, picked up his blade.

"You must not fight him, Master!" cried Arlene. "Do not fight!" cried Tina.

Arlene was dragged to the iron post and knelt beside it. Her wrists, rudely, were lifted and snapped into the slave bracelets dangling at the ring. Then she knelt as did Tina, as what she was, as a slave girl, at the post, with her hands lifted and fastened above her head to the ring.

"Please, Masters!" they cried.

"Be silent, Girl," said Ram to Tina.

"Be silent, Girl," I said to Arlene.

"Yes, Master," said Tina.

"Yes, Master," said Arlene.

Ram and I met, as we had with our previous antagonists, in the center of the oval.

Then, after a moment or two, the man with us in the center of the sand withdrew.

"Place each of you your right heel on the wooden rim of the sand oval," he said, grinning.

I looked about the tiers. There were some six of the tubular weapons in evidence. Most of the men, however, were armed, as were Ram and myself, with the short sword.

I looked across the sand to Ram. We lifted our blades to one another, in salute.

"Fight!" cried the judge, or controller of the combat.

I leaped into the tiers, slashing and striking. I sped toward those who held the tubular weapons. Ram, on his side of the room, cut his way upward, buffeting and kicking. There was much screaming, and blood. I shook loose from two men. I stabbed another. Two of the tubular weapons clattered down. I cut the neck of a man who reached for one. I kicked a fellow in the face who reached for the other. Two men leaped on me, causing me to fall down the tiers. I heard blades leaving the sheaths. The girls screamed. More men fell, struggling to rise and draw their weapons. I heard a fearsome hiss and something smoked past my head, sinking into the sand. A moment later there was a burst from under the sand and sand and wood splinters blasted upward. I freed myself from the men with whom I was entangled, and slipped the blade through one. I shielded myself from one fellow with a tubular weapon while striking at another. I met two men with blades on the sand, felling one and slashing another, who reeled away. I leaped to the side to hack down at four men who were struggling with Ram. He leaped up, freed of them. He had lost his sword. Another hiss smoked past me and I saw, across the room, almost at the same instant, a six-inch dart sink part way into a steel wall and part of the wall, screeching, burst back, a four-inch hole, blackened, in it. I kicked a sword to Ram, and he seized it, meeting and defending himself against an attack. I passed my sword through the body of the man who had been in charge of the combats. I heard two more hisses, and part of the benches in one tier burst apart and I saw another dart disappear into the body of a man and I saw his eyes wild and the scarcest instant later he seemed to blow apart. I was then conscious of a whitish gas falling from the ceiling. I cut a man down by the door

362

and tried to force it open. It was steel, and locked. I coughed and choked in the gas. It was hard to see. I reeled back from the door, and met the blade of another man, and cut him down. I saw Tina and Arlene, braceleted at the iron posts. They were agonized, trying to breathe. A steel dart, fired from one of the riflelike weapons, caromed about the steel walls, leaving an explosive scar of blackened metal, a foot long, where first it struck. A man backed away from me, shaking his head. He could not well see me. I called out to Ram, who spun about, felling a man who would have struck him from behind. I defended myself against two other men, but, in the foglike mist, in a moment they were elsewhere. I heard a man pounding on the steel door. "Let us out!" he cried. I saw Tina and Arlene, in their collars, slumped unconscious at the posts, their small wrists still obdurately captive in the inflexible slave bracelets which secured them so perfectly at the ring. I saw a man topple unconscious from one of the tiers. Another man I saw groping for one of the dart-firing weapons, it fallen on the tiers. I looked upward, at the impassive mirrorlike window in the wall. I could see the milky smokelike gas reflected in it. I defended myself against another attacker. He stumbled backward, bloody. Some four men now sank to their knees and sprawled among the tiers. The man had the tubular weapon now, and was trying to steady it. I did not have time to reach him. I threw myself to the sand and, dropping the sword, rolling, seized up one of the weapons. Another man seized it, too, and I kicked him from it. I whirled, choking, straining to see through the gas. The man on the tiers had lifted the weapon to his shoulder but he did not fire it. My finger hesitated on the circular press-switch. He wavered and the muzzle of the weapon declined and he fell unconscious. I looked about, as I could. Ram lay sprawled in the sand near me. I was then the only man on my feet. I stumbled, and then straightened myself. I shook my head, trying to clear it. The gas was thick about me. Oddly, though the room was filled with a whitish gas, it seemed to be turning dark. I struggled to lift the muzzle of the weapon toward the mirrorlike window. Then I fell unconscious in the sand.

31   HALF-EAR

"In here," said the man in the brown and black livery of those men in the service of the Kurii. He indicated the metal door.

I had walked with them through the steel halls. There had been two of them. Neither of them was armed, nor was I.

I could have done little more in the steel halls than kill them.

One of the men opened the metal door. He then stood to the side, and gestured that I might go within.

I entered the door, and it was closed, and locked, behind me.

I looked about the room. It was domed, and some forty feet in height. It seemed simply furnished. It contained a few objects, mostly at the edges of the room. There were some tables, and cabinets and shelves. There were no chairs. Some chests, too, were at the side of the room. I stood upon a rug of some sort. Its nap was deep. It would give good footing to a clawed foot. The room was rather dark, but I could see dimly. There appeared to be a shallow basin of water sunk in the floor to one side. In the sides of the room, here and there, there seemed windows like portholes. Yet I did not think they opened onto the outside. I could see neither the bleak, moon-lit ice of the north beyond them, nor even the lights of stars. Looking up I saw above me, beginning some ten feet from the floor, a network of widely placed wood and steel rods. Oddly, certain portholes, or apertures, or whatever they might be, were set high, too, some twenty feet from the floor, ring-ing the dome. One could not, given their height, look through them from the floor. By feel I determined that one of the walls, that to my right, as I had entered the room, as was the floor, was lined with some heavy ruglike substance. Thus, something suitably clawed, I supposed, could cling to it. On a table to the side, toward what I took to be the front of the room, there was a dark, boxlike object, about six inches in height, and a foot or so in width and length. At the center of the room, toward the front, there was a wide, low, circular platform. On this something lay.

I sat down, cross-legged, some twenty feet in front of the platform, and waited.

I watched the thing on the platform. It was large, and shaggy, and curled upon itself, and alive.

I was not sure, initially, if there were one or more things on the platform. But then I became confident it was only one thing. I had not realized he was so gigantic.

I sat quietly, watching it breathe.

After a time it stirred. Then, with an ease, an indolent smoothness of motion startling in so large a beast it sat up on the platform, regarding me. It blinked. The pupils of its eyes were like dark moons. It yawned. I saw the double row of fangs, inclined backward in the mouth, to move caught meat toward the throat. It blinked again, and began to lick its paws. Its long, dark tongue, too, cleaned the fur about its mouth. It turned away and went to a side of the room where it relieved itself. A lever, depressed, released water, washing the waste away. The animal scratched twice on the plates near where it had relieved itself, as though reflexively covering its spoor. It then, moving on all fours, lightly, moved forward, around the platform, and went to the sunken basin of water in the room. It put down its cupped paws and splashed water in its face, and then shook its head. Too, it took water in its cupped paws, and drank. With one paw it gestured that I should approach, and palm open on the appendage, indicated that I might use the water. Crouching down I took a bit of water in the palm of my hand and drank. We looked at one another across the sunken basin.

The animal, on all fours, withdrew from the edge of the basin.

It projected its claws and scratched on the ruglike substance on the walls. Then, claws catching in the heavy material, it moved up the wall, stretching and twisting its body. Then it dropped down to a pole in the scaffolding. It sat there for a moment, and then, lightly, swung from one pole to another, and then returned, dropping lightly, for an animal of its weight, to the floor before the platform. It stretched again, catlike. And then it rose to its hind feet and looked down at me. It was more than eight feet in height. I would have conjectured its weight at some nine hundred pounds. Then it dropped again to all fours and moved to the table on which there reposed the dark, boxlike object.

It moved a switch on the box. It uttered sounds, low, guttural, inquisitive. It did not use human phonemes and so it is difficult, if not impossible, to convey the quality of the sound. If you have heard the noises made by great cats, such as the Bengal tiger or the black-maned lion, and can conceive of such noises articulated with the subtlety and precision of a civilized speech, that will provide you with an approximation of what I heard. On the other hand, the vocal apparatus of the beast was not even of Earth origin. Certain of its sounds, for example, were more reminiscent of the snort of the boar, the snuffling of the grizzly, the hiss of the snake, than those of the large cats. The phonemes of such beasts are unmistakable, but they are, truly, like nothing Earth has prepared one to hear. They are different, not of Earth, alien. To hear these noises, and know they are a speech can be initially very frightening. Evolution did not prepare those of Earth to find intelligence in such a form.

The beast was then silent.

"Are you hungry?" I heard. The sounds, separate, had been emitted from the dark, flatish, boxlike object on the table. It was, then, a translator.

"Not particularly," I said.

After a moment a set of sounds, brief, like a growl, came from the translator. I smiled.

The beast shrugged. It shambled to the side of the room, and there pressed a switch.

A metal panel slid up. I heard a squeal and a small animal, a lart, fled from within toward the opening. It happened quickly. The large six-digited paw of the beast closed about the lart, hideously squealing, and lifted it to its mouth, where it bit through the back of its neck, spitting out vertebrae. The lart, dead, but spasmodically trembling, was then held in the beast's mouth. It then, with its claws freed, opened its furs and, by feel, delicately, regarding me, fingered out various organs which it laid on the floor before it. In moments it had removed the animal from its mouth. Absently, removing meat from the carcass, it fed.

"You do not cook your meat?" I asked.

The translator, turned on, accepted the human phonemes, processed them, and, momentarily, produced audible, correspondent phonemes in one of the languages of the Kur.

The beast responded. I waited.

"We sometimes do," he said. It looked at me. "Cooked meat weakens the jaws," it said.

"Fire, and cooked meat," I said, "makes possible a smaller

jaw and smaller teeth, permitting less cranial musculature and permitting the development of a larger brain case."

"Our brain cases are larger than those of humans," it said. "Our anatomy could not well support a larger cranial development. In our history, as in yours, larger brain cases have been selected for."

"In what way?" I asked.

"In the killings," it said.

"The Kur is not a social animal?" I asked.

"It is a social animal," it said. "But it is not as social as the human."

"That is perhaps a drawback to it as a species," I said.

"It has its advantages," it said. "The Kur can live alone. It can go its own way. It does not need its herd."

"Surely, in ancient times, Kurii came together," I said.

"Yes," it said, "in the matings, and the killings." It looked at me, chewing. "But that was long ago," it said. "We have had civilization for one hundred thousand years, as you would understand these things. In the dawn of our prehistory small bands emerged from the burrows and the caves and forests. It was a beginning."

"How can such an animal have a civilization?" I asked.

"Discipline," it said.

"That is a slender thread with which to restrain such fierce, titanic instincts," I said.

The beast extended to me a thigh of the lart. "True," it said. "I see you understand us well."

I took the meat and chewed on it. It was fresh, warm, still porous with blood.

"You like it, do you not?" asked the beast.

"Yes," I said.

"You see," it said, "you are not so different from us."

"I have never claimed to be," I said.

"Is not civilization as great an achievement for your species as for mine?" it asked.

"Perhaps," I said.

"Are the threads on which your survival depends stouter than those on which ours depends?" it asked.

"Perhaps not," I said.

"I know little of humans," it said, "but it is my understanding that most of them are liars and hypocrites. I do not include you in this general charge."

I nodded.

"They think of themselves as civilized animals, and yet

367

they are only animals with a civilization. There is quite a difference."

"Admittedly," I said.

"Those of Earth, as I understand it, which is your home world, are the most despicable. They are petty. They mistake weakness for virtue. They take their lack of appetite, their incapacity to feel, as a merit. How small they are. The more they betray their own nature the more they congratulate themselves on their perfection. And they put economic gain above all. Their greed and their fevered scratching repulses me."

"Not all on Earth are like that," I said.

"It is a food world," it said, "and the food is not of the best."

"What do you put above all?" I asked.

"Glory," it said. It looked at me. "Can you understand that?" it asked.

"I can understand it," I said.

"We are soldiers," it said, "the two of us."

"How is it that an animal without strong social instincts can be concerned with glory?" I asked.

"It emerges, we speculate, from the killings."

"The killings?" I asked.

"Even before the first groups," it said, "we would gather for the matings and killings. Great circles, rings of our people, would form in valleys, to watch."

"You fought for mates?" I asked.

"We fought for the joy of killing," it said. "Mating, however, was a prerogative of the victor." It took a rib bone from the lart and began to thrust it, scraping, between its fangs, freeing and removing bits of wedged meat. "Humans, as I understand it, have two sexes, which, among them, perform all the functions pertinent to the continuance of the species."

"Yes," I said, "that is true."

"We have three, or, if you prefer, four sexes," it said. "There is the dominant, which would, I suppose, correspond most closely to the human male. It is the instinct of the dominant to enter the killings and mate. There is then a form of Kur which closely resembles the dominant but does not join in the killings or mate. You may, or may not, regard this as two sexes. There is then the egg-carrier who is impregnated. This form of Kur is smaller than the dominant or the nondominant, speaking thusly of the nonreproducing form of Kur."

"The egg-carrier is the female," I said.

"If you like," said the beast, "but, shortly after impregnation, within a moon, the egg-carrier deposits the fertilized seed in the third form of Kur, which is mouthed, but sluggish and immobile. These fasten themselves to hard surfaces, rather like dark, globular anemones. The egg develops inside the body of the blood-nurser and, some months later, it tears its way free."

"It has no mother," I said.

"Not in the human sense," it said. "It will, however, usually follow, unless it itself is a blood-nurser, which is drawn out, the first Kur it sees, providing it is either an egg-carrier or a nondominant."

"What if it sees a dominant?" I asked.

"If it is itself an egg-carrier or a nondominant, it will shun the dominant," it said. "This is not unwise, for the dominant may kill it."

"What if it itself is potentially a dominant?" I asked.

The lips of the beast drew back. "That is what all hope," it said. "If it is a dominant and it encounters a dominant, it will bare its tiny fangs and expose its claws."

"Will the dominant not kill it then?" I asked.

"Perhaps later in the killings, when it is large and strong," he said, "but certainly not when it is small. It is on such that the continuance of the species depends. You see, it must be tested in the killings."

"Are you a dominant?" I asked.

"Of course," it said. Then it added, "I shall not kill you for the question."

"I meant no harm," I said.

Its lips drew back.

"Are most Kurii dominants?" I asked.

"Most are born dominants," it said, "but most do not survive the killings."

"It seems surprising that there are many Kurii," I said.

"Not at all," he said. "The egg-carriers can be frequently impregnated and frequently deposit the fertilized egg in a blood-nurser. There are large numbers of blood-nursers. In the human species it takes several months for a female to carry and deliver an offspring. In the same amount of time a Kur egg-carrier will develop seven to eight eggs, each of which may be fertilized and deposited in a blood-nurser."

"Do Kur young not drink milk?" I asked.

"The young receive blood in the nurser," he said. "When it

369

is born it does not need milk, but water and common protein."

"It is born fanged?" I asked.

"Of course," it said. "And it is capable of stalking and killing small animals shortly after it leaves the nurser."

"Are the nursers rational?" I asked.

"We do not think so," it said.

"Can they feel anything?" I asked.

"They doubtless have some form of sensation," it said. "They recoil when struck or burned."

"But there are native Kurii on Gor," I said, "or, at any rate, Kurii who have reproduced themselves on this world."

"Certain ships, some of them originally intended for colonization, carried representatives of our various sexes, with the exception of the nondominants," it said. "We have also, where we knew of Kurii groups, sometimes managed to bring in egg-carriers and blood-nursers."

"It is to your advantage that there be native Kurii," I said.

"Of course," he said, "yet they are seldom useful allies. They lapse too swiftly into barbarism." He lowered the bone with which he was picking his teeth and threw it, and the remains of the lart, to the side of the room. He then took a soft, white cloth from a drawer in the table on which the translator reposed, and wiped his paws. "Civilization is fragile," he said.

"Is there an order among your sexes?" I asked.

"Of course there is a biological order," he said. "Structure is a function of nature. How could it be otherwise?

"There is first the dominant, and then the egg-carrier, and then the nondominant, and then, if one considers such things Kur, the blood-nurser."

"The female, or egg-carrier, is dominant over the nondominant?" I asked.

"Of course," he said. "They are despicable."

"Suppose a dominant is victorious in the killings," I said. "Then what occurs?"

"Many things could occur," he said, "but he then, generally, with a club, would indicate what egg-carriers he desires. He then ties them together and drives them to his cave. In the cave he impregnates them and makes them serve him."

"Do they attempt to run away?" I asked.

"No," he said. "He would hunt them down and kill them. But after he has impregnated them they tend to remain, even when untied, for he is then their dominant."

"What of the nondominants?" I asked.

"They remain outside the cave until the dominant is finished, fearing him muchly. When he has left the cave they creep within, bringing meat and gifts to the females, that they may be permitted to remain within the cave, as part of the dominant's household. They serve under the females and take their orders from them. Most work, including the care of the young, is performed by nondominants."

"I do not think I would care to be a nondominant," I said.

"They are totally despicable," he said, "but yet, oddly, sometimes a nondominant becomes a dominant. This is a hard thing to understand. Sometimes it happens when there is no dominant in the vicinity. Sometimes it seems to happen for no obvious reason; sometimes it happens when a nondominant is humiliated and worked beyond his level of tolerance. It is interesting. This occasional, almost inexplicable transformation of a nondominant into a dominant is the reason our biologists differ as to whether our species has three, or four sexes."

"Perhaps the nondominant is only a latent dominant," I said.

"Perhaps," he said. "It is hard to tell."

"The restriction of mating to the dominants," I said, "plus the selections in the killings, must tend to produce a species unusually aggressive and savage."

"It tends also to produce one that is extremely intelligent," said the animal.

I nodded.

"But we are civilized folk," said the animal. It rose to its feet and went to a cabinet. "You must not think of us in terms of our bloody past."

"Then, on the steel ships," I said, "the killings, and the fierce matings, no longer take place."

The animal, at the opened cabinet, turned to regard me. "I did not say that," he said.

"The killings and the matings then continue to take place on the steel worlds?" I asked.

"Of course," he said.

"The past, then, is still with you on the steel worlds," I said.

"Yes," it said. "Is the past not always with us?"

"Perhaps," I said.

The beast returned from the cabinet with two glasses and a bottle.

"Is that not the paga of Ar?" I asked.

"Is it not one of your favorites?" he asked. "See," he said. "It has the seal of the brewer, Temus."

"That is remarkable," I said. "You are very thoughtful."

"I have been saving it," he told me.

"For me?" I asked.

"Of course," he said. "I was confident you would get through."

"I am honored," I said.

"I have waited so long to talk to you," he said.

He poured two glasses of paga, and reclosed the bottle. We lifted the glasses, and touched them, the one to the other.

"To our war," he said.

"To our war," I said.

We drank.

"I cannot even pronounce your name," I said.

"It will be sufficient," he said, "to call me Zarendargar, which can be pronounced by human beings, or, if you like, even more simply, Half-Ear."

32   I HOLD CONVERSE WITH ZARENDARGAR

"You see?" asked the beast, pointing upward, it seemed at a starry sky above our heads.

"Yes," I said. I did not recognize the patch of the heavens above us.

"That was our star," he said, "a yellow, medium-sized, slow-rotating star with a planetary system, one small enough to have sufficient longevity to nourish life, one large enough to have a suitable habitable zone."

"Not unlike Tor-tu-Gor, or Sol," I said, "the common star of Earth and Gor."

"Precisely," he said.

"Tell me of your world," I said.

"My world is of steel," it said. It seemed bitter.

"Your old world," I said.

"I never saw it, of course," he said. "It was, of course, of a suitable size and distance from its star. It was small enough to permit the escape of hydrogen, large enough to retain oxygen. It was not so close to the star as to be a ball of scalding rock nor so far as to be a frozen spheroid."

"It maintained temperatures at which water could be in a liquid form."

"Yes," it said, "and the mechanisms, the atomic necessities, of chemical evolution were initiated, and the macromolecules and protocells, in time, were formed."

"Gases were exchanged, and the hydrogen-dominated atmosphere yielded to one in which free oxygen was a major component."

"It became green," it said.

"Life began its climb anew," I said.

"Out of the two billion years of the wars and the killings, and the eatings and the huntings, came my people," it said. "We were the triumph of evolution in all its heartless savagery," it said.

"And the doom of your world," I said.

"We do not speak of what happened," it said. It moved to the wall and, passing its paw before a switch, caused the projection on the ceiling to vanish. It turned then to look upon me. "Our world was very beautiful," it said. "We will have another."

"Perhaps not," I said.

"The human being cannot even kill with its teeth," it said.

I shrugged.

"But let us not quarrel," it said. "I am so pleased that you are here, and I am so fond of you."

"Out on the ice," I said, "we saw, or seemed to see, in the lights in the sky, your face."

Its lips drew back. "You did," it said.

"The lights are most normally seen in the fall and spring," I said, "near the time of the equinoxes."

"That is clever of you," it said.

"What we saw then," I said, "was artificially produced."

"Yes," it said, "but it is not unlike the natural phenomenon. It is produced by saturating the atmosphere with certain patterns of charged particles. These patterns may be arranged in given orders, to correspond to alphabetic characters, either in a Kur tongue or, say, in Gorean. The lights, apparently a natural phenomenon, are thus used as a signaling device to Kur groups and their human compatriots."

"Ingenious," I said.

"I permitted my visage to be depicted in the lights to honor you, and welcome you to the north," it said.

I nodded.

"Would you like another drink?" it asked.

"Yes," I said.

"Your complex," I said, "is doubtless impressive. Would you show me about it?"

"I can do so without leaving this room," it said. It then, turning various dials, illuminated what I had taken to be the darkened portholes, or some other sort of aperture, in the walls, which I now saw were recessed screens, coordinated with various, movable cameras, operated from the room. By means of these cameras, and the various screens, I was given to understand the immensity and intricacy of the complex. Some of the screens were over my head but, lifted to the poles, those above, I, clinging to the poles, could see well. The beast moved easily on the poles beside me.

"It is very impressive," I said.

"It is mostly automated," said the beast. "We have only two hundred humans here and some twenty of our people."

"That is incredible," I said. Clearly the complex was tiers in depth and pasangs in width.

"It was simple to gyroscopically stabilize and mine an ice island," it said. "We have created this within the ice, and the mined ice is simply shredded and discarded in the sea, attracting no attention."

"You wanted to close the tabuk off in their northward migration to drive the red hunters south and away from the area?" I asked.

"Particularly before the winter," it said, "when they might roam too far northward on the ice."

"There is a fantastic amount of stores here," I said.

"Electrical equipment, explosives, weapons, supplies, vehicles," it said. "And much, much more."

"It would take years to assemble this depot," I said.

"It did," it said. "But only recently did I assume command."

"The Kur invasion then, using this staging area, is imminent."

"We did not wish to risk the great fleet," it said. "With this depot we need bring in, in the fierce strike, little more than the hibernated marches." A march is a Kur military expression. It refers to twelve bands and their officers. It consists of between twenty-one hundred and twenty-two hundred animals.

374

"In twelve Kur hours, all cities on Gor can be destroyed," it said.

"What of the Priest-Kings?" I asked.

"I do not think they can meet an attack in force," he said.

"Are you sure of that?" I asked.

"I am sure," he said, drawing back his lips about his fangs. "Though not all are sure," he said.

"That is why the great fleet is not being risked?" I asked.

"Of course," he said. "I could urge the launching of the great fleet. But then I am only a simple soldier. Others stand higher on the cliff than I."

"Troopships, beaching their personnel, should be sufficient," I said, "given the supplies present here."

"Yes," he said, "on the assumption that the Priest-Kings are as weak as I speculate."

"Why do you think them weak?" I asked.

"The Nest War," he said. "Surely you have heard of it."

"I have heard stories," I said.

"I believe them true," he said. "Now is the time for the People to strike." He looked at me. "Oh, I could have your mind torn open, and could break you, or kill you, as anything can be torn and broken, or killed, but, in the end I, at best, would know only what you believed to be true, and that may or may not be true." He dropped down to the floor, and I dropped down beside him. "Priest-Kings are clever," he said.

"I have heard that," I said.

"I think I could not break you," he said. "I think I could only kill you."

I shrugged.

"You are like a Kur," he said. "That is why I like you." He put a heavy paw on my shoulder. "It would be wrong for you to die in the machine of truth," he said.

"There are many valuable supplies in the complex," I said. "What if they should fall into the hands of the Priest-Kings?"

"There is an arrangement to prevent that," he said.

"I had thought there would be," I said. Not all areas in the complex, I was confident, had been scanned by the cameras I had seen. The overhead tracks, too, those controlling the movements of neck-chained slaves, presumably did not reach to all areas.

"What are Priest-Kings like?" asked the beast. "Are they like us?"

"No," I said, "they are not like us."

"They must be fearsome things," said the beast.

I thought of the lofty, delicate, golden creatures. "Perhaps," I said.

"Have you ever seen one?" he asked.

"Yes," I said.

"You do not wish to speak?" he asked.

"No," I said. "I would prefer not to speak."

He put both paws on my shoulders. "Good," he said. "You are loyal. I will not press you!"

"Thank you," I said.

"But someday," he said, "we will know."

I shrugged. "Perhaps," I said. "I do not know."

"Let us speak of less sensitive topics," he said.

"Agreed," I said.

We returned to the table, on which reposed the paga.

"How was I captured?" I asked.

The beast poured another glass of paga for each of us. "That was simple," it said. "A gas was introduced into your shelter of snow, from the outside, rendering you, and the others, unconscious."

"Imnak was on guard," I said.

"The red hunter, like Karjuk?" he asked.

"Yes," I said.

"Karjuk spoke to him and he, a rational fellow, in the light of economic and prudential considerations, joined us promptly."

"I never doubted that Imnak was a man of decision," I said.

"Do not be bitter," he said.

"What would you think if a Kur betrayed his own kind?" I asked.

He looked at me, startled. "It could not happen," he said.

"Surely Kurii, in their own wars, have occasionally demonstrated treachery."

"Never to men, never to another species," said the beast. "That is unthinkable."

"Kurii, then," I said, "are in this regard nobler than men."

"It is my supposition," it said, "that in all respects Kurii are nobler than men." It looked at me. "But I except you," he said. "I think there is something of the Kur in you."

"In the room of the dueling," I said. "There was a large mirror."

"An observation port," it said.

"I thought so," I said.

"You fought splendidly," he said. "You are very skilled with that tiny weapon."

"Thank you," I said.

"I, too, am skilled in weaponry," it said, "in various weapons traditional with my people, and in modern weapons, as well."

"You maintain, even with your technology, a dueling tradition?" I asked.

"Of course," it said. "And the tradition of the fang and claw is continued as well."

"Of course," I said.

"I am not fond of modern weapons," it said. "An egg-carrier or even a nondominant could use them. They put one at too great a distance from the kill. They can be effective, and that is their justification, but they are, in my opinion, boring. They tend to rob one, because of their nature, of the closeness, the immediacy, the joy of the hot kill. That is the greatest condemnation of them. They take the pleasure out of killing." It looked at me. "What can compare," it asked, "with the joy of real victory? Of true victory? When one has risked one's life openly and then, after a hard-fought contest, has one's enemy at one's feet, lacerated, and bleeding and dying, and can then tear him in victory and feast in his body, what can compare with the joy of that?"

The eyes of the beast blazed, but then the fierce light subsided. It poured us again a glass of paga.

"Very little, I suppose," I said.

"Do I horrify you?" it asked.

"No," I said.

"I knew I would not," it said.

"How did you know that?" I asked.

"I saw you fight," it said.

I shrugged.

"You should have seen your face," it said. "You cannot tell me you did not like it."

"I have not told you that," I said.

"In time the war will be finished," it said. It looked at me. "If we should survive it, there will be afterwards no use for such as we."

"We will, at least," I said, "have known one another."

"That is true," it said. "Would you like to see my trophies?" it asked.

"Yes," I said.

33 I LEAVE THE COMPLEX

It was chilly in the low, steel room, one serving as a port to the outside ice.

Near the circular, heavy door, now closed, stood the white-pelted Kur, that which had rings in its ears, that which had accompanied Karjuk, the traitor to his people. It held a leather harness looped in its paw.

I donned the furs.

I was to be taken outside and there, some distance from the complex, out on the ice, slain. It would seem as though the sled sleen had turned upon me. If I was found, it would be conjectured that the death, violent though it might have been, was not one unnatural for the Gorean north. I would have been lost in the north, apparently lost in a fruitless, misguided venture, one ill-fated from the beginning, one in which nothing but a meaningless, bloody conclusion would have been encountered. If there were a search for me, or curiosity concerning me, it would terminate when the carcass, torn and frozen, was found.

No sleen would draw the sled, of course.

The beast looped the harness about me, and I stood, waiting, in the harness, before the sled.

Its teeth would be sufficient to mock the predations of a reverted, starving sleen upon my body. He must be sure, however, to leave enough to be found, some bones and furs, the broken sled, some chewed traces.

I was pleased to have met Zarendargar, or Half-Ear. We had talked long.

Strange that I could converse with him, for he was only a beast.

I think he regretted sending me out upon the ice, to be rent by the white Kur. Zarendargar, or Half-Ear, I think, was a lonely soldier, a true soldier, with few with whom he could speak, with few with whom he could share his thoughts. I suspect there were few, if any, in that steel complex, even of his own breed, with whom he could converse warmly, excitedly, swiftly, in detail, as he did with me, where a word might suggest a paragraph, a glance, a lifted paw signify what might with a less attuned interlocutor require hours of converse to convey. He seemed to think we were, in some sense, kindred, that despite alien evolutions, remote origins and diverse histories. How preposterous was that concept! One does not find one's brother upon the shores of foreign worlds. "The same dark laws which have formed the teeth and claws of the Kur have formed the hand and brain of man," had said Half-Ear. This seemed to me, however, quite unlikely. Surely the same noble, high laws which had formed the lofty brain and useful hand of man could not have been responsible for the fangs and claws of the predatory Kur. We were men and they were beasts. Was that not clear to all?

I felt the leather of the sleen harness being drawn more tightly about me. It was cinched upon my body.

I thought of the melting of copper, the flame of sulphur, the structure of salt, of jagged Eros in its orbit, of the crags of Titan, of the interactions of compounds, the stirring of molecules, the movement of atoms, the trajectories of electrons. How formidable seem the implacable correlations. Perhaps what is alien to us is only ourselves in a different visage. Perhaps the other is not different but, ultimately, the same. When we seek the unknown is it ourselves for which we truly search?

Then I dismissed such foolish thoughts.

Surely it could not be that the dark rhythms and the brotherhoods of diverse chemistries could have combined to produce on an alien sphere those who were our brothers. He had spoken of convergent evolution. I had scoffed at this. One need only use one's eyes to see the difference between a Kur and a man. We were men, they were beasts, no more. Yet I had not been unfond of Half-Ear. I had felt, in meeting him, that I had known him for a long time, and I felt that he had had similar feelings. It was strange. We were so different, and yet, somehow, not so unlike as one might think. Then I reminded myself again that I was a man, and he a beast, no more. How shamed I was that he should compare himself to me. How offensive I found his allegations!

One need only use one's eyes to see how different we were!

How incredible it would be if one landed upon a foreign shore, a planet remote from our own, and found, emerging from its dark forests, shambling toward one, its eyes blazing, one's brother.

The white Kur stepped back. I was harnessed to the sled.

Last night I had been locked in my cell. It had not been unpleasant, however. Half-Ear had seen to that. Delicate viands, and furs and wines had been placed in the cell for me. Too, two slave girls, in pleasure silk, perfumed and collared, had been thrust into the cell for my use. I read the collar of each. The collar of each said, "I belong to Tarl Cabot." They had knelt at my feet, weeping. But that night I had well taught them their slavery. In the morning, when the white Kur had come to fetch me, and I had left the cell, both Arlene and Constance had had to be beaten back from the gate with whips. Then they were locked behind me in the cell. They had thrust their arms through the bars, crying out, weeping. With whips they were driven back further in the cell. I saw them, beautiful, inside the bars. They were not permitted to touch them. "Master," they wept. "Master!" They fell to their knees. "Master!" they cried. "Master! Master!" I turned and left the larger room, that in which the cell was located. I did not look back.

The white Kur reached to the lever which, rotated, would swing back the thick, circular steel hatch.

"Greetings, Tarl, who hunts with me," said Imnak, grinning, entering the room.

"Greetings, Traitor," I said.

"Do not be bitter, Tarl, who hunts with me," said Imnak. "One must look out for one's own best interest."

I said nothing.

"I want you to know that I, and all the People," he said, "will be forever grateful to you for having freed the tabuk."

"That is a comforting thought," I said.

"One in your position can probably use a comforting thought," speculated Imnak.

"That is true," I said. It was difficult to be angry with Imnak.

"I hold no hard feelings toward you," said Imnak.

"That is a relief," I said.

"I have brought you something to eat," he said. He lifted up a sack.

"No thank you," I said.

"But you may grow hungry before you reach your destination," said Imnak.

"I do not think so," I said.

380

"Perhaps then your companion," said Imnak, indicating the Kur with his head, "might enjoy something to eat. You must not be selfish. You should think of him, too, you know."

"I will not be likely to forget him," I said.

"Take the food," said Imnak.

"I do not want it," I said.

Imnak looked stricken.

Suddenly I was startled. My heart leaped.

"Sleen like it," said Imnak, hopefully.

"Let me see it," I said. I looked into the sack. "Yes, I will take it," I said.

The Kur came away from the lever which controlled the hatch to the outside. It smelled the sack and looked within. It handled the chunks of meat, large and thick, in the sack. It satisfied itself the sack contained no knives or weapon.

"It is for me," I said to the Kur.

The lips of the Kur drew back. It took the sack and put it on the sled. It then went back to the lever and rotated it. The hatch opened slowly. I could see the darkness, the moonlit ice beyond. The temperature in the steel room, almost immediately, fell thirty or forty points in temperature. Wind whipped into the room, blowing the Kur's fur, and Imnak's black hair about his head.

"Tal," said Imnak to me, not as though bidding me farewell, but as though greeting me.

"Tal," said I to him.

The Kur took his place behind the sled. I leaned forward and, putting my weight against the traces, drew the sled over the steel plates and out onto the ice.

34 WHAT OCCURRED ON THE ICE

As I had anticipated it was the intention of Half-Ear that my mutilated body be found at a considerable distance from the complex.

We trekked northward. The wind was twisting and swift. The cold was intense.

The complex was more than an Ahn behind us.

"I am hungry," I said to the Kur, half shouting, pointing to my mouth.

Its lips drew back. It lifted the whip. Again I put my weight against the traces.

When I, drawing the sled, had left the complex I had turned and looked upon it. I had stood there for a moment in awe. It was indeed an ice island, and one of considerable size. It towered more than a thousand feet above the surface ice in which it was now locked. It would extend, below the surface, much farther, probably some seven thousand or so feet. In width it was some four pasangs, I would conjecture, and in length some ten pasangs. It was not the only such island in the vicinity.

The Kur had lifted the whip behind me, and I had then turned to continue the journey, the cliffs of the ice island rearing high above and behind me.

It had been kept stabilized in its position gyroscopically during the summer. It would be located by the invasion fleet by virtue of its position.

I looked up at the stars. Already, I supposed, the troopships, with their hibernated marches, engines flaming, quiet in the near vacuum of space, burned their silent, purposeful way toward the shores of Gor.

"I am hungry," I said to the Kur.

Its lips drew back, this time in a snarl. It bared its fangs. I saw that it was considering killing me. But it would be obedient to its orders, if the situation would permit it. It was not what it seemed, a simple ice beast. It was a ship Kur, once bound by the discipline of the steel worlds, the pledges of crews and the necessary rigors of strict report lines. Unless I forced it to do so, it would not kill me until the time and place mandated in its instructions.

Yet it was displeased with me.

I saw it lift the whip. It could, of course, lash the furs from my back. But if it did so, I would soon freeze; too, the cut fur, sliced by the whip, would belie the deception of a sleen attack. It might kill me now, but then it would have to draw the sled itself, my rent body upon it, to the place or distance at which it was to be abandoned.

The Kur took the sack of meat in its paw. I reached out for it. It drew the sack back, and its lips went back about its fans. It then crouched itself upon the sled, the sack of meat before it, snarled, and lifted the whip.

I looked at it, as though in dismay. "How can I draw the sled with such weight upon it?" I asked. "Please," I said.

It reached into the sack and drew forth one of the large, heavy chunks of meat. It extended it towards me, but, when I went to take it, it drew it back and bared its fangs. I stepped back. It slipped the large chunk of meat into its mouth. I saw it swallow. Its lips drew back. Then it snarled and lifted the whip.

"Please," I said.

I saw its eyes blaze. Then it threw another piece of meat down its throat.

I turned away, and, now struggling, put my weight against the traces. The beast was indeed heavy, and it was not easy to draw the sled, its weight upon it, over the roughness and jagged contours of the ice.

Half of an Ahn later, weary, my legs heavy, my back sore, I turned once more to see the beast. It snarled and again lifted the whip. The sack which had held the meat lay empty on the sled. The beast seemed, however, generally content. Its eyes were half closed. It seemed sleepy.

I turned about and again drew the sled. It was now a matter of time.

My major fear had been that the beast would have swallowed the meat into its storage stomach, in which it would not be digested until, at the beast's will, it was disgorged into the true stomach, or chemical stomach. I did not think, however, he had swallowed the meat into the storage stomach. First, there was sufficient food at the complex, and Kurii usually do not carry excess food and water in their body except when anticipating periods of scarcity. The additional food, of course, is a weight burden and impairs performance. Secondly, the beast seemed sleepy and content, which suggested to me that it had fed, and pleasantly, to its satisfaction. The metabolism of the Kur, however, does tend to be more under its control than it is with many organisms. Even in the true, or chemical, stomach, it can, by regulating the flow of digestive juices, hasten or protract the process of digestion. For example, it commonly digests at its leisure, but, if it anticipates proximate exertions, it can hurry the process. A Kur, thus, requires a smaller time interval than many species between eating heavily and engaging in demanding physical behaviors. This trait, doubtless, has been selected for in Kur evolution. I was not particularly worried, however, for, even at a slow

383

rate of digestion, I was confident there would be time for the meat to accomplish its dark work. The sack which had been filled with meat was empty. It must have contained fifteen or twenty pieces of meat.

Suddenly the sled was lighter, for the Kur had stepped from it. I was suddenly alarmed.

It stood behind the sled, looking about. We were in a wide place, almost a shallow bowl, some hundred yards or so in diameter. It was a relatively clear place among the crags and projections of ice. From the air it might be easily identified, I supposed, even from a considerable altitude.

The Kur seemed satisfied. I began to sweat. I pulled down the collar of the parka, habitually. One does not wish to sweat in the north. One does not want it to freeze on one's body, but, even more dangerously, one does not wish one's furs to become wet and then freeze, thus robbing them of their thermal efficiency and, indeed, increasing the likelihood of a break or tear in the hides. A rent in a garment, not soon repaired, can be extremely dangerous. A needle and thread can be as important in the north as a means to make fire.

The Kur's lips drew back, in a Kur grin, seeing my action. It was foolish, in the circumstances, I supposed. Yet it is a kind of thing one does, even without thinking, when one is wise to the north.

I looked about at the shallow, moonlit bowl, in whose center we stood, the sled between us.

It seemed to me, too, objectively, a sensible place for the Kur to address himself to his hideous task. It was relatively open, easily identifiable, or as easily identifiable as any area might be in the ice, and was at a suitable distance from the complex.

It was difficult to fault the judgment of the Kur. It was an intelligent animal.

The Kur indicated that I should free myself of the harness. I did so, with my mittened hands.

We stood apart from one another. The wind had subsided now. It was very cold and desolate in that place. Its lips drew back. I saw expectoration form at the corner of its mouth, an anticipatory salivation. It froze almost immediately into beads and he broke them away from the fur about its jaw with a movement of its paw. Its breath was foglike about its head and fangs. A soft vapor, like steam, clung about its form, then wafted away, where the cold air had made contact with the warmth of that large, terrible body. It gestured that I should approach it.

I did not do so.

With one paw it struck the sled to the side, from between us.

It gestured again that I should approach it. Again I did not do so.

I backed away from it. I had no illusions that I could outrun a Kur.

It dropped down to all fours. I saw it begin to tremble in anticipation. Then it threw back its huge, shaggy head and, jaws widely distended, it long fangs white, exposed, gazed savagely upon the three calm moons of Gor. Then to the moons and to the frozen world about us, to the ice and the sky and stars, it uttered a wild, fearsome, howling cry, a long, horrifying cry. The origins of that cry, I conjecture, are lost in the vanished antiquities of the prehistory of the Kur, or of the beast that, in time, became the Kur. It was a cry that was both territorial and imperial. It was the challenge of a predator and carnivore to a world. It said, "I am here. This is my place." Too, it seemed to say, "This meat, this kill, is mine. Dispute it with me who will." It was a cry that might once have been heard in the mouths of caves, or in the darkness of forests. I had little doubt but what, eons ago, on the native world of the Kur, that cry had antedated speech and fire. Man, doubtless, has forgotten such cries. The Kur has not.

The beast turned about, twice, happily, almost leaping; then again it faced me. Its claws emerged. It scratched delightedly at the ice. It gazed upon me. It uttered a shriek anew, but one of pleasure. Its breathing was swift. It could scarcely contol itself.

I backed away, further.

It watched me, alertly, with pleasure. It growled softly, almost a purrlike sound, but more intense, more excited.

Then its ears lay back against the side of its head.

I stumbled backward, and it sped toward me, swiftly.

I struggled, seized in its arms. I saw the blazing eyes. It lifted me from the ice, lifting me toward its mouth. It held me, looking at me for a moment. Then it turned its head to one side. I struggled and twisted futilely. Its breath was hot in my face, and I could scarcely see it for the vapors of our mingled breathings. Then its jaws reached for my throat. Suddenly and so suddenly for a moment I could not comprehend it there was a hideous shriek from the beast and I could hear nothing else for a moment and it was one of surprise and pain and I was momentarily deafened and then, too, at the same time, reflexively I was flung from it the stars and ice suddenly wild and turned and I struck the ice and rolled and slid across it. I scrambled to my knees. I was more than forty feet from the beast.

It stood, not moving, hunched over, looking at me.

I rose unsteadily to my feet.

It tried to take a step toward me, and then its face contorted with excruciating pain. It lifted its paw toward me.

Then, suddenly, as though struck from the inside, it screamed and fell, rolling, on the ice. Twice more it cried out, and then lay, motionless, but alive, on the ice, on its back, looking up at the moons.

The digestive juices, already released into the true stomach, continued with their implaccable chemical work. Bit by bit, loosened molecule by loosened molecule, in accordance with the patient, relentless laws of chemistry, the sinew slowly dissolved, weakening the bond which held the compressed, contorted, sharpened baleen, until the slender bond broke. The beast screamed again.

Thoughtlessly the beast must have devoured fifteen or twenty of the hidden traps.

I thought now I had little to fear.

I went to the sled. There seemed little of use there.

Fortunately I glanced upward. Somehow it was again on its feet.

It stood hunched over. It looked at me. How indomitable it was. It coughed, wracked with the pain of it, and spat glots of blood on the ice.

Slowly, step by step, it began to move toward me, its paws outstretched.

It then screamed with pain, bent over, as another of the wicked traps sprang open.

It stood there, whimpering on the ice. For a moment I felt moved.

Then, scrambling, on all fours, it charged. I overturned the sled between us. It fell screaming against the head of the sled and, with one paw, swept the sled to one side. It rolled on the ice, leaving it dark with blood. It coughed and screamed, and raged. Then two more of the treacherous baleen traps sprung open. It looked at the moons, agonized. It bit its lips and jaws in pain. It tore at its thigh.

I moved warily away from the beast. I did not think, now, I would have great difficulty in eluding it.

It was bleeding now, profusely, at the mouth and anus. The side of its mouth was half bitten through. The ice was covered with blood, and defecation. Too, it had released its water on the ice.

I moved away from it, drawing it in a circle from the sled. I then doubled back and, taking up the traces of the sled, turned back toward the complex concealed in the ice island.

I pulled the sled, returning toward the complex. The beast, step by painful step, bloody in the snow, followed. I did not let it approach too near.

Judging by its cries, those uttered before, and those which it uttered as it followed me, it must have taken nineteen of the traps into its body. It amazed me that it was not content to lie still and die. Each step must have been torture for it. Yet it continued to follow me. I learned something from it of the tenacity of the Kur.

At last, on the return to the complex, some four Ahn later, it died.

It is not easy to kill a Kur.

I looked down at the huge carcass. I had no knife. I must use my hands and teeth.

35 I RETURN TO THE COMPLEX; WHAT OCCURRED IN THE COMPLEX

"It is not a Kur!" cried the man. "Fire!"

Then I had my hands on his throat, and threw him between me and his fellow. I heard the dart enter his body and I thrust him back and away from me and I saw him, rent and scattered, burst apart. The other fellow, also in what seemed to be a suit of light plastic, with a heating unit slung at his hip, fumbled with the weapon, to insert another charge in the breech. I dove toward him and the breech snapped shut and the weapon, struck to the side, discharged and I flung him to the ground, we both half tangled in the white fur of the Kur. With my left arm about his neck I struck his head to the side with the flat of my right hand. He lay still, the neck broken. It is a thing warriors are taught.

I looked up. It seemed quiet. Yet two weapons had been discharged. The tubular weapons discharge with a hiss. It is not particularly loud. The explosion of the darts, however, timed to detonate an instant after fixing themselves in the target, is much louder. The first explosion had been muffled in the body of its victim. The second, however, might have been heard. It had burst, after a long, parabolic trajectory, over a thousand feet below, showering ice upward more than two hundred feet into the air.

I had returned to the complex, crossing the ice near it, with the sled. This would assure me, I hoped, that I would not be mistaken for a common ice beast. I did not know what signs and countersigns, or signals, the white Kur might have had at its disposal to protect itself in this regard. I, at any rate, had none. Ice beasts, or common ice beasts, of course, do not use sleds. I think the sled let me approach more closely than I might otherwise have been capable of doing. The fur of the Kur, too, in the uncertain light, of course, was helpful. I had kept, too, as I could, to the cover of the pack ice. I had left the sled at the foot of the ice island and, with the fur of the Kur as a camouflage, had climbed, crag by crag, projection by projection, foothold by foothold, to the height of the island. The hatch through which I had exited did not have an obvious opening from the outside. Again, I did not know any signs or countersigns, or signals. I had climbed the height of the ice island looking for some mode of ingress to the complex. I was interested not so much in official thresholds, of a sort which I supposed would be provided to facilitate the work of lookouts and guards, as apertures more practical to my purposes, apertures unguarded through which passage would not require any system of recognition devices. The air in the complex had been fresh. It was my hope that there would be ventilation shafts. If the Kurri relied on a closed system I must take my chances with more standard portals.

It seemed quiet. I reached again for the fur of the Kur.

It came so swiftly I was not sure I saw it. I may have heard or sensed it the object cutting the fur of the parka and lodging a foot behind me in the ice and I flung myself away from

388

it and the ice shattering and exploding outward and the blast and ice pushing me like a hand and I struck a projection of ice and slipped downward, and then I saw them coming two of them both armed and I slipped and lay contorted at the foot of the ice projection.

"He's dead," said one of the men.

"I shall put another dart into him," said the other.

"Do not be a fool," said the first.

"Can you be sure he is dead?" asked the other.

"See?" said the first. "There is no breath. If he were alive his breath, its vapor in the cold, would be clearly visible."

"You are right," said the second man.

Neither of these men, I gathered, had ever hunted the swift sea sleen. I was pleased that once, in kayaks, with Imnak, I had made the acquaintance of that menacing, insidious beast.

"Aiii!" cried the first man, as I leaped upward, striking him aside with my right hand. It was the second man whom I must first reach. He was the more suspicious, the more dangerous of the two. His weapon contained a dart, at the ready. The weapon lifted swiftly but already I was behind it. The other man had not reinjected a dart into the riflelike contrivance he carried. I turned to him when I had finished the first. I did not realize until later he had struck me with its stock from behind. His scream was long and fading as he fell to the ice below the cliffs.

I quickly sorted through the accouterments of the second man. I must move quickly. Not only was dispatch of tactical significance but exposure to the arctic winter could bring a swift death on the summit of the ice island. In moments I wore one of the light, plastic suits, with hood, with the heating unit slung at the hip. I did not know how long the charge in the unit would last but I did not expect to be needing it long. I then took the sack of darts from the second man and threw it, on its strap, about my shoulder. I gathered in the two weapons which they had carried.

Another object lay on the ice, a small, portable radio. A voice, in Gorean, was speaking urgently on the device, inquiring as to what was occurring. I did not attempt to respond or confuse the operator. I thought it better to let him ponder what might have happened high above on the surface of that rugged island of ice. If I responded I was sure I would be soon marked as a human intruder. If my voice would not betray me surely my failure to produce code words or identificatory phrases would do so. As it was the operator could speculate on possibilities such as a transmitter malfunction, an accident, or an attack of wandering ice beasts. An investigatory party would soon be sent forth to investigate. This did not displease me. The more men there were outside the complex the fewer there would be inside. The various hatches, also, I was confident, would not open from the outside. If they did, the mechanisms could always be jammed or destroyed. I knew I had at least one ally within, Imnak, who would risk his life to protect me. He had already done so.

In short order I managed to find one of the ventilator shafts through which fresh air was drawn into the complex; there was a system of such shafts, some for drawing in fresh air and others for expelling used, stale air. Kurii, with their large lungs, and the need to oxygenate their large quantities of blood, are extremely sensitive to the quality of an atmosphere. Ship Kurri, crashed or marooned on Earth, have usually made their way to remote areas, not simply to avoid human habitations but to secure access to a less polluted, more tolerable atmosphere. Kurii, incidentally, because of their unusual lung capacity, can breathe easily even at relatively high altitudes. They have little tolerance, however, for pollutants. Kur agents on Earth are almost always humans.

I could not remove the grating at the top of the shaft. It was fixed into the metal, welded therein.

I stepped back and depressed the firing switch on one of the tubular weapons. I then set another dart into the breech. It was not, however, necessary. The metal was broken loose and twisted crookedly upward. The opening was not too large, but it would be enough. I felt around inside the darkened shaft with my hand, and then with the barrel of a weapon. I could find no handholds or footholds. I did not know the depth of the shaft, but I supposed it must be a hundred or more feet, at least. I had no rope. I slipped into the shaft, sweating, my back against one side, my two feet against the other side. Thus began a slow and tortuous descent, inch by inch. The slightest mistake in judgment, as to position or leverage, and I would plummet within the shaft, helpless, until I struck its bottom, however far below it might be.

It took more than a quarter of an Ahn to descend the shaft.

The last twenty feet I slipped and, pushing and thrusting, fell clattering to its bottom.

The grille at the lower end, some seven feet above a steel

floor, and opening into a hall, was not fixed as solidly as the one above. Indeed, to my amazement, I lifted it out.

"What kept you?" asked Imnak.

He was sitting on two boxes, at the side, whittling a parsit fish from sleen bone.

"I was detained," I said.

"You were very noisy," said Imnak.

"Sorry," I said.

I saw that the screws holding the lighter grille in place had been removed. That is why it lifted out.

"You removed the screws from the grille with your knife," I said.

"Would you have preferred to kick it loose?" asked Imnak.

"No," I said. Then I said, "How did you know to find me here?"

"I thought you would have difficulty explaining your right to enter to the guards at the hatches," said Imnak.

"Surely there are many ventilator shafts," I said.

"Yes," said Imnak, "but not many with people crawling down them."

"Here," I said, handing Imnak one of the tubular weapons, and several of the darts from the bag which I carried.

"What good is this?" asked Imnak. "It blows apart the meat, and there is no place to put a line on the point."

"It is good for shooting people," I said.

"Yes," said Imnak, "it might do for that."

"It is my intention, Imnak," I said, "to locate and detonate the device concealed in this complex which is intended to prevent the supplies here from falling into the hands of enemies."

"That is a long thing to say," he said.

"I want to find a switch or lever," I said, "which will make this whole place go boom bang crash, as when the dart hits a target and makes a big noise."

"I do not know the words 'boom' and 'bang'," said Imnak. "Are they Gorean?"

"I want to make a thing like thunder and lightning, crash, crash," I said, angrily.

"You want to cause an explosion?" asked Imnak.

"Yes," I said.

"That seems like a good idea," said Imnak.

"Where did you hear about explosions?" I asked Imnak.

"Karjuk told me," said Imnak.

"Where is Karjuk?" I asked.

"He is somewhere outside," said Imnak.

"Did he ever speak to you of a device to destroy the complex?" I asked.

"Yes," said Imnak.

"Did he tell you where it is?" I asked.

"No," said Imnak. "I do not think he knows where it is."

"Imnak," I said, "I want you to take this weapon, and get yourself, and as many of the girls as you can, out of the complex."

Imnak shrugged, puzzled.

"Do not dally," I told him.

"What about you?" he asked.

"Do not worry about me," I said.

"All right," said Imnak.

He turned to leave. "If you see Karjuk," I said, "kill him."

"Karjuk would not like that," said Imnak.

"Do it," I said.

"But where will we get another guard?" he asked.

"Karjuk does not guard the People," I said. "He guards Kurii."

"How do you know what he guards?" asked Imnak.

"Forget about Karjuk," I said.

"All right," said Imnak.

"Hurry, hurry!" I told him. "Leave! Hurry!"

"Is it all right if I worry a little about you, Tarl, who hunts with me?" he asked.

"Yes, yes," I said, "you can worry a little."

"Good," said Imnak. Then he turned about and hurried down the hall.

I looked upward. In the ceiling where the slave tracks, those steel guides determining, by virtue of the steel spheres and neck chains, the permissible movements of various girls.

At that moment, down the hall, coming about a corner, were two men, in brown and black tunics.

"Why are you in the suit?" they asked me.

"I came from the surface," I said. "There is trouble up there."

"What sort of trouble?" asked one.

"We do not know yet," I said.

"Are you in security?" asked one of the men.

"Yes," I said.

"We do not see much of you fellows," said one.

"It is better that you fellows know only your own sections," I said.

"There is greater security that way," said one.

"Yes," agreed the other.

"If you see anything suspicious, report it," I advised them.

"We shall," said the first man.

"In the meantime, see that the grille on that shaft is replaced," I said.

"We'll take care of it," they said.

"Why is it open?" asked one.

"I was checking it," I said.

"Oh," said the other.

"You forgot to turn off the heat unit on your suit," said one. "That will use up the charge."

I pushed in the button which was more raised than its fellow on the panel of the device.

"I forgot that once," said one of the men. "It is easy to do, the suit maintaining a standard temperature."

"Perhaps they should have a light on the panel," I said.

"That would show up in the dark," said one of the men.

"That is true," I said.

I then left the men and they, behind me, set themselves to replace the grille in the ventilator shaft.

I encountered few humans in the corridors. Once I did encounter some twenty men, in a column of twos, moving swiftly down one hall. They were led by a lieutenant and were all armed.

I assumed they were on their way to the surface, to aid in the search and investigation which must now be underway high above.

It would be only a matter of time until the blasted ventilator grating, some two hundred feet above, at the height of the shaft, would be located.

The girl approaching me down the corridor was very beautiful. She was, of course, slave. She was barefoot. She wore a brief bit of transparent brown slave silk, gathered before her and loosely knotted at her navel. She was steel-collared. She carried a bronze vessel on her right shoulder. She was brown-haired, with long brown hair, and brown-eyed. She was a sweet-hipped slave. A chain, some feet in length, was attached to her collar, which slid easily behind her, she drawing it, as she made her way toward me. If she were to stand under the sphere holding the chain above her in its track the chain would fall, gracefully looped, behind her, almost to the back of her knees, whence it would rise again to its lock point on her collar. This slack in the chain makes it possible not only for the girl to kneel but for her to be put on her back on the steel plates.

I stopped walking in the corridor, and she continued to approach, until she was about ten feet from me. At that point she knelt, putting the bronze vessel to one side. She knelt back on her heels, her knees wide, her hands on her thighs, her back straight, her head down. It is a beautiful and significant position. It well betokens the submission of the female to the free man, her master. She was at my will.

I observed her for a time, noting her helplessness and her beauty.

"Master?" she asked, not raising her head. I did not beat her.

She lifted her head. "Master?" she asked, trembling.

"Are you so eager to feel the whip?" I asked.

"Forgive me, Master," she said. She put her head down.

"I am new in the complex," I said. "I would have information."

"Yes, Master," she said.

"Stand, and approach me," I said, "and turn the other way."

She did so. I pushed her head forward and threw her hair to the side. A heavy steel padlock was attached to the chain. The tongue of this lock had been placed about the steel collar, between the metal and the back of her neck, and snapped shut. The tongue was thick and the lock must have weighed a quarter of a pound. "This must not be comfortable," I said.

"Is Master concerned with the comfort of a slave?" she asked.

"It was merely an observation." I said. The tiny hairs on the back of a girl's neck are very exciting.

"There are various sorts of collars," she said. "Some have a ring on the back, to take the lock. I think they did not realize, in the beginning, how many girls they would bring here. Some of the chains have links wide enough to simply use the chain itself, looped and locked about the girl's throat."

"This is an adapted slave collar," I said, "though it is a size too large for you."

"That is to accommodate the lock tongue, when it is shut into the lock," she said.

"There are two tiny yellow bands on your collar," I said.

"That is because I am a "yellow girl," " she said.

"There are also two yellow bands on the lock," I said.

"Our collars are color coded to the locks and chains," she said.

"And you are a "yellow girl,' " I said.

"Yes, Master," she said.

"What is your name?" I asked.

"Belinda," she said, "if it pleases master."

"It is a lovely name," I said.

"Thank you, Master," she said. I would not beat her for not having a pleasing name.

"What other sorts of girls are there here?" I asked.

"There are five color-coded collars," she said, "red, orange, yellow, green and blue. Each color permits a girl a different amount of freedom in the tracks."

"Are you kept constantly on these chains?" I asked.

"No, Master," she said. "We wear them only when sent on errands."

"And when you are not on errands?" I asked.

"We are kept safely under lock and key," she said.

"Are all girls in coded collars?" I asked.

"No, Master," she said, "the true beauties are kept in steel pleasure rooms, for the sport of the men."

"Explain to me the color system," I said.

"Blue is most limited," she said. "Green may go where blue may go, and further. I am a yellow. I may go where blue and green may go, but, too, I have access to areas beyond theirs. I may not go as far as the orange collar permits. Where I am stopped, they may continue. The maximum amount of freedom is enjoyed by a girl who wears a collar with two red bands."

She looked at me, over her shoulder.

"But surely Master knows these things," she said.

I turned her about, facing me, and threw her back against the steel wall.

"Forgive me, Master," she said.

"Place the palms of your hands back, against the wall," I said.

She did so.

"You are not of the complex," she said, suddenly. "You are an intruder," she whispered.

With the barrel of the tubular weapon I tore open the loose knot holding the pleasure silk together at her navel. It fell, parted, to either side. She winced, backed against the steel wall. The barrel of the riflelike contrivance, deep in her belly, held her in place.

"Do not kill me, Master," she said. "I am only a slave."

"Slaves sometimes speak much," I told her.

"I will not speak," she said.

"Kneel," I said.

She did so.

"I will not speak," she said. "I promise I will not speak, Master!"

"You are very beautiful, Belinda," I told her. I held the barrel of the gun at her face.

"I will not speak," she whispered. "I will not betray you."

"Take the barrel of the gun in your mouth," I told her. She did so, timidly.

"You know what this can do to you, do you not?" I asked.

She nodded, kneeling, terrified.

"You are not going to speak, are you?" I asked.

She made tiny, terrified, negative movements of her head. Her mouth was very beautiful about the steel. She had not been given permission to release it.

"Yes, very beautiful," I said.

With the barrel of the weapon I guided her downward, to her side, and then lay the weapon on the plates. Her head was turned to the side. She did not dare to release the weapon. I then began to caress her. To my amazement, almost immediately, she began to respond helplessly, spasmodically. "What a slave you are," I chided. She moaned, and wept and whimpered, but could not speak. When I stood up, and took the weapon from her mouth, she looked at me, startled; she half rose from the floor, turning on her left thigh, her right leg drawn up, the palms of her hands on the floor, her lovely body deeply mottled, a terrain of crimson, with the intense capillary activity which I had induced in her. "Your slave," she said.

I turned about. I did not think she would speak.

I continued on down the halls. Some more men passed me, and two girls. I checked the collars on the girls. One was blue, and one was yellow.

I moved swiftly, and yet the complex was a labyrinth. I did not think any of the humans in the complex would be likely to know the location of the device for which I sought. And I did not think any Kur would reveal it.

I sped rapidly down the hall.

A siren began to whine. It was very loud in the steel corridor.

I slowed my pace to pass a fellow in the brown and black tunic of the personnel of the complex.

"There is an intruder above," I said loudly to him.

"No," he said. "A ventilation shaft grating was found blasted on the surface. There is reason to believe he may now be within the complex."

"Of course," I said, "the siren. It is an internal security alert."

"Keep a close watch," said the fellow.

"Be assured I shall," I said.

We hurried apart from one another. I kept my eyes on the overhead track system. Then I came to a branching in the corridor. The overhead track system, which I had hoped to follow to its termination, also branched at this point. Further, I could see other branchings further away, down each of the corridors. The track system doubtless reached to the far corners, or almost to the far corners, of this level, and, descending and ascending, above stairwells, to various other levels, as well. The siren was loud, persistent, maddening. I cursed inwardly. Here and there in the corridors, and here, too, where I now stood, there was a surveillance lens mounted high in the ceiling, on a swivel. I saw it move, remotely controlled from somewhere, in a scanning pattern. The guard's garb which I wore had been, until now, apparently, suitable disguise. I started off down one of the corridors, intent not to appear indecisive or vacillating. I wished it to seem that I knew my way about. When I glanced back the lens was oriented in a different direction. It had not been trained on me. Two more men passed me in the hall. Each carried one of the dart-firing weapons.

I cursed inwardly. It could take a great deal of time to explore the remote areas of the complex. I did not know, first, where the most remote areas accessible to the overhead track lay or where the surveillance devices, which might be available to human beings, might not scan. The destructive device I sought, I was confident, would lie in an area beyond the reach of the overhead track system and, I conjectured, in an area not public to the surveillance system. I recalled that no such device had been revealed by the monitors in the private chamber of Zarendargar, Half-Ear, war general of the Kurii.

I recalled the girl I had left on the steel plates far behind me, the chain dangling down from the overhead track system to the collar on her neck.

She was a "yellow." I needed a "red."

I looked up at the track above me, angrily. At one of its terminations, doubtless the most remote, lay the area which I sought.

The siren stopped whining, and a voice, over a speaker system, in Gorean began to speak. "Secure all slaves," it said. "All personnel report to their stations." This message was repeated five times. Some men ran past me. There was then silence in the halls.

It was an intelligent arrangement. In times of danger Gorean slaves are often chained or confined that they may in no way effect the outcome of whatever action may ensue. They will helplessly await their eventual disposition at the hands of masters. That all personnel were to report to their stations would provide the leaders in the complex with an accounting of their forces and suddenly make the surveillance system of the complex effective. A lone figure would be easily identified as the intruder.

I thrust open a door in the hallway. I saw a man within who was securing slaves. He had thrust them, ten girls, naked, in a row, kneeling, belly tight against a steel wall. On short neck chains, with collars, he fastened them in place. Their wrists, at the sides of their heads, in light manacles fastened to wall rings, were similarly secured. He looked up. "I'm hurrying!" he said, angrily. I did not speak. He snapped the right wrist of the last girl on the line in its manacle. He then slipped the key in his pouch and, looking at me angrily, hurried out of the room.

The girls, bellies and bodies tight against the wall, were frightened, but they made not the least sound.

To one side, aligned on the wall, were several track chains, with their attached locks. I found one which had a heavy lock, its key attached, which had on it two red bands. Its chain would fit the longest tracks in the complex.

I then went to the girls, to check the graceful, slender steel collars they wore, those lighter, characteristic slave collars about which the heavy iron wall collars had been closed.

I found two that were marked in two tiny red bands.

"Where is the key to your chains?" I asked one of them.

"Our keeper has it, Master," she said.

I had feared it would be the case. I had not attempted to kill or detain their keeper. His failure to report at his station would surely have localized my whereabouts in the complex.

I looked about, angrily.

I could not free one of the red-collar girls. Both had been

well chained by a Gorean master. There was no time to test and play with the locks, and each wench was secured by three devices, each sufficient to hold her. The explosive darts at my disposal, addressed to their bonds, would surely have destroyed them.

I turned about and, taking one of the chains, sliding it in its track, left the area where the girls were secured. If I were successful in detonating or initiating the trigger sequence on the apparatus I sought I hoped that it would destroy only those parts of the complex in which the munitions and supplies were stored. Perhaps Imnak would succeed in finding and freeing them, somehow. I had wanted him to evacuate as many girls as possible from the complex. And yet, nude, or in their silks, would they last more than an Ahn outside in the polar night? There were probably many such girls in the complex, now helplessly chained, beautiful, secured slaves. They would be, presumably, innocent victims in the wars of beasts and men. Then I dismissed them from my mind; I was again Gorean; I had work to do; they were only slaves.

I re-entered the hall, sliding the chain with me. I had little doubt I would soon be noticed.

I wondered how long was the track in which the chain slid. Such a chain, without its secured beauty, would be sure to attract attention.

I passed various doors in the hall. There were training rooms, exercise chambers, apartments. If I chose merely to hide it would take the men of the complex a good deal of time to find me. But I could accomplish little by such an action.

I descended some stairs to a lower lever, following the path set by the sliding chain.

I heard some men about a corner, running in step. I let the chain dangle and, hastily, took refuge in a side room, a pantry. I took a roll from a basket and fed on it. The men passed. They had brushed aside the chain, paying it no attention. Perhaps a girl had been removed from it for chaining by the nearest guard when the instructions concerning slave security had been issued over the speaker system. When I was about to re-enter the hall I suddenly stepped back. A guard and a free woman, in robes of concealment, had passed. I had not understood until then that such women might be in the complex. There was an intruder in the complex. She was being conducted, doubtless, to a place of greater security. Perhaps this level was being cleared for purposes of conducting a close search. I finished the roll taken from the basket and left the pantry area.

Outside I encountered two more pairs of individuals, two guards and two more of the free women. I gathered they might be being trained in the complex for their duties later.

"He's not in there," I said to the men, gesturing with my head to the pantry from which I had emerged. Then I said to them, "Hurry!"

They hurried on.

I caught sight of a flash of ankle beneath the heavy robes of concealment worn by the women. It was a trim, exciting ankle. I smiled. I supposed they had not been told that when their political and military work for their faction was completed they would be silked and collared and kept as slaves.

Another man hurried by, running a slave girl on her neck chain before him. She was a yellow-collar girl, as Belinda, whom I had earlier had in the halls, had been. She was still in a snatch of slave silk. "She should be secured," I said to the man, sternly.

"She will be," he said.

I heard another man coming, from behind me. I spun about, covering him with the weapon I carried.

"Do not fire," he said. "I am Gron, from Al-Ka section."

"What are you doing in this area," I said.

"I have come to fetch the Lady Rosa," he said.

"In what apartment is she," I demanded.

"Forty-two," he said, "Central Level Minus one, Mu corridor."

"Correct," I told him, lowering the weapon.

He breathed more easily.

"I will fetch her," I said. Indeed, I had need of a wench. "Return to Al-Ka section."

He hesitated momentarily.

"Hurry," I said, angrily. "A condition of possible danger exists."

He lifted his hand, acknowledging this, and turned about. He soon disappeared down the corridor.

I soon determined that I was in Mu corridor, from Gorean markings high on the wall near a point where the corridor branched in two directions. It seemed probable to me that I was on the appropriate level as I had encountered the man at some distance from the nearest stairway.

I saw no others at that time in the corridor. I slid the chain along beside me.

Soon I had come to the steel door marked forty-two. I saw that a branch of the recessed chain track, above, entered the apartment, doubtless so that the Lady Rosa could be served by appropriately secured female slaves. I opened the door and slid the chain, on its track, within the opening. Inside the apartment was luxurious, plush and silked. It was dimly lit by five candles in a tall floor stand. There was much ornate, intricate carving in the room. A woman, startled, leaped up from the large, rounded bed on which she had sat. She wore the robes of concealment. She whipped the silken sheath of a veil across her features.

"You should knock, you fool," she said. "I had scarcely time to conceal my features."

She looked at me, her eyes flashing over the veil. Her features were, even veiled, not particularly concealed. Her face was narrow but very beautiful. She had extremely dark eyes, and dark hair, even bluish black, which, under the hood of the robes, I could see was drawn back about the sides of her head. Her cheekbones were quite high. Her face was regal, aristocratic, and cold. She was angry.

"You are the Lady Rosa?" I asked.

She drew herself up coldly. "I am the Lady Graciela Consuelo Rosa Rivera-Sanchez," she said. "What is going on?" she asked.

"There is an intruder in the complex," I said.

"Has he yet been apprehended?" she asked.

"No," I said. "How long have you been in the complex?"

"Four months," she said. Then she said, "Four Gorean months, not yet completing the fourth passage hand."

"Are you familiar with the chain-and-track system, for controlling the movements of slaves?" I asked.

"Of course," she said.

"At its remotest terminations?" I asked.

"Yes," she said, "but humans are not allowed beyond those points."

I smiled.

"How could an intruder penetrate the complex?" she asked.

"By means of a ventilator shaft," I said. "You speak Gorean rather well," I said, "though with a distinct accent."

"I have been intensively trained," she said.

That accent, I thought, which was aristocratic and Castilian, would not be objected to by most Gorean masters.

"I have high linguistic aptitudes," she said, coldly.

I thought that that was fortunate for her. She would more quickly be able to understand and please a master in the subtleties of his pleasure, once she was totally owned by one. On the other hand, almost any girl, in a condition of slavery, learns quickly. She must. Slave girls are incredibly alert to the subtlest and most delicate nuances of a master's speech. The tiniest inflection can tell her whether her master is joking with her or, if she does not do something differently almost instantaneously, that she is to be mercilessly whipped. Girls in collars strive to learn well the language of their masters. Differences among them in the swiftness with which the various proficiency levels are attained are functions, generally, of native aptitude and exposure conditions. The slave girl is, doubtless, among the most highly motivated of female language students. Yet, if they begin to learn Gorean as adults, or young adults, they will almost always retain traces of their native tongue. I have encountered girls on Gor who spoke Gorean with a variety of Earth accents.

"What does the intruder want in the complex?" inquired the woman.

"At the moment he needs a woman," I said.

"I do not understand," she said.

"Remove your clothing," I said.

She looked at me, startled.

"Or I shall do it for you," I said. "I am the intruder," I explained.

She backed away. "Never," she said.

"Very well," I said. "Lie on the bed, on your stomach, with your hands and legs apart." I drew forth the knife at the belt of the garment I wore. It is not wise to try to tear away the garments of a free woman with one's bare hands. They may contain poisoned needles.

"You're joking," she said.

I gestured with the knife to the bed.

"You would not dare," she hissed.

"To the bed," I said.

"I am the Lady Graciela Consuelo Rosa Rivera-Sanchez," she said.

"If you are pretty enough," I said, "perhaps I will call you Pepita."

"You would take away my clothes, wouldn't you?" she said.

"I am Gorean," I told her. I took a step toward her.

"Do not touch me," she said. "I will do it."

402

Her small hands reluctantly went to the hooks at the throat of the garments.

"The veil, and hood, first," I said.

She brushed them back, with a movement of her hand, a toss of her head.

"You would bring a high price," I told her.

She looked at me in fury.

"Step from your slippers," I told her.

She did so. She was then barefoot.

"Continue," I told her.

Her hands again went to the hooks at the throat of the garments. Angrily, deliberately, she loosened the hooks, one by one.

She pulled the garments down a bit from her throat. Her throat was slender and lovely. It would take an engraved steel collar, bearing her master's name, beautifully.

Her hands were at the two outer robes. She looked at me.

"We do not have all day," I told her.

They fell about her ankles.

"Between the third and fourth robes," I told her, "there is a sheathed dagger, concealed in the lining. Keep your hands away from it."

"You are observant," she said.

A warrior is trained to look for such things.

The third and fourth robe slipped to the floor, about her ankles.

There remained now but the fifth robe, and the light, sleeveless, greenish-silk, sliplike undergown.

Her hands hesitated at the throat of the fifth robe.

"Off with it," I told her.

It, like the others, fell about her ankles.

"Step from the robes," I said.

She did so.

She was very slender, and exquisite, in the sheath of green silk.

"Do not make me strip further, I beg of you," she said.

"Turn about," I said.

With the knife I cut the cord binding back her hair.

"Excellent," I said.

Her flesh was very light; her hair, long, reaching below the small of her back, thick and lovely, was marvelously black. It contrasted vividly with the remarkable paleness of her arms, her shoulders and back. I wondered if she realized that women of her paleness and beauty had, in effect, like certain

403

other types, been sexually selected, over generations, even on her native world, a world which seldom consciously thought of itself as a world breeding slaves. Many strains and types of beautiful women, of course, had been developed on Earth. The Lady Rosa was an excellent specimen of one such type. Earth women have been bred for love and beauty; it is unfortunate that they are educated for frustration.

I found a comb on a nearby vanity. Sheathing my knife and holding her by the back of the neck with my left hand I swiftly, but with some care, combed out her hair.

She sobbed in anger when the tiny, cloth-enfolded needle, tipped with kanda, fell from her hair, caught, and drawn out, by the teeth of the comb of kailiauk tusk.

I turned her about, roughly.

I looked down at her.

She looked up at me, her eyes flashing. "I am now defenseless," she said.

"Yes," I said.

With my knife I cut the thin shoulder straps of the sheathlike garment of greenish silk. With the back of the knife to her skin I moved the garment down and away from her, until it was at her ankles. She shuddered when the coldness of the knife blade moved against her flesh. She looked down at the knife, apprehensively. "What do you want me for?" she said. "Are you going to rape me?"

She looked at the large, round bed, soft and deep, covered with green silk. Well could she conceive of herself upon it, at my mercy, rightless, abused for my pleasure.

"You would have to earn your right to serve upon such a bed," I told her. "A wench such as you would have to first learn your lessons in the dirt or on straw, or on a fur thrown over cement at the foot of a master's couch, under the slave ring."

I took her by the hair and pulled her to the side of the room, near some chests.

There, from a chest, I took two sandal strings. With one of these I tied her hands behind her back. A sandal string is more than sufficient to hold a female. The other sandal string I tied snugly about her belly. I then took forth a long, linear face veil; it was red; it was an intimacy veil; any given layer of this veil is quite diaphanous; its opacity is a function of the number of times it is wrapped about the face; a free woman, entertaining an anxious lover, might detain him for days, each night permitting him a less obscure glimpse of her

features, until the shattering moment when she perhaps permits him to gaze upon her unclothed face. Such nonsense, of
course, is not tolerated from a slave girl. She is simply ordered to the slave ring. The intimacy veil, I detected, had
never been worn by the Lady Rosa. Its presence in her
wardrobe was doubtless merely a function of the desire of
her employers to assure its completeness and her adequate
familiarity with Gorean customs, a familiarity she might have
to develop in order to prosecute certain missions which might
be expected of her on Gor.

I looped the intimacy veil about the back of her neck and
crossed it above her breasts and drew it to the sides, over her
breasts, and then took both lengths around her body and behind her back, again crossing them, then looping them about
the sandal string tight on her waist; I then took the two loose
ends and passed them between her legs, drawing them up
snugly and passing them behind and over the sandal string at
her belly. I straightened the two layers of loose cloth in front;
they were about six inches in width and fell beautifully below
her knees.

She looked at me with horror.

"It will do for slave silk," I said.

I pulled her by the arm before a large mirror in the room.

She moaned, regarding herself.

"Note the slip knot on the sandal string," I said. "The
string may be removed by a simple tug."

"Beast!" she wept.

I observed her slim, lovely thigh. I thought it would look
well incised with the standard Kajira mark of Gor; it is the
first letter, in cursive script, of the word 'Kajira', the most
common word for a female slave in the Gorean lexicon; it is
a simple, rather floral mark, simple, befitting a slave, lovely,
befitting a woman.

She struggled before the mirror, but I held her in place by
her left arm.

Yes, the mark would look well on her thigh.

"I have put you in red silk," I said. "Is it appropriate?"

"It certainly is not!" she said.

"Perhaps it soon will be," I said.

She struggled fiercely, futilely. Then she stopped struggling.
"I will give you gold, much gold, to free me," she said.

"I do not want your gold," I said.

She looked at me, startled, frightened.

I dragged her to the threshold of her apartment. It was

there that the chain dangled from its overhead track, within the door.

"What do you want of me?" she begged. "The tiles are cold on my feet," she said. "Untie me," she said. "No!" she cried.

I had lifted the chain and was looping it about her neck. I did so, four times. She would feel its weight. The loops would conceal to some extent that she wore no collar. The chain was color coded with two red bands. I thrust the heavy tongue of the stout padlock through two links of the chain. I then snapped it shut. It, too, was color coded with two, tiny red bands. I looked at her. She was now a component in the chain-and-track system of the complex.

"I am the Lady Graciela Consuelo Rosa Rivera-Sanchez," she said.

"Be quiet, Pepita," I said.

She gasped. Then she said, "No! Do not force me outside the apartment clothed like this!"

I thrust her through the door, out into the corridor. She looked at me with misery, the chain dangling behind her. She realized that she would be marched anywhere, if and as I pleased.

I looked at her. I carried the dart-firing, riflelike contrivance with me.

I now had my guide.

The red silk would diminish suspicion. A red-silked girl in a Gorean fortress is a not uncommon sight. Suspicion, if any, would be most likely generated by the fact that she was not, under the security alert, in close chains, in a holding area. Her modesty had made it unlikely that many in the complex would recognize her body or features, which had, I gathered, been generally kept from view by the multitudinous robes and veils of concealment common to the Gorean free women of the high cities.

She sank to her knees in misery.

I expected that Kurii would be manning the lensed monitors in the hall. I did not think they would notice, with the resolution available to normal scanning, that she lacked the small brand on the thigh. They would have been more suspicious had her thighs been covered. Similarly I did not expect them to note, under the loops of chain, with the standard lens resolutions they would use, similar to those in Half-Ear's compartment, I supposed, that she lacked the slender steel collar of the Gorean slave girl.

406

"On your feet," I said.

She struggled to her feet, and stood, regarding me.

"On the red-collar system," I said, "which is the most extensive in the track, is there any termination more remote than any of the others."

"Yes," she said.

This surprised me.

"Take me to it," I said.

She drew herself up, proudly. "No," she said. She winced, the barrel of the riflelike contrivance thrust into her belly. I forced her back until she was pinned against the wall. "You would not," she said.

"You are only a woman," I told her.

"I will take you!" she said. "But it will do you no good, for humans are not allowed beyond that point!"

"Which way?" I asked.

Her eyes indicated the direction.

I thrust her, roughly, stumbling, with the side of the riflelike contrivance, in that direction.

"Faster," I told her.

We proceeded swiftly down the corridor.

"If we pass men," she said, "you know I need only cry out to them."

"Do so," I said, "and half of you may remain on the chain." I had not gagged her, for that, surely, would have provoked suspicion.

"Faster," I ordered. I prodded her with the barrel of the riflelike contrivance and she cried out with pain, stumbling, and hurried her pace.

Soon she was gasping. She was an Earth girl. She was not in the condition of the Gorean slave girl, with her almost perfect diet, imposed by masters, her muscles toned by a regime of exercises, her legs and wind toughened by long hours of training in sensuous dance.

I saw one of the lens monitors rotate on its swivel in our direction.

"Hurry, Kajira," I said. "It is long past the time when you should have been secured."

The monitor turned away.

For several Ehn we hurried through the halls. Sometimes we descended stairwells. She was sweating and gasping. The chain was heavy on her neck and shoulders. "Hurry, pretty Pepita," I encouraged her.

407

Then, on a given level, four below the central level, we saw four men approaching.

"Walk," I told her.

I walked beside her, obscuring her left thigh.

She shuddered, seeing how the men looked at her. One of them laughed. "A new girl," he said.

In less than four Ehn, from that point, the track system terminated.

"This is the farthest reach of the track system," she said. The chain dangled downward, then looped up to her neck. Her small wrists twisted futilely behind her in the encircling, knotted sandal string, that simple device which constituted her bond. "Humans may not go further."

"Have you seen those who are not humans?" I asked.

I knew there were few Kurii in the complex.

"No," she said, "but I know them to be a form of alien. Doubtless they are humanlike, perhaps indistinguishable from humans."

I smiled. She had not seen the beasts she served.

"I have brought you here," she said, "now free me."

I opened the padlock and freed her neck of the chain. The attached padlock, with its key, I snapped about a link of the chain, between some four and five feet from the floor. This is the inactive position of the chain, lock at collar level, chain terminating with a closed loop, the loop about a foot off the floor, an arrangement permitting a girl to be quickly and conveniently put on the chain and permitting the chain, if no girl is upon it, to be slid in its track without dragging on the steel plates.

She turned about, holding her bound wrists to me, that I might unbind them. Instead I took her by the hair and walked her, bent over, beside me, sliding the chain along with us, backward, until I came to a branching in a hall. I slid the chain a distance down that hall, and then, still holding her, returned to that point at which the track system terminated.

"Free me," she begged. "Oh!" she cried, as my hand twisted in her hair.

"You are too pretty to free," I told her.

I then thrust her ahead of me, down the corridor, beyond the termination point of the chain-and-track system.

She turned about, terrified. "Humans may not go beyond this point," she said.

"Precede me," I told her.

408

Moaning, the bound, silked girl turned about and preceded me.

I saw that no more of the lensed monitors covered this portion of the corridor. I grew uneasy, for it seemed matters proceeded too simply. A steel door lay at the end of the corridor. I had speculated that the destructive device would lie beyond the reach of slaves, and in an area secret to the monitoring system, which might be available at times to humans. Yet, now, I was apprehensive.

I tried the door at the end of the corridor. It was open. I thrust it back with the butt of the riflelike contrivance I carried.

I looked at the girl. I nodded to her to approach me. She did so. I held my left hand open, at my waist. She stiffened, and looked at me, angrily. I opened and closed my left hand once. I saw her training in Gorean customs had been thorough. But she never thought that such a gesture would be used to her. She came beside me, and a bit behind me, and, crouching, put her head down, deeply. I fastened my hand in her hair. She winced. Women are helpless in this position. I carried the dart-firing weapon, loaded, in my right hand. I looked cautiously about the frame of the door. I entered, conducting the girl. The room, large, seemed deserted.

It seemed a normal storage room, though quite large. It was filled with boxes, the markings on which I could not read. Some of the boxes were in the nature of open crates. They seemed to contain machinery and parts for machinery. There were corridors among the boxes.

I heard a sound and, releasing the girl, lifted the weapon, with both hands.

A figure, in black, stood up, high, atop several boxes. "It is not here," he said.

"Drusus," I said. I recalled him, he of the Assassins, whom I had bested on the sand of the small arena.

He carried a dart-firing weapon.

"Put aside your weapon, slowly," I commanded him.

"It is not here," he said. "I have searched."

"Put aside your weapon," I said.

He put it at his feet.

"What are you doing here?" I asked.

"I suspect the same as you," he said. "I have searched for the lever or key, or wheel, or whatever it may be, which, manipulated or turned, will destroy this place."

"You serve Kurii," I said.

"No longer," said he. "I fought, and was spared by one who was a man. I have thought long on this. Though I may be too weak to be an Assassin, yet perhaps I have strength sufficient unto manhood."

"How do I know you speak the truth?" I said.

"Four Kurii were here," he said, "to guard this place, to intercept him who might attempt to attain it. Those I slew."

He gestured to an aisle in the boxes. I could smell Kur blood. I did not take my eyes from him. The girl, turning about, shrank suddenly back, desperately, futilely, trying to free her small hands, tied behind her back, and stifled a scream.

"Four times I fired, four I slew," he said.

"Report what you see," I told the girl.

"There are four beasts, or parts of beasts," she said, "three here, and one beyond."

"Take up your weapon," I said to Drusus.

He picked it up. He looked at the woman. "A pretty slave girl," he said.

"I am not a slave girl!" she said. "I am a free woman! I am the Lady Graciela Consuelo Rosa Rivera-Sanchez!"

"Amusing," he said. He descended from the boxes.

"I had thought the destructive device, if it exists, would be here," I said.

"I thought so, too," he said.

"If you trip or trigger the device," said the girl, "we will all be killed!"

"The invasion must be stopped," I said.

"The device must not be detonated," she cried. "We would all be killed, you fools!"

I struck her back against the boxes, blood at her mouth, and she sank to the floor.

"You think and act as a slave," I said.

She put her head down, trembling, frightened, an instinctive gesture for a slave.

"You are a slave," I said. "I can tell."

She looked up at me, frightened.

"Perhaps it would be well for you to ask permission before you speak in the presence of free men," I said.

She put her head down.

"She would look well naked, on an auction block," said Drusus.

"Yes," I said.

"What shall we do now?" he asked.

At that moment the large steel door, through which I had entered the room shut. It must have been done automatically. We saw no one. The wheel on our side of the door, hummed and spun, locking the door. At the same time, from the ceiling, a filtering of white, smoky gas began to descend.

"Hold your breath!" I cried. I leveled the dart-firing weapon I carried at the door, and pressed the firing switch. The dart, like an insidious bird, sped to the steel, smoking, and pierced its outer layer. An instant later, as I flung myself downward, near the girl, Drusus with me, there was a ripping of steel which tore at my eardrums. I gestured the others to their feet, and, together, we ran through the smoke and gas to the door. It lay twisted, half wrenched from its hinges, half melted. We lowered our heads and slipped through the opening. The girl screamed as the hot metal brushed her calf. We were then free in the hall. Some eight Kurii were hurrying toward us.

Drusus lifted his weapon, calmly. A dart hissed forth. The first Kur stopped and then, suddenly, burst apart. Another reeled away from him. Another tore the blood and flesh from his face, half blinded, roaring with fury. A dart hissed above our heads and rent in its explosion the metal behind us. I fired a dart and another Kur spun about hideously, scratching at the metal, and then, before our eyes, erupted as though it had engorged a bomb. The six Kurii remaining, one with an arm dragging on the floor, hung to its body by torn shreds of muscle, scrambled backwards, snarling. Then they disappeared about a corner.

"Hurry!" I cried.

We sped forward, and, at the first branching in the corridor, turned left.

We had no desire to again encounter the Kurii.

Scarcely had we left our original corridor than we heard a great slam of steel. Looking backward we saw that it had been sealed.

"Let us move quickly," I suggested.

We hurried up a flight of stairs.

We saw no one.

We began to ascend another flight of stairs. Near its top the girl stumbled and fell, bound, rolling, down several steps. She was bruised and sobbing.

I took her in my arms.

"Did you see the beasts!" she cried. "What are they?"

"They are those whom you served," I informed her.

411

"No!" she cried.

"But you will now serve others, pretty slave," I told her.

She looked at me with horror.

I threw her over my shoulder and ascended the stairs.

"Who goes there!" cried a man. Then he spun away from us, roiling and spattering backward.

"The way is now clear," said Drusus. "Let us hurry."

Another steel panel slammed down behind us. The siren then began to whine in the steel halls.

"Perhaps there was no destructive device," said Drusus.

"I know where it is now," I said. "We have been fools! Fools!"

"Where?" he asked, puzzled.

"Beyond the reach of slaves, beyond the scope of the monitoring devices," I cried. "Where no one may reach, where no one may see!"

"We have journeyed already to the termination of the slave track," he said.

"Where do all the slave tracks terminate?" I asked.

"All?" he asked.

"Yes," I said.

"In the center of the complex," he said.

"At the chamber of Zarendargar," I said.

"Yes," he said.

"I have seen that chamber," I said. "It contains monitors, but it itself is not monitored."

"Yes," he said. "Yes!"

"Where but in the chamber of the high Kur would lie that terrifying mechanism?"

"Where no one may reach, where no one may see," he said.

"Saving Zarendargar, Half-Ear, himself," I said.

"Yes," he said.

"We have failed," said Drusus.

I nodded in agreement. The strange common project of two men, of diverse and antagonistic, yet strangely similar castes, an Assassin and a Warrior, had failed.

"What is now to be done?" he asked.

"We must attempt to reach the chamber of Zarendargar," I said.

"It is hopeless," he said.

"Of course," I said. "But I must attempt it. Are you with me?"

"Of course," he said.

"But you are of the Assassins," I said.

"We are tenacious fellows," he smiled.

"I have heard that," I said.

"Do you think that only Warriors are men?" he asked.

"No," I said. "I have never been of that opinion."

"Let us proceed," he said.

"I thought you were too weak to be an Assassin," I said.

"I was once strong enough to defy the dictates of my caste," he said. "I was once strong enough to spare my friend, though I feared that in doing this I would myself be killed."

"Perhaps you are the strongest of the dark caste," I said. He shrugged.

"Let us see who can fight better," I said.

"Our training is superior to yours," he said.

"I doubt that," I said. "But we do not get much training dropping poison into people's drinks."

"Assassins are not permitted poison," he said proudly.

"I know," I said.

"The Assassin," he said, "is like a musician, a surgeon. The Warrior is like a butcher. He is a ravaging, bloodthirsty lout."

"There is much to what you say," I granted him. "But Assassins are such arid fellows. Warriors are more genial, more enthusiastic."

"An Assassin goes in and does his job, and comes out quietly," he said. "Warriors storm buildings and burn towers."

"It is true that I would rather clean up after an Assassin than a Warrior," I said.

"You are not a bad fellow for a Warrior," he said.

"I have known worse Assassins than yourself," I said.

"Let us proceed," he said.

"Agreed," I said. We, together, I carrying the girl, made our way up another flight of stairs.

"Wait," I said.

"Yes," he said.

"The most obvious approaches to the chamber of Zarendargar," I said, "will probably be heavily guarded. Thus, let us circle about and climb upward. Perhaps we can eventually cut through from the level above."

"For a warrior," he said, "you are not totally without cunning."

"We have our flashes of inspiration," I informed him.

We climbed up two more levels. Then we began to circle about, far to our right. We wanted another stairway, one more remote, to ascend yet higher.

We had scarcely attained the second level than we heard the cry, "Halt!"

Drusus spun and fired a dart, swiftly, from the hip. Men scattered. The dart caromed off a wall and exploded near them. We darted about the corner of a wall. Four darts hissed past, exploding in a succession of bursts some fifty yards from us. I threw the girl from my shoulder to my feet. We heard running feet, coming from another direction. We looked wildly about. I took the girl at my feet by the hair and yanked her to her feet. We then ran, I running the girl beside me, at my hip, to the nearest corridor.

"This is an outer corridor," said Drusus. "In it are doors to the outside."

We sped along the corridor. We heard feet behind us, coming down the corridor we had just vacated. Then, ahead of us, some two hundred yards away, we saw some more men.

We continued to run.

I looked back. The men behind us now seemed wary. They were not ready, apparently, to pursue us into this corridor. Similarly, the fellows in front of us, apparently trapping us, did not try to approach.

We slowed our pace, puzzled.

"Over here, Tarl who hunts with me!" called a familiar voice.

"Imnak!" I cried.

We entered a recessed, broad room, which gave access to one of the hatchways that led to the outside of the complex. To one side there was a large wheel, that operated the door. It was cold in the room. Outside was the arctic night. A man turned about. "Ram!" I cried. "Imnak freed me," he said. I saw several of the dart-firing weapons in the room, indeed a crate filled with them, on small wheels. Too, there were several kegs of darts, wrapped in packages of six. "Oh, Master!" cried Arlene, clinging to me. "I so feared for you." I raped her lips as a master, and she yielded, melting to me as a slave. "Master," said she who had been the Lady Constance of Lydius, then Constance, my slave. How beautiful she was, blond, in her wisp of slave silk. I took her in my other arm, and let her lick at my neck. I felt lips at my leg. Audrey knelt there, her head pressed against my calf. Barbara knelt, too, at my feet, putting her head down to my boots. I saw Tina with Ram, and Poalu with Imnak. Besides these there were some fifteen other slave girls in the room, frightened. The only males there were Drusus, myself, Imnak and Ram.

There were, too, some furs and food. "I took what women, and weapons, and things, I could," said Imnak.

"But you did not leave the complex," I said.

"I was waiting for you," he said. "And for Karjuk."

"Karjuk?" I said. "He is an ally of the Kurii."

"How can that be?" asked Imnak. "He is of the People."

"We have failed to find the destructive device," I said to Imnak. "I think it is in the chamber of Zarendargar, the high Kur in the complex, but it does not matter now," I said. "Nothing matters any longer. All is lost."

"Do not forget Karjuk," said Imnak.

I looked at him.

"He is of the People," Imnak reminded me.

"Where did you find this new slave?" asked Arlene of me, not too pleasantly, regarding the slim, beautiful girl I had brought with me.

"I am not a slave, Slave," said the pale, aristocratic, black-haired girl.

Arlene looked at me, frightened.

"She is not yet a legal slave," I told Arlene, "so treat her with the technical respect due to a free female."

Arlene fell to her knees before her, her head down, and the girl straightened herself, proudly.

"Get up," I said to Arlene. She did so. "Though this girl is not yet a legal slave," I told Arlene, "she is actually a true slave." The girl recoiled. "Thus," I said, "she need not be treated with particular respect."

"I understand perfectly, Master," said Arlene. She regarded the pale, aristocratic girl, who shrank back. The other girls, too, regarded her. The Lady Rosa shuddered, not daring to meet their eyes. She knew that there was not one girl in that room who was not assessing her, frankly considering her, and comparing the quality of her flesh to their own. "She will make good slave meat," said Arlene.

"But not so good as you, Wench," I assured her.

"Thank you, Master," said Arlene, putting her head down, smiling.

"Check the prisoner's bonds," I said.

"Did you tie her, Master?" asked Arlene.

"Yes," I said.

"Then she is well secured," said Arlene. But she checked the Lady Rosa's wrist bonds as I had instructed her to do. She did so a bit roughly. "She is perfectly secured," said Arlene to me, smiling innocently. The Lady Rosa tossed her head and looked away.

"There are furs here," I said to Imnak. "I think it best that you and Ram, and the women, try to leave the compound, and make your way across the ice."

"What of you?" asked Imnak.

"I shall remain here," I said.

"I, too," said Drusus.

"I, too, will remain!" cried Arlene.

"You will obey, Slave," I said to her.

"Yes, Master," she said, tears in her eyes.

We then heard pounding on the outside of the broad hatch. "Surrender! Open! Open!" called a voice.

"We are surrounded," I said.

"There is no escape," said Drusus.

"Stand back from the hatch," I said, "lest they blow it in towards us."

We stood back, dart-firing weapons ready.

Suddenly we heard a scream from the other side of the hatch. Then a cry of rage. Then we heard pounding, frightened, on the other side of the steel. "Help! Help!" we heard. "Let us in! Let us in!" There was more frenzied pounding. "We surrender! we heard. "Please! Please!" There were more screams. We heard something sharp strike against the steel. We heard a dart-firing weapon discharge its bolt. "We surrender! We surrender!" we heard. "Let us in!"

"It is a trick," said Drusus.

"It is certainly a convincing one," I averred.

We heard another man scream with pain.

Then, from the other side of the steel, we heard a voice call out. It spoke in the language of the People. I could understand very little of it.

Imnak beamed, and ran to the wheel. I did not stop him. He turned the wheel. The large, squarish hatch, some ten feet in height and width, studded with bolts, slid slowly to the side.

Ram let forth a cheer.

Outside, on the dim, polar ice, many on sleds, drawn by sleen, were hundreds of the People, men, and women and children. More were arriving, visible in the reflection from the moons on the ice. Karjuk stood near the entranceway, his strung bow of layered horn in his hand, an arrow at the string. Other hunters stood about. Men from the complex lay scattered on the ice. From the backs and chests of several

416

protruded arrows. Red hunters stood about. Some of the men from the complex had been downed by lances. A few cowered, their weapons discarded, herded together by domesticated snow sleen, ravening and vicious, on the leashes of their red masters. Some men of the complex were thrown to their stomachs on the ice. Their hands were jerked behind them and were being tied with rawhide. Then their suits were being slit with bone knives. "We will freeze!" cried one of them. The red hunters were putting their enemies completely at their mercy, and that of the winter night.

Karjuk called out orders. Red hunters streamed in, past me. Imnak handed the dart-firing weapons to some of them, hastily explaining their use. But most simply hurried past him, more content to rely on their tools of wood and bone. The men with the domesticated snow sleen passed me. I did not envy those on whom such animals would be set. Drusus, with a dart-firing weapon, joined one contingent of hunters, in their vanguard, to cover them and match fire with whatever resistance they might encounter; Ram, seizing up a weapon, joined another contingent. I looked outside the hatch, or port. Even more of the People, women and children as well as hunters, were making their way across the ice to the complex. They were detaching many of the snow sleen from the sleds, to be used as attack sleen.

Karjuk continued to stand by the port and issue orders, in the tongue of the red hunters.

"There must be more than fifteen hundred of the hunters," I said.

"They are from all the camps," said Imnak. "There are more, before they have finished coming, than twenty-five hundred."

"Then it is all the People," I said.

"Yes," said Imnak, "it is all the People." He grinned at me. "Sometimes the guard cannot do everything," he said.

I looked at Karjuk. "I thought you an ally of the beasts," I said.

"I am the guard," he said. "And I am of the People."

"Forgive me," I said, "that I doubted you."

"It is done," he said.

More red hunters streamed past us.

I saw two men from the complex being prodded through the halls, toward a room. Their hands were bound with rawhide, behind them. A woman was being dragged along by

417

the hair. Her clothing had been removed. Already her captor had put bondage strings on her throat.

"I would alter the garments you wear, if I were you," said Imnak, "for you might be mistaken for one of the men of the complex."

I removed the suit I had worn. I donned boots and fur trousers. I did not wish to wear a shirt or parka in the complex, because of its heat.

More hunters came past us. Imnak explained to some of them the nature of the dart-firing weapons.

The prisoners, captured outside, shuddering, half-frozen, were herded within the complex, bound.

"Go to where it is warmer," I told the girls shivering in the recessed room.

Arlene, Audrey, Barbara, Constance, and the others, hurried to a place of greater shelter.

Karjuk went then to direct the operations within the complex. He was accompanied by Imnak.

I stepped outside, into the arctic night, though bare-chested, to survey the rear of our position.

I checked the ice cliffs, the ice about, to see if any organized sortie might be obvious. I saw nothing. If men of the complex fled the complex I did not think they would last long in the arctic night. The power units in their suits would eventually be exhausted, and they would then be at the mercy of the snow and ice.

I looked about, and, suddenly, saw that the port to the complex was being slowly closed. Swiftly I re-entered. The Lady Rosa, startled, turned toward me, from the wheel which controlled the panel. She backed away, shaking her head. Her mouth had been on the wheel.

Not speaking I went to her and put her to her knees. With my knife I cut a length of her hair, about a foot in length, and crossed and tied together her ankles. I then dragged her by the arm across the steel, out through the portal, and onto the ice. "No," she screamed, "No!" I left her on her side on the ice. "No!" she screamed.

I returned within the complex and, with the wheel, closed the heavy, sliding hatch.

I heard her screaming on the other side of the steel. "Let me in!" she cried. "I demand to be let in!" Her cries could be heard with some clarity. She had doubtless twisted and squirmed frenziedly, until she must be, on her knees, just outside of the steel.

"I am a free woman!" she cried. "You cannot do this to me!"

I did not think she would last long outside in the arctic night, silked as she was.

She had tried to kill me.

"I will be your slave," she cried.

She did not know if I were still on the other side of the door or not.

"I am your slave!" she cried. "Master, Master, I am your slave! Please spare your slave, Master!" She wailed with misery and cold. "Please spare your slave, Master!" she wept.

I turned the wheel, opening the hatch.

She fell inward, across the threshold, shivering. I drew her within the room, and spun shut the hatch.

I looked down at her, shuddering at my feet. She looked up at me, terrorized. "What manner of man are you, my Master?" she asked. I looked down at her. She struggled to her knees and put her head down, to my feet. She began to kiss them, desperately, in an effort to placate me. "Look up," I said to her. She did so. "You will be whipped severely," I told her. "Yes, Master," she said. "I tried to kill you."

"You did that when you were a free woman," I told her. "I discount it."

"But then why would you have me whipped?" she asked.

"You kiss poorly," I told her.

"I beg instruction," she said.

"I will have a girl try to teach you some things," I told her. Experienced slave girls are often useful in teaching a new girl, fresh to her condition, how to please men.

"I will try to learn my lessons well," she said.

I threw her to my shoulder, to carry her within the complex to a holding area. "You will learn your lessons well," I told her, "or you will be thrown to sleen for feed."

"Yes, Master," she said.

"The complex is secure," said Ram, "save for the chamber of Zarendargar, Half-Ear. None has entered there."

"I shall go in," I said.

"We can blast our way in," said Ram. "Let us do that," said Drusus.

I walked down the long hall toward the chamber of Zarendargar. Behind me, some hundred yards or so, were Ram, and Drusus, and Karjuk and Imnak, and numerous red hunters.

I carried a dart-firing weapon in my hand. It seemed a long way down the hall. I had not remembered it as being that far. The overhead track system stopped some forty feet or so from Zarendargar's chamber. I looked at the monitor lens in the ceiling. Doubtless my approach had been observed on it. The interior of the chamber, though it contained monitors, was not itself monitored.

At the door to Zarendargar's chamber I paused, and lifted the dart-firing weapon. But the door seemed ajar.

The fighting in the complex had been sharp and bloody. Men of the complex, and red hunters, had fallen. The resistance had been led by the giant Kur, whose left ear had been half torn away. But there had been too many red hunters, and too many weapons. He had, when the battle had turned against him, freed his Kurii and his men to flee or surrender as they would. No Kur had surrendered. Most had been slain, fighting to the last. Some had departed from the complex, hobbling wounded away into the arctic night. Zarendargar himself had withdrawn to his chamber.

The door there seemed ajar.

I thrust it open with the barrel of the dart-firing weapon.

I recalled the chamber well.

I slipped inside, furtively, but then lowered the weapon.

"Greetings, Tarl Cabot," came from the translator.

On the furred dais, as before, I saw Zarendargar. There was a small device near him.

The great shape, stiffly, uncurled, and sat there, watching me.

"Forgive me, my friend," it said. "I have lost a great deal of blood."

"Let us dress your wounds," I said.

"Have some paga," it said. It indicated the bottles and glasses to one side.

I went to the shelves and, looping the dart-firing weapon over my shoulder, by its stock strap, poured two glasses of paga. I gave one of the glasses to Zarendargar, who accepted it, and retained the other. I went to sit, cross-legged, before the dais, but Zarendargar indicated that I should share the dais with him. I sat near him, cross-legged, as a Warrior sits.

"You are my prisoner," I said to him.

"I think not," he said. He indicated, holding it, the small metallic device which had lain beside him on the dais. It nestled now within his left, tentacled paw.

"I see," I said. The hair rose on the back of my neck.

"Let us drink to your victory," he said. He lifted his glass. "A victory to men and Priest-Kings."

"You are generous," I said.

"But a victory is not a war," he said.

"True," I said.

We touched glasses, in the manner of men, and drank.

He put aside his glass. He lifted the metallic object.

I tensed.

"I can move this switch," he said, "before you can fire."

"That is clear to me," I said. "You are bleeding," I said. The dais on which I sat was stiff with dried blood. And it was clear that so small an effort as rising to meet me, and touching his glass to mine, had opened one of the vicious wounds on his great body.

He lifted the metallic object.

"It is this which you sought," he said.

"Of course," I said. It was that object which lay beyond the reach of men, and where it could not be scanned by the monitoring system.

"Did you know it would be here?" he asked.

"I understood that it would be here only later," I said.

"You will not take me alive," it said.

"Surrender," I said. "It is no dishonor to surrender. You have fought well, but lost."

"I am Half-Ear, of the Kurii," it said.

It fondled the metal device, looking at me.

"Is there so much of value here," I asked, "that you would be willing to destroy it?"

"The supplies here, and the disposition maps, the schedules and codes, will not fall into the hands of Priest-Kings," it said. It looked at me. "There are two switches on this mechanism," it said. It lifted the mechanism.

There were indeed two switches on the mechanism.

"When I depress either switch," it said, not taking its eyes from me, "a twofold, irreversible sequence is initiated. First, a signal is transmitted from the complex to the steel worlds. This signal, which can also be received by the probe ships and the fleet, will inform them of the destruction of the complex, the loss of these munitions and supplies."

"The second portion of the sequence, simultaneously initiated, triggers the destruction of the complex," I said.

"Of course," he said.

His finger rested over the switch.

"There are several humans left in the complex," I said.

"No Kurii save myself," he said.

"True," I said. "But there are humans here."

"Free," he asked.

"Some are free," I said.

He shrugged. The great furry shoulders then hunched in pain.

I could smell blood.

"Some of the humans here," I said, "prisoners, were among your cohorts."

"My men?" it asked.

"They fought bravely," I said.

The beast seemed lost in thought. "They are in my command," he said. "Though they are human, yet they were in my command."

He depressed the second of the two switches.

I tensed, but the room, the complex, did not erupt beneath me.

"You are a good officer," I said.

"The second switch was depressed," he said. "The signal to the worlds, the ships, the fleet, is transmitted. Secondly the destruct sequence is now initiated."

"But it is a second destruct sequence," I said.

"Yes," said Half-Ear, "that which allows for the evacuation of the complex."

"How much time is there?" I asked.

"Three Kur Ahn," he said. "The device is set on Kur chronometry, synchronized to the rotation of the original world."

"The same chronometry which is used in the complex?" I asked.

"Of course," he said.

"That is a little more than five Gorean Ahn," I said.

"Two Ehn more," he said.

I nodded. The Kur day was divided into twelve hours, the Gorean day into twenty. The periods of rotation of the original Kur world and of Gor were quite similar. That was one reason the Kurii were interested in Gor. They wished a world which would be congenial to their physiological rhythms, developed in harmony with given environmental periodicities of darkness and light.

"But I would advise you to be better than a Kur Ahn afoot away before the time of destruction," he said.

"I shall act quickly," I said. "You must accompany us to safety."

The great Kur lay back on the dais, his eyes closed.

"Come with us," I said.

"No," it said. I could see the blood emerging from the large body of the animal.

"We can transport you," I said.

"I will kill any who approach me," it said.

"As you will," I said.

"I am Zarendargar, Half-Ear, of the Kurii," it said. "Though I am in disgrace, though I have failed, I am yet Zarendargar, Half-Ear, of the Kurii. "

"I will leave you alone now," I said.

"I am grateful," it said. "You seem to know our ways well."

"They are not dissimilar to the ways of the warrior," I said.

I poured him a glass of paga, and left it near him on the dais.

I then turned away and went to the portal of the chamber. He wished to be left alone, to bleed in the darkness, that no one might see or know his suffering. The Kurii are proud beasts.

I turned at the portal. "I wish you well, Commander," I said.

No response came from the translator. I left.

36 TO THE VICTORS BELONG THE SPOILS; I LIFT A GLASS OF PAGA

Orders were swiftly given.

In two Ahn we were ready to withdraw from the complex. Sleds were readied; prisoners, men of the complex, now in furs, some forty of them, were tied, their hands behind them, their necks linked by a long rope of rawhide, placing them in coffle. There was no fight left in them; they knew that on the ice, away from the technology of the complex, they could survive only if the red hunters chose to let them do so. Some would be sold to traders in the spring; others might be kept in the camps, to serve the red hunters; they, male slave beasts, would be stronger than female slave beasts. Perhaps eventually a hunter would take a trading trip south and take them with him, bound, to dispose of them in, say, Lydius, with his furs and other trade goods.

I regarded fifteen women who had been in the complex, women being trained as Kur agents for work in their cause. All were kneeling naked; most already had bondage strings on their necks; those that did not the hunters could sort out or do contest for.

"Put them in the sacks," I said.

Each was thrust in a deep furred sack, which was then placed within another heavy fur sack, larger than the first. There was an opening in the sacks only for the head, which was then rimmed with a hood, so that only the face was exposed, and that could be withdrawn to protect it from the cold. The rawhide straps on the sacks were then drawn tight, looped about, and tied tightly behind the hoods; the women could not reach the straps; they were, thus, effectively imprisoned.

"Tie the sacks on the sleds," I said. It was thus that the women would be transported.

The women moaned as they were carried helplessly to the sleds.

They would eventually learn to serve red masters.

She who had been the Lady Rosa was not, of course, with them. She was elsewhere, where I wanted her.

"Are we ready for departure?" I asked Imnak.

"Almost," said Imnak. Poalu, already furred, was with him.

"Come with me," I said to Imnak. "And bring, too, the bravest and best of your hunters, who performed for our cause in this place the best and noblest works of war."

There was a cheer.

"Surely Karjuk stands highest among them," he said.

"Come with us, Karjuk!" I cried.

"Go on without me," he said. He smiled wryly. "I am a sour and solemn man."

"Surely you would like a little thing to warm and pleasure you in your house?" I asked.

424

"I might grow too fond of it," he said. He bent down, tying a bundle, which he would put on his sled.

Imnak winked at me. "Come along, grim friend," said he. "You can help us make our choices."

"I know little of such matters," said Karjuk. "I am a lonely man."

"Come along," said Imnak. "Surely you can tell us which would be best at pulling sleds."

"You must look at the legs," said Karjuk. "Strong legs are important."

"Come along," said Imnak.

"Very well," said Karjuk.

We walked along a hallway. With us were many of the red hunters, some seventy or eighty, and Ram, and Drusus.

We entered a large room, off the hall.

In the room, alone, in its center, knelt a young red woman, her head down. She had been the only woman of her race, other than Poalu, who had been slave in the complex. She had been found in security chaining, in one of the slave rooms. She looked up.

"No one wants this one," said Imnak. "She has been a slave to white men."

There were tears in the girl's eyes. She was very pretty. She was short and plump like most of the women of the red hunters.

"What are you going to do with her?" asked Karjuk.

"Put her out in the snow," said Imnak. "She shames the People."

"I live apart from the People," said Karjuk.

"Do you want her?" asked Imnak.

"Of course not," said Karjuk, quickly. "She is too pretty for me."

"Do you know her?" asked Imnak.

"She was Neromiktok, of the Copper Cliffs Camp," he said. The word 'Neromiktok', in the language of the People, means 'Smooth-and-Soft-to-Touch'. I had learned this from Imnak. I had learned, too, that she had once been the beauty of the Copper Cliffs Camp.

"Do you know him?" inquired Imnak, innocently, of the girl.

"He is Karjuk, Master," she whispered, "once of Bright Stones Camp, who became the guard."

"It is said he left the camps and became the guard," said

425

Imnak, "because his gifts were once refused by a proud girl of the Copper Cliffs Camp."

She put down her head.

"How did you become a slave," asked Imnak.

"I was too good for men," she said.

Several of the red hunters with us laughed, to hear a slave so speak.

"I ran away from Copper Cliffs to avoid an unwanted match," she said. "I was captured. I was made a slave."

"Are you still too good for men?" asked Imnak.

"No, Master," she said.

"You have shamed the People," said Imnak sternly.

"Yes, Master," she said, her head down.

"What sort of woman are you?" asked Imnak.

"One who wants to kneel at the feet of men, and love them," she said.

"Shameful! Shameful!" cried Imnak cheerfully.

"Yes, Master," she said, sobbing, not raising her head.

"Do you know the fate for shaming the People?" he asked.

"Please, no, Master!" she said.

"Seize her," said Imnak, to two of the red hunters. They seized her, each taking an arm, and dragged her to her feet.

"They are going to put me out in the snow!" she cried to Karjuk, agonized.

"Are you going to put her out in the snow?" asked Karjuk.

"Of course," said Imnak.

"But she has strong legs," said Karjuk.

The girl struggled in the arms of the red hunters. They released her and she flung herself to her knees before Karjuk, head down, sobbing, holding his legs.

"I suppose she could draw a sled," said one red hunter.

"Perhaps," said another.

"She might be pretty in the furs," said another.

"Keep me, Master! Keep me, Master!" begged the girl of Karjuk, sobbing. "I beg of you to keep me, Master!"

"No one wants you," said Imnak.

"Please, Master!" begged the girl, tears in her eyes, looking up at Karjuk.

"You are too good for me," said Karjuk.

"No, No, Master," she cried, "I am only a slave, a slave!"

"You are very pretty," said Karjuk.

"A slave is pleased if her master should find her pleasing," she said.

"What do you want?" he asked.

426

"To kneel at your feet, and to serve you and love you," she wept.

"Shameful!" cried Imnak.

"One cannot have everything," said Karjuk, defensively.

"Please, Master," she begged.

"Let us consider important things," said Karjuk. "Can you sew, and cook?"

"Yes, Master!" she cried.

"Can you make a good sleen stew?" he asked.

"Yes, Master," she said. "And though I know you are above such things I can show you wonders in the furs, which I have been taught as a slave."

Karjuk shrugged. "It is not wrong to broaden one's experiences," he said.

"Keep me, Master," she begged.

"I will call you Auyark," he said.

"I am Auyark," she said, joyfully, putting her head against his leg, weeping.

He looked down at her. "I think you will make a summer in my house," he said. Auyark is a word in the language of the People which means Summer.

"Look up at me," he said, "Girl."

She looked up at him.

"I will keep you," he said, "but you must understand that you are kept as a slave, completely as a slave, and only as a slave."

"Yes, Master," she said.

"And if you are not pleasing," he said, "I will put you out into the snow."

"Yes, Master," she said.

"Come now," he said. "On your feet. We must load a sled."

She stood up.

"Let me load the sled, Master," she said.

He looked at her. "Yes," he said. "You will load it, lovely slave."

They left the room, he first, she following.

"Imnak," I said, "you arranged this entire thing."

"It is not impossible," he said. "But, hurry, there are other wenches to distribute, and there is little time."

I looked down at Arlene, kneeling in line, with the other girls. She was in the first line. There were four such lines, of

427

fifty or so girls each. They were the girls who had been slaves in the complex.

"We are your spoils," said Arlene.

All the girls were stripped. All knelt in the position of pleasure slaves.

She who had been the Lady Rosa knelt to one side, similarly exposed and positioned.

She, too, was a slave girl.

"Yes," I said to Arlene.

"Women have always been the spoils in the victories of men," she said, "the tokens, symbols, the fruits and prizes of their conquests."

"Of course," I said. "How do you feel about that?"

"I find it indescribably thrilling," she said.

"Kneel straighter," I said.

"Yes, Master," she said.

"Why are Thimble and Thistle," I asked Imnak, "in with the flesh loot?" The two Earth girls, Audrey and Barbara, knelt near Arlene.

"I have Poalu," said Imnak.

The girl Belinda, whom I had used on the steel plates of the corridor, while she wore her long neck chain, fastened in the overhead track system, knelt a few girls away, in the second row. She lifted her body to me, her eyes pleading, but did not break position.

Constance, the lovely blond-haired slave from Kassau, whom I had imbonded in the fields south of the Laurius, knelt in the fourth row.

She was very beautiful.

Chains were brought, sirik chains, with their collars, and wrist and ankle loops, all attached, strung on an individual hold chain.

I threw six sirik chains over my left shoulder.

"Let us begin," said Imnak.

I threw two of the sirik chains to the tiles, one after the other.

Arlene and Audrey, swiftly, rose to their feet and ran lightly to kneel before me.

They looked up at me.

"I am a slave. I beg your chains," said Arlene.

"Pick them up," I said, indicating a sirik to her. She lifted up the chains.

"I am a slave. I beg your chains," said Audrey.

"Pick them up," I said, indicating the other sirik. She

picked up the chain, with its collar, and wrist and ankle rings. I saw her lift it, tears in her eyes. Gently, head down, she licked and kissed the metal. I smiled. As I had thought, the former rich girl was the first to lick and kiss her chains.

Arlene, angry, lifted the chains to her lips. She, looking at me, pressed the chains to her lips and kissed them. Then, delicately, touching the chain with her small, soft tongue she licked the metal. Then she kissed it again. Then she held the chain diagonally in her mouth, her small, fine white teeth gently closed upon it. She then removed it from her mouth. "You see, I can lick and kiss my chains even better than she, Master," said Arlene.

"Oh, oh," said Audrey, softly. Her body trembled. She looked up from the chain. She was almost in orgasm.

"But do you understand the meaning of it?" I asked Arlene.

Suddenly Arlene shuddered, and looked at the chain. She held it in her small hands. It, locked on her body, would confine her obdurately, making her helplessly the rightless slave of a master. Every organism has its place in nature. That of woman is at the foot of man.

"I love being a woman, Master," she said. She held the chain against her bared beauty.

"Now lick and kiss the chain, Slave," I said.

"Yes, Master," she whispered.

She bent her head to the chain and, delicately, sobbing with emotion, licked and kissed at the metal. Her tears fell among the links.

I locked the sirik on Audrey. She looked at me, desperately.

"Later," I said.

"Yes, Master," she said.

"Go to the sled, Slave," I said.

"Yes, Master," she said.

They, still in sirik, would be fastened in fur sacks and tied on sleds. Later, after the first ice camp had been constructed, they would be freed from sirik, and used in the huts. Later, given garments, they would trek, in neck coffle, beside the sleds.

I took the chains from Arlene, pulling them from her, and, with five snaps, locked them roughly on her body.

I smelled the womanhood of her. She looked at me. "Later," I said. "Go to the sled, Slave."

"Yes, Master," she said, moaning.

Men about me were enacting similar ceremonies of en-slavement with other imbonded wenches. Ram, I saw, took none. He was satisfied with lovely Tina, who had been the Lady Tina of Lydius. Drusus, I saw, had put a pair of beau-ties in sirik. He sent them to the sled on which he had been alotted space for his belongings, including two slave girls.

I threw another sirik to the floor before me.

Barbara, the blond Earth girl, knelt before me. "I am a slave," she said. "I beg your chains."

"Pick them up," I said.

She did so, and kissed them.

I locked them on her.

"Go to the sled," I said.

"Yes, Master," she said.

I threw another sirik to the floor before me.

Constance, the Gorean slave, blond and lovely, knelt be-fore me. "I am a slave," she said. "I beg your chains."

"Pick them up," I said.

She did so, and kissed them.

I locked them on her.

"Go to the sled," I said.

"Yes, Master," she said.

I threw the fifth of the six sets of chains which I held on my shoulder to the floor.

Belinda, whom I had used in the corridor, hurried to me, kneeling before me.

She was joyful. I would permit her, at least for the time, at my feet.

Soon, in sirik, she made her way toward my sled.

I threw the last sirik to the tiles before me.

The graceful and aristocratic girl, she who had been the Lady Rosa, came and knelt before me. "I am a slave," she said. "I beg your chains."

"Pick them up," I said.

She did so, and, looking at me, pressed them to her lips. Then she put her head down and, delicately, licked and kissed them.

I locked the collar on her neck, and the two wrist rings, one after the other, on her small wrists. I then took the chain between her legs and, crouching behind her, snapped the two ankle rings shut on her fair ankles. I then stood up and stood before her. I looked down at her, my hands on my hips. "Whose slave are you?" I asked. "Yours, Master," she said. "Go to the sled, Slave," I said. "Yes, Master," she said.

"We must hurry," said Imnak. "In two Ahn this place will be no more."

Outside the room which had been used for slave selection by the victors, I took a dart-firing weapon from one of the red hunters.

"Where are you going?" asked Imnak.

"To the chamber of Zarendargar," I said. I slipped one of the darts into the weapon's breech, and let the bolt spring shut.

"Why?" he asked.

I shrugged. "In the disruption consequent upon this place's destruction," I said, "his death would be hideous."

I went to the chamber of Zarendargar, the weapon in hand. Imnak followed.

At the chamber of Zarendargar I pressed open the portal with my foot and lifted the weapon, to fire at the figure which would be recumbent upon the blood-soaked, furred dais.

I was startled. I leaped into the room. Weapon in hand I scanned the room, the walls, the high poles threaded over my head.

I shook.

Zarendargar was gone.

"I will have the rooms and halls searched!" cried Imnak. He hurried away, out of the room.

I walked slowly to the stained, furred dais. I had placed on it a glass of paga before I had left the room. I saw, against a steel wall, the shattered remnants of such a glass. But on the dais there was another glass, it, too, filled with paga.

I laughed loudly.

I bent and picked up the second glass. I lifted it to the empty room, in both a toast and a salute.

Then I downed the paga. Then I threw the glass against the steel wall, where it shattered, and fell, its fragments showering downward, mingling with those of the other glass.

I turned about and left the room. Outside Imnak was trying to organize a search of the complex.

"There is no time," I said.

"But the beast," he said.

"There is no time," I said. "We must make away."

"Yes," said he, "Tarl, who hunts with me." He hurried away, calling to the red hunters.

The snow sleen were already harnessed.

I paused there, alone, at the portal of the chamber of

Zarendargar, Half-Ear, war general of the Kurii. I looked within, once, at the blood-stained dais, and the steel wall, at the foot of which, mingled, lay the fragments of two glasses.

Then quickly I turned about and strode from the area. The trek must be initiated.

37 WE HAVE LEFT THE COMPLEX; WE WILL MAKE OUR WAY TOWARD THE PERMANENT CAMP

"Look!" cried Imnak.

I turned the sled about. Others, too, turned about, the long sleds, like clouds, on the bleak ice.

Many of those with us cried out in wonder and alarm.

Behind us, in the winter sky, looming, streaming hundreds of pasangs upward into the sky, shimmering and flickering, extended vast, subtle curtains of chromatic lights, yellows, and pinks and reds.

"It is not the season," said a hunter.

Then men cried out with awe. Some women screamed. Children hid their faces.

For an instant, in that lofty, panoramic display, there had appeared, only for an instant, etched in light, the gigantic head of a Kur. One ear, the left, had been half torn from its head. The lips drew back, exhibiting the Kur's fearful sign of pleasure. Then the fearsome head was gone.

We then saw, I, and the others, and the People, on the pack ice more than an Ahn's trek from the complex, a blast of light which, in the darkness of the polar night, made us cry out with pain, half blinded.

For a terrible instant it had seemed as bright as day, with a brightness that most of the People, in their northern regions, had never known, a brightness that might have struck the white sands of the blazing Tahari or the green jungles of the rain forests of the eastern Cartius.

Then the lights in the sky were gone and the polar night

had returned, save for a long, shimmering volume of yellowish smoke that reared from the distant ice.

"Lie down!" I cried to those standing about me. "Behind the sleds!"

The shock wave of the blast, in some seconds, struck us. It drove ice and pelting, granular snow before it. It tore at our furs. I held the sled, bracing it against the blast. Arlene cried out with terror as the sled twisted and half-tipped. She, like others of her kind, women, slaves, and slaves to be, was absolutely helpless. She was confined in two fur sacks, one placed within the other, the layer of warm air between them acting as insulation. She could not escape from the two sacks, and they were tied on the sled. Within the sacks she was naked, and in sirik. There was no danger that women such as she would escape on the ice. The sleen harnessed to the sled squealed with fury, scratching, thrown from its feet, twisted and tangled in the traces. We were in the blast of air for only some seven seconds. And then it passed as quickly as it had come.

I cuffed the sleen on its snout and, holding it by the harness, jerked it up, disentangling it from the traces. A single sleen is kept in two traces, or a double trace. When more than one sleen, or girl, pulls the sled, they are commonly kept on a single trace. This conserves leather and diminishes the amount of tangling that might otherwise occur.

I turned the sled back to face where the complex had been. I stood on the rear runners, lifting myself for a better look. Arlene struggled, as she could, to see. My other girls, Audrey, Barbara, Constance, Belinda, and the girl who had once been the Lady Rosa, were tied on the sleds of other hunters. Arlene had been quite proud that she had been the one I had chosen to bind on my own sled. Too, she was the first one, of all the loot girls, on whom I had locked my chains. After the first camp we would remove the girls from sirik and use them; when we set out again they would be furred, and in neck coffle. Sometimes I thought I might let Audrey lead the coffle, and sometimes Arlene. I would enjoy playing the two Earth girls off against one another, each one striving more desperately, more helplessly, to please me than the others.

I smiled.

Women with deep feminine needs are mercilessly exploited by Gorean men.

It was a pleasant game. They are so helpless.

And yet how lovely they are. One must strive to remain strong with them.

I touched the side of Arlene's head with my mitten. Her head was within two hoods, parts of the fur sacks, tied on the sled, within which she lay chained.

She turned her head to look up at me, and smiled.

"Do you want to be respected?" I asked.

"You will never respect me," she laughed. "I am a slave."

"Do you want to be respected?" I asked.

"No man respects a woman who knows what else to do with her," she said.

"It is a Gorean saying," I said.

"I know," she said.

"You are an insolent wench," I said. "Perhaps I should whip you."

"I know that you will whip me, if you wish to do so," she said. "And that thrills me. Also, it makes me determined to try to please you, completely, and totally, so that you will not wish to do so."

"Good," I said. I looked at her. "Would you like to be returned to Earth?" I asked.

"Master jests, I trust," she said.

"Of course," I said, "for you are a luscious slave, fit for chains and markets."

"No," she said, "I would not like to be returned to Earth. I have never been so sensuously alive as here, at the mercy of men. I pity even the free women of this world, who cannot know the joys and loves of the female slave. I do not wish to return to Earth, to adopt again the role of pretending to be a man. What has Earth to offer that is worth more than joy and happiness?"

"I may sell you," I said.

"You may do so if you wish, Master," she said, "for I am only a slave. If you do sell me, I shall hope that I will please another."

"You speak scarcely like an Earth girl," I said.

"I am no longer an Earth girl," she said. "I am a Gorean slave girl."

"True," I said.

She snuggled down in the furs. I saw the furred sacks, in which she was confined, move under the ropes which bound them on the sled. I heard the small sound of the chain from within the furred sacks.

"You have not answered my question," I said.

"What question?" she asked.

"Do you want to be respected?" I asked.

"No," she said. She smiled up at me. "I want to be loved, and treasured. I want to be mastered."

I laughed.

"I want to be a woman," she said.

"Do not fear, lovely slave girl," I said. "This is not Earth. This is Gor. On Gor you, in bondage, will be given no alternative other than to fulfill the deepest and most profound needs of your sex."

"Yes, Master. Yes, Master," she said.

Red hunters were turning their sleds about. "Look!" said Imnak. I saw that the sleen was lifting its paws, water dripping from them.

"It is only hot air," I said, "hugging the ice, low, from the destruction of the complex."

"No," said Imnak, "there!"

He pointed far off. There, steam roiled upward from the water.

I saw piles of layered pack ice slipping into the water.

"See the ice," he said. "The water is boiling!"

Suddenly, near us, a lead, a great crack in the ice, broke open.

I looked back to the complex. Smoke billowed upward. In the upper atmosphere, it had now spread out, broadly, like an umbrella opened in the thin air. The mushroom-shaped cloud was disconcertingly familiar. A nuclear device, or a nuclear-type device, it seemed, had been involved in the destruction of the complex.

I watched the great mountain of ice, which had been the sheathing of the complex, slip downward into the sea.

"The water there is boiling!" cried Imnak.

"Nothing could live in it," I said.

"The beast is dead," he said.

"Perhaps," I said.

"You saw the face in the sky," he said.

"The mechanism to project that image," I said, "could have been preset."

"The beast is dead," said Imnak. "If it did not die in the rooms and halls, surely it died, scalded or drowned, in the surrounding waters."

"Nothing could live there," said a hunter.

"The beast is dead," said Imnak.

"Perhaps," I said. "I do not know."

The ice beneath our feet began to buckle and groan.

"Hurry!" cried Imnak.

I took one last look at the distant, churning, steaming waters, erupting and boiling, where the polar sea, as though offended and startled, hissing in indignation, recoiled from the fiery touch of a mechanism contrived paradoxically by the wit of rational creatures.

The Priest-Kings have set limits to the devices of men upon this world. They favor the spear and the bow, the sword and the steel of the knife. But Kurii lived not under their ordinances. I wondered from what shaggy Prometheus, long ago, Kurii had accepted fire. I wondered at what it might mean, fire kindled in the paw of a beast.

"Hurry!" cried Imnak. "Hurry!"

Nature transcended is perhaps nature outraged.

"Hurry!" cried Imnak. He shook my shoulder. "The beast is dead!" he cried. "Hurry!"

I recalled the chamber of Zarendargar, and two glasses, drained of paga, dashed against a wall of steel.

I lifted my hand to the roiling, steaming waters in the distance, beneath the high, spreading cloud.

"Hurry!" cried Imnak.

I turned the sled about, and cracked the whip over the head of the sleen. "On!" I cried. "On!"

The sleen, clawing and scratching at the ice, threw its weight against the harness.

The ice split behind me, and my foot, protected in its sleenskin boot, splashed in water, and I thrust the sled up and onto solid ice, and, crying out at the sleen, cracking the whip, sped away.

38   I SHALL RETURN TO THE SOUTH

I gently closed the door of the feasting house. I did not think my departure would be noticed.

Inside the people of Imnak's camp disported themselves.

There was much boiled meat and stew. Inside there was laughter and song. Outside a gentle snow had begun to fall. I could hear the noises of pleasure from within the low, half-buried feasting house. I looked out to the shore of the polar sea, that northern extending branch of Thassa. The stars were bright in the moonlit sky.

I made my way to the sleds.

Inside the feasting house Imnak was singing. This pleased me. No longer was he intimidated by the mountain which had once seemed to rear before him. No longer did he fear to sing, for now the mountain welcomed him. "No one knows from where songs come," as the People say. But now songs had come to Imnak. He was no longer lonely of songs. They welled from within him, like the surfacing of the great Hunjer whale, like the dawning of the sun after the long night, like the bursting of the tundra into flower, the tiny white and yellow flowers emerging from their snowy cocoon-like buds.

In the feasting house Imnak sang. Poalu was there, too. I checked the harness on the snow sleen on my sled.

"I am not greater than the mountain," said Imnak, "and yet the mountain cannot sing without me. It is only through me, and others, too, that the mountain can see, and can sing. Only through me can the mountain know how beautiful it is. I must tell the mountain of its beauty. Songs come from me now, telling me their names and stories. One is glad that they come. One is pleased to be a friend of songs. No one can climb to the top of the mountain. One climbs a little higher than another, but that is all. It is enough for a hunter, one small and frail, to stand on the lower slopes and sing. No one climbs much higher than another, and no one can truly speak the glory and beauty of the mountain. It is enough to stand on the lower slopes and sing. Who could ask more from life than the opportunity to stand for a time on the slope of the mountain and sing?"

The harness on the snow sleen was secure. The beast was restless.

There were some eight sleds there. Ram and Drusus had their sleds, and, besides mine, there were the sleds of five hunters, men who would accompany us south, across Ax Glacier. Tied by the neck to the left-hand, rear upright of Ram's sled, clad in furs, was Tina. Tied by the necks to the left-hand, rear upright of the sled of Drusus, clad in furs, were the two beauties he had selected and chained in the complex of the Kurii. Various girls were tied similarly to the sleds of the hunters who would accompany us. They were girls from the complex, some of whom had been free women, who would be taken south as trade goods. Tied to the left-hand, rear upright of my own sled, too, was a coffle line. On it, neck-secured, were six girls. It was a double coffle line; the last girl is placed on it first; the double line is knotted about her neck and then the two strands are taken forward; the fifth girl was next neck-knotted into the line and the two strands taken forward again, and so on; when the first girl is put in the coffle, the two strands are then taken forward again and knotted about the left-hand, rear upright of the sled; this way the only free ends of the bond, by means of which it might be untied, knotted together, fall at the left hand of the driver, and are easily within his view. This is a useful coffle tie when the girls' hands are not tied behind their backs. We wanted their hands free to help with the sled, when it became necessary to haul or push it over rough ground or through heaps of ice or broken snow.

The coffle line looped up to the neck of the first girl. She was Alrene; the second was Audrey; the third was Barbara; Constance was fourth; Belinda was fifth; she who had been the Lady Rosa was sixth. They were all clad in furs. The snow blew gently about them.

I went to the rear of the coffle line and took the last girl on the line gently in my arms. I put my lips, gently, to hers. They were cool, in the cold night. Yet beneath mine they yielded, as a slave's. Already had she who had been the Lady Rosa learned much. There is a difference between the kiss of the free woman and the kiss of the slave girl; the slave girl yields to her master; the difference is unmistakable. It is said that he whose lips have never touched those of a slave girl does not know, truly, what it is to hold a woman in his arms.

"What shall I call you?" I asked. "Rosita? Pepita?"

"Call me whatever you wish, Master," she said. "I am wholly yours."

I touched her thigh through the furs. "When we reach Port Kar," I told her, "I will brand you."

"Yes, Master," she said.

I went to the fourth girl on the coffle, Belinda, whom I had obtained in the complex, whom I had first enjoyed in the steel corridors of the complex, while her throat was still chained to the overhead slave track. I took her in my arms, gently, and kissed her, as I had the last girl on the line.

"You are already branded," I told her.

"Brand me a thousand times," she said, "each time I will be more yours."

"One brand," I said, "is enough to make clear the slave of you."

"Yes, Master," she said. "But each time you touch me you brand me. Each time you touch me you make me more a slave. Each time you touch me I am the more yours."

"You are a slave," I said. "It would be the same for any master."

She put her head down. "Yes, Master," she said.

I pushed up her chin with my thumb. She was crying. "Hope that you will one day fall into the power of your love master," I said. "For there is in you, I sense, a superb love slave."

"Thank you, Master," she said. She pressed her lips to the back of my mittened hand.

I went to Constance, who was the fourth girl on the coffle.

I kissed her.

"You, like Belinda, are already a branded slave girl," I told her.

"Yes, Master," she said. "Master," she said.

"Yes," I said.

"You were going to sell me in Lydius," she said.

"Yes," I said.

"Are you still going to do so?" she asked, frightened.

"No," I said. "I will take you back to Port Kar," I said.

"Thank you, Master," she breathed.

"Port Kar has excellent markets," I told her.

"Will you not keep me?" she begged.

"Perhaps, for a time," I said.

"I will try so hard to be pleasing to you," she said.

"You will do so, or you will wish that you had done so," I said.

"Yes, Master," she said.

I looked at her.

"It is said the women of Kassau make excellent slaves," I said.

"I will show you that it is true, Master," she said.

"Properly trained, you might make an excellent gift for one of Torvaldsland," I said.

She looked at me, frightened. "We women of Kassau fear the mighty raiders," she said.

"You would look well at their feet," I said.

She shuddered.

I regarded her. Perhaps I would have her trained as an exquisite pleasure slave, trained in sensuous dance and the thousand arts of pleasure. She might then be sent, formerly of Kassau, now trained, perfumed and silked, to one of the fierce Torvaldsland rovers. Perhaps Ivar Forkbeard, my friend, might enjoy her licking at his boots. Girls make lovely gifts. I usually kept some in my house, in Port Kar, for such purposes.

But perhaps I would keep her, for a time. Or, perhaps I would put her on a block in Port Kar.

I did not know.

"I will try to please you," she said.

"In Port Kar," I said, "a girl who is not pleasing is not unoften bound hand and foot, and thrown naked, as garbage, to the urts in the canals."

"I will try to be pleasing," she smiled.

I laughed, and gently cuffed the side of her head. She kissed at my mitten.

"When I sell you," I said, "if I should sell you, I will sell you south, into a perfumed slavery."

"Thank you, Master," she said.

I was fond of Constance. Why should she herd verr and churn butter in Torvaldsland? Let her serve naked and loving, bangled, perfumed, made-up, on the multicolored tiles of some southern domicile. Let her crawl naked, collared, to the feet of a southern master.

It would be sufficient.

But perhaps I would keep her. I did not know. I could decide that later, at my convenience.

I went to Barbara, and took her in my arms, and kissed her, gently.

"I will brand you in Port Kar," I told her.

"I await the iron with eagerness, Master," she said.

I then went to the second girl on the coffle line, Audrey. I took her in my arms and, gently, kissed her.

She clutched me. "I beg your brand," she said, hoarsely.

"Are you not the former rich girl of Earth?" I asked.

"I am a Gorean slut and a slave," she said. "I beg your brand."

She looked up at me, tears in her eyes. "All my wealth on Earth," she said, "could not buy me a collar, or a brand. Here I have nothing and yet they will be put upon me, because men please to do so."

440

"Yes," I said.

"Brand me," she said.

"I will," I said.

"I dare not ask your collar," she said. "After I am branded discard me or sell me, if you will. I shall always remember with joy the moment of pain in which I knew that I, though only a lowly slave, had been found worthy of your iron."

"I will keep you for a time, at least, in my collar," I said. "You are not without interest as a female slave. My men may find you amusing. And perhaps I will occasionally permit you to serve me in my quarters."

"Thank you, Master," she said.

"Then I think I will sell you," I said. "I think you will profit from knowing many masters, and many slaveries, for you are superb and exquisite slave meat."

"Thank you, Master," she said.

I went to Arlene, who led the coffle. The double line looped up to her throat from the left-hand, rear upright of the sled.

She looked up at me. I brushed the hood, fur-trimmed, back about her shoulders. How incredibly beautiful she was. There was a light snow about. Some of the snow fell in her hair. I brushed back some hair from the left side of her face.

"My thigh has not been marked," she said. "Will Master brand me, too, in Port Kar?"

"Yes," I said.

"A girl is pleased," she said.

"Truly?" I asked, holding her head between my hands.

"Yes," she said, "it is a great honor for a girl to be branded by a Warrior, and one who is a Captain."

I shrugged. I supposed, objectively, what she said was true. I was of a high caste, that of the Warriors, and was a captain. A boast among slave girls is "My brand was put upon me by a Warrior." Another is, "I was found beautiful enough for a Warrior to brand!"

Suddenly she held me, closely. "Oh, Master," she wept, "it has nothing to do, truly, with caste. It has to do, rather, with the kind of man you are. You could be a Peasant, an Iron Worker. It would not matter. When you look at a girl she wants your brand. When your eyes fall upon a girl she wants to be your slave. Girls dream of being branded by a man such as you. We dream of being the slaves of men such as you."

"Those are the dreams of slave girls," I said.

"Of course," she said.

"Slave girls should beware of speaking their dreams," I said, "lest they be overheard by a master."

"Every slave girl should boldly speak her dream," she said.

"But a master may be listening," I said.

"Let us hope, for her sake, that he is," said she. "Why else should a slave girl cry out, if not to be overheard by a master?"

"I find women mysterious," I said.

"The answer to our riddle," she said, "is a strong man, and a collar."

"I think it is true," I said.

"I had no real choice," she said. "In the snow you made me a slave."

"Of course," I said.

"I love you for it," she said, "—Master." I kissed her, gently, on the lips. She looked up at me, her eyes moist. "Will you keep me?" she asked.

"For a time, perhaps," I said.

"Yes," she said, ruefully, "I know—perhaps to amuse your men, and perhaps occasionally, if you are so moved, to serve you in the furs."

"Perhaps," I said.

"And then perhaps you will sell me," she said.

"Perhaps," I said.

"And then I would have to go to whom I am sold, and serve him—and as a complete slave, in the fullest sense of the word."

"Of course," I said.

"My own desires and feelings would be meaningless," she said.

"Of course," I said. "You are a slave."

"Yes," she said, "I am a slave." She wiped a tear away from her cheek. "Doubtless," she laughed, "I, like Audrey, would profit from many masters, and many slaveries."

"Doubtless," I agreed.

"For I, like Audrey," she asked, "am superb, exquisite slave meat?"

"Yes," I said.

"On Earth I was nothing," she said. "Here, at least, I am valued for my qualities as a slave."

"In so far as a girl has value," I said.

"Yes," she said, "—so far as a girl has value." Suddenly

her eyes flashed. "Surely I would bring a high price!" she said.

"You could, currently," I said, "be bought and sold for a handful of copper coins."

"Oh," she said.

"You are untrained," I pointed out.

She bit her lip.

"But I would see that you had a bit of training before I would put you on the block," I said.

"It would help me survive," she said.

"Yes," I said. "It would also raise your price."

"I see," she said.

"There is in you, and in these other girls," I said, surveying the coffle, "a superb love slave. If you pass through many hands, and many slaveries, your chance of being acquired by one who will be to you your true love master is much increased."

"Do you sell us because you are cruel, or because you are kind?" she asked.

"If I sell you," I said, "it will be done as I wish, when I wish, and because I wish."

"Yes, Master," she said, putting her head down.

"I could sell you to make money," I said. "I could sell you because I am tired of you. I could sell you because it amused me. I could sell you because I would be curious to see what you would look like standing naked in the sawdust on an auction block."

"Yes, Master," she said.

"I have sold girls for all of those reasons, and many others," I said.

"Of course, Master," she said. "Forgive me. We are slaves."

I pulled the hood of her parka up, over her head. "Fasten the hood," I said. "The trek will be cold."

"Yes, Master," she said.

I lightly kissed her lips. Our lips, momentarily, lingered together. Then I took her fully in my arms, and lengthily kissed her. "I will try to be pleasing to you, Master," she said.

I heard the sleen scratching at the ice. Ram coughed. The red hunters set their mittened hands to the uprights on their sleds.

"Be silent, Slave," I said, pushing her from me.

"Yes, Master," she said. She stumbled back, the double coffle line on her neck.

I turned about, to look once more behind me. It is a trick of red hunters, to see what the return journey will look like. But I did not think I would come this way again.

I saw the ice of the polar sea, and the stars, and the feasting house, within which Imnak sang.

Then I turned about and lifted my arm. To my left, in the east, was the first, tiniest glimmering of light, a dawn that would begin the long day of the arctic spring and summer. The night was over.

I lowered my arm. "On!" I said. "On!" The eight sleds left the area of the camp. I moved behind the sled. The girls, behind the sled, and to its left, moved with me.

Our departure was not noticed.

Don't miss the great novels of Dray Prescot on Kregen, world of Antares!

"Although Kregen has many aspects of Barsoom, it is more reminiscent of John Norman's Gor."—Erbania

☐ **TRANSIT TO SCORPIO.** The thrilling saga of Prescot of Antares among the wizards and nomads of Kregen. Book I.
(#UY1169—$1.25)

☐ **THE SUNS OF SCORPIO.** Among the colossus-builders and sea raiders of Kregen. Book II.   (#UY1191—$1.25)

☐ **WARRIOR OF SCORPIO.** Across the forbidden lands and the cities of madmen and fierce beasts. Book III.
(#UY1212—$1.25)

☐ **SWORDSHIPS OF SCORPIO.** Prescot allies himself with a pirate queen to rescue Vallia's traditional foes! Book IV.
(#UY1231—$1.25)

☐ **PRINCE OF SCORPIO.** Outlaw or crown prince—which was to be the fate of Prescot in the Empire of Vallia? Book V.
(#UY1251—$1.25)

"For sheer pageantry and character development, Akers far outshines any other writer writing this type of story. . . ."
—Jackson (Tenn.) Sun

If you wish to order these titles,

please use the coupon on

the last page of this book.

Recommended for Star Warriors!

The Dorsai Novels of Gordon R. Dickson

The Commodore Grimes Novels of
A. Bertram Chandler

The Dumarest of Terra Novels of E. C. Tubb

The Daedalus Novels of Brian M. Stableford

If you wish to order these titles,

please see the coupon in

the back of this book.

DAW PRESENTS MARION ZIMMER BRADLEY

"A writer of absolute competency . . ."—Theodore Sturgeon

☐ **THE FORBIDDEN TOWER**
"Blood feuds, medieval pageantry, treachery, tyranny, and true love combine to make another colorful swatch in the compelling continuing tapestry of Darkover."—**Publishers Weekly.** (#UJ1323—$1.95)

☐ **THE HERITAGE OF HASTUR**
"A rich and highly colorful tale of politics and magic, courage and pressure . . . Topflight adventure in every way."—**Analog.** "May well be Bradley's masterpiece."—**Newsday.** "It is a triumph."—**Science Fiction Review.**
(#UJ1307—$1.95)

☐ **DARKOVER LANDFALL**
"Both literate and exciting, with much of that searching fable quality that made **Lord of the Flies** so provocative."
—**New York Times.** The novel of Darkover's origin.
(#UY1256—$1.25)

☐ **THE SHATTERED CHAIN**
"Primarily concerned with the role of women in the Darkover society . . . Bradley's gift is provocative, a topnotch blend of sword-and-sorcery and the finest speculative fiction."—**Wilson Library Bulletin.** (#UJ1327—$1.95)

☐ **THE SPELL SWORD**
Goes deeper into the problem of the matrix and the conflict with one of Darkover's non-human races gifted with similar powers. A first-class adventure. (#UY1284—$1.25)

☐ **STORMQUEEN!**
"A novel of the planet Darkover set in the Ages of Chaos . . . this is richly textured, well-thought-out and involving."
—**Publishers Weekly.** (#UJ1381—$1.95)

☐ **HUNTERS OF THE RED MOON**
"May be even more a treat for devoted MZB fans than her excellent Darkover series . . . sf adventure in the grand tradition."—**Luna.** (#UW1407—$1.50)

To order these titles,

use coupon on the

last page of this book.

Presenting JOHN NORMAN in DAW editions . . .